ONE BETTER

Also by Rosalyn McMillan
Knowing

ROSALYN McMILLAN

ONE BETTER

WARNER BOOKS

A Time Warner Company

Warner Books, Inc., 1271 Avenue of the Americas,
New York, NY 10020

⬤ A Time Warner Company

First Printing: September 1997
10 9 8 7 6 5 4 3 2 1

Library of Congress Cataloging-in-Publication Data

McMillan, Rosalyn.
    One Better / Rosalyn McMillan.
        p.   cm.
    ISBN 0-446-52242-2
    I. Title.
PS3563.C3866054   1997
813'.54—dc21   97-26259
                                                          CIP

To my daughters, Ashley Shaylynn and Jasmine Danielle, and especially to all the beautiful little children who have brought their mothers tears of pain as well as tears of joy.

$\mathcal{A}$CKNOWLEDGMENTS

$\mathcal{I}$ am blessed with loving friends like Elmira Johnson, Angela King, Angela Wynn, Fredrica Crowe, Veronica Busby, and Sheila Baker, who offer their time and help at a moment's notice. I appreciate all of you.

City Councilmember Anita R. Ashford, of Port Huron, Michigan, sent me hundreds of facts about Detroit's empowerment zone. Thank you, my friend.

Even though I'd done my research on my characters' medical and drug histories, it is still impossible to write your story without interviewing those gifted doctors and nurses who deal with life-and-death situations every day. I offer a special thanks to Kathy Kosta in the critical care unit at Crittendon Hospital and Dr. Ira H. Mickelson (Dr. Mike). Jean Quenby, at Oakland Family Services, sent me tons of information about alcoholism and the dynamics of female alcoholics. What was really key was a dissertation that she sent me about the social and psychological aspects of African American alcoholics.

Denise Stinson, my agent and friend, is a creative genius. Her suggestions and ideas have been invaluable.

My new editor, Claire Zion, has been a joy to work with. She scolded me, taught me, praised me, and kept my story, my story. Bless you.

What is especially gratifying is when a publisher makes a commitment to its author. Thank you, Maureen Egen.

A warm thanks to firefighters Kimberly Bell and William France Jr., who risk their lives daily to save the lives of so many children, as well as the lives of others. You truly are our heroes.

A loving thanks to my two sons, Shannon and Vester Hill Jr., who helped me tremendously with young folks' slang.

Saving the best for last, I'd like to thank my husband, John D. Smith, who insisted that the dialogue for my male characters sound as if a man actually said it, instead of a woman saying what she wished her man would say. To my lover, my friend, my companion, know the depth of my love. The living water of our love flows through my body, my soul, like a lake, ever creating, forever creating . . . us.

Part One

They {the Negroes} will endure. They are better than we are. Stronger than we are. Their vices are vices aped from white men or that white men and bondage have taught them: improvidence and intemperance and evasion—not laziness: evasion: of what white men had set them to, not for their aggrandizement or even comfort but his own. . . . And their virtues . . . Endurance . . . and pity and tolerance and forbearance and fidelity and love of children . . . whether their own or not or black or not.

—WILLIAM FAULKNER

SPICE

Children begin by loving their parents; as they grow older they judge them; sometimes they forgive them.

—Oscar Wilde

$\mathscr{D}$ozens of cars were lined up for the valet service at the corner of University Drive and Pine Street in downtown Rochester, Michigan. By 8:30 A.M. BMWs, Mercedes, and Acuras began being parked by the finest red-jacketed valets money could hire. By 8:50 A.M. the lot was packed. Anyone new in town would have thought there was a party going on.

Locals knew that 9:00 A.M. was when the four-star, multimillion-dollar gourmet restaurant Southern Spice, known for its superb southern cooking, opened for breakfast. The five-story, 27,000-square-foot Victorian mansion that housed the restaurant was originally constructed with sixty-three rooms, thirteen bathrooms, two hundred and thirty-two windows, and twenty-

3

two fireplaces. Its Gothic exterior featured a dramatic gable roof and decorative tiles in different shapes and colors. The same tiles were repeated above doorways and over the tops of the dozens of bay windows. The roof's steeply pitched sides, topped with pointed spires and turrets, added to the exaggerated opulence. "Southern Spice" was inscribed in beige script over the grand brick-tiled entranceway.

Once inside, the scintillating aromas from the kitchen would cause many a belly to rumble. Orange and pineapple juice were freshly squeezed every morning. Country-cured ham from Virginia, bacon with the rind on, and egg-white shrimp omelets with a tropical citrus butter sauce were some of the house favorites on the breakfast menu.

People went out of their way to dine at Southern Spice because the food and service were both unparalleled. There was always something different on a menu that changed with the seasons. Southern Spice was elegant enough to serve Russian Seruga caviar and down-home enough to have fresh catfish for breakfast.

It was also a place where the Pistons' Grant Hill and Joe Dumars and legendary superstars such as Aretha Franklin and Anita Baker could eat without interruption from people asking for their autographs.

"Rosa Parks, the Winans, Mayor Quincy Cole . . . hmmm," Spice read to her friend Carmen from the morning paper as she sipped her coffee. "There's quite a few more black folks on the list this year."

Taking a break from preparing a celebratory brunch for her elder daughter in her private apartment upstairs from the restaurant, Spice was reading the *Detroit News*'s "Michiganians of the Year" list. The honor roll had begun in 1978, and for the third year in a row Spice Witherspoon was among the lauded Michiganians. As owner of the renowned restaurant, Spice had received numerous culinary, civic, and philanthropic awards over the past ten years.

Even though Spice knew she made the Michiganians list because of her achievements as a restaurateur, she was still most proud of the fact that her efforts in the community were appreciated. Hard work and charity were virtues she lived by.

The two women were two floors above the restaurant, preparing a small feast in Spice's personal kitchen. The left side of the huge room was a well-equipped commercial kitchen with a double glass-door Traulsen refrigerator and the La Cornue $14,000 range with twin smoked-glass ovens. The far corner was filled with a wide butcher's block curio cabinet that held an assortment of All-Clad pots and pans. Arranged along the cream Corian counters above dozens of stained-glass cabinets were various sizes of cutlery and the latest Cuisinart and mixers. In the center of the room was a long island, with back-to-back twin black porcelain sinks and a wine rack. On the right-hand wall was an arched barbecue pit and brick fireplace, with a low fire, now softly scenting the air with hickory, and right next to it floor-to-ceiling built-in bookshelves filled with cookbooks. The kitchen was Spice's favorite space in her two-story duplex, carved and refurbished from fourteen of the mansion's original rooms.

As Spice read the paper, the aroma of smoking meat brought her mind back to when her daughters were in school. She'd loved preparing large breakfasts and then walking her children to the bus stop on the corner. By living upstairs in the converted mansion, she'd been able to stay close to work without compromising the amount of time she spent with her children.

Of Spice's two daughters, Mink, the straight-A student, had always been organized, with daily homework assignments ready for her mother to check and sign. But her younger daughter, Sterling, was another matter altogether. Though Sterling's grades mirrored Mink's, her priority, even at age six, had always been her appearance.

Only David, Spice's now deceased husband, thought Sterling's obsession with her looks was cute. Everyone else saw it as saying a lot about Sterling's future character.

Spice and David were married on June 9, 1972, at the courthouse in Midnight, Mississippi. David, at twenty-six, was eight years Spice's senior, and Spice could still recall how badly his hands were shaking as they stood before the minister.

"Having second thoughts?" Spice remembered asking David.

There were tears in his eyes when he answered her. "Of course not. I love you."

David knew that when she agreed to marry him, Spice hadn't loved him. With two small children she needed a husband, security, and a home; David offered all three. Looking back now, Spice remembered the exact moment when her feelings had shifted.

Spice remembered the grueling eighteen-hour days that she and David used to work in the early years of the restaurant. Spice was the head chef then, and with the help of only three waitresses, David had to manage everything else. One evening, while David was cleaning the kitchen after the restaurant had closed, Spice looked over at him. Suddenly a warm pool of feeling filled her insides, and she realized then and there that he was the only man she would ever love.

"Baby, you're exhausted. I'll finish." She kissed him lightly on the neck. "You go on upstairs."

"No. You're exhausted, too." He loosened her apron and wrapped his arms around her, hugging her tightly. "I'm okay. Now go on. I'll be up in about an hour."

Hesitantly Spice walked away. Just before opening the door, she stopped and turned back. As softly as a shadow she said, "I love you, David."

"I know," he answered, smiling.

ONE BETTER

For twenty years, their marriage had been perfect. Spice's love had grown so deep for David that it surprised her. With the girls entering college, Spice and David had begun fantasizing about grandchildren and how they would fit into their potentially glorious future.

But it was not to be. On his way home from a weekend trip to Midnight, David had fallen asleep on the freeway and run into the back of a semi. He'd been killed instantly, he and his white Lincoln crunched up like an accordion. To protect her, David's brother, Otis, begged Spice to let him identify the body.

Now, widowed for five years, Spice knew that she would never again feel such an honest love as the one that she'd shared with David.

"Who else made the list, Spice?" Carmen asked, wiping a piece of loose hair from her forehead. After dipping the wooden spoon back inside the bowl, she finished sprinkling English toffee over the top of the caramel pie cooling at the stove and then placed it inside the refrigerator.

In eight months Carmen would be forty-five. Her small body, with tiny breasts and hips, and even her full head of naturally curly hair, cut in a sixties shag, resembled a child's. Carmen wasn't just thin; she looked undernourished. The bones of her gentle, latte-colored hands looked like trembling branches. It hurt Spice to see her friend's frailty.

Spice called off five more names, listed alphabetically, and stopped at the last entry: Reverend Golden Westbrook. "I'm not familiar with that name. I wonder—"

"Mr. Westbrook is the pastor at Divinity Baptist in Detroit. He's the president of the Detroit chapter of the National Alliance for the Advancement of the Black Race. He's been getting a lot of attention because of the NAABR elections this fall," Carmen explained as she began to pace the kitchen floor.

"Really? I wonder if he's looking for a wife." Spice continued reading the morning paper and sipping her coffee. "Now that's the kind of man Sterling should be dating."

"Sterling?"

"She may be needing a husband sometime soon." There was a bitter tone in Spice's voice. "She'll be twenty-six the end of February, and she's still costing me a fortune every month. I'll support her for one—" Spice stopped. She was becoming increasingly irritated by Carmen's pacing back and forth. "I'm starting to feel a breeze across my face from you walking so fast. You're making me nervous, Carmen," she said as she flexed the paper forward. "Sit down and take a break, will you? We've got plenty of time." She waited until Carmen was seated. "I'll pay her bills for one more year, until she gets her degree. *If* she gets a degree, which I doubt. Degree or not, one year, then she's on her own."

Carmen uttered a short laugh. "I can just see Sterling with a preacher." She removed a flask from her apron and took a quick sip of vodka.

Spice turned her mouth up in a half smile. "I think it's time for Sterling to make some changes, don't you?" she said, putting the paper away.

"What about you, Spice?" Carmen smiled. "Are you going to make some changes? When are you getting married again?"

"I'm not ready." Spice watched Carmen's smile fade. "April marks the fifth anniversary of David's death. And to be perfectly honest with you, I enjoy my freedom and making all the business decisions around here." Her voice was emotionless. "I married David because I needed a man to take care of me and my kids. My kids are grown now. I've since learned how to take care of myself. I don't *need* a husband anymore."

Although their friendship spanned decades, Carmen had never questioned Spice's motives. Spice missed David terribly at times but could not afford to reveal her vulnerability. Though few people knew it, Southern Spice was opening a second restaurant in downtown Royal Oak. And with it Spice was being launched into the rough-and-tumble world of business development. She had to appear as a woman with a man's strength and a woman's creativity.

When the timer went off, Spice removed the roast from the oven. Immediately the kitchen filled with the fresh scents of apricots, pecans, and thyme. She added a splash of bourbon to the robust sauce simmering on the range, the last step in the preparation of the succulent apricot-pecan-stuffed pork loin. Soft steam formed on the windows, clouding the outside view as the women worked. With the subject of husbands dropped, the two women moved on to a safer topic—food.

"Don't you think this is a lot of food for four people?" Carmen asked while stirring three pounds of fresh jumbo shrimp and lobster into the bubbling red pot of gumbo on the stove's front burner.

"Of course not! It's time for a celebration." Spice paused. "How often does a mother see her black child promoted to captain with a major airline? And a female child at that." She expertly sliced the piping hot pork roll and began arranging the dual circles of meat over a circular base platter of roasted new potatoes, leeks, and baby carrots. "However," she added, "whatever food is left over, we can wrap up and deliver to Mother Maybelle's Soup Kitchen downtown in the morning." As she poured a hefty amount of the hot glaze into a separate dish, Spice brought a finger to her lips and gingerly sampled the tangy bourbon sauce. "Mmmm," she said, "perfect."

Carmen gave the gumbo one final stir, then replaced the cover on the pot, lowering the flame. "Everything for the brunch should be ready in about fifteen minutes."

Spice moved to the refrigerator and looked inside at its contents once again. On the top shelf, a spinach salad with apple-onion vinaigrette glistened in a glass bowl. She checked

Carmen's work of art on the lower shelf: five lotus-shaped stemware pieces filled with peach Melba.

"I haven't even worked my usual shift, and I'm exhausted," Carmen said, sitting down, putting her feet in the opposite chair, and once again removing her small flask from her apron pocket.

Spice and Carmen had been cooking since 6:00 that morning. It was now 11:12 A.M. and the brunch was set to begin in just under two hours.

As she spoke, Spice's voice was inflected with the hurt she felt inside. "Carmen, I'm really having a problem with you not taking part in today's celebration." She slipped on a pair of oven mitts and lifted one of the chafing dishes filled with scrambled eggs, bacon, and sausage. The center island and counters in the kitchen were covered with eggs Benedict, ham, corned-beef hash, biscuits and gravy, homemade waffles with strawberries and whipped cream topping, and fresh Danishes completing today's meal. "You know how important you are to this family. It won't be the same without you."

"Not today, Spice." Carmen placed the dish she'd transferred from the kitchen beside Spice's in the living room. Stepping back, she automatically smoothed the swirled gold moiré skirt draping the buffet table that she and Spice had lavished with gold silk bows. Ornate Russian Fabergé silverware was laid out next to red china. Ivory linen napkins were rolled through cylinders of jewel-studded bracelets. "However," Carmen said teasingly, "if you'd like to offer me a bottle of your private cognac, I could be persuaded into accepting one of those."

"Of course," Spice said, moving hesitantly toward the bar.

Reflected in the mirror along the well-lighted bar was an elegant black lacquer Yamaha piano facing the south wall. Spice's most prized possessions were two papier-mâché gilt, mother-of-pearl, and cane side chairs with a similarly painted papier-mâché mother-of-pearl *cave à liqueurs* that were carefully positioned beside the piano for a stunning effect that added to the flamboyance of the room. Though she rarely drank, Spice kept the bar well stocked. There were several bottles of Dom Pérignon and Cristal along with the usual variety of liquors.

But what Spice was particularly proud of was the case of Louis XIII cognac, valued at $1,355 a bottle, that had been given to her by David on their fifteenth anniversary.

"Now, Spice," Carmen said, resting her hands on her narrow hips, "I was just kidding about the cognac, girl." She chuckled. "I could have sworn you'd say no, knowing how much those bottles mean to you."

Spice exhaled and felt her body relax. Truly, she would have given Carmen anything she wanted, but she was thankful that her friend didn't feel the need to test her loyalty that way. She hugged Carmen's tiny body, then said seriously, "If you change your mind . . ."

"Spice, I know I'm family, but today should be a celebration for kin, your brother-in-law, and your daughters. Anyway, it's been a while—"

"Since I've seen Mink and Sterling. I know," she said softly. "Otis called yesterday and said that he wanted to talk to Sterling about something. It might have been about a job." She shrugged it off. "Anyway, I've forgotten the conversation, I've been so busy with this new project."

She removed her apron and gloves and sat at the kitchen table. Carmen joined her and listened as Spice told her about her latest entrepreneurial adventure.

Foxphasia, the $38 million hotel and office center, was located on the northeast corner of I-696 and Woodward in Royal Oak on a 6.8-acre site. Along with two other investors, Spice had founded the Foxphasia Corporation to develop three office buildings of three, five, and fifteen stories, respectively, a five-story condominium, and a three-story cultural children's museum with a pedestrian bridge that would be built between the

Detroit Zoo and the 154-bed office-hotel that housed Southern Spice's sister restaurant on the first level. When Spice finished explaining her version of the completed project to Carmen, she clapped her hands like a child and exclaimed, "It's getting exciting, I can tell you that, girl!"

"I'd like to see it one day."

"Why wouldn't you? Anytime, kiddo." Then Spice added, "Even though my daughter is talented, I made a mistake in commissioning her to design the children's cultural museum."

"Sterling?"

"Yes. It took all of Otis's and my pull to get her hired temporarily at Zuller Architectural Firm. She had to work through one of their senior architects because she's not licensed yet. And she still hasn't finished the plans. She seemed so excited about it last summer. Now she's a month behind for the bank's deadline for approval of the plans. And the cold shoulder I've received lately from Zuller might never thaw."

"Don't worry, she'll come through." Reaching across the table, Carmen touched Spice's hand. "You need someone to help you with all this."

"Otis has offered many times to help me. But I don't want him involved. I see him enough already. Daily contact would be too much." She leaned back in her chair and turned to gaze outside. "I had planned on discussing my future plans for the development with the girls. You know, let them see the possible benefits of building a family empire. Otherwise, it just doesn't make any sense to work so hard for much longer."

"Marriage is still an option."

"As I said earlier, I'm still not ready." Spice turned to face her friend. "So it's not. But if I can convince Sterling of the importance of her career, and how it'll tie in with our Foxphasia Corporation projects, maybe she'll get serious. You know how Sterling thinks soul food is another name for slave food and refuses to eat it. She feels no matter how you fix it, or serve it up, it's still slave food, which is why I decided not to encourage her to take an active role in the restaurant part of the business."

"Sterling knows how to get to you, Spice. But she'll come through."

"I'm not so sure anymore about anything. In twenty years I'd like to know that at least a son-in-law or a grandchild is being groomed to take over."

"Spice, I don't think you're being fair to yourself or the girls by not get—"

"I'll tell you what. I won't discuss anything that serious today. We're just going to eat heartily and have a laughter-filled afternoon." Spice forced a smile that faded quickly.

With her hand still in the center of the table, Carmen touched her friend's arm. "Is there something you're not telling me?" she asked.

Spice looked Carmen squarely in the eye and held it before saying, "No."

"You've been acting funny ever since your birthday." Carmen turned her head to the side. "Personally, I partied through most of that year. So I really can't remember how I felt. But I've heard that turning forty-three is worse than turning forty."

Spice could smell the liquor on Carmen's breath as she spoke. "I'm not a believer in that myth," she said, turning away and hearing but not seeing Carmen take another sip from the flask. "It's never the physical that concerns me most. It's my mental attitude—staying on top of things, being in control. Life has been good to me, but I don't want the girls to make the same mistakes that I made."

"Mistakes teach us about life, Spice."

"David and I worked hard to build this business, and we assumed they would want to keep it going." Spice removed the bread pudding from the oven and placed it on the butcher block to cool. "Mink's got her own career—" She added quickly, "Of course I'm happy for her. But Sterling . . . Sterling . . ." She shook her head. "What am I going to do with her?"

"She'll learn."

"When? Sterling doesn't care about anything but shopping." Spice sighed. "I keep making excuses for her not delivering the plans at the bank, but I'm running out of lies. I didn't raise her to be a loser. I know I made some mistakes early on, but—"

"You did what you had to do, Spice."

Their eyes locked, and the silent understanding they shared was enough right now. "I'm surprised that Otis hasn't arrived yet. He loves to catch me off guard."

"Nervous?"

"No," Spice lied. "Yes. Otis has been pressuring me a lot lately about dating again. He feels it's time I moved on with my life. I'm certain dating isn't like it used to be back in our day." She felt Carmen's smile on her back as she checked the clock above the double ovens: fifteen minutes before twelve. "They'll be here pretty soon—"

"And you'd better get dressed." Carmen scrambled from the chair and began stacking the dishwasher. "I'm just about to leave for home, but I'll call you later to see how everything went."

Spice whispered a warm "Thanks" in Carmen's ear, then ruffled her curly locks before leaving the kitchen.

Sterling arrived first. Using her key to Spice's private-access elevator and residence, she entered the duplex and hung up her coat in the front closet. "Spice?" she called out to her mother. "Spice," she said louder, "it's me, Sterling."

"Hi, baby. I'll be down in a few minutes," Spice yelled from her bedroom doorway. "Open a bottle of champagne while you wait."

Sterling checked out the spread of food and sampled a piece of toffee before removing one of three chilled bottles of champagne on ice. She took it upstairs to the library. Just as she was settling into a relaxing glass of champagne, she heard the elevator stop, followed by the sound of a key unlocking the door.

A few seconds later Mink peeked into the library. "Hello, Sterling," she said, giving her sister a hug. After setting her purse on the lower shelf of a bookcase, she asked Sterling, "Where's Spice?"

"She's still dressing, and Otis hasn't arrived yet." Sterling sighed. "Join me in a glass of champagne," she said, reaching inside the liquor cabinet for another crystal goblet. She poured a drink for her sister, then toasted her, saying with a smile, "Congratulations on your promotion."

"Thanks."

"I'll be back in a sec," Sterling said, setting down her empty glass. "Gotta take a trip to the bathroom." As she stood, she smoothed and adjusted her cuffed sleeves just so. Every gesture showed that she knew how she shimmered in her stunning ivory Christian Lacroix pantsuit with three rows of lustrous bubblegum-sized pearls hanging from her neck. Wearing all muted opalescent tones, poised and lovely in pastel nylons, pumps, and a softly painted mouth, she didn't need anyone to tell her that she looked terrific.

As beautiful as both women were, they couldn't have looked more different. Mink stood five feet nine to Sterling's five feet one. Sterling wore her hair long, in waves of autumn gold; Mink wore a perfectly shaped half-inch afro. Sterling's complexion was ivory, like a delicate lily; Mink's flawless skin was a rich chocolate brown. Sterling's eyes, a striking gray that at first glance appeared blue, made many people think of the goddess Athena; Mink's eyes were a deep sepia that mirrored the stars in midnight waters. The stunning high arch of Mink's sculpted cheekbones, her broad nose and full lips, called attention to her exotic appeal; Sterling's high, sophisticated forehead, sleek brows, aristocratic nose, and narrow lips gave her a classical, 1930s beauty.

Throughout Sterling's and Mink's lives, their hobbies, choices in men, and recently their career paths were as dissimilar as their physical features. It was obvious they had different fathers, though neither woman thought much about it—and that was lucky for Spice.

The master suite was decorated in the same theme as the rest of the apartment: rich creams, taupes, brass and glass in the furniture, thick white carpeting, and bold, black velvet walls. Leaning over her dressing table, Spice reapplied her makeup for the third time. She'd underestimated how nervous she'd be and couldn't get her hands to stop shaking. Consequently, at 1:22 P.M., she still hadn't finished dressing.

Finally, expelling a last sigh in a futile effort to calm herself, she left her room and headed toward the familiar sound of her daughters' voices. She hesitated for a moment and took a deep breath just outside the entrance to the library. Just as she was ready to go in, she was stopped in her tracks by the catty tone in Sterling's voice as she spoke to her elder sister.

"You'll probably hear about it next week," Sterling said loftily. "The dean's wife caught her husband and me together."

"Did she catch you in his bed or yours?" Mink's voice practically roared. "Never mind, I don't want to hear the vulgar details."

"Neither," Sterling answered with what sounded like pride. "In the backseat of his car in the school's parking lot."

"Jesus!" Mink exploded. "How stupid can you get? How stupid could *he* get?"

As Sterling began detailing how their affair had begun, there was no remorse in her voice.

Steadying herself, Spice walked into the room. "Hello, girls," she said, kissing Mink and then Sterling on the cheek. As she stood back to appraise them, she said, "You both look stunning."

"So do you, Spice." Mink poured her mother a glass of champagne.

"Thank you," she said, accepting the drink from Mink. And with her eyes fastened on Sterling, she said, "Finish your story," then took a seat on the velvet couch.

Mink took a seat beside Spice and patted her on the knee.

"Anyway, the wife called security, and since a half gram of cocaine was found in the car, the university decided to suspend me."

Spice had learned long ago not to react to Sterling's outlandish, self-destructive behavior. The more she showed she cared, the more her younger child rubbed her nose in her failure as a mother. When the telephone rang, Spice jumped, tipping the bubbly beverage over onto her lap, staining her silk dress.

"Hello," she said angrily while reaching for a handful of tissues to dry her soiled dress. She listened to her head chef explain why he'd called. "What kind of emergency, Travis?" From the corner of her eye, she could see Sterling lighting a cigarette and listening to her every word. "I'll be right down." She slammed down the receiver and rolled her eyes at Sterling.

"I've got to go," was all she said before quickly leaving the room.

She knew that I'd been planning this for months, Spice thought, nervously twisting her gold wedding band, which she wore on her middle finger, back and forth. She was positive that Sterling had staged the whole affair to draw attention to herself. They had played this game many times before. Losing another opportunity? And drugs? Again? Spice was fed up with Sterling's secondhand theatrics. She was so angry, she welcomed the excuse to escape—not an unfamiliar feeling, unfortunately.

Spice had tried to teach her daughters that they could be more—more intelligent, more talented, more attractive—one better than anyone, just by being themselves. But somehow the message hadn't gotten through to Sterling.

Pushing the button for the elevator to the restaurant, Spice thought back to another incident just four years earlier, on Sterling's birthday. All the preparations had been made at Southern Spice for Sterling and her boyfriend Bennie's wedding. Though Spice and Mink knew that Bennie Locke was the human embodiment of Narcissus, they'd had no luck convincing Sterling how awful her future would be with him.

And no one discussed that Sterling's real motive for her early graduation from Rochester High School and subsequent marriage plans had more to do with Mink's eloping with Dwight immediately after her twentieth birthday than with Bennie.

Anyway, there hadn't been a ceremony that day. Bennie had never shown up. The young bride-to-be was "all dressed up with nowhere to go." Sterling had been overwhelmed with embarrassment and filled with rage. Unfortunately, it had not proven to be the last of Bennie in their lives.

When the elevator stopped on the main level, Spice stepped onto the pink-and-white checkerboard flooring of Southern Spice's main kitchen.

She waved at the employees as she made her way toward the head chef's office.

Just as she entered Travis Foxx's office, Spice heard a rumbling, rolling noise, then the sound of a file cabinet drawer clicking shut, telling her that Travis was wearing his manager's hat at the moment. Travis had filled some of the tasks left by David's death. But Lord knew he was no David.

From the moment she sat down, Spice felt his eyes visually undressing her. "What's the emergency?" she asked.

She caught the snide smile on Travis's face as he moved from behind his desk and, facing her, rested his buttocks against the desk and leaned forward. He was a carbon copy of Will Smith on *Fresh Prince of Bel Air*, especially the ears. Spice had slipped once and called him "Will," which had pissed him off.

"If you'd come downstairs with me a moment, I'll show you."

They took the elevator to the basement. All the way down,

Travis complained about the freezer, which was costing a fortune in repair bills. His immediate bugaboo was with the new compressor system that currently ran their freezer and refrigerator. He'd voiced his concern over the hassles caused by the system last year. The system took up too much room and used double the electricity that a more compact unit would cost. Now they had the bills to back him up.

At Travis's suggestion, Spice peered at the overburdened circuits. She tried to make some sense of what she was looking at. She'd never been able to grasp the necessity for all the wire and tubing that extended off into a zillion directions.

With a sudden movement, Travis was behind her, gently cupping her buttocks.

"Don't." Spice checked each breaker inside the circuit box to see if any were in the off position. Travis, ignoring her, massaged her breasts from behind.

"Look," she said, pulling from his embrace, "I made a mistake. It's over. It can't happen again."

She watched his sly smile as he released her.

"You've got the most exquisite body that I've ever seen. Naked or clothed."

"I hope this isn't why you called me away from Mink's celebration."

"You don't give a rat's ass about that and you know it."

Travis's words stung.

"Travis, how I love my daughters is none of your damn business. Now if there is no legitimate reason for me to be here, I'm gone."

After four years of celibacy, Spice had longed for sexual satisfaction without the emotional entanglements. She'd assumed that a young man like Travis could enjoy occasionally bedding an older woman without strings. But after one week of intoxication, she'd found that it just wasn't possible; he was too demanding of her time, and his lack of discretion as her employee

19

hadn't helped. Just like today, acting amorous while on the premises was typical of his immature behavior throughout their brief fling. So she had ended it.

At twenty-six Travis was an asset to her business. He had the perfect ingredients of good chef management: culinary creativity, menu vision, manpower efficiency, and discipline. Combine these attributes with reason and common sense, and Travis was the epitome of a professional chef.

Spice chastised herself silently. She'd allowed Travis to take one too many trips around her mulberry bush. It was time to show him how pussy and power prevailed and that a mere set of balls had to step back when it came to running her business.

STERLING

*Whether it be for good or evil, the education of a child is princi-
pally derived from its own observation of the actions, words, voice
and looks of those with whom it lives—the friends of the young,
then, cannot be too circumspect in their presence to avoid every and
the least appearance of evil.*

—JOHN JEBB

---

*S*terling was livid. She poured another glass of champagne
and quickly gulped it down before asking Mink, "Can you believe that bitch left us here?"

"Spice is our mother, Sterling. She's not a bitch. I think
you've got the two confused."

"Fuck that. What kind of mother would walk out on her
daughter's party and go to work?"

"I'm sure it was important. She'll be back in a few minutes."

"Bullshit. She didn't have to leave. Travis knows this business inside and out."

Mink was silent.

"Tell me, Mink, is there anything more important to her than that fucking restaurant?" Sterling asked, fuming.

"Maybe she's upset about your news."

"I've told Spice all along that I didn't think I could make it at Crown." Sterling paused to light a Salem, then blew out a thin veil of smoke between them. "She wouldn't lis—"

"Hold on, little sister," Mink said, coughing. "You *can't* make it. Period." She fanned the smoke out of her face and, taking a step back, crossed her arms beneath her breasts. "Quit making these pitiful excuses. You're just plain lazy. You've never worked a day in your life. All that's expected from you is to get a degree, and you can't even do that."

Cocaine and sex were Sterling's passions; they were good servants, but ungodly masters. And both had been key to her escape from responsibility and reality since age sixteen.

Like all addicts, Sterling felt she was always in control of her drug use. But now she was not able to fool herself, or anyone else; she was hooked on red rum heroin. That was the right name for it: murder spelled backward.

"I'm not an overachieving martyr like you, Mink. If someone would just let me explain—"

Mink's face was full of anguish as she stood up abruptly. "It's cold in here," she said, retrieving her purse and moving downstairs to the living room.

Sterling followed a few feet behind her sister.

"Go on, I'm listening," Mink said as she moved toward the fireplace. Carefully she hoisted two logs into the fire, reviving the smell of burning hickory. Warmth quickly filled the large room.

Sterling's eyes rested on the fine details of the room. She remembered how Spice had meticulously chosen the flawless pieces for the black suede wall panels that were framed by cream gilded floor and ceiling moldings; the two nineteenth-century Chinese chairs; a pair of chic ebonized gilded stools, and several Chinese porcelain figures. Sterling had been quite young when she'd realized that the "junk" Spice fussed over was worth a lot of money. To Sterling, it was still junk.

Nothing's changed, Sterling thought. She'd been talking for the past five minutes with not one response from her sister. As usual, Mink hadn't been listening. No one ever listened to her. Suddenly bored, she moved to the piano bench and began toying with the keys. In a piece of music, there were separate notes broken up by air. Sterling felt there was a lifetime of stale air between herself and her sister. As she started in on a childhood melody, Mink startled Sterling with a question.

"You're forever talking about how painful your relationship is with Spice. What you don't realize is that the drugs are causing you the pain. Not Spice. Can't you see that they're destroying your life?" Mink stared intently at her sister. "Each and every time you're run out of school, drugs are the bottom of the problem."

"I enjoy drugs the same way you enjoy professional status," Sterling stated calmly. "Can't you see what that game is doing to *your* family?" The corner of her lips curled up in a knowing smile.

Mink scowled. "You ain't doin' nothin' but burning up brain cells that you won't ever be able to recover." She shook her head. "Why do you put yourself through this? Why do you put Spice through this?" She tried to camouflage her frustration and sound compassionate. "Whatever problems you have, drugs aren't the answer. You're high right now, aren't you? You don't have to answer. I can see it in your eyes."

"Girl's gotta do what a girl's gotta do."

"Why don't you try doing what you gotta do with your own money? Don't you care how hard our mother worked for that money? Of course you don't—you've never worked a day in your life. So obviously you can't identify with the black struggle."

"That's the problem between you and me; you try so hard to

be black. Why? If you're so down, so ethnic, why do you have to go around proving it to everyone?"

Mink rolled her eyes. "Uh-huh, and you're not trying to pass—"

"I'm not black or white. I'm just *me*." Sterling changed the song that she was playing. "I remember every song that David taught me."

"Give Spice the respect she deserves. David's gone. And after all, he wasn't really—"

Sterling began playing the music louder, drowning out Mink's words. "This is a classic tune that David taught me when I was five." She swayed her body back and forth as her fingers moved swiftly over the keys. "Remember?" She slowed the tempo. "David was more of a parent than Spice could ever be." Although the statement was spoken quietly, the words were filled with bitterness.

"Can't you be honest for once? I'm your sister, Sterling, for God's sake. I'm trying to help—" Mink stopped in midsentence, looking resigned.

"Why don't *you* try being honest for a change? You hide behind that uniform, but underneath you're a whore just like the rest of us."

"Where in the hell did you come up with some stupid shit like that?" Mink started.

Sterling stopped playing and swung around to face Mink. She began to laugh. "And the funny part . . . what's really funny is that you're so jealous of me it's pathetic."

"You must be outta your mind, girl," Mink said, rising.

"The fuck I am. You bring your ass over here and I'll show you who's crazy."

"You don't know who you're fucking with, girl."

"Come on, big sista!" Sterling started to laugh again. "Come and get some of this," she said, rotating her open hand into her chest and bobbing her head forward. Sterling started shadow-boxing as she moved toward Mink. She stopped for a moment and said with a smirk on her face, "Oh, by the way, Mink. I have *worked* today. The only kind of work I plan on doing—on my back." She paused, sneered, then sniffed the air. "I still got dick juice on me from this morning."

"You low-down slut—"

"Slut?" She walked toward Mink. "Who the fuck you callin' a slut? Ol' bitch-ass trick!" she screamed as she grabbed Mink's lapel, then swiveled her torso and right arm back in preparation to slap her. Sterling's open palm was halfway to her sister's face when Mink caught her wrist with her right hand, then grabbed Sterling's chin in the crook of her left elbow. Sterling felt Mink's arm slide down her neck and apply pressure on her throat and larynx, cutting off her air. Sterling struggled, trying to slip her petite body from Mink's tight grasp, then managed to loop her foot around Mink's calf and tug. Surprised by Sterling's strength, Mink lost her balance and slipped on the thick pile, bringing Sterling down with her.

"Lemmego, muthafucka!" Sterling yelled in Mink's ear as she tried to break free.

Neither would relinquish their tight grip. Struggling for leverage, they moved like serpents, their curved bodies sliding, rolling on top of each other along the black carpeting. The girls were clawing and scratching each other, returning blow for blow and tearing the room apart while they fought. Sterling grunted and let out a loud moan just as one of the Ming vases fell from the mantel and cracked. The papier-mâché chairs were knocked on their backs as they tumbled over them without noticing. Mink pushed in Sterling's face with one hand and snatched a clump of her gold tresses with the other.

"Ouch!" Sterling hollered, trying to shake her hair free from Mink's grasp.

Scrambling to her knees by the buffet table, Mink tried to pull herself and Sterling to their feet, but before she could, Sterling managed to grab one of the red china plates and break it over Mink's head. Mink winced but didn't shout as the plate connected with her skull.

Mink's suede heel caught on the edge of the tablecloth as she tried to stand, and an avalanche of gumbo, rice, eggs, and meat in warm chafing dishes came tumbling down onto the both of them.

Pieces of rice stuck in Mink's hair like maggots. Clumps of lobster slid down between her breasts. "I hate you!" Mink shouted as she grabbed a fistful of Sterling's angora sweater.

Together they rolled over and over, through the porcelain shards and food, struggling for position. Finally Mink managed to get her foot at Sterling's crotch. She pushed hard, pumping her heel against Sterling's pubic bone, until tears formed in Sterling's eyes.

"Now that was some shit!" Sterling shouted between clenched teeth. She managed to break away from Mink and scrambled to the other side of the room. She snatched a bottle from the top shelf of the bar and cracked the neck open on the side of the baby grand piano. Wagging the top half of the broken bottle toward Mink, she licked a drop of blood from the side of her mouth with her tongue. "Now you come and get some of this," she hissed.

"Spice is going to kill you," Mink said, looking around the room.

"Fuck her! Fuck you. Fuck all y'all mutherfuckas." Sterling dropped the broken bottle, turned, and started throwing bottles of champagne at Mink.

Mink dodged the battery of bottles aimed at her, but one bottle hit the toe of Otis's shoe just as he entered the room.

"Ouch! Dammit, Sterling!" Otis shouted. "What the fuck is going on in here?"

Sterling froze.

"Good God," Mink said, surveying the destruction of the room.

"Go home, Mink. The party's over," Otis said grimly as he

grabbed Sterling's arm and released the unbroken bottle from her grasp.

Quietly, without a glance in Sterling's direction, Mink gathered her things and left.

Otis released the inside button of his elegant black-and-white-houndstooth Versace jacket and steered Sterling to the sofa. After turning over one of the chairs, he sat across from her as she busily brushed food fragments from her hair.

The sharp smell of champagne grew stronger as it seeped through the room. "Damn, it stinks like hell in here." Otis snatched a handkerchief from his pocket and wiped off his shoes.

"Maybe it's your cologne," Sterling offered with a snide smile.

"You breathe trouble," Otis said, straightening his lapel. "You know that?"

Sterling's gray eyes were slippery with tears. She was exhausted, sore all over, and she just wished that someone would wrap his arms around her and say, "Everything's going to be all right, baby."

Instead her uncle Otis smoothed his Ho Chi Minh mustache, leaned back in the chair, appraising her and the room, and said, "You've fucked up all around this time."

Sterling pushed her red Viper to sixty in a thirty-five-mile-per-hour zone as she drove toward Pheasant Ridge, her condominium complex in Rochester Hills, just five miles from her mother. Until yesterday, the weather in Michigan had been quite warm, if snowy, for January, but today the temperature had plummeted to the teens, causing an explosion of new potholes on every major road surface. Slow spangles of thick snow, a symphony in white, began falling in a rhythmic bossa nova.

She touched the cut on her mouth with her tongue. It burned. She took a couple of deep breaths, then dialed Bennie's number on her cell phone. He picked up on the first ring.

"Yeah."

"Bennie. It's Sterling." She paused. "Can you come over?"

"I'm kinda busy. I was just on my way out."

Lighting a Salem, she slowed at the traffic light.

"Sterling? You still there?"

"Sure." She blew out the smoke, thinking fast. Her head was sore. Every strand of hair felt as if it were pulsating. "I really need you to stop by today. Can you make it? *Please.*"

"No can do, baby." His voice was hurried and without sympathy when he asked, "You need some dope?"

Sterling was hurt by his curt response. Why did he always offer drugs to soothe her needs rather than himself? Like millions of women, she knew she loved too much. She was a woman who refused to let go, who had used her sexuality to snare a man even though she knew she would be better off without him. She was a woman who allowed what the man in her life thought of her to become what she thought of herself. She was a woman who had gotten involved in a relationship that was a re-creation of painful memories from her childhood—yet, knowing this, she still couldn't break free. No more than she could break free of her need for drugs.

"Yeah, I'm almost out," she lied, hoping it would prompt him to come see her. "Can you drop something by while you're out?"

"I'm headed the other way, baby. If you need it today, I'll have my partner, Jamie, swing it by this evening. You remember Jamie, don't you?"

"Um-hm. Crater-faced fellow." Sterling balanced the phone with her chin and pressed the buttons to open both front windows. As the smoke escaped from the open windows, she welcomed the rush of cold fresh air that flowed across her face. Straining to listen to the sounds in the background, she was certain that she heard a woman's voice. "I don't want Jamie. I want you," she demanded.

"Seriously, I've got business to take care of today."

"So you'll be at my place tomorrow, then?"

"Look, Sterling. Someone's waiting. I've got to run." He hung up without waiting for her to answer.

She inhaled deeply and let the wind whip away the unwanted tears as she steered her Viper toward the back of the complex and parked in her usual spot.

Once inside, she took a long shower and washed the food out of her hair. She glanced at the answering machine while she dressed, disappointed that there weren't any messages. She'd half expected Mink to call to at least apologize.

Sterling poured a glass of Courvoisier from the small bar in her bedroom. She picked up her cigarettes, lighter, and deck of tarot cards on the table in the hallway and closed the blinds in the living room, shutting out the afternoon sun. The ultramodern black-and-white condo was approximately two thousand square feet, and every item in it was shimmeringly new. Her huge collection of crystal animals glittered on glass tables throughout the living room. No one understood the attraction, but the figurines reminded Sterling that animals were free spirited, honest, and simple—all the things she could never be again.

She shuffled the tarot cards, then turned on the television set to the Home Shopping Network and lit a Salem. The smoke curled in her eyes and stung as she placed the first card on the coffee table.

It was the Death card. Her body tensed. In the five years that she'd worked with the cards, she'd never turned this one on the first draw. "Bullshit." She shrugged it off, took a long draw from her cigarette, then continued turning the cards.

Her mind drifted back.

If you let her get through this, Lord, I will always love her. . . .

Those were the words Spice had uttered by Sterling's hospital bedside last year. Spice had thought Sterling was asleep. Sterling hadn't known at the time that she was ten weeks to term with an ectopic pregnancy—Bennie's baby. One of her fallopian tubes had burst, and she had nearly died because of the infection. A few hours after the surgery, the doctor and Spice stood by her bedside, discussing the prognosis. The doctor said she would probably never have a baby. Certainly not without complications.

Sterling hadn't wanted this baby, didn't even like kids, but suddenly it seemed important.

If you let her get through this, Lord, I will always love her. . . .

Sterling remembered how much it had hurt to hold back the tears until Spice had left her room. In those words, Sterling had heard her mother's confession—she had never loved Sterling before.

Even as a child she'd suffered at Spice's hand; Spice had always whipped her harder than Mink, had always yelled at her louder.

"Your truths are not my truths," Sterling had told Spice when, at sixteen, she'd questioned her about the unfairness she experienced during her childhood. Spice disagreed with Sterling's version and told her that it was all in her imagination. But Sterling believed her mother was lying. Through her teens she drew away from her mother and sister. Once her stepfather, David, was gone, she was left all alone.

The degree in architecture she sought was Spice's vision, not hers. Her only aspiration was to be part of a loving family.

Was having a goal so important in life? Did it say who you were or give your life meaning? She didn't understand her mother's and sister's obsessions with their goals, which only underscored how she felt that she just didn't fit in, that she wasn't a part of anybody. She had just herself, but she was determined to make that enough.

"I hate you, Spice," Sterling whispered as she stared down at the tarot cards.

She didn't want to be alone tonight. Tossing aside the cards, she picked up the telephone. On a whim, she called Travis Foxx and invited him over. Travis had come on to her often, and now was as good a time as any to find out if he could be a possible diversion when Bennie wasn't available.

ONE BETTER

By the time the doorbell had rung for the second time, Sterling had gotten her fix and was floating.

Wearing a gold satin hostess gown cut low in the front and high on the sides, Sterling fluffed her hair before opening the door. "Won't you come in, Travis." There was a playful sexiness in her voice that he couldn't miss.

Travis kicked the snow from his feet, handed her a package, and stepped inside. "Nice place," he said, looking around, then handing her his coat. He removed his shoes, even though she hadn't asked, and sat on the sofa.

"Suppose we make a drink first. Is the bar that way?" he asked, pointing toward the kitchen.

"Mm-hm. Glasses on the top right-hand shelf." She opened the package. "How'd you know?" There was a fifth of Courvoisier inside.

"Wild guess." After he prepared his drink, he offered to freshen the one she held in her hand, then joined her on the sofa.

"I was glad to get your call. I've thought of calling before, but it was never the right time," he said, handing her the glass.

She smiled. "I'm flattered." She clinked glasses with him, took a sip, then picked up the tarot cards. Turning her head to the side, she watched him ease comfortably back against the fullness of the sofa, stretching out his legs. After shuffling the cards, she placed them in the center of the table. "Has anyone looked into your future lately?"

With his eyes fastened boldly on her exposed breasts, Travis leaned forward, picked up the cards, and shuffled them again. "How about if I read yours?"

"I'd enjoy that."

"Of course, you might not like my way," he said, forming the cards into three piles, "but I think it's effective." He smiled. "I bet you've got all the cards memorized."

"Don't you?"

"Uh-huh." He looked her directly in the eyes. "It's not good to memorize the cards. You can interpret the meaning wrong."

"How so?"

Travis drew the first card; it was the Death card. "Don't get so defensive," he said, watching her eyes grow round. "I told you, when you memorize the meaning of cards, you don't get an accurate interpretation of what's happening. This tells you what kind of vibrations are going on in a person's life—the changes that are taking place." He placed more cards around it. "Let's see."

"What is it?" she asked quickly.

"It seems that you're in for a change in your love life. And . . . and in your work life."

"I'm not employed."

"And . . . yes . . . you need to change that flippant attitude of yours and be more serious."

Sterling laughed lightly. "No card says that." Then she decided to observe him in silence. She could tell a lot about Travis by the way he moved his body while he talked, the way he let his eyes linger a second too long.

An hour later Travis had shown his avid pupil two more spreads, the Celtic Cross and the Diamond, which Sterling preferred over her simpler version.

"My, that's interesting," she said to Travis, staring boldly at his crotch as she moved closer to him on the couch.

"What?" he asked.

"That double-barrel shotgun you're carrying between your legs," she said. "Is it loaded?"

"Always," he confirmed with a smile. With the tips of his fingers, he gently lifted her head at the same moment he lowered his, and their lips met in a kiss.

Sterling broke away, picked up the tumbler of Courvoisier and ice, and after pressing it against her lips, moved it down her neck to her breasts, then stopped, letting the wet moisture from the glass coat the swell of her cleavage. Seeing that she'd gotten his full attention, she slowly untied the gold satin gown, revealing her nude body underneath.

No more words were needed. Travis reached out and caressed the beautiful breasts that peaked and strutted proudly before him. With a sultry smile on her lips, Sterling drew his head against her breast and felt his cool lips encircle her nipple.

Pushing her back on the sofa, he kissed her, sliding his tongue inside her hot mouth. Hearing a low moan from the back of her throat, Travis ran his tongue over her lips, then her breasts, indulging himself in the softness of her flesh, kneading, sucking each breast until he heard a pleased sigh escape from her lips.

"Mmm, you smell like heaven," he whispered in her ear. "As fresh and fragrant as the breath of an angel."

Sterling blushed, then giggled to herself. *Damn! That sounds good. How'd you think of that shit?*

Cupping her head with one hand and kissing her, he reached down to tease the tight curls of her womanhood, then eased two fingers into the warm center. She gasped, then, with her hands pressed against his, guided him to push farther, deeper. She felt her clitoris swelling; her legs became rigid, and the back of her throat went bone dry as his fingers moved in and out, out and in, until she felt her muscles grabbing, tugging him back inside.

Her first orgasm was as if the sweet earth had floated out to sea on a warm, gentle wave. She didn't care if she drowned.

Travis reached behind him and grabbed one pillow and then another, pushing each beneath Sterling's hips.

Not a word was spoken between them; their heated breathing was their only communication.

Travis spread Sterling's legs wide, kissing her belly, running his hands all over her thighs. Desire rose up in her as he moved his head down. Sliding both hands on the sides of her hips, he pulled her closer toward him. His tongue outlined the fluffy triangle, making lazy circles, tickling the tiny gem. Hearing her breathing quicken, he plunged his tongue inside.

Delirious with need, Sterling reached out and clutched the back of his head. She felt a tingling warmth travel from her abdomen to her inner thighs. Moaning with pleasure, she pumped her hips toward the pressure of his throbbing tongue. A flame shot through her. She was on fire.

Her small jewel began to tingle, then tighten. Suddenly she felt a sweet deliciousness take her over. She shivered. Her body felt as if it were levitating, riding on the crest of clouds until it floated downward, slowly, and slower, until she felt as if she'd disappeared.

Wanting to give him as much pleasure as he'd given her, she guided his head back to her mouth. Matching the intensity of his kisses with her own, she reached down and pressed a damp hand against his hardness. Sterling unzipped Travis's pants, releasing his swollen member. With the heat of his penis in the palm of her hand, she stroked him up and down, feeling his vein throb, then feeling it harden and melt little drops of semen on her nimble fingers.

The thirst of her desire was so high, she felt punished by it and nearly ripped Travis out of his clothing. Every inch of his chest was covered with thick chestnut hair. "Mmmm," said Sterling, licking her lips and finally breaking the silence between them. "I can't wait." She kissed the burgundy nipples peaking out beneath his chest hair and stroked the hardness pressing against her thighs. How desperately she wanted to kiss him below, to taste the tangy fluid oozing from the tip and taunt him with her hot tongue.

"Where's the bedroom?" he asked.

"This way," she said, taking his hand. She led Travis through the darkened hall and into the ivory blackness of her bedroom. Opening the drapes, she let the light of the moon flood the room. After pulling back the sheets, she lay back and reached for him.

"Wait," he said, sliding on the condom.

Seconds later he lay on top of her, his eyes searching her face, his chest against her full breasts. The closeness of their young bodies felt like completion, until he entered her, stretching himself deep inside until he felt her vagina contract.

Sterling stiffened.

"Something wrong?"

"No," she whispered. *It hurts!* she wanted to scream. He was much larger than Bennie and the other men she had known. Instead she said in a husky whisper, "Your cock makes me so hot, I can't hardly stand it. I want to fuck you all night."

"Damn, baby, I'm about to come." Travis pulled back, waiting until his passion subsided, controlling his breathing, then began again.

She bit her bottom lip as he plunged deeper and deeper inside her. Oh, God, she thought, it's gotta stop hurting in a minute. Just relax.

He found her mouth once again, and she could taste the light tang of whiskey as his tongue traced her lips, softly parting and then swiftly surging inside. The pain finally subsided. Pleasure suffused her thoughts as liquid love lubricated her vagina.

Travis seemed mesmerized by Sterling's eyes. He looked almost grateful, pleading, as he weaved in and out, stroking her and simultaneously stimulating her clitoris. She smiled and stroked his buttocks with her long nails, reaching down to tease his testicles, then finding his anus and gently rubbing it until he moaned.

Something clicked. Her moist palms touched him everywhere, her mouth opened at the curve of his neck, licking, sucking. By the time Travis had gotten his second orgasm, and she'd sworn that she'd gotten her third, his penis was still as hard as marble.

"Mmm," he said, turning her buttocks around and entering her from behind. "Yeah, baby," he said, stroking. "Ain't that good?"

"I can't hardly stand it, it's so good, baby," she said through gritted teeth.

As he propelled his pelvis forward more and more sharply, he gave out small cries until suddenly he thrust fiercely and came.

The sounds he emitted were louder, whining, nearly sobbing, and he stayed drooped over Sterling like a wilted flower, heaving, his wet face against her pale back.

When he finally eased himself out of her, he fell onto his back, sinking his head back against the soft pillows.

"That was great," she breathed. Sterling straddled Travis's sweat-soaked body and kissed the glistening hairs on his chest. "Am I better than Spice?" She felt him flinch before he spoke.

"Say what?"

Her high was wearing off by then, and even though she had thoroughly enjoyed having sex with Travis, it somehow didn't compare to what she felt when she was with Bennie. In a way, it was too easy: no meat, just heat.

Maybe she could still have a little fun. She reached for him, her eyes penetrating his, and pressed him back inside her. "Tell me that I'm better than she is." She worked her pelvis and squeezed until she felt him stretching himself deeper and deeper inside her. "I want to know," she demanded. "Am I better?"

"Yes," he said, but she felt his interest dwindle. He slapped the back of her buttocks gently and lifted her small body to lie beside him. "Mind if I sleep for a few minutes before I go?" He yawned.

"You don't have to leave." She stroked his shoulder and wedged her chin along the side of his neck. "Is there anything I can get you?"

"No thanks." He pulled the sheet to his waist. "I just need thirty minutes"—he yawned again—"then I'll be fine."

"Sure, take all the time you need," she said, watching him close his eyes.

In twenty seconds he was asleep. His soft snore was a pleasant sound, she thought. If she'd loved him, it would be sweet music breathed softly into the ear of her dreams.

While he dozed, she thought again of Bennie, her lover who never once thought of protecting her by using a condom. She sighed as she slipped into a kimono and, after watching the tempo of Travis's even breathing, left the room.

Her hands shook as she scavenged the bathroom for her heroin. Finding it, she took a sniff, then washed her face with ice cold water. She stood against the sink, gripping the sides. In minutes she felt the wave of pleasure flow through her body. When she released her hands, she could barely feel the tips of her fingers. She stared at them stupidly, then laughed.

She sat on the closed toilet seat, and though she tried to resist, her mind floated back to that afternoon. What happened to the love? she thought. What happened to the beauty of a family?

She remembered how many nights as a young child she'd listened to David telling her an old nursery rhyme when he put her to bed.

The family is like a book—the children are the leaves, the parents the covers. At first the pages of the book are blank and purely fair, but time soon writeth memories and painteth pictures there. Love is the little golden clasp that bindeth up the trust. Oh, break it not, lest all the leaves shall scatter and be lost.

Minute by minute her naked body, and second by second her naked heart, felt the oncoming coldness from the eyes, the voice, the feelings of a single touch, by a woman she'd grown to hate as much as love. The floating vision of Spice appeared before her, then disappeared and left her feeling the chill of abandonment.

Sterling was unaware of how long she had been sitting there when the ringing of the doorbell made her get up.

"Just a minute," she called out.

It was just past eleven o'clock and she was hoping that it was Bennie so she could make him a little jealous. She mussed her hair a bit more, then opened the door.

"What took you so long coming to the door?" Spice said,

wiping her feet on the rug and looking around Sterling's apartment. Her hooded black velvet cape swirled around her. "And your hair—" She stopped.

"Have a seat." Sterling's first thought was the rush she would feel if her mother found Travis in her bed.

The large room was spotless, except for the cards and a pile of clothes falling off the sofa and onto the floor in front of it. Spice walked over to the black leather chair across from the sofa and sat down. She then said, "I came to apologize."

"Why? Just because you're totally wrapped up in your own needs and refuse to consider anyone's feelings? What's new about that, Spice?"

"Don't be ridiculous."

"I don't have time for this shit tonight. Let's drop it, okay? It's late. Why didn't you phone first? I could have saved you a trip."

When Spice reached down to pick up the cards, her cape fell open, revealing white satin pajamas underneath. "I couldn't sleep," she said, pressing the pajama top closed with nervous fingers. She spoke each word carefully. "I want to put this mess—"

"This really isn't a good time." Sterling arranged the cards in a pile on the table, then stumbled on the corner of the couch as she reached down to gather up the strewn pieces of clothing. "I've got company," she said pointedly.

"I see."

Sterling sniffed. "Look, I'm thinking I'm done with school. I'd like to work off the books for Zuller." Her words were somewhat slurred when she continued, "It's pointless for me . . ." She stopped. "Did you say something?"

"No. But it's somewhat difficult for me to believe that Zuller would still consider hiring you after you blew off the museum designs."

Laughing, Sterling said, "Didn't Paul Zuller tell you *why* we didn't finish the plans?" Paul Jr. had fired Sterling without his dad's permission before the design was even started; he'd caught her using drugs on company property. It took a bit of cunning, but she'd fixed Junior's butt but good. She giggled to herself as she remembered Paul Sr. getting high with her; but later his wrinkled body had ridden on top of her, and that was disgusting. After that, she couldn't face the museum's plans anyway. "Whatever—school's out."

"You're making a mistake, Sterling."

"I thought everyone had concluded by now that I *am* a mistake." Her voice was slurred, but the bitterness in her words was clear.

Spice swallowed hard and picked up her purse to leave. Wrapping the cloak around her shapely frame, she moved toward the door. "Please think about it, Sterling," she pleaded. Slowing her steps as she spotted the familiar coat on the chrome stand by the door, she turned back around to face her daughter. Her voice was filled with regret. "He's not good enough for you, Sterling."

"How would you know?" Sterling cocked her head to the side and frowned at her mother. "Tell me, Spice, did you enjoy sampling the hired help? I've been told you're not as good as—"

"Don't you dare talk to me like that." Spice turned to leave. "Do you enjoy behaving like a common whore?"

Tears bubbled up in Sterling's eyes. She balled her fists, and her knuckles whitened. "Like mother, like daughter," she said.

Spice faced her, stunned. "Stop it!" she screamed. "Coming here was a mistake. I'm leaving."

"Oh, don't leave now. The show's just starting." Sterling pushed her mother's stiff body back down in the chair. "I mean don't *you* fucking move!"

Spice froze, shocked by her daughter's sudden rage.

Sterling giggled, then the expression on her face turned serious. Placing both hands on the chrome arms of the chair, she was face-to-face with her mother. "Yeah. I know all about you. Those lies you've been telling us for years. And that bullshit about your mother passing for white somewhere in Tennessee—the one who supposedly looks just like me?" She spat out, "Ha!" She shifted her weight, watching Spice intently. "Remember that damn picture you cut out of the newspaper of the woman who resembled you so much—the one you told Mink and me was your *mother*?" She threw up her hands when Spice lowered her head. "Look at me. I'm talking to you!" she screamed. "My God, how could you lie to us like that?" Sterling stepped back, puffing wildly, one hand on her hip. "I didn't believe a word of that shit. Neither did David. He told me he only hired the private detective because he felt sorry for you. He never believed that he could find a woman that's been missing for nearly forty years."

Sterling didn't see or care about the tears that fell from her mother's eyes. She moved to the kitchen and poured two fingers of Courvoisier into a glass tumbler while she continued. Spice appeared to be petrified, rooted in her seat. "Bullshit! It's all bullshit! Lies. You just wanted him to feel sorry for your 'abandoned' ass."

Spice's tall form seemed to shrink several inches. She made an attempt to collect herself and speak, but the words wouldn't come. Her lips trembled and tears fell from her olive black eyes.

Sterling would never forget the look on Spice's face. Every detail, every scowl, would be etched in her memory. She fled, slamming the door to her bedroom. "You bitch," was all she could think of as angry tears streaked her face.

But suddenly the thought of going back to bed with Travis made her feel hollow.

Was there no one who could love her enough?

 C<small>ARMEN</small>

*What shall I tell my children? . . . You tell me—'Cause freedom
ain't freedom when a man ain't free.*

— L<small>ANGSTON</small> H<small>UGHES</small>

---

*B*efore she had left Spice's duplex for home, Carmen had
rinsed and refilled her flask with Absolut, which she hated. She
preferred Popov vodka, but her supply was depleted at home,
and she didn't feel like a trip to the party store.

Once inside her apartment, she felt a wave of nausea and
rested on a footstool for a moment.

Looking around at her "fun furniture" living room, as she
called it, Carmen was temporarily warmed by the bright blue,
red, and yellow sofas and chairs and the colorful Crayola rugs
sprinkled over shiny hardwood floors. She shrugged off her coat
and thought back to her conversation with Spice.

Carmen couldn't understand Spice's fears. Her friend's home

was filled with beautiful treasures and loving memories. The girls might bring her trouble, but on the other hand, there was so much possibility. Even now, Mink's daughter, Azure, was a special source of pleasure.

Carmen had warned Spice when Sterling disappeared for a week immediately following David's funeral that unless her problems were dealt with, Sterling's grief would boomerang back at Spice. Carmen knew. For the past twelve years she'd lived in the nine-hundred-square-foot garage apartment that was part of the mansion adjoining Southern Spice. She'd always had a good view from which to observe Sterling and Spice. She'd seen how each was suffering from a longing for affection and how both were too stubborn to show how they needed the other. Carmen felt that she was the only one who could make Spice understand that the resentment and anger Sterling expressed through destructive actions were really a desperate cry for her mother's love. And that was why Sterling demanded more from Spice than Mink. But how could Carmen lay this on Spice without hurting her?

Funny, Carmen thought, they'd both started out in Midnight on equal footing, with equal problems, yet Spice was now rich and successful and Carmen was still struggling to come to terms with the ephemeral illusions of her past. What could have happened to those pretty dreams?

The thought of a quick drink got her up as far as her purse, and she poured a double shot from the flask into a tumbler, then turned on the television.

A rerun from *Little House on the Prairie* was on. Often, when she watched the show, Carmen was brought to tears. Pa, Michael Landon's character, was a believably perfect father who seemed capable of solving any problem that faced his family. Carmen smiled, watching his handsome face and easy smile as he kissed his wife on the cheek.

Having never been married, and not seeing the possibility of marriage in her immediate future, and now without a child of her own, Carmen at times could not contain her resentment of Spice, who had it all.

Resentment, she knew, was a union of sorrow and malignancy. She detested the passionate jealousy she felt toward her dear friend's fortune. Surely Spice had paid her dues and then some. Carmen wished she could rid herself of her envious feelings. Spice had shown her nothing but love, and Carmen couldn't help feeling guilty. She took another drink.

It was a quiet night, as serene as a meditating nun. But the plush dark sky outside her kitchen window offended Carmen. As the moon's crescent shone through the skylight, Carmen wondered when Spice was going to stop and pause and thank God for the blessings that she had and just be happy. As she downed the last of the booze from her flask and set down her empty glass, her eyes again scanned the stark white walls of her apartment.

"How has my world been reduced to this walled-in space?" she said aloud. She stood and moved to the window. Somewhere in the back of her mind, thoughts of her son, now gone, surfaced once again, and she felt moisture coat her eyes. Despite the two sweatshirts, her body began to tremble and her teeth chattered. She couldn't shake the bone-chilling cold that had crept inside her soul.

Back in the kitchen, she opened the bottle she always kept on reserve and consumed two more quick drinks. At first she felt normal; then, as she turned to move back to the living room, she could feel her body moving as if in slow motion.

"Just one more shot." She poured a tiny bit more into the glass.

You've got to take better care of yourself, Carmen. . . . That's what Spice always told her, even when they first met.

Twenty-seven years ago Carmen had been living in Midnight,

Mississippi. She and Antoinette Green, as Spice was known then, had shared a large home with three other single mothers. Carmen had one son, and Spice one daughter, Mink. All the women received county checks. Spice and Carmen were close, got along like sisters. Both were determined to get off welfare and wanted a better environment for their kids. They found work as cooks at one of the local chicken shacks. Within a few months they agreed to pool their money and move in together. That way they could schedule their hours at work so they could baby-sit each other's children.

The two worked as short-order cooks in a restaurant popular with truck drivers. They were paid cash under the table at $2 an hour, well below minimum wage back then. But the big tips and free lunches made the trade-off worth it. Often they talked of how long it would take to save enough to tell the government what to do with their paltry checks. They figured two years would do it. Meanwhile they lived in their three-bedroom farmhouse three miles from town and enrolled in a local cooking school, both working toward a chef's license. They got off welfare. Though Carmen was nearly two years older than Spice, it was clear from the beginning that Spice was the more stable of the two. Even then, Carmen had liked her booze too much.

After a few months, Carmen and Spice discovered that they were both pregnant. They had been ashamed to admit their stupid mistakes to each other. Plagued with uterine complications from the beginning, Spice was bedridden the last two months of her pregnancy and forced yet again to live on welfare.

But her luck changed when she met David Witherspoon, who was visiting his family in Midnight the summer after Sterling was born and stopped in at the Silver Spoon diner. Spice was on duty, and from his counter seat, David watched Antoinette add her own mixture of spices to the food he'd ordered. She'd told him that she learned about spicing from reading the periodicals from France in her doctor's office. From then on, David came in frequently to see Spice, and one day he teased her that she was "the spice of his life." The nickname stuck—it suited her.

Spice's special seasonings, which she shared with Carmen, had become so popular in town that the church began asking them to cater events. Soon the affluent white folks asked that Carmen and Spice cook for their dinner parties. Before they knew it, their catering business flourished.

David had fallen in love with Spice, as well as with her two young daughters, Mink and Sterling, and he soon asked Spice to marry him and move back to Detroit, where he worked as a carpenter for General Motors. Spice agreed, telling Carmen that she admired David for his levelheaded maturity and his habit of banking ten percent of every paycheck.

It was the combination of David's maturity and Spice's ambition that made Carmen love and yet envy them so much. Even then Carmen knew they were a couple who could accomplish anything.

Carmen had to give it to the man; even though he was three inches shorter than Spice and his nose was a bit large for his dark face, his mouth a bit too small, and his eyes seemed to bulge from their sockets, David didn't look bad, just interesting. When you took into account his wide shoulders and thick legs and thighs, he was surprisingly attractive. In fact, the more Carmen looked at him, the better looking he became.

David pulled Carmen aside before he left for the city with Spice. Privately he told her that she would always be welcome in their home. Their pleasant conversation ended with a discussion about marriage. She left that day with an impression of a good man who believed that marriage was supposed to be for a lifetime.

It would take a lifetime for her to forget him.

Carmen never did stop loving David. But as time went on, she loved him like an older brother. She had grieved beyond measure when he passed away. But so much had happened in be-tween.

A rerun of *Good Times* failed to make her laugh, or even smile. Bored, empty, and lonely, she dialed Spice. There was no answer; the voice-mail box was full. She thought about calling Sterling or Mink but changed her mind. Maybe they would think she was butting in on their business. After all, she was an aunt in name only.

After she'd hung up her clothes, she tried calling Spice once again. Still no answer. *I'll see her at work in the morning.*

Dressed in zinc white flannel pajamas, Carmen lay back in bed for an hour, listening to the wind still howling outside. She was restless. No amount of booze calmed her anymore.

Her mind haunted her, going back in time.

After Spice had left Midnight for Detroit with David and her two daughters, Carmen fell into a depression. Her drinking problem worsened. She lost her job as a cook, and without Spice, she couldn't handle the catering business. Ultimately she was evicted from their apartment, and the state helped her and her son, Adarius, move into a small house in a run-down part of town. There, Carmen met and fell for a man who introduced her to drugs.

In and out of flophouses and rehab facilities for four years, Carmen had given up on life when the social workers finally put her son into a foster home. She was eventually picked up and jailed for possession of heroin.

"Enriquez!" the bailiff of the correctional facility had hollered.

The big-breasted woman had stopped in front of Carmen's cell. "Me?" she had asked. "No one knows . . ." She had accepted the thick letter through the bars. Carmen's hands had shaken. It had been the first letter she'd ever received from anyone since she'd landed in jail.

It had been from Spice, of course, whose letter rushed

through the events of the past few years. Spice had described in detail the life she and David had built for themselves in Michigan. They'd been married for over six years and had finally fulfilled their dream of opening a classy soul-food restaurant. Spice had explained how they'd gotten started when the opportunity came to purchase a ruined Victorian house. With his expertise as a carpenter, David had bartered his services with other skilled trades to aid him in completing the work on the mansion. Now, Spice had said, their business was growing. Despite their struggles, they had obviously been happy.

Each month thereafter, Carmen had received a letter from her friend. How Spice had found her or why it took six years to get in touch were questions never to be answered. The point was, Spice was back beside her in her heart. Spice's letters had lovingly described the renovation of the Painted Lady, which proceeded even after the restaurant had opened. Spice clearly had put her stamp on each room. Each even had its own fireplace masoned of varying stones. Sterling and Mink had helped Spice select the colors for the vast rooms, many of which were circular and all true Victorian in style. They had painted the walls in shades from dark rose to sage avocado. Spice had complained in her letter that the ceilings were at least twelve feet high and it took twice as long to paint them.

Close to the time of her first parole hearing, Carmen had received a letter from eight-year-old Mink, neatly printed with enclosed Crayola drawings from six-year-old Sterling. Both girls had addressed her as "Aunt Carmen." How those letters had made her cry! Looking back, she knew again the warmth of Spice's friendship. Her friend had not forgotten how important it was to Carmen to feel a part of Spice's family.

Even back then, Carmen remembered, Spice had worried over Sterling. While Mink did her best to help her mother, Sterling, two years younger, did nothing but create a mess. Even through the letters, Carmen could tell that Sterling was making a bid for attention. When would this child be more secure? Hadn't they—Carmen and Spice—done their best in that little apartment on Beale Street? Every time Sterling had cried, someone was there to hold her, comfort her. She had been rocked to sleep, sung to, loved. What was missing for Sterling?

Spice had always ended her letters with "Promise me you'll take better care of yourself, Carmen. Love, Spice."

Carmen picked up the quilt from the end of the bed and carried it with her to the sofa in the living room. She changed the channel to CNN and set up the electric coffeemaker, then waited for it to brew.

Everywhere she looked in her apartment there were reminders of children. A sixty-year-old baby buggy filled with porcelain dolls was next to the bookshelf in the far left corner. An eight-by-ten smoke-stained baby photo with a pair of bronzed baby shoes attached sat on top of the television. *Not tonight.* Quickly Carmen moved her gaze away. Pictures of Mink and Sterling at different ages were on the walls, as well as on the surfaces of tables and shelves.

Her hands shook as she tried to balance the hot coffee on its saucer. She made it to the sofa and sipped the cooler liquid from the saucer before setting it down. When had the tremors gotten so bad?

Around one o'clock in the morning, Carmen was awakened by the wild wind whistling past her bedroom window. Thick flakes of snow had begun to fall seemingly from nowhere. The wind picked up speed steadily, and minutes later beautiful star crystals and snowflakes swirled, forming a mist.

Through the open window, she watched the splendor outside. The pristine visage that fresh snow brought always renewed her spirit, releasing her childlike side. "Hey there, little fellow," she called to the brown rabbit making tracks in the snow, "what's your hurry?" She felt surrounded by life's wonders—beauty available to every human being. But it was rare that she could take it in, appreciate it.

Like most alcoholics, Carmen suffered from mood swings— the high of booze before the stupor set in and the depression of dealing with reality whenever she attempted sobriety.

Once out of bed, she knew nourishment was essential. But as she tried to force down a bowl of vegetable soup with crackers, she was appalled by the taste and replaced it with two double shots of vodka before taking a shower. Her small form had grown frail as alcohol had become the only calories her body received.

Closing her eyes, she hugged herself and prayed once again that her frigid heart would awaken. As she sipped her coffee, she knew that even if she hadn't slept well, at least she'd be sober when she went to work.

Mink

With children we must mix gentleness with firmness. . . . They must not always have their own way, but they must not always be thwarted. . . . If we never have headaches through rebuking them, we shall have plenty of heartaches when they grow up. . . . Be obeyed at all costs; for if you yield up your authority once, you will hardly get it again.

—CHARLES HADDON SPURGEON

"Wake up, Mommy." Azure's grip was insistent as she shook her mother's narrow shoulder.

Tick, tick, tick—*frooom.* The furnace rumbled as the heat kicked on. Mink turned over, her thoughts coming together with each clink of hot steam filling the pipes. She could feel her tongue, thick and dry, before she spoke.

"I'm up," she said with her eyes still closed. She reached over and felt the cool empty space beside her. "Where's Daddy?" she asked, suddenly opening and adjusting her eyes to the bright overhead light.

Azure was three and a half years old. Nicknamed "Baby-Z" by her father, Dwight, she had her daddy's crooked smile, wide nose, and broad forehead. Her small ears, like Howdy Doody's, were positioned on a head that seemed to be waiting for the rest of her tiny body to catch up. Her long fingers, thin and flat like the black row of piano keys, and narrow feet were the only features she had inherited from her mother. And then there was her dark fuzzy hair, brushed in an afro puff that her daddy loved to fix for her, which enhanced her pixielike appearance.

"Dunno." Azure climbed into the rumpled bed beside her mother and tugged on her arm. "I'm hungry, Mommy. Fix me breakfast, please."

From just outside the doorway, Mink could hear Jelly Jam, Azure's Yorkie puppy, panting heavily. When Mink moved to the end of the bed to grab her robe, she felt a jolt of pain, a reminder of the fiasco with Sterling. "Shit," she shouted as a broken fingernail got caught in her sleeve. Jelly immediately backed up. He knew better than to enter her room. "Isn't Erma up yet?" Mink glanced at the clock on the nightstand. Good Lord, it was just past eight A.M. *"Damn,"* she muttered. She'd planned on sleeping till nine.

"She won't wake up," Azure said quickly.

Mink, wearing one of her husband's gray PowerHouse Gym T-shirts, sat up in bed and felt an instant throbbing at her temple. She checked her face in the mirror from across the room. From twenty feet away she could see that the bruise on her forehead from the fiasco with Sterling had deepened into varied shades of violet. "Did you wash your face and brush your teeth yet?" she asked as she walked into her private bath.

"No."

"You go and take care of that," Mink said, shoving Azure's

little body out of the bathroom. "Then I'll meet you downstairs in the kitchen."

Azure ran back to give her mother a long hug, kissed her on both cheeks, then stopped. "What happened to your face, Mommy?" she asked.

"This?" She touched the bruise, flinching. "Oh, nothing, really. Last night I accidentally bumped my head on the bathroom door." She was taken off guard by her daughter's concerned expression and added, "But I'm okay. It doesn't hurt a bit—now scoot."

Since her recent promotion with the airline, Mink's duties had escalated. Beyond the normal responsibilities of an airline captain, there was the burden of paperwork. It was a challenge that took an extra hour each night—whether she had flown or not. In just over a month of being a captain, she was emotionally and physically exhausted. But she couldn't complain; she had asked for and gotten just what she'd wanted.

Within minutes Mink was down the hall, knocking on her housekeeper's door. "Erma?" she called out. "Erma, are you okay?"

Mink heard the bed creak, then a sleepy voice answered, "Come in."

"Good morning." Mink took a seat beside the bed as Erma scrambled for her glasses on the nightstand, then turned on the light.

"You okay?" Erma asked, noticing Mink's bruise.

"Um-hm. Popped my head on the door. It's nothing."

"Put some ice on it, you hear?" When Mink nodded Erma smiled warmly, then said, "Your husband called late last night."

"Dwight? I didn't hear the phone." Dwight Majors had been a firefighter for the city of Detroit since before he'd married Mink.

"I could tell when you came home last night that you were exhausted, so I didn't waken you." Erma yawned. "He's working a double shift at the fire station. I was dreaming so good, I didn't get up to leave you a message."

"Oh, yeah," Mink said, remembering, "it's your day off. I had completely forgotten."

"I'll get the baby's breakfast," Erma said, pulling back the covers.

Rising, Mink stopped her. "No. You sleep in. I can handle things today." Ordinarily she rarely went into Erma's room. Erma seemed to know without discussing it that Mink wanted to keep her distance. Over a four-year period, they had developed a grandmother-granddaughter type of relationship. Even though Mink never wanted to make it any friendlier than that, she had come to rely on the older woman's wisdom.

Azure was scolding Jelly Jam when Mink entered the kitchen.

"No," she said, waving her finger in front of Jelly's face, "you're not getting German chocolate cake, either." Azure went to the lower cabinet and pulled out a big box of dog biscuits, ignoring Jelly's whimpers for his favorite snack, which was in a covered dish on the counter.

After Jelly got his biscuit, Mink opened the back door and let the dog outside, then began looking inside the cabinets. "You want strawberry Pop-Tarts this morning?" Mink asked, still searching.

"I don't like Pop-Tarts anymore."

Mink reached behind the short boxes and took out a large yellow one. "How about Honeycomb cereal?"

"I don't like that, either."

Mink's anger was beginning to rise. "All right. What *do* you like to eat for breakfast?" Normally Dwight's job, breakfast wasn't a meal Mink could remember preparing for her daughter. She hated to cook.

"Cap'n Crunch."

"We're in luck, then. Here's a brand-new box."

ONE BETTER

Azure was silent while watching her mother place the bowl before her and drown the cereal with milk.

Jelly scratched at the door, wanting back in. When Mink returned, she saw that Azure's bottom lip was trembling and her eyes were full of tears.

"What's wrong now?"

"Daddy and Erma know that I don't like Cap'n Crunch without the Crunch Berries."

Mink was amazed at her own instant fury. "Why didn't Erma buy the Crunch Berries kind?"

"She didn't buy that cereal. You did, Mommy."

Mink was about to argue, then remembered last week when Erma had been sick and she'd gone shopping. She'd been so irritated about doing the task, she'd barely checked the list that Erma had written out for her. Holding her temper, she took a few deep breaths. "Let's start over," she said, making her voice light. She removed the unwanted cereal and poured it down the disposal. While Mink filled the coffeepot with tap water, she turned and said briskly, "Tell me what you'd *like* for breakfast."

Azure knew that tone of voice, and silent tears fell down her chubby cheeks. She turned her face away so her mother couldn't see. "I want my daddy," she said, sniffing. She ran from the kitchen, with Jelly trailing fast behind.

"Spoiled brat," Mink said under her breath. "I'm not putting up with this shit—not today."

Agitated, Mink dialed the fire station and slurped some coffee after dousing it with cream. "Can I speak to Dwight Majors, please?"

In a minute or two Dwight answered, "Firefighter Majors here."

"It's Mink."

"Didn't count on the overtime, sweetie. How was the brunch?"

Mink hadn't seen her husband in two days. "Terrible," she answered, annoyed. Her next trip for Pyramid would begin before Dwight was off duty. "We can talk about that later."

"Do you want to talk when I get home?"

"That's the problem. You're not home. Forgive me for being a little selfish, but I don't get to talk shit with the guys all day at work—I've got a real job."

"Don't start this again, Mink."

There was a long silence as both felt the familiar argument coming. Mink was complaining Dwight didn't pull his weight; Dwight was defensive, accusing her of rubbing his nose in shit.

"Listen, Azure's in her room. She won't eat breakfast. She probably won't eat lunch, either. And I'll be damned if I'm making dinner."

"As I said earlier, we'll talk when I get home."

Through gritted teeth she added, "I won't be here when you get home. I've got a four-day trip scheduled to leave tonight. So who's supposed to take care of your spoiled-ass daughter? It's Erma's day off!"

Half an hour later, with a persistent throbbing at the base of her head, Mink left the house and her daughter, teary eyed after a scolding over the phone from her daddy, in Erma's care. It was worth paying Erma overtime. Relishing the idea of a day of pampering and getting away from her maternal responsibilities, Mink gathered her coat and purse for a trip to the European-style spa in Farmington Hills. It was a place where her body would be rubbed with a cream of crushed pearls, her hands dipped into hot peach-scented paraffin, and her feet would luxuriate in an aromatic foot bath. For four hours every effort would be made for the Estee client to achieve a better harmony among the body, mind, and emotions.

Once inside the four-car garage, Mink started her new ice blue Jaguar convertible and let it warm up for a few minutes. To her right was the Audi station wagon used to chauffeur Azure to her numerous activities. (Azure was never allowed in the

Jaguar.) Occupying the last two stalls were a dump truck and landscaping equipment. Though she berated Dwight about his attachment to the firefighters, the truth was she merely resented his time with the boys. In her saner moments, Mink knew how Dwight worked hard to build his landscaping business while keeping his city job.

As stupid as it seemed, as Dwight's business continued to grow with each new year, Mink knew herself that she was becoming more shrewish. She kept bugging him to rent a garage for the growing clutter. His answer was always the same: he wanted his expensive equipment where he could guard it, at home.

Their landmark mansion was situated on two acres at the end of Arden Park Boulevard in the historic Boston-Edison district in Detroit. Most of the mansions in that area, though huge in square footage and cheap to purchase, were expensive to maintain. But the mansion meant more than home to Mink—it represented achievement, that she was at least as good as her mother. And that was important enough to carry the heavy burden of maintaining the old house.

As Mink backed out the driveway and into the falling snow, she ignored the snowman decked out in Kenté cloth, surrounded by dozens of identical pairs of footprints—one set large and one tiny.

When the opportunity had come for Mink to be promoted from co-pilot to captain, she had understood the sacrifices she would have to make to be successful. Even before she'd obtained the title, she had been constantly away from home. It took years to build her experience, log flying time, and close in on the three thousand hours required for the commercial license that she had hoped to achieve by age twenty, and had. That was the first step in a succession of steps that had led to her position today. She felt it important for other African American females following her to set a standard of excellence.

Rosalyn McMillan

A recent article in *Ebony* magazine hailed Mink as the first black female captain to work for a major airline in the history of the United States. At the beginning of 1997, there were approximately ten thousand pilots and co-pilots. Only seventy-five were black. Of the six hundred female pilots, only twelve were black.

At age ten, Mink had gone on her first airplane trip. She and Spice were visiting Aunt Carmen in Mississippi. Mink was mesmerized as she gazed at the fluffy clouds and landscape below, and the dream of being a pilot instantly became her passion. With the help of one of Spice's affluent customers who owned a plane, Mink began flying lessons at fourteen.

For years Mink juggled classes at high school and lessons at flying school, then endured the tediousness of working as a flight instructor to accumulate hours. Married by age twenty, Mink had at that time already managed to secure a position as flight engineer. During a period of massive hiring in the early nineties, she gained seniority and ultimately was able to secure the position of captain at age twenty-seven.

But Mink had other lessons to learn. She had to ignore the sexism and racism from her fellow employees and the dirty looks she received from some of the passengers she greeted as they boarded.

Passengers didn't realize that most black pilots were more experienced than their white counterparts because of having been repeatedly passed over for the position. Often the black pilots were steadily accumulating hours and experience while they awaited employment.

So Mink just went about the business of achieving her dream while ignoring the barbs of others. But it was hard, and sometimes she felt that no one—least of all Dwight—understood. What had he ever been up against?

With two high-profile jobs in their marriage and a young child to raise, Dwight's flexible hours as a firefighter fit perfectly into their schedules. He was a great father—no question. When Azure was born, it was Dwight who interviewed over two dozen applicants for a live-in housekeeper, finally settling on Erma. And that was just the start of it. In fact, fatherhood was so high on his list of priorities that Mink had conceived Azure as quickly as possible to fulfill her obligation to Dwight and then get on with her life.

Mink arrived at Estee Mira's Spa in the City in Farmington, signed in, and picked up a magazine. The receptionist was busy explaining the rudiments of a spa day to a new client.

The waiting room was full, so Mink stood against the wall.

"May I help you?" the receptionist finally asked Mink after she'd been shifting from one leg to another for over five minutes.

"I'm here to see Randi. Could you please tell her Mrs. Majors is here?"

"She's with a client." The receptionist turned the appointment book around and checked for Mink's name. "Uh, Mrs. Majors—"

Mink snapped, "I don't care who she's with. I asked you to call her."

"I'm sorry, if you don't have an appointment, I can't interrupt—"

Mink waved her hand in front of the young woman's face. "Just tell her that Mink Majors is here. I'm sure she'll see me."

"As I said, Mrs. Majors—"

Mink walked around to the other side of desk, ignoring the woman's protests to stop. She shouted, "Randi! Randi!" up and down the corridor. After Randi made polite explanations to her client, she drew Mink to the side. Neither could see Grace Ujamis, the manager, fast approaching, along with the receptionist, who wore a strained smile on her face.

"This isn't really a good time—" Randi started.

"Is there a problem, Mink?" Grace cut in, nodding to Randi. "I'll handle it," she said, and led Mink to the side of the hall.

"I wanted to speak with Randi. I know that I don't have an appointment, but—"

"I'm sure that we can fit you in." Grace led the way back to the reception desk. "What would you like to have done today, Mink?"

"The works: a manicure, pedicure, facial, herbal wrap, and massage." Mink moved back around to the other side of the desk and watched Grace flip the appointment book pages back and forth. She tapped her broken nail nervously against the counter, waiting.

"Let's see." She turned to Cindy, the receptionist. "Would you tell Pauline that I'd like to see her for a moment, please?"

"But I want Randi—"

"Settle down, Mink. I can accommodate you this morning."

Mink caught her noticing the bruise, Sterling's little gift. Good, maybe the bitch will think I'm battered and cut me some slack, she thought to herself.

Grace quickly looked back down at the filled pages. "But you'll have to work with us." She motioned for a technician who had just appeared. "Darlene, would you take Mrs. Majors's coat, please?"

"Thank you," Mink said, easing out of her vibrant red-dyed fox stole. She heard snatches of the hurried conversation at the reception desk and rolled her eyes as she handed Darlene her coat.

"Darlene can take you for your pedicure in room three in just a few moments," Grace said to Mink and added cheerily, "Would you like a cup of coffee, Mrs. Majors?"

"No, thank you." She picked up her purse and went to use the telephone in the corner. "I'll be right over here, Grace."

Grace nodded and continued writing in the book, informing the technicians of the revised schedule.

Mink dialed Spice's number, catching her just as she was on her way out. "Did you get your box yet?"

"Um-hm," Spice said, a smile in her voice.

"I'm so sorry, Spice. I wish I could get the vases repaired—"

"Stop it! The last thing I expected today was a case of cognac and champagne. Thanks, it really wasn't necessary."

"No. My fault. I shouldn't have let Sterling work me up like that." Mink paused, exhaling. "Have you heard from her today?"

"No. But I expect to. Soon. I've cut her monthly allowance by a grand a month, and canceled all of her credit cards."

"That sounds good. What made you do it?"

"My accountant called. Sterling was ten thousand overdrawn on her account. Of course I was pissed, but I told him to go ahead and pay it." She sneezed. "He reminded me, 'Spice, you've done this four times already this year.' I'm constantly giving her ultimatums, and she's not paying attention. I've got to draw the line somewhere! He told me by his calculation of Sterling's account, her bills are running more than mine."

"She's not going to take this—" Mink overheard Kia, Spice's secretary, telling her to hurry, the car was waiting.

"Look, I've got to run. I'll talk to you later. And thanks again," Spice said before hanging up. Mink was quite used to Spice's busy schedule.

Mink found a vacant seat and flipped through another magazine, checking her watch. Ten minutes passed. Twenty. Twenty-five. She jumped up and stood back at the counter. "Grace assured me that I'd wait just a few moments. I've been waiting almost thirty minutes!" she hollered.

The receptionist turned three shades darker than Mink's fox coat. She opened her mouth to speak, then quickly clamped it shut and rigidly tapped her balled fists against the counter.

"This is exactly why I need to have someone come to my home," Mink said in an arrogant voice. She leaned across the counter and tapped the open book with force. "I don't know who you think—"

The receptionist spoke through clenched teeth. "If you'll follow me, Mrs. Majors, Darlene just called for you."

When Mink arrived at Pyramid Airlines that evening, after four luxurious hours at the spa, she felt great. "Welcome aboard Pyramid Airlines," she said, greeting the oncoming passengers.

Mink hadn't missed one sneer as she watched the condescending eyes of some of the passengers. The gold-winged nametag that read "Captain Majors" spoke for itself—a black woman was in control. Just a year ago she remembered submitting over a hundred résumés to secure this position. During that time, she'd received only two inquiries—she would never forget that. Nor would she forget who she was, what color she was, what gender she was.

During the interviewing process, Mink had gone through days of tests. The vision test was a breeze. Then there was the general aeronautical knowledge test about weather. She passed with scores much higher than average.

The psychological exams were extensive; there were three hundred and sixty true and false questions. This interview was trouble. A psychiatrist asked her about her childhood, and she lied, saying she'd been raised by her natural parents in a two-parent home.

She'd been warned by a few black pilots—those who weren't put off by a female getting ahead—that the psychiatrist was notorious for concluding that the interviewee did not fit the airline's psychological profile for reasons that were arbitrary. And there was a long list of pilots rejected for one reason or the other to prove this theory.

The interview with the shrink had been in a room smaller than a bathroom. The doctor was white, he wore white, the room was white. Everything in that room was white except her.

"Tell me about your home life as a child," the psychiatrist had said, "and start from the beginning."

Mink tensed. Beads of perspiration started to form above her eyebrows. More sweat broke out on her toes and buttocks as she shifted in her seat. *I'm going to need a straitjacket when they carry me out of here.* Several possible answers stuck in her throat. Then an idea came to her, and she recounted a story she'd read in *Essence* years back about a child star. She wrapped it up with a teary account of how wonderful her parents had been in encouraging her to pursue this career.

Apparently he believed her. His smile seemed genuine when he asked, "Which parent did you love best, your mother or your father?"

When Spice married David, Mink was old enough to know that David wasn't her natural father. Though she had loved him, she knew her feelings weren't as deep as her love could have been if he were her blood father. "I love them both the same," Mink said, thanking God that a lie detector band wasn't attached to her fingers.

Mink's entire body felt as though it had been immersed in water—she was sweating bricks. She had no idea who her real father was, yet she didn't hesitate to lie, telling the doctor that she was from a sound, loving environment and that her parents were in sync with each other about her education and future. What did it matter if she only had a mother and a stepfather? she thought to herself. *But in the eyes of white America, it did.*

To this day, each time she stood to greet Pyramid's passengers, she thought about those tests. Now her family's financial future was secure with the $270,000 she earned yearly. Like the other employees at Pyramid, she owned a piece of the airline, thanks to a strike two years earlier. There was also the 401(k) retirement plan that the company had offered that provided for an annual pension of seventy-five percent of her salary. The struggle to get here had been worth it, even if occasionally her daughter and husband got the short end of the stick.

She came back from her reverie as the last passenger boarded. Mink waved at Julie, the flight attendant she'd known for years.

"Later," Julie said hurriedly.

"Sure. See ya."

There had been ugliness between captains and flight attendants during the recent strike, but Mink felt comfortable with Julie.

After shutting the cockpit door, Mink took the seat opposite her co-pilot, Harrison Fielding. She'd never flown with him before and was mildly curious about him. Harrison was an African American male, approximately fifty to fifty-five years old, Mink guessed. With a fiery copper complexion as smooth as a rose petal, his barber-trimmed mustache and hairline made him look every bit the professional. He must be just under six feet tall, Mink guessed.

Mink always liked to let her crew get settled comfortably before she took her seat. "Hello," she said tentatively, feeling out the vibrations, "I'm Captain Majors."

"I know." His voice was guarded. "Harrison Fielding," he said, extending his hand. "I've seen the press releases about you."

"Who hasn't," Mink said in a self-mocking voice, thinking of the *Ebony* article. "I wonder if they'll ask me to do a piece for *Wired* next." Luckily Fielding got the joke. "Let's have a good flight, Harrison."

"Agreed," he said, smiling.

Mink locked both seat belts and checked the interior equipment. She moved through the normal procedure of setting her side of the control panel for departure, then checking the navigation and information systems. As she went through the routine of checking the safety items, she simultaneously monitored Fielding's preparation and reviewed the log book to make sure the aircraft was legal for take-off.

Mink's co-pilot went through his own routine, while he also kept his eyes on Mink's preparation. Obviously he wasn't as friendly as he pretended. They were two nervous enemies watching each other, Mink thought. They confirmed radio frequency, received procedure for the airport, received clearance from traffic control, and waited for departure time. As ground control guided the aircraft from the tarmac, Mink felt Fielding scrutinizing her every move.

When the ground crew instructed Mink to start the engines, the stars sparkled in the black sky.

As she moved the plane down her designated runway, she savored the feel of the power building. She was controlling and riding a 250,000-pound beast. The high was indescribable.

Mink thought about her daughter and husband, as she always did during take-offs. After the skirmish over breakfast, Azure had kissed her mother good-bye and told her she'd miss her while she was away. Mink wished now that her fight with Dwight was over—forgotten. How could she tell him that when she'd said, "Leave me alone," she'd really meant she was afraid to be alone? That when it seemed she loved him the least, she needed him the most? How could she let him know that the moment she left on a trip, she counted the minutes that would bring her back to him? Even though the professional side of her knew that she was a whole person, the other side of her never stopped questioning, Do you love me as much as I love you? Will you always love me?

Mink wondered if Fielding could tell by looking at her crimsoned lips, her stockinged legs, her manicured nails, that inside she was not together. She felt the skeptical eyes of her co-pilot as they took to the air.

Whoosh! A clean take-off. Mink felt her adrenaline surge, and she relaxed.

Mink took in Harrison's smile like a warm embrace. As she turned away to look outside the window, she felt an indescribable sense of calm around her, as gentle as infant love.

Now, as the jet soared through a reef of clouds while they ascended, she felt yet another rush. A part of her could almost inhale the clean scent of the air outside lifting them higher, toward heaven.

Under the canopy of the twinkling stars, the jumbo jet's nose appeared as black as a thundercloud as the machine bulldozed through the dark night. The effect for all the passengers who were watching, she knew, was just as heady as it was for her, no matter how often she might fly.

The rush she felt at just the moment when they climbed to cruising altitude always triggered her libido; she invariably wanted sex—right then, floating in midair. It was, of course, an unfulfilled fantasy. She couldn't exactly fly a plane and have sex at the same time!

As they leveled off at thirty-five thousand feet, Mink imagined she could hear the silence of the snow falling from the clouds to the ground below outside her window.

They were scheduled to land in Tampa, Florida, at 11:45 P.M., leaving hours to fill with polite conversation. Mink, noticing Harrison's wedding band, broke the silence.

"How long have you been married, Harrison?" Mink asked.

"Twenty-seven years," he said, beaming. "My wife's name is Jennifer."

"Congratulations. Being away so much must be pretty hard on your wife."

"She's got a pretty hectic schedule herself, even though she's a housewife. Jenny does volunteer work three times a week at the University of Shiloh Hospital, where both our son and daughter were born."

Mink didn't miss the admiration in his voice.

A housewife. That was pretty rare. Though she would never admit it, she felt envious of women like Jennifer. She couldn't imagine being in that kind of marriage, being totally dependent on someone. Yet she fantasized about having someone take care of her. It was just one of the battles raging inside her, pulling her in different directions.

ONE BETTER

Mink, in turn, told Harrison about her and Dwight's upcoming eighth anniversary this summer. And, of course, she had to brag about Baby-Z.

"How about your parents?" Harrison asked. "What does your dad do?"

What dad? Mink thought fast. "He's a research chemist."

"Oh." He seemed stunned by this. "What a family!"

Mink kept her gaze ahead as she inhaled the scent of him, as fresh as morning sunshine. He also seemed totally unaware of his natural sensuality. Coming up through the ranks, she'd had a mentor, an older pilot. He'd warned her not to talk about herself. But she felt herself relaxing with Harrison.

"What do you do for fun?" he asked.

"Fly," she said in a dreamy voice. "I own a 310 twin-engine Cessna," Mink added casually.

Now *that* was the truth.

OTIS

The child's heart curseth deeper in the silence than the strong man in his wrath.

— ELIZABETH BARRETT BROWNING

All of Detroit's best contractors were currently lusting after the so-called empowerment zone, Detroit's hot spot of redevelopment for minority neighborhoods. Otis Witherspoon was sitting in the catbird seat. As senior inspector in the building and safety and engineering department, he had the power to halt or give the go-ahead to every building under construction in the city of Detroit. His enviable position garnered him a lot of friends over his twenty-eight years in the field, as well as a passel of enemies. But the rush on the empowerment zone properties had his brain spinning with ideas and his pockets loaded with cash from those eager to persuade him in a friendly way.

Otis answered the phone on his desk on the fourth ring while filling in the final entry on his daily route report. He listened as he wrote. "Send him in, Doris."

With the tax advantages of building in the eighteen-square-mile zone, developers naturally had rushed in to buy, which had resulted in a shortage of available land. Only one year after the zone's creation, all hell was breaking loose.

At the moment Golden Westbrook, briefcase in one hand and a mound of paperwork clutched in his other fist, loomed in the entrance of Otis's small office, located on the fourth floor of the City-County Building in downtown Detroit.

"Can I help you, Westbrook?" Otis asked calmly.

Golden tossed three sheets on the desk in front of Otis. "Is this your signature?"

Without giving it a side glance, Otis stated, "I'm certain that it is. Problems?"

"Yesterday you issued a stop work notice to my foreman on my Sand Dollar Court Condominiums."

Otis shuffled through the papers on his desk as he mumbled the name of the complex. "Yep," he said, finally looking up, "the interior walls going up in Sand Dollar were installed before the inspection was made on the electrical system." His voice hardened. "I've warned your man Bond on several Westbrook Renaissance projects in the inner city not to try this stunt again. Apparently he didn't listen."

Golden leaned against the door and waited until a group of men passed by the office. "I don't want to have to file a complaint. But if necessary I—"

Otis laughed lightly. "Whatever. We'll both do what we have to do."

"Don't try and intimidate me, Witherspoon." Nearly all developers doing business in most metropolitan areas knew that building inspectors took kickbacks. But Reverend Golden wasn't just any developer. "I may wear my collar backward, but make no mistake, I'm a serious businessman. And I only do business in a proper manner."

"Hold up, Westbrook." Otis feigned righteous indignation, though in truth he was getting angry. He kicked his chair back and stood face-to-face with Golden. "Are you suggesting that I'm guilty of malfeasance, sir?" Otis knew that Golden's Renaissance Development Corporation was currently $3 million over-budget. Any delay was costly at this point, and both men knew it. This project, located in downtown Detroit, was expected to cost nearly $50 million and create 250 town houses for lower-income families, renovate 5 apartment buildings, and build a 37,000-square-foot retail strip and a 58,000-square-foot Farmer Jack grocery store.

"I'm told you've overlooked first-level electrical inspections in the past," Golden said quietly.

Before Otis could continue, Golden cut him off with a wave of his hand. "Look, I'm thirty days behind schedule on Wind-star, thirty days on Pinewood Villas, and ninety days on Shore-line Condominiums because of this office." He breathed deeply before adding, "And one of my main investors is ready to back out. If you don't pull that stop work order, I'm done for, and you know that my Renaissance project makes up almost half of the empowerment zone. Work with me, Witherspoon." All the Westbrook properties, which collectively fell under the title Renaissance, were created to upgrade the zone. Golden didn't understand how Witherspoon could deny his own people.

Otis felt agitated. He didn't want to help this preacher, not if the preacher wasn't going to help him. He returned to his seat. "Why don't you take this up with the inspector in charge of complaints, Mr. Westbrook." With each flex of his arm as he straightened his desk, each fold on Otis's Armani charcoal gray suit slipped subtly back in place. His time was as expensive as the clothes he wore.

It wasn't the city's bimonthly paycheck that enabled Otis to afford his closet full of expensive suits, the Lexus SC 400 he drove in the winter, and the Cadillac Seville in the summer. Nor did his $55,000 salary pay for his six-figure home or the two vacations he took a year. No, it was men in Westbrook's position who allowed him to live so luxuriously.

With a chronic backlog in the inspection department, both men knew that politics played into everything. It was about who you knew, or who you were paying on the side, that enabled you to sidestep the bureaucratic bullshit. "I've inspected all three of your development projects this week," Otis said to Golden. "I could have cited your company ten violations. Several of the structures, besides Sand Dollar, weren't in compliance with the building codes."

Golden looked at Otis skeptically. "In a matter of three minutes, you've managed to thwart three years of work." It was clear that Golden was trying to hold his temper. "Don't you have any kind of conscience for the citizens in the city of Detroit?"

"Most definitely," Otis said. "I am also aware that the city's tax base is at a disadvantage when we overbuild low-income housing projects."

For a brief moment the two men stared at one another. Clearly the lines had been drawn, and Otis was in the power position. Golden extended his hand toward Otis and said, "I'll look into that complaint. Good afternoon, Witherspoon." And Golden Westbrook walked out of Otis's office.

After Otis checked his messages and made a few calls, he locked the door to his office and headed for the elevator. He was surprised to see that Golden was still in the building, ahead of him down the hallway. *Maybe he did file that complaint.*

"Westbrook—" Otis Witherspoon called out. "Hold up."

Dressed in a moderately priced black suit and white shirt, with a multicolored bow tie and brocaded vest, Golden looked every inch the upstanding preacher-businessman. He continued to walk ahead of Otis a few feet, stopping at the elevator. After setting his briefcase on the floor, he slipped on his overcoat, then checked his watch.

"What is it, Otis?" Golden asked wearily. "I'm on my way to a dinner engagement. As it is I'm going to be late."

"Oh, a date?" Otis pressed the elevator button.

"No," Golden returned quietly. "Dinner with a few NAABR committee members."

Otis knew who would be there, and he relished the opportunity to meet them tonight. "Mind if I tag along? It's possible we *may* be able to work something out. Besides, I'm starved."

"Certainly," Golden said flatly.

"By the way, I got the word on my way out that the plumbing division has pulled your plans on that riverfront property. You're out of spec again." He tried to make his tone concerned. "But if you can be in my office by, say, nine A.M. tomorrow, I'm sure we can have everything taken care of by ten, ten-thirty."

"I'm tied up tomorrow. Maybe Mon—"

"Tomorrow's the best I can do," Otis said firmly. "Otherwise I have no choice but to write a new report and recommend a superseding notice."

Otis was giving Golden another chance to play ball, as he'd been trying to do since he'd first met the man.

Just last year Otis and Golden had been through a similar scenario. For six solid months Renaissance Properties had problems with the city's engineering department. One problem involved soil samples from Golden's Galleria Town Houses, situated a half mile off the Detroit River, which came back with extremely high levels of contamination. Golden said he distrusted the results.

"The costs and time involved in correcting the problem are unrealistic!" Golden had screamed at Otis. Luckily for him, Golden had known better than to accuse Otis of contaminating the samples. "Someone inside the city is deliberately manipulating the figures."

Each time a Renaissance property came to him, Otis gave Golden the opportunity to start playing by Otis's rules. For the soil samples, Otis had explained he had put his top people to work on the project and that they'd rechecked the numbers. When Golden still wouldn't come through with any incentive for Otis, Otis saw to it that Golden's riverfront property was tied up with the safety division for quite a while.

So why was Golden making the same mistake now? What would it take to bring the good reverend around?

When the clamorous elevator doors opened, Otis waited for Golden to gather his briefcase and step inside. "Did you watch the Lions kick San Francisco's butt Sunday night? They were awesome, weren't they?" he said, smiling.

He'd known Golden on a strictly professional basis for years but was certain that the man had never watched a complete game of sports of any kind in his life. Just the same, Otis carried on the conversation about football, then moved on to the latest hockey match until they reached the parking lot.

The darkness thickened like a brooding thundercloud as Otis traveled south on Interstate 75 toward Rochester, trailing Golden by at least two car lengths. January's frozen breath had made the misty falling snow as slick as wax. It was obvious they were headed toward Spice's restaurant.

Otis and Golden arrived at the restaurant close to six. After checking their coats, Golden gave the maître d' his name. As they followed the black-jacketed gentleman into the restaurant, an outburst of laughter from a large party in the center of the dining room rose above the jangling of silverware and dishes. Seconds later the two men joined four others previously ensconced in a two-room private dining suite, already enjoying their appetizer.

"Sorry I'm late," Golden said as he took a seat. "Some of you may already know Otis Witherspoon, the building inspector for the city."

Otis said hello and then added casually, "I'm also a thirty-year member of NAABR." The men nodded in affirmation.

Otis was impressed. The men at the table were definitely heavy hitters: Pastors Kevin Booker and Josh Taylor, both with political clout in the community; business executive Arthur Simmons, an entrepreneur who'd bought an insignificant car dealership and made it worth millions; and Erik Cain, who worked double duty as Golden's manager and accountant. Cain spoke first.

"Hello, Otis. Good to see you," he said, shaking the other man's hand.

Otis studied the eager-looking young man. In the years Cain had worked for Golden, he and Otis had had business dealings, although not the kind that Westbrook would approve of.

Pellets of snow turned to rain and began streaming against the windows. Seconds later shrieks of thunder revved up behind the rain as Otis was personally introduced to the remaining NAABR members. He easily joined in the conversation about the organization's elections already in progress.

"First and foremost we have a spiritual thrust as our mandate." Pastor Booker lifted his cup and sipped his coffee. "With Westbrook's dual roles as Detroit's chapter president and the pastor of a large church—whose congregation is sixty percent NAABR members, I might add—he is in a good position as our candidate to restore core spiritual values." He smiled as he placed his cup back on the table. "Another point of emphasis is the quest for economic justice for our people."

Founded in 1913 by four black scholars and a handful of liberal whites concerned about racial injustice, the National Alliance for the Advancement of the Black Race was an advocacy group for civil rights and litigated thousands of national and local discrimination lawsuits. After two years of heavy negotiating, Golden and the NAABR members present at this meeting had recently been triumphant in winning a landmark $700 million settlement for commercial loan commitments with the National Bank & Trust of Detroit and the Fair Banking Alliance. The money was earmarked for minority businesses.

"I agree," Pastor Taylor broke in. "Booker and I—and I'm sure I speak for Golden as well—don't look at our roles in the committee as being strictly political, but a holistically spiritual one that administers to the needs of our constituency." He scanned the nodding faces surrounding the table before saying, "Our goal, gentlemen, is to mobilize voters and get them involved."

With one ear turned to their conversation, Otis watched Henry, the elderly waiter, pour his glass of water. He knew Spice kept him on because Henry would die of loneliness if he didn't have this job. In the years Otis had known Henry, they'd never held a two-sentence conversation and his face was always as blank as a blind man's.

Smoothing his beard, as he had a tendency to do when he was thinking, Otis appraised the tempting selections that were being laid out on the Biedermeier sideboard.

"Help yourselves, gentlemen," the waiter said. "If you desire anything else, please press the buzzer on the floor beside the table." He smiled, nodded at the table of men, then discreetly rolled the silver cart outside the room, closing the carved pocket doors behind him.

The table was beautifully set, flanked by an allegorical hand-painted screen and large ferns. The men formed a line, and each helped himself to the spread of turkey and dressing, ham, fried chicken, pheasant, collard greens, turnip greens, grits and greens, macaroni and cheese, coleslaw, mashed potatoes and gravy, candied yams, homemade rolls, and biscuits. Information and conversation was exchanged as the men enjoyed their meal.

In ten short months the elections for the office of president of the Detroit NAABR chapter would be held, and it was clear to Otis that Golden was spending time and money necessary to be reelected.

Otis was aware that various members of Golden's campaign team assembled for dinner on a regular basis at restaurants to talk strategy for the ensuing election. Now Otis wanted to see what these men were up to, what kind of money they really possessed. It was always a good idea to be widening his net of influence. If these guys were going to open their pockets to Golden, maybe Otis could somehow share in the wealth.

The heady aroma of ginger, basil, and sage filled the room. A quiet rustle of people talking and tittering about could be heard just outside their private chambers. After he'd finished a warming cup of coffee, Otis stretched his legs and sat back leisurely in the cushioned seat, listening to Golden stress the importance of the church's involvement with politics.

"Gentlemen, you are all aware that in the African American community, the church has always been at the vanguard of social justice and public policy. Out of the black church have come our colleges and universities. Out of the black church have come our black businesses and trade associations. The church was the incubator for the civil rights movements in America."

To Otis, the passion in Golden's voice seemed genuine as he paused for a second to wipe the sweat from his brow. "We know that developing businesses in our communities helps to build the tax base for providing public goods and services, helps the economy, and helps to provide jobs." At this Otis and Golden locked eyes. "Our chapter is dedicated to coming up with specific programs designed to encourage our young people to be entrepreneurs."

Preach, brother, preach! You just might get me to step inside a church yet. Otis chuckled quietly at his own joke, keeping his eyes on Westbrook so as not to be stared down.

Golden folded his arms across his chest and leaned back in his chair in conclusion. "We can get more for small-business development if we go about it the right way. We can look at this as a vehicle of economic independence and break the cycle of government dependency."

For the next half hour the group of men shared their ideas and visions on how they could obtain the endorsement from the thousands of UAW voters, who had the power to significantly determine the outcome of an election. Then the men pulled out their checkbooks. Even Otis. He wrote his check out for $100.

"My Lord," stated Pastor Booker, "we should meet here more often." He held his large belly and laughed gleefully. "If these ain't the meanest greens I've ate in years, my name ain't Kevin *Sasquatch* Booker."

The team of businessmen and pastors concurred with a hearty laugh. Erik Cain, obviously stuffed to the gills, pushed his plate forward, his chair back, and belched. "Excuse me," he said with embarrassment.

Otis snickered as he gulped down the remainder of his coffee. "Kevin? Josh? Any of you gentlemen like more coffee?" he asked, noticing the brown shadows in their white cups. Without waiting for an answer, he pressed the buzzer for Henry. When the elderly gentleman didn't appear, he opened the pocket doors and stepped into the circular dining room.

"Miss! Miss!" Otis called to the waitress nearby.

Watching the shapely woman shift her weight on her left hip, Otis knew who she was before she turned around.

Upon hearing the call for service, Spice raised a single finger above her head, signaling Otis to wait a moment. She was obviously critiquing a trainee.

"Yes, sir . . . I've got it," the trainee said. "You and your wife will have the pecan-crusted turkey cutlets with wild rice, and sautéed sweet peppers. And your son here would like turkey and dressing with broccoli instead of the turnip greens. Cornbread all around, or confetti muffins with your orders?" The family requested both. She thanked the customers and slid the menus under her right armpit. Spice gave Beverly a pleased smile as the young woman headed for the kitchen.

The staff's evening attire at Southern Spice was black tuxedos and crisp cream shirts for the men, and long black high-slit skirts with soft, off white, organdy cuffed blouses with a high neck and cameo for the women. Spice wore a black velvet evening gown and was obviously, this evening, working as hostess.

Just as Spice started to turn in Otis's direction, he felt the walls shudder, and the lights went out.

Bright light from sizzling veins of lightning sliced through the curtained windows.

"The lights will be back on in a moment," Spice shouted into the room, but the patrons weren't worried about the semidarkness. The temporary loss of light merely made their dinner more romantic under the soft glow of the candlelight on every table.

As Spice made her way toward the private dining room, he saw the golden glow of candles bathing the contours of her face. She was carrying a candelabra.

"Hello, gentlemen." She hiked an eyebrow when she spotted Otis. "Hello, Otis," she said, smiling, "I didn't know you were here." She gave him a quick hug. "Excuse me," she said to the group, "Otis is my brother-in-law." She let her hand rest on Otis's shoulder. "Now, gentlemen, may I be of service?"

"I'm fine. The grits and greens were sublime," Kevin said, almost humming.

"Perfect," said Pastor Booker, pulling the napkin from his thick neck. "Please extend our compliments to the chef."

"I'd like to suggest the next time you visit us you try the Parmesan collard casserole," Spice proposed. "Our guests *love* it."

Josh Taylor, with biscuit in hand, was busily scooping up the last drop of gravy on his plate. "The southern fried chicken is worth a trip back. Never had fried chicken quite like that before—but don't tell my wife." Otis saw Spice was truly charmed by the compliment. "What's the secret?"

Spice looked around the table, engaging all eyes to focus on her. "Buttermilk. It's marinated in buttermilk overnight. I trust you won't tell anyone." She winked and pressed her fingers against her lips. "If everyone's wives knew our secrets, we'd be out of business." She winked again at Josh, then turned her attention back to Otis, whose eyes had never left her face.

"Everything is exceptional," a voice said, pulling her attention back to the room at large.

"The food, the restaurant. It's lovely," said Erik Cain with a broad smile.

"It's all in the presentation," Spice said, now looking at Golden, the one man in the room she'd never met personally before.

"You haven't told us your name," Golden stated in a calm manner.

Before she could answer, Henry was at her side with a message from Representative Donna Bradley, asking for her. "Tell her I'll just be a minute." Spice paused, glancing through the door to the congresswoman's table. "And Henry, see that couple right there? Send a cake over to table eighty-nine with my compliments." She nodded at the couple. "It's the McCormicks' twenty-fifth anniversary."

"Sure thing, Ms. Spice," Henry said, making a notation on his pad.

"Spice as in Southern Spice?" Golden asked.

She blushed. "The same."

"And you work the tables?" Josh Taylor jumped into the conversation. "All the years I've been coming here I never knew it." The other men concurred.

"Sometimes, like tonight, I play the part of hostess," she said, turning away from Otis and Golden to face the younger man. "Occasionally, I like to cover the floor and talk one on one with the customers—see if they're pleased or displeased with their meal or the service. Oftentimes I don't let them know that I'm the owner. This evening, however . . . I didn't think it proper, given the company of such reverent men, to hide the truth." With a final smile for the room, she turned back to her brother-in-law. "Otis, you were asking something?"

"Yes, we need more coffee, my dear."

They all smiled. "With pleasure." Spice turned to go, stopped only by Golden's amber-speckled eyes. "I'll be back with a pot of fresh coffee. Help yourself to dessert," she said, gesturing to the sideboard. She smiled at Golden. "And gentlemen, dinner's on me this evening." She ignored their protests about accepting the free meal.

Henry appeared to clear the table.

"Shall we move to the adjoining room for brandy, gentlemen?" Pastor Booker offered after their hostess had gone. "There's a warm fire burning, and that leather chair a few feet away seems to be calling my name."

Otis wanted this opportunity to speak with Golden alone and pulled him to the side. "I'd like to be of help to your campaign, Westbrook."

"But your check is enough. Thank you," Golden said.

Glancing over his shoulder at Cain, who was watching them nearby, Otis lowered his voice before speaking. "If you'd consider adding another partner to the Sand Dollar project, I could guarantee at least fifteen thousand city votes—not to mention getting your approvals. My influence—"

Just then a polite knock sounded at the door. "Excuse me, gentlemen," Spice said, reentering the room. "Fresh coffee. Help yourselves."

Envy, like a cold prison, benumbs and stupefies. Otis didn't miss the connection of Spice's eyes lingering too long on Westbrook. He also didn't miss Golden's husky response when he said, "Yes. Thank you."

81

Otis was outraged. Spice was flirting openly with the man! There could be no mistaking what he saw. He knew all her moves, all her gestures.

"I appreciate your offer, Otis," Westbrook said, continuing their conversation. "However, may I get back to you after I've discussed this with my election committee?"

"Certainly," Otis said. They watched as Spice sashayed out of the room. Both men knew the subject of a partnership would never be discussed again.

SPICE

There's a time when you have to explain to your children why they're born, and it's a marvelous thing if you know the reason by then.

—HAZEL SCOTT

---

*A*t 10:30 P.M. Spice retreated upstairs to her private quarters. She was exhausted from standing on her feet all night, rushing around the restaurant, playing hostess, restaurateur, and chef adviser.

Now her intercom was buzzing. What could they want now! "Who is it?" Spice asked wearily.

"It's Otis, Spice." He breathed slowly. "Can I come up?"

"It's late, Otis. I can only spare a few minutes." She didn't understand why she gave in to her brother-in-law so easily.

"Thanks."

Otis smiled at her as she met him at the front door. "Evening, Spice. I won't stay long."

Spice clasped the front of her black peignoir closed and stepped to the side. "Come on in," she said, giving Otis a limp hug.

He followed Spice to the lower living room, made himself a drink, and offered Spice one.

"No thanks. Excuse me a moment. I'll get myself a glass of wine instead." Knowing how obsessive Otis was about her private life, Spice went back upstairs and turned down the volume on her answering machine. Not that she had secrets to shock him; it was just none of his business who called her. Stopping in the kitchen, she poured a glass of cold Zinfandel from the refrigerator, then joined Otis sitting by the fireplace.

His clear eyes glittered like sapphires as he studied her face. "Have you given my suggestion any more thought?"

Spice sighed. She knew Otis was frustrated. He was a widower, and at least three times a year, since one year after David died, Otis would plead his case. Spice would turn him down and ask him to stop pressuring her, because her answer would never change. Then he'd start in all over again.

"Really, Spice, I think you've been a widow long enough. Haven't you changed your mind yet?"

"No," she said, turning away from his piercing stare, "I haven't."

"Spice . . ." Otis turned her face toward his and looked into her eyes. "I could be here for you, for the girls. Sterling's giving you nothing but hell—"

"I'm sorry you had to witness that the other day," she said, and shrugged it away. "But Sterling is my concern."

He reached out and pulled her into his chest, caressing her neck and shoulders. "When you have problems, I want you to come to me."

Spice shrugged off his heavy hands and turned around to face him. "Thanks, but I'm managing okay by myself."

"Spice," he said slowly, "I could help you with everything."
He paused. "I could make you forget—"

"Otis, Otis . . . don't."

"You need a man here. A man living here with you." He took
her hand in his. "You know I've always been crazy about you,
Spice. David's gone. Why can't we—"

"I will not—" Spice stood, covering herself as much as she
could with the flimsy material of her robe. "I will not start a relationship with my husband's brother."

"There's nothing wrong with that. What's the harm—"

"Just the thought makes me feel guilty." Spice knew that in
some cultures it was actually a tradition, but not in her book.

"You're a young woman, sweetheart. You can't continue to
punish yourself by being alone. David would want you to be
happy. He would want you to find love again."

"You talked to him lately?" Spice asked jokingly. The simple
truth was, she was attracted to Otis. Why wouldn't she be? He
was good-looking, intelligent, and confident. This last quality
was the main attraction.

Otis stroked his goatee and gazed deeply into her eyes.
"We're both lonely. We need each other. I know I'd be good for
you, Spice. I just need a chance to prove it to you."

Just as she looked up into his face, Otis captured her mouth
and pressed his lips softly against hers. Feeling his arms wrapping around her, she let him pull her toward him. She felt his
arousal pressing her thigh as she responded to his touch. Tilting
her head back to welcome his kiss, she felt his tongue slide inside her mouth, igniting a flame of passion in her that made her
ache with desire. The kiss deepened, and when she felt his lowered hands caress her buttocks and inner thigh, she relaxed,
until she felt his hands moving even higher.

"I need you, Spice," he whispered in her ear as his fingers fon-
dled the outer lips of her vagina.

"Mmm," she said, backing away from his kiss and shoving his hands away. "Please go, Otis."

He stroked her hair and kissed her briefly once more to be sure she was sure she wanted him to leave. "I won't rush you, Spice. I can wait."

As he boarded the elevator down the hall, he held back the door and asked, "You sure you want me to leave?"

Her chest heaved as she struggled to answer. "I'm sure," she said finally.

"When you're ready, you call me." With a cocky smile on his face, he blew her a kiss as the elevator doors closed.

Spice descended from her apartment, arriving in Southern Spice's kitchen to the cacophonous commotion of the weekly delivery trucks unloading meat, fish, cheese, fresh produce, and all the other necessary products for the day's business. It was Monday morning.

Since David's death, Spice's life day-to-day had changed dramatically. Gone were the peaceful days of bone-tiring work without any other demands. Now her appointments were updated daily by her secretary and publicist, and almost every minute of her day was packed.

After exiting the elevator, Spice did a quick assessment of faces and places. She made it a point to acknowledge each of her employees, not just to be pleasant, but to keep track of absentees. Of the one hundred and twenty-five workers who were employed on two shifts, twenty-two of whom were part-time, she knew where every face and body belonged and when. In addition, each year Spice selected two African studies majors from Oakland University, a college she always supported, to work in the gift shop—Victorian Spice—in the front of the restaurant.

The gift shop, decorated with fresh interpretations of Victorian style, was 750 square feet of wall-to-wall treasures: yards of antique laces, sterling silver wallflower holders, porcelain jewelry boxes, velvet bags for perfume bottles, antique chairs painted gold and covered in dried flowers, with matching stools, lace and needlepointed tapestry pillows, silk-fringed antique lamp shades, old jewelry, and mementos of the restaurant such as silver-plated engraved matchbooks.

As Spice passed into the largest area of the first-level kitchen, she waved to the team of cooks in charge of vegetables, which ranged from tender collard greens and buttered cabbage to fricassée des carottes. She said good morning to the crew in charge of entrées. Today's were grilled duck with orange sauce, pecan-crusted turkey cutlets, braised duckling with turnip sauce, honeyed barbecue spare ribs, and Southern Spice's famous southern fried chicken with gravy.

The workers hurriedly moved in sync with one another, knowing their jobs and most obviously loving them, probably because they did them well. Time was an important factor in the food business. The staff knew they had approximately four and a half to five hours to prepare the food daily.

Throughout the week, sixty-three cooks alternated cooking lunch and dinner. After completing their jobs, they were responsible for cleaning their table area, including at least nine square feet of their respective circular stations. The kitchen could serve as a blueprint for a commercial kitchen. The walls of sanitized space held sparkling aluminum griddles, deep fryers, steamers, boiling pans, pressure cookers, grills, mobile convection ovens, and conveyorized infrared ovens, each stored in the place most convenient to its use.

There was another kitchen on the second floor, with a dumbwaiter that Spice often used for late night snacks. It was smaller and used primarily for pastries and baking. Specially made chocolate candies in beautifully wrapped boxes were created fresh daily, along with the ethereal desserts, the odors of which billowed blissfully throughout the upper-level kitchen. These treats were also sold in the gift shop.

Spice took pride in the fact that all the vast varieties of cob-
blers and pies had crusts made from scratch. Preparing the flaky
patisserie was one of Carmen's chief responsibilities as chef
patissier. And Spice knew that no matter how much vodka Carmen imbibed, the crust was always perfect. In the winter season
Carmen would create a five-layer black forest cake, a maple leaf
pie with pecans, fruit crumble with prune plums, and her specialty—apricot Napoleon, a crisp pastry layered with vanilla
bean custard and caramelized fresh apricots, served with blue-
berry compote and crème anglaise.

During the summer months Carmen would prepare fresh
fruit in red wine syrup, fruit sorbets, peaches au vin rouge, and
poached pears in port. Her other duties included supervising
three members of the bakery crew in preparing three dozen
fruity desserts, along with a half dozen each of caramel, German
chocolate, chocolate, coconut, lemon, and pound cakes.

Now, as Spice walked through the salad section, which was
separate from the main kitchen on the first floor, she heard a familiar voice.

"You okay this morning, young lady?" asked Effie, one of her
elderly employees who'd never missed a day of work in ten years.

"Just skippy," Spice said, returning the smile. "How 'bout
you, Miss Effie?"

"Right fine." She smiled and then continued dicing up the
meat and vegetables that went into the eight types of omelets
the restaurant offered.

"Morning, Ms. Spice," Develle said. He was the stockman on
the first shift; his duty was to rotate the supplies stored in the
basement to the daily supply they housed in the kitchen for the
week.

"Morning, Develle. Any problems?" He shook his head no,
but she felt his long dark stare on her as she sauntered away.
There was a seductive power exuded from being the proprietress

of such a big business. Anyone in such a position demanded respect and a little adoration, she'd found.

The existence of these perks hadn't occurred to her early on, certainly not when David was alive. Her mind went to Mink. Did her supersuccessful daughter share these goodies—and could she handle them?

As Spice breezed through the next cooking station, she inhaled the honeyed scent that emanated from the smothered short ribs of beef Travis was preparing. She walked toward him, and when their eyes met, she hooded hers, wanting to send the message that she meant business.

Travis leaned against the counter, his hips thrust forward slightly, his feet a few inches apart. In response to Spice's lowered gaze, he slowly inserted his thumbs firmly in his apron pockets and brought his fingers around to point down toward his genitals.

"I'm scheduled to attend a seminar, 'Strategies for Opening Your Own Business for Professional Chefs,' in Philadelphia next week. Care to join me?"

"I'll pass, Travis."

"Okay . . . another time, maybe. However, I feel that the time to discuss a five percent raise in my salary is long overdue." His body was poised for play, but his eyes were serious. "I've been working my ass off, Spice."

She could see that he was gauging her response. "I'll have to think that one over." Truly, with the numerous advances against his salary she'd given him to support his increasingly expensive tastes, she hadn't expected this from him. She had lent him fifty thousand as it was, even though she knew he was using it to start the ball rolling on his own restaurant.

Travis watched as Spice finished her kitchen rounds. Then he followed her as they moved toward his office near the elevator. "When you return, I'd like for you and me to go over some of the problems we're having with the downtown restaurant. Some of the equipment that's being delivered for the kitchen isn't what you and I ordered."

Where was he going with this? she wondered. Knowing Travis, she was sure there was some reason he was whining about the discrepancy. She knew he wanted control of the new business. That was no problem—she'd told him so. But nit-picking wasn't Travis's style. There had to be a more personal reason why he was staking his claim so early on in the restaurant. She did not want to think he would try to skim money off the equipment, as it was returned and they were credited. All head chefs knew that even though their lauded culinary skills brought in customers, they could always be replaced by aggressive, newer talent.

The owner always maintained control. Spice instinctively moved away from him just as Travis reached out for her. Without question, the fluctuation of emotions she experienced around him was disturbing, particularly since he was obviously bedding her daughter. "Weren't you at Sterling's last night?"

"I stopped by for a couple of drinks."

"Nothing else?"

"Nothing worth mentioning."

"So there wasn't anything intimate that happened between the two of you?"

"As I said, nothing worth mentioning happened."

"I'm not interested in your personal business, Travis, but because of what had transpired between you and me I didn't want—"

"Don't worry about it." He paused. "More important, we should be discussing the continued absenteeism of your friend Carmen."

"She didn't show up for work this morning?" Spice stopped, thinking. Was this Travis's way of pushing her buttons?

"I'm positive that she's at home drunk. Lately, she's been

struggling to finish her work on time. If you ask me, she can't handle her alcohol."

"I *didn't* ask you." Her tone was bitter. "As a matter of fact, you could use a fresh-breath mint to camouflage your own boozy breath."

They were interrupted by Develle. "Ms. Spice?"

"Yes, Develle," Spice said, answering the faint knock at the open doorway.

"Can I speak to you privately for a moment?" Develle asked.

"Sure." She turned to Travis, stiffly. "We'll finish our discussion later." She checked her watch and headed out the door, followed by Develle.

Develle asked if he could have an additional table brought in for his anniversary dinner the following evening—as usual, the place was fully booked. She assured him that she'd take care of it. *If only all my problems were this easy.*

At 9:25 A.M. Spice and Carrie, the food and beverage manager, reviewed the bar inventory. Since David's death, she'd fired six managers. Apparently they thought she didn't check the stock against the bar tabs. All six had been drinking or stealing gallons of liquor a week.

The inventory took twenty minutes, at which point she rushed through her paperwork with her personal secretary and publicist, Tracey Allen.

As tall as Spice, Tracey was a thirty-one-old Caucasian female with thick blond shoulder-length hair, a high forehead, and soft gray eyes. Tracey possessed a movie star quality. In truth, the reason Spice hired her eight years before was that she reminded her so much of Sterling. Her relationships with the press and polite professionalism handling VIPs was the primary reason so many celebrities continued to make Southern Spice the number one restaurant in the area. Tracey was single. With all the intense publicity she garnered for Southern Spice and all her energy focused on business, it wouldn't take long for her to open up her own public relations firm. And when that time came, Spice would wish her well.

Spice's office was located just down the hall from the bar and second kitchen. The elevator was accessible only to the employees who worked in the inner sanctum. When she entered her office, she sighed at the mounds of paperwork covering her desk. Cherrywood raised paneling covered the entire office, and her antique half-moon-shaped desk was also made of cherrywood. There was an ornamental rug in red, black, and gold that balanced a tufted burgundy leather couch and high back matching armchairs. A lighted Romare Bearden painting hung above a cast-iron gas fireplace surrounded by marble-and-cherrywood paneling. Spice had left the office totally intact since her husband's death, and it reflected his simplicity as well as his masculinity. She loved it that way.

She rifled through the telephone messages, made the necessary calls, and gave a few directives to Tracey. Then, gathering the papers she'd need for the planning committee meeting and placing them into her briefcase, she prepared to leave.

Kia, her assistant, strolled into the room, carrying a steaming cup of coffee for her boss. "The car will be downstairs in fifteen minutes."

"Thanks. You're a gem." Spice snapped her briefcase shut, then opened her gold-and-diamond-encrusted Carolee necklace watch, checked the time, and clicked it shut.

"Ms. Witherspoon?" Kia asked while removing a cold cup of coffee from her boss's desk.

"Yes, Kia?"

"The interviews with the CERC applicants went well, don't you think?"

"Extremely," Spice said with a relaxed smile. The Committee for the Employment of Retarded Citizens was a cause dear to her heart. "We'll begin the training program in two weeks. Think you can handle it?" Twelve CERC men and women presently

92

worked at Southern Spice; she was adding eight more. And she planned on hiring between forty to fifty applicants to work in the new restaurant, Royal Oak Spice, and the attached hotel.

"Absolutely."

"Good girl." She winked and picked up the phone.

Through the open blinds in her executive office, Spice watched the snowflakes continue to build a thick screen. Turning away, she glanced at the cardboard sketches of the Foxphasia project in Royal Oak that took up a considerable part of the wall. For some reason they seemed more realistic in the office than on the actual construction site.

While Kia was busy straightening the papers in Spice's office, Spice dialed Charles Kentwood, one of the partners in Zuller, the architectural firm. His secretary put Spice on hold while he concluded his previous call.

As she waited, her mind drifted. Spice realized that she hadn't heard a peep from either of her daughters in days. Then Kentwood was on the phone. Just as she said hello, Kia buzzed in over the intercom: "Your daughter's on line two." It looked as though her psychic powers were working today.

"Just a minute, Charles," she said. Then, "Which one?" to Kia. She massaged her temples and waited.

"It's Mink, Mrs. Witherspoon."

"Thank you," she said to Kia, breathing a sigh of relief. Having Sterling call *her* would catch Spice off guard. For some silly reason she wanted to do the calling. Be in command of the conversation. "Please tell her I'll call her back in ten minutes."

Resting her head against the back of the chair, she returned to her call with Charles Kentwood. Soon it turned into a conference call with Morgan Belder, the builder. The Foxphasia complex in Royal Oak was two weeks behind schedule. There was a problem with building codes. She'd have to meet them at the construction site. Foxphasia was not in the empowerment zone. *Damn, if Otis worked for Royal Oak, I wouldn't have this problem.*

As their conversation continued, Spice's mind wandered. She hated the new designs for the children's museum. She'd specifically commissioned Sterling for the museum because she loved her daughter's original ideas to have an Egyptian exhibit, a medieval castle, a dollhouse exhibit, a children's theater, interactive library stations, light beams, waterfalls, traveling exhibits, and a special toddler area. But since Sterling hadn't delivered on time, she had no choice but to request Zuller to put another architect on the project. When the blueprints came in, she could only smile and say, "I love it." But Morgan kept running into problems executing the architect's dream (more like a nightmare, Sterling had pointed out). What had been the beginning of a happy marriage between builder and designer had turned into a fury of accusations on the unprofessionalism of each. She listened to their childish threats and wondered to herself why she was doing this. And why on earth was she doing it alone?

Spice concluded her last meeting at six P.M. and went directly home, only to find a tearful message from Sterling on her voice mail. She had warned Sterling under no uncertain terms that her credit cards would not be reinstated until she got some part-time work, plus went back to school and was stable for at least three months. Spice reached for the phone to call her back, then changed her mind.

After changing into a pair of navy knit pants and long top, Spice moved into the library and picked up a stack of the last six issues of various food magazines that she hadn't found the time to read.

Spice felt the library was her special room, more so than any other in her home, and she retreated there nightly. The room was private—small but quiet, nestled near the back of the duplex, and furnished with a hand-carved Italian chest and curved built-in bookcases that flanked an Ethan Allen entertainment cabinet complete with glass lighted bar. To Spice, the room felt romantic, with a sumptuous taupe velvet sofa and circular ottoman, tapestried side chairs with yards of matching tapestry, and velvet drapes hanging on the three huge windows. On the floor a swirling, circular-patterned Axminster carpet in shades of avocado, gold, and taupe made dozing, reading, or relaxing on the floor a definitely dreamy option.

While flipping through her favorite couture periodical, *W* magazine, she pulled the tasseled throw from the back of the sofa over her legs, then tore out several outfits that she planned on purchasing.

If I were truly in the dating mode, she thought, I would be dressing right about now instead of sitting here alone cutting out pictures of expensive clothes. First I'd serve cocktails in the library, and then we'd leave by seven-thirty for our eight o'clock dinner reservations at the Golden Mushroom. I would be extremely closemouthed about my businesses because most men are . . . are . . . She yawned.

I didn't realize how sleepy I've gotten.

The buzzer to her private elevator rang.

"Spice. It's me, Travis. There's a man here who says he knows you and wants to know if he can come up."

Fighting the grogginess in her voice, she said, "Who is it?" She heard Travis asking the man his name.

"Westbrook, something."

The preacher? "Put him on the speaker, Travis. I'd like to talk to him."

"Ms. Witherspoon . . ."

"Yes," she breathed into the intercom.

"It's Golden Westbrook. Are you busy? I'd like to speak with you for a few minutes if it's not too inconvenient."

"Come on up." Knowing that she had two full minutes before he'd be at her front door, she dashed into her private bathroom, brushed her hair, gargled, put on a fresh coat of lipstick, and was back at the door before he'd made it. Spice invited him to take a seat on the sofa.

"I won't take up too much of your time. I realize you're a busy woman."

Taking a seat directly across from him on one of the tapestried chairs, Spice said, "Would you like coffee?" *Damn. He's younger than I thought. He can't be over thirty-five.*

"No, thank you. Nothing."

"Sparkling water, maybe?" *My Lord, you fool, he just said nothing!*

Spice couldn't believe how nervous she was. When he shook his head no, she observed a kind of peacefulness in his eyes. It was as if a river somewhere down inside of him fed her thirst. And then she felt peaceful, too. When she'd met him briefly at the dinner she'd thought his eyes ordinary, chocolate colored. But now, closer to him, she saw that they were flecked with amber, like sparkling ginger ale with the sun filtering through it. They were alluring eyes that looked as if they had just left the bedroom and were anxious to get back. With their gaze still connected, she could feel something special was happening.

"I'm here on business, Ms. Witherspoon."

"Please, call me Spice." Steepling her fingers, Spice tapped them back and forth—waiting. For what, she wasn't sure.

"I've spent the past four days at the International Building, tracking down the owner of the property on Lafayette and Eighteenth in Detroit."

"That parcel sounds familiar."

"It should." He opened his briefcase and removed a sheet of paper. "Your late husband was the lien holder, and I assume it now belongs to you." He handed her his copy of the title search.

"I take it this property has some value to you personally?" she asked, accepting the paper he handed her. Unconsciously she ran a finger around her earlobe as she read the information, then looked up at him.

"Of course. It's a prime spot, perfect for developing two- and three-bedroom low-income houses with a bicycle trail, small park, and playground for children. I'd like to make you an offer."

Suddenly she felt naked and looked away. Was it possible he hadn't touched her with anything but his eyes?

"I remember this parcel now." David had begun developing the property for Alfred, a retired co-worker from General Motors. When Alfred's financial backing fell through, David hated to put a lien in for the work he'd already started, but his expenses were too high to ignore. "I'll have to speak to my attorney about this before I—"

"I'm prepared to make you a substantial offer, well over the amount due."

Yes, she was impressed with Mr. Westbrook.

Oh, Spice thought, so he's a little aggressive. I like that. "Mr. Westbrook, if I'm not mistaken, my husband had planned on building a senior citizen complex on that site. The plans were already approved."

"I've tracked your development company . . . Spice." He gathered his papers back inside the briefcase. "Originally, I'd planned on developing that property into one- and two-bedroom track homes for the minority middle class, so our thoughts run in a similar direction." He stopped, blushing. "Maybe you and I can come to terms on a joint venture."

"Why should I become a partner with you? I don't need—"

"I didn't mean to imply that you're financially strapped. I felt that you might be interested in working with me on other projects in the city as well."

Spice thought, Who better could she trust than a preacher? The property was just lying there anyway.

Before he closed his briefcase, she spotted a set of tapes.

"Are those gospel tapes?"

"No," he said, handing them to her. "These are copies from this morning's service at Divinity Baptist. Would you like to listen to them?"

Spice blushed when she admitted that she hadn't been to church in years.

Then Golden said, "Keep the tapes, listen to them over and over until you understand the meaning of the message. It's never too late to start, Spice. Come when you're ready. Come when you feel good, and you'll feel better when you leave."

She wasn't sure why she'd said yes to this handsome preacher. Did she really need yet another development project? Wasn't Foxphasia, with all its complications, enough right now? Why hadn't she said no? *Who are you kidding?* Spice could hear Carmen's voice in her head: *You just want an excuse to rub up against that handsome young preacher.* Well, so what? Spice glanced at the phone, but it was too late to answer Carmen for real. *You told me it was time, my friend. Maybe you're right.*

After Golden had left, Spice went downstairs to her office. She unlocked the desk and removed David's old papers from the lower desk drawer. She hadn't looked at them in years. Sure enough, his plans for the Lafayette property, along with several ideas he planned to develop in Detroit, were there. Reading his notes brought back so many pleasant memories, she lost track of the time.

It was eleven thirty-five when Spice returned home. She took a shower and readied herself for bed. But first she needed a midnight snack. Sticking her head inside the refrigerator, she searched the shelves for something sticky and sweet. She finally settled for a fruit salad and took a small bowl into her bedroom. After opening the doors to the entertainment center, she slipped the tape into the slot.

Before getting into bed, she turned off the ringer on the telephone. She took one spoonful of fruit and sat cross-legged in the middle of the bed with the bowl plopped in her lap. For a few moments she allowed herself the pleasure and indulgence of being alone. Out loud, she told herself and the black velvet walls that held years of silent knowledge, "Damn, I'm cold!"

ONE BETTER

She left the bed and turned up the heat. Yet when she returned, she knew that the coldness she felt wasn't outside her body, it was inside. She wanted to feel the warmth of a man tonight. She heard the last car leave the parking lot. "Hmmm," she breathed. Each taste of fruit felt like a caress as she luxuriated in the thought of something far sweeter and more pleasurable.

Feeling the onset of desire, she placed a hand beneath the soft satin folds of her gown and stroked her nipple until it hardened. She wet her lips with her tongue and, using both hands, stroked her breasts with gentle determination until she felt herself melt and moan with pleasure. She imagined the sweet sounds of sex between a man and a woman and felt the warm fluid building between her legs. Releasing one of her hands to probe the moist center, she jumped when she saw the red light blinking, indicating someone was trying to call on her private phone line. After four rings the voice-mail message started. The red button seemed to scream at her as it flashed on and off five more times while the clock changed from 11:59 to 12:02.

The tremor of her desire had come and gone, and she retreated to the bathroom. When she returned to the bed, she picked up the remote for the tape player and pushed play. As she scooped up the last chunks of melon, the ripe scent of cantaloupe filled the air.

Music faded in low at first, then louder, until a full choir broke into song. Seconds later Spice heard the harmonic voice that was familiar to her from just hours earlier.

"When you speak the truth, you're speaking God's language." His voice was so provocative, so smooth, that Spice leaned forward in bed to listen. "Study what you see with your mind and not with your emotions, and you will learn. If you have love and truth, you will be free. Love comes naturally. You can't buy love because love is truth. . . ."

Spice was mesmerized. Ordinarily she wasn't moved by messages. Especially those made by preachers. But she felt something different now. She turned up the volume, finished her fruit, and listened.

"You can buy happiness temporarily if you're a rich man. You can buy a real Rolex, diamonds, furs. But not love. God is love—truth, they are all connected. If you are a liar, love is not for you."

Spice thought of all the angry energy she'd used to gain financial security and how the feeling wasn't what she'd expected. Golden's message tapped into her disappointment, her emptiness, the feeling she'd been cheated. When would her real life begin?

"Look to God as your spirit, not at the church. God is real. You can be powerful in Spirit walking in God's spirit. We are God's diplomats. Love and truth are God's gift to us. We let our ego get in the way of truth."

Truth, thought Spice. Why were there so many secrets? She hadn't been honest with her children about her past life, about anything, about who she was and where she came from. Truth. Secrets.

Spice had always felt she could take better care of her secrets than anyone else could. And *truth*? Moral truths, like human beings, she'd come to learn, changed their aspects the way chameleons changed color.

Spice fell asleep listening to Golden's voice: "Love is natural. Love is free. Love is the essence of God."

STERLING

I have never felt myself to be an honest part of anything since the world of childhood deserted me.

—GEORGE LAMMING

---

*S*tepping from the shower, Sterling toweled off, then blow-dried her hair. After dousing her body with perfumed lotion and liquid talc, she stepped back from the mirror, admiring her small but nicely proportioned figure.

She removed her robe from behind the bathroom door and went into her bedroom. Just then the phone rang.

"Hello?" she said, answering.

"Are you asleep?"

"Bennie! Where have you been all week?" What did it matter? His voice drowned out all her doubts and fears. He was here now.

"I'm sorry, baby. I've been working double shifts—mail's crazy—must be everyone paying off their Christmas bills."

"Or getting ready for Valentine's Day," she teased, and then said, "Do you realize that God equipped each of us with some talent of one sort or another? A talent is a kind of emotional muscle. It must be constantly exercised. Ignore it, and it will atrophy. Of course you know where my talent lies."

"How soon can you get here?"

Sterling believed that the connection between Bennie and her began with the erotic and emanated from there. She worked to keep that connection going. "Twenty minutes."

"I've got something special to ask you, baby. But that'll wait—meanwhile, hurry, baby, I don't want to come before you get here," Bennie said, breathing heavily into the phone.

Arriving in a full-length black diamond mink coat and a black silk chiffon nightie, Sterling discarded her fur in the outer hall. From the bare windows soft moonlight poured pale enchantment over her skin, casting a dramatic glow as she moved into the living room of Bennie's riverfront apartment.

"You got something for me?" Sterling asked in a husky whisper, then eased into his arms and kissed him on the mouth.

Realizing that Bennie was capable of reading her every motion, she hoped that he hadn't noticed her jittery fingers. She needed a hit—bad—but she didn't want him to know.

Bennie pushed the door shut behind her, and after kissing her on the mouth, closed his arm around her waist and handed her a small white packet. When she returned from the bathroom, he lowered his eyelids, then slowly lifted them before saying, "You better get your juicy coochie on back in that room. The lemon sherbet ice cream is just starting to melt."

"Did you remember the champagne?"

"Mm-hm. We got work to do." He patted her on the behind and steered her toward the bedroom.

They began by placing two scoops of sherbet and cold champagne into crystal flutes until golden bubbles foamed and peaked just above the rim. Glass in hand, Sterling sipped and eased herself back on the bed. With each movement, the desire to connect, to feel, and to caress each other strengthened between them.

Easing his lips apart with her tongue, Sterling kissed him, the sweet liquid feeling cold inside her mouth. She enjoyed the softness of the flesh inside his mouth and the nubby texture of his tongue against hers. Placing her left ankle in his palm, he reached to massage her foot and toes. The clean scent of soap and the faint hint of perfume mingled with his Tommy Hilfiger cologne. The earthy tang of arousal from their bodies blended to create an aphrodisiac aura.

Relaxing against the pillows, Sterling watched Bennie dip her toes, one by one, in the creamy mixture. She thought that she would go berserk with the thrill as he gently kissed and licked off the sweet liquid. Seconds later he eased his nude body over her, dripping the cool liquid along the expanse of her legs. She trembled with anticipation, knowing where this was leading.

He stopped, the glass empty, and waited. Her nails dug into the sheets. The hands on the bedside clock seemed to freeze until she felt his cold tongue touch the hot folds of her vulva. He spoke to her with each flicker of his tongue: "This is how much I desire you, when I touch you here. This is how bad I want to sink inside you, when I touch you there."

When at least his mouth found hers, Sterling stroked his head, his neck, his buttocks, his back. She ran her fingers along his face, his ears, then locked her fingers over his buttocks, forcing him to enter her.

He thrust into her, watching her face, and sank deeper into the freshness and wetness of her. The rhythm was slow, and slowed further to a tempo of touch, wait, tease, the hesitation, the anticipation, building now until they passed into a higher plane of being where nothing mattered except the infusion of joy brewing within their bodies as they quickened the pace to a climactic beat of power and stroke, and they came together, melting into a single pulse.

They fell into a deep sleep. Upon awakening, Sterling turned to admire Bennie's handsome face as he lay on his back. Nude, she stretched in the center of the white velvet coverlet on Bennie's circular bed, amid rumpled sheets on a pillow for one, but shared by two. How she loved the sharp contours of his jaw and chin and the way his lips sort of curved up at the corners in a mock grin. And she knew she would always want to kiss his lips, and she did so now. It was eleven-fifteen. When she felt his body moving, she knew that it was just a matter of time before he'd awaken totally.

"Bennie?" Sterling saw him open his eyes and touched her lover's face with her finger.

"I'm sorry. I dozed off." He kissed both of her eyes, then eased back to his previous position.

"I love you," Sterling said, touching each baby-fine hair on his chest. She caressed the tender skin over his perfect copper-colored cheekbones. His face was smooth as brown silk. With a smile she offered her tongue, teasing the curves of his lips.

Bennie caressed her shoulders protectively, then whispered in her ear, "I love you, too, baby." He slowly turned down the lights by the remote next to the bed. The room seemed more beckoning with each rotation of the dial.

The sound in her ear was like a seashell—breezy, hollow, echoing. She said nothing, just moved her body closer to his raw heat. Sterling knew well how to use her body. She knew how to soften the silent call of his body until it harmonized with hers— her hypnotic hips guiding him, promising ecstasy. Sterling's obsession with her own lust was her weakness. It was also her strength. The application of her power between the sheets was what kept it going between them.

Placing her hand on his, she rubbed his palm over her buttocks, her thighs, and let it rest on her moist center. Her body was like his song; with his instrument he played the melody. Their bodies were in perfect sync, which improved their harmony.

Early morning's hush veiled their unending phantasmagoria. At ten after five they were still making love. And there was still fire between them. Their unavoidably kindred spirits lured them to the brink of insanity.

Releasing her, Bennie turned on his side and lit a cigarette. He swiveled his body around and sat on the edge of the bed. Blowing a cloud of smoke into the air, he looked back over his shoulder. His eyes drifted over her as she turned slowly to face him. "It's always good between us."

Running a hand over her narrow buttocks, he said, "You know, you got some good stuff, baby. Don't tell nobody. You hear?" He smiled at her with affection tinged by sexual connection.

Sterling touched the corner of Bennie's mouth with her finger and smiled back. She felt completely comfortable as she brought that same finger down to her private place, inserted it, arousing herself, twirled it around, and watched Bennie looking on intently. "When you have the best piece of ass around, you don't have to brag about it. I ain't never seen this motherfucka, all I know is that I'm wearing it."

Bennie chuckled. "If a woman ain't never fucked herself, how she supposed to know how good her pussy is?"

"You told me." She paused. "And maybe one or two others as well. . . ." She yawned and then asked, "Do you think my car's safe?" She looked out the window of Bennie's apartment in the dull gray light. Across the Detroit River she could see the brilliant city lights of Ontario.

"You're not in the ghetto, Sterling. We've got excellent security in downtown Detroit, for God's sake."

Sure, you've got nothing to worry about. It's not like anyone would think about stealing your old Mazda. "So I'm cautious about my vehicle. I love that—"

"Look. I can take you home," Bennie said angrily. It was a problem between them. Whenever she visited him, she felt unsafe—as if he lived in a bad neighborhood. She couldn't always hide it. But Sterling couldn't help it if she came from the other side of town.

She had no intention of going home. It seemed to her that no matter how good their lovemaking was, something would always happen to spoil their reunion.

Not bothering to cover herself, Sterling left the bed and retrieved the package that Bennie had on the dresser. Determined to make their time together a success, she inflected a gay tone in her voice. "Get this ready while I make us a drink." She tossed him the package and exited the bedroom, slowly. She loved for Bennie to look at her body.

When she returned from the living room with two tumblers of cognac, she could tell from Bennie's serene smile he was already one snort ahead of her. She sat the drinks on the nightstand and snorted the heroin that he offered her.

"Mercy!" Sterling shouted. She giggled for no reason in particular and felt as light as a feather, falling back into the comfort of ten fluffy white pillows. "Wow!" She exhaled and closed, then opened, her eyes. "Mmmm." She crossed her arms behind her head, closed her eyes. "You've been holding out on me, Bennie." Reaching over to massage his penis, she added, "This is not the same shit Jamie brought me last week. Mmmm," she repeated, marveling in the exquisiteness of the drug. "I want some more." She licked her tongue over the top of her lip, unsure if the drug was turning her on or if it was Bennie's hardening member.

Tapping her hand back, Bennie scolded, "Not yet. We've got business to discuss."

Sterling opened her eyes. "What?"

ONE BETTER

"I need a favor."

"Anything." She placed her hand on top of Bennie's and guided it over her breasts, her thighs, and then the opening of her vagina.

"Stop it, baby," he said, pulling his hand from hers, "this is serious." He lit another cigarette, then walked over to the closets and opened one. He came back to the bed with two neatly taped and tied packages the size of a shoebox.

"What's that?" Sterling asked, sitting up in bed.

"A million dollars in cash." Bennie set the box of cash on the bed beside Sterling. He didn't bother to open the other package, just shifted the box from one hand to another. "This package is filled with heroin. It's worth, I'd say . . . about a quarter of a million." Sterling had been around heroin enough to know that one kilo ran about $150,000.

The phone rang and Sterling answered it, grateful for the intrusion. She could tell from the look on Bennie's face that he didn't appreciate her answering his phone. "It's Sandy," she said, walking toward Bennie and handing him the cordless phone. She rolled her eyes as Bennie talked to the mother of his son. She could tell from their conversation that something was wrong with the baby.

B.J. Jr. was Bennie's twenty-two-month-old son. He'd impregnated Sandy almost three years earlier, when Bennie and Sterling had called off their third try at an engagement. The whole situation tried her patience, but she knew she had to convince Bennie that she liked children.

The call reminded her of the time last year when Bennie had slapped her.

"You lying son of a bitch, you promised to take me—" she had been complaining.

"Sandy said that little Bennie isn't getting any better. The pneumonia has spread to both lungs."

"That's the lyingest bitch I've seen in my life," Sterling had shouted, wild with jealousy.

Bennie had slapped her so hard, her head spun halfway around to her back. "Don't you call the mother of my son a bitch!" he'd screamed.

When Sterling had raised her hand to slap him back, Bennie had stopped her. "Don't ever try no shit like that again. I don't want to hurt you, Sterling."

That was a year ago. And while he'd never struck her again, he had hurt her with words over and over. But the problem with B.J. and Sandy went even further back than last year. Sterling remembered right after B.J. was born the bitter conversation that she and Bennie had had.

"I think you should get a blood test, Bennie."

"Why?"

"I don't think it's yours."

Bennie was furious. "Just because he resembles Sandy's side of the family doesn't mean that he's not mine."

Sterling was so upset when she saw the hurt look on his face. But it was too late, the damage had already been done. "I'm sorry."

"Listen, I make a good living at the post office. Just because I won't marry his mother doesn't mean that my own son is going to do without."

To top everything off, Bennie had given Sterling syphilis. She'd felt humiliated when the doctor had asked her to name every man she'd had sex with in the past year. Even though she'd told the doctor that Bennie was the only man she'd slept with at the time, she still felt like a whore when the doctor looked as though he didn't believe her story.

Bennie had given Sterling a tearful apology and then made love to her all night long. In the morning, he had suggested that Sterling try something. It was then that he'd introduced her to heroin. When they'd made love that morning, sex was better than it had ever been.

Within two months Sterling was strung out. But getting the drug was never a problem; Bennie was a dealer. He'd sold Sterling on the idea that drugs couldn't hurt her if she didn't overdo them.

Now, Sterling left the room to take a shower. When she returned Bennie was still on the telephone, talking to Sandy. He'd turned on the lights and was writing down a series of numbers on the message pad. "I'll be by the hospital in a half hour. Don't cry, Sandy, B.J.'s been through this before."

"How is the little tyke?" Sterling asked, forcing a smile. Several of B.J.'s pictures were tucked in the seams of the dresser's mirror. Personally, Sterling thought B.J. looked just like one of the Ewoks from *Star Wars*. No way could a man as good-looking as Bennie have fathered such an ugly child. It couldn't possibly be his, she thought, and not for the first time.

"Is it his asthma again?" Last year, just five days before Christmas, Sandy had played the same scenario with B.J.

"I'm sure she's making it sound worse than it is." Bennie turned on the shower. "Anyway, I've got next weekend off, and I thought the three of us—"

Dammit, not this bonding shit again! Sterling half listened to Bennie's plans as he talked over the glass shower stall. *I've told him I'm not changing nobody's shitty diapers. Why is he doing this? Doesn't he realize that I love him and not that damn baby?*

"Is that cool with you, Sterling?" Bennie asked as he dried himself off.

"Mm-hm."

Watching Bennie now as he dressed in jeans and a T-shirt, she saw his mouth moving but didn't hear a word that he said. She tried to focus. "Do you think you can do it?" Bennie asked for the third time. "Sterling?"

"Sure. I can do it." Sterling thought he meant changing B.J.'s diapers; she was willing to give it another try. Hell, if it took being a surrogate stepmother to tie Bennie to her, she'd play the role. Temporarily.

Bennie walked through every room in the all white apartment, opening all the drapes and letting in the dull morning light. "The first pickup is in Texas." He stopped. "Are you sure you can pull it off?"

Sterling was shocked. What was he talking about? No way did she want to run drugs. What else did she have to do to prove how much she loved him? "Maybe. But what's in it for me?"

"Cash, and an unlimited supply of drugs. I'll deposit the money in your account."

Suddenly all Sterling saw was green: the assorted green silk plants that were perfectly placed in every corner, the meadow green carpet that her toes had sunk into, the army green T-shirt that Bennie now wore. The box of green money on the bed.

Like a jaundiced eye, something in the corruption transferred its color onto all the objects she beheld. Everything around her, including the pristine white sheets, seemed stained green and impure. Sterling stood next to Bennie with her hands on her hips. "Exactly how much cash?"

"Oh, that's negotiable. I've got pickups in Arizona and Texas. The feds have been getting closer to our shipping the stuff through FedEx and the postal service. That's all I need—I'd be right on the front line. So now we're back to using runners. I knew I could count on you."

"No problem," she said, and died a little.

The sky was dull gray as she exited the Harbortown apartment complex. Throughout the quiet night a light snow had fallen and lay twinkling at dawn. The engine purred like well-fed kitten as she let her car warm up, using the time to brush the snow from the entire surface of her Viper.

As she drove west on Jefferson Avenue toward the John C.

Lodge Freeway, the deserted streets intimidated her. At any minute she thought a dirty crack addict might jump out and stick her up. There were pieces of newspaper, empty bottles, and crushed paper cups along the sides of the streets. The potholes were so large and black, they looked like moon craters.

Most of the city's streetlights weren't operational. Sterling hated Detroit. She couldn't understand why anyone in their right mind would want to live in the city. The taxes were exorbitant, and the services were terrible. Sterling had thanked her mother many a day for having the foresight to know she needed to raise her daughters outside the city.

Fifteen miles and twenty-two minutes later she pulled into the almost vacant parking lot of the Kmart on Ford Road in Dearborn.

The first item on her list was a douche bag. Although Sterling loved Nieman Marcus and Lord & Taylor, any woman in her right mind wouldn't shop for a douche bag at any other place than Katiejoe's.

Knowing a Comerica Bank was a few miles away, Sterling pulled off the Southfield Freeway on Nine Mile Road. She checked her balance; it was less than $1,000 thanks to Spice's embargo. Pissed, she withdrew $400 from the twenty-four-hour teller and sped off. After taking a snort from the stash that she'd stolen from Bennie, she took a deep breath, rubbed her nose with the back of her hand, and then smiled.

Just in case Bennie did another disappearing act with no calls or visits to her place, she thought, looking inside her purse at the packets of heroin, I'm set for a while.

Back on the freeway, Sterling flew on wings as she turned east on Interstate 696 to I-75 north to Rochester. Home.

Less than a mile from her condo, she pulled into a car wash, yawning. It was now seven-thirty in the morning. There wasn't a piece of trash on the road or addicts to jump out at her. She felt safe. But just as she gave the attendant her keys, she spotted trouble. Travis was a few feet behind her.

"Sterling?" He walked up beside her and placed a hand on her shoulder. "Are you okay?"

Sterling snatched her shoulder away. "Excuse me."

"I was a little concerned. You seem—"

Straightening her body, she paid the $7.50 charge and dropped the change inside her purse. "I'd like my tires, rims, and carpet done, please."

"That'll be five dollars more, miss."

"Why don't you let me follow you home?" Travis offered.

"Are you crazy?" Sterling looked him up and down and frowned, then walked through the next set of glass doors. She didn't like Travis's patronizing attitude. She didn't need his help!

She sat at the triple set of plastic chairs, waiting for the work to be completed on her car. Through the glass windows, she watched Travis pay his bill. He turned, and his eyes met hers.

The drugs were fast, and her mind wasn't functioning too clearly. She couldn't remember how much she'd snorted on the freeway. She smiled at Travis and then left the world behind.

Sterling woke up in her apartment that Sunday evening around eleven o'clock in velvet black darkness. *Where am I?*

Travis. Travis, was all she could remember.

Sterling dialed his home.

"It's Sterling. Did you bring me home?"

"Yes. I drove your car home, put you to bed, and caught a taxi back to the car wash. I can't talk now, Sterling. I've got company." He lowered his voice to a whisper, though his voice still seemed louder than a yell. "I just have one thing to say to you— stop the drugs. They're a total turnoff. You could be so much *better* than most women your age. You could be *better* than just someone's occasional plaything. You could be *better* than just a druggie." He stopped. "Don't you know that?"

The hum from the dead line seemed to pulsate through her veins. Through her fog, Sterling tried to make sense of what Travis had just said. Better? She could be better than the rest?

No one had ever told her that. Well, no one but Spice, and she'd never sounded convinced.

Sterling took a long bath, changed into a pair of pink sweats, and took out her sketches.

Her mind filled with images of the perfect shelter for a perfect childhood, she spent the next three hours working on the multilevel floor plans for a dream home that she'd begun two years earlier.

"This is the home that I'm going to live in one day." But as she said the words, she knew that she would never live in this house. Every room, every detail, spelled love. Spelled Spice.

During the days that followed, Sterling thought about Bennie's drug run. She was almost broke, but she'd work something out, and maybe it served Spice right. But deep down, Sterling knew that was about as mature as wetting her bed. As far as money went, she would work something out. She didn't need drug money. Maybe Otis could get her a job in another architectural firm? With that thought in mind, she worked on the sketches of residential and commercial designs that she'd thought up in her head.

From the beginning, Sterling took to architecture the way some people got religion—through a series of epiphanies. After "designing" her first structure in a class she'd taken freshman year at Columbia (the semester before she got kicked out), she experienced something akin to Emerson's perfect exhilaration—gladness to the point of fear.

She missed school. Missed networking with other students, energized by the power of creating a structure, which was like an infant, a baby, that one molded from inception. It was a rush to bring a design to perfection; what one imagined as perfect sometimes turned out to be just that—perfect. Where else was life like that?

Never mind the suspensions and dismissals—through it all, she continued to sharpen her design skills. As she did so, she felt another strange experience. Mind, body, and building connected, became singular. This year, at Crown, when Patrick Wynn, one of her teachers at the architectural department, complimented her broad intelligence and comprehensive talent, Sterling was amazed by his recommendation to put her on an accelerated track.

Then, as always, as she got into the groove of her work, she'd begin to spiral out of control. She'd start missing classes, self-destructing with sex, and doing more drugs. She was told by the dean to clean up her act, so she seduced him. Nevertheless, four months later she was gone from Crown.

Sterling didn't want to think of that now.

When she wasn't drawing, Sterling did her nails. Every two days she changed the design, composing and creating something more spectacular than the last. A graphics workstation with a heavy-duty magnifying lamp was in the center of her study, which was also lighted by a large picture window. Dozens of sharpened pencils, paints, and brushes filled a Rover caddy she could easily roll from wall to wall. Two El Greco French easels flanked the opposite ends of the room; one she used for drawing and one for nails.

Often, like today, she would be surprised herself by the clarity of her designs. Each seemed more elaborate and yet more integrated than the last.

And when Bennie kept calling, she didn't return his calls. For once she had the upper hand. The amount of heroin she'd stolen from Bennie was enough to last her for about a month. When that ran out, she had another source, Horacio, she could call. True, he was a scuzzball and his dope was shit, but he would do in an emergency. She'd be a damned fool if she let herself believe that she could depend totally on Bennie for her every need, especially her growing drug needs. And the more she thought about him asking her to run drugs, the angrier she became. She was done with Bennie, she told herself, once and for all.

During their estrangement, Bennie sent Sterling a dozen white roses daily. A total romantic when the situation demanded it, Bennie obviously remembered that white roses were Sterling's favorite. After a week, he started to penetrate her crustaceous soul.

Getting high alone wasn't fun anymore. Even though Bennie wasn't perfect, the only thing he ever demanded from her was easy—just sex. He never got into her head and needed to know the reasons why he hurt her. Their relationship was simple. It was like Snuggle fabric softener: it fluffed up pretty, smelled good, never had any static electricity. This was why Sterling continued to believe she would win his love—and him—from Sandy in the end. Their relationship was entangled, messy, and though Bennie loved B.J., his romantic side, the lover and free spirit in him, belonged to Sterling—she was sure of it.

She missed Bennie. He tugged at something inside of her that seemed to be made of pure love, innocence, need. She could never explain, or understand, the attraction, other than knowing that she needed to be needed by him.

On Friday a huge gift basket of lotions, soap, and bath salts arrived, along with three dozen buttery soft yellow roses—yellow for please come home. Mindful of the prickly thorns, Sterling pulled back the green foliage, brushed the velvety softness of the petals against her cheek, and inhaled the heady scent of the rose before pressing it against her heart.

She picked up the telephone, then quickly hung it back up. She did this twice more before going to bed. It was too soon.

The following week, Sterling was tapped out on designs.

Without assignments or that one commission from Spice that she had blown, it was hard to work. She needed a goal. Bored with changing her nail color, she picked up a few books from a small bookcase in her study and flipped through the pages. She selected one by Erica Jong, *Any Woman's Blues*. Just as she plopped down on the white sofa, the once beautiful yellow roses seemed to hang their withered heads in shame, their dying scent permeating her senses.

She read the tearful saga about a woman's emotional addiction to her lover. When she finished the novel, she was shocked by how much she identified with the main character, Leila. She too was helpless before this obsession. With tears in her eyes, she was unable to wait a second longer. She dialed Bennie's number.

"Hello?" A wobbly tear slid between her closed eyes when she heard his voice. Listening to his familiar breathing, Sterling felt her heart stop and pressed her hand against her bosom "It's me. How's B.J. doing?" she asked.

"How's *my* baby?" he countered.

The heat was on. When she hesitated, he let go a deep gulp. In record time he was at Sterling's condo. He left his clothes at the front door. Apologies weren't necessary. Armed with the best cognac and the purest heroin, the young couple screwed until their bodies were sore with love and memories. It ended with tears and apologies.

"Tell me about the deal again. I can do the Texas thing. Tell me where to drop the rental car. First, I rent the car, and put the bag of cash in the trunk. Then I take Interstate 77 to Brownsville, Texas, cross the border there into Mata . . . Mata . . ."

"Matamoros, Mexico, baby."

She was struggling, stumbling, but she managed to convince Bennie that she had indeed been listening but had tuned him out because she was scared. Scared of his reactions, of his turning against her if she was caught. She would have no one. No one. It was eerie. It was terrifying. It was a fact.

"I love you, Sterling. Honestly. I really need your help. You're the only one who can help me."

Sterling looked into Bennie's soft brown eyes and wanted to believe him. She was desperate to trust him, to believe that he loved her, that she was the one who could help him, that she mattered to him.

"I'll do anything, Bennie."

Sterling pushed aside the dope, took both of Bennie's hands in hers, and rubbed them over her heart.

"Don't ask questions, just do as I say." He took a deep breath and continued. "Ordinarily, if you're a steady customer with the Mexican cartel, chances of somebody knocking you or your runner off are slim. I've dealt with Gus, Ricardo, and Henriquez in Mexico for eight years, and have every confidence in their safe delivery of high-quality drugs, but this is a cruel business. Even though I've never had a problem with them, you can't hardly trust nobody." He placed his hand over hers.

"Bennie? Is there anything else I need to know?"

Sterling felt him flinch. She didn't understand. There was something he didn't want her to know about this. He seemed too guarded.

Outwardly Bennie looked like the prime example of a hard-working young man. He had a steady job as a supervisor in Detroit's main post office. He owned a five-year-old Mazda and owned a co-op in Harbortown—a yuppie's dream. With his meager salary of just over $35,000 a year, anyone would think that he was just an average young man leading an average life.

Sterling knew that Bennie had been in the drug business for well over nine years, and she wondered what he did with all of his money. He'd hinted over the years that he had stashed a lot of it away somewhere.

When she took the plane to Texas a week later, on the seventh of March, she was totally high. With some of the up-front money Bennie had given her for the run, Sterling had secretly ordered an exorbitant amount of the eighty percent heroin from Horacio. Even though Bennie promised to give her all the drugs she wanted, Sterling felt it was better if he didn't know exactly how hooked she actually was.

She had half a million dollars in cash in a navy Dooney & Bourke bag when she arrived at the Houston airport. Bennie had gone over the scheme a dozen times with her. Once over the border, Sterling had to drive about ten miles to Castellano's Garage outside Matamoros. Bennie told her to look for a man with a jade-and-silver elephant earring in his right ear. She was supposed to tell him that she needed her tire changed. When he took out the spare tire, he was going to remove the bag of money and replace it with a spare tire filled with drugs. Afterward she was supposed to shop at a nearby store and pick up a few pieces of jewelry and souvenirs, then drive back across the border and into Texas.

Shit, this was easy. Just 1,830 miles in thirty-three hours and she'd be back home. To Bennie. She could make it. She had to.

CARMEN

Blessed be the hand that prepares a pleasure for a child, for there is no saying when and where it may bloom forth.
                              —DOUGLAS WILLIAM JERROLD

---

*M*y goodness gracious," Spice said, putting down the scissors and massaging her hands. "I hadn't realized how strenuous this job was."

Carmen smiled and dropped a large mound of baby food labels in front of her. "Two more bundles and you're finished."

"Can't we start our rounds now," Spice pleaded, "and let the younger volunteers clip coupons?"

"Come on, honey bunny, don't give up on me now. We'll be finished soon."

For years the Heinz Baby Food Company had given St. Anthony's Children's Hospital six cents per label. Concerned citizens sent in thousands of labels that had to be cut, counted,

counted again, and then put into bundles of one hundred. Once Heinz's check came, the hospital put its money toward research.

"Ready to go upstairs?" Carmen asked Spice enthusiastically.

"I don't understand it, Carmen."

"What?"

"How you can be so happy to see so many children suffering."

Carmen paused, buttoning up her blue smock. "The head nurse told me that even though there are two hundred and fifty other volunteers, it takes just one to make a child's stay at St. Anthony's less frightening."

As they left the small office and passed the blue logo of a boy and girl's silhouette holding hands, she smiled. "I take pleasure in thinking that I'm that person. The most precious thing you can give somebody is time, and it doesn't cost nothing."

Their first stop was the intensive care unit. "Hi," she said, going into the room with a pile of books tucked beneath her arm and addressing the little faces there. "How's everybody today?"

A little girl who appeared to be about five years old frowned. With a plastic oxygen tent encasing her tiny body, the young girl, whose every breath seemed painful, was probably suffering from pneumonia. Carmen approached her bed and said, "Tell you what, how about if I read you a story? I've got several here. I'll call off the names and you nod when you hear one you'd like me to read, okay?"

Carmen pulled up a chair beside the bed. "How's about *Alice's Adventures in Wonderland*?" She watched the girl hesitate, then shake her head no. " 'The Three Little Pigs'?" Still no luck. Carmen shuffled through the books, then said, "I know. You're a big girl, right? You'd prefer big girl stories."

Scooting her chair closer to the bed, Carmen smiled and said, "Look here. I've got a wonderful story about a little girl. It's called *Meet Danitra Brown*. Danitra, that's a pretty name." The little girl smiled. "It says here that Danitra is a truly remarkable little girl." Carmen looked at the child's eager eyes and added,

ONE BETTER

"She's probably a lot like you." A bigger smile this time. "Danitra only wears purple because she thinks that one day she might be a princess, and everybody knows purple is the royal color. Would you like me to read you this story?"

Racked with coughs that reverberated like bad music, the little girl couldn't answer immediately. In a remarkably quick reversal, her face became bright with anticipation.

Carmen's heart leaped. These kids, no matter how ill they were, no matter how much they suffered, were little troupers. Who couldn't help but be inspired by their courage?

"Are you okay, baby?" When the child nodded, Carmen opened the book and showed her the pretty picture on the first page, then began to read. When she left, the young girl had fallen asleep with a serene smile on her face.

She visited nineteen other patients on that floor, stopping to read to those patients who weren't yet asleep. Now it was time to visit the burn unit, and this was the part that always made Spice freeze. Frequently Carmen covered this unit herself, but not tonight.

The unit was relatively empty, and most of the kids were already asleep by the time they got there. Still, throughout their visit she could feel Spice's every reaction. One little boy awoke while they were there and Carmen refused to look at Spice—but still she felt her resistance.

It was late Sunday evening by the time they finished at St. Anthony's. Both wore their blue lab coats over their jeans and white tops. "We're home," said Spice, pulling into Carmen's driveway.

"I like the one about the makeup the best," Carmen said, unbuckling her seat belt.

They had been listening to *Talk of the Town,* with Darby Mitchell, the late night deejay on WJLB-FM 98, and had laughed most of the way home.

"Wait—" Spice placed a hand on Carmen's wrist. "Listen . . ."

121

"You know you're ghetto when the rims on your ride cost more than your car," said the deejay, reading a fax from a listener.

The two women laughed together as the deejay put another caller on the air.

"You know you're ghetto when you cut off your Barbie's hair and use it as bangs for your weave." Even the deejay was howling in response to the joke.

Spice turned off the ignition, laughing.

The wind and snow wailed in furious gusts, lifting the border of Spice's velvet cape as they climbed the stairs leading to Carmen's apartment above the garage.

"Hungry?" asked Carmen once they were inside, hanging up her coat and reaching for Spice's cloak.

"Starved."

"I'll make sandwiches."

"Great. Make them *spicy*," she teased. Spice whipped off her black-and-white horsehair boots and sank back on the cozy sofa.

"I had the pleasure of an unexpected visitor stopping by my place a week ago."

Carmen recognized a new excitement in her friend's voice. "Mr. Westbrook?"

"Yeah." Spice hiked an arched brow. "Are you surprised?"

"No, not really. I'm surprised you kept it a secret so long." Carmen shrugged, then smiled easily. "He knows a good woman when he sees one."

Both were lost in their own thoughts for a minute, but the silence between them was comfortable. Spice closed her eyes. "Did you see that little boy?" Her eyes were still closed, as if she didn't want to look her friend in the eye.

In a kind of flashback, Carmen experienced again Spice's feeling in the unit. "Who?" she said, lighting the stove and taking an Italian sausage out of the refrigerator. She washed her hands, talking to Spice over the sound of the splashing water. "See who,

Spice?" she asked again, hoping that Spice didn't notice the shrill note in her voice. Unconsciously she banged the skillet against the gas eye, then added three caps of canola oil in the center.

"That little boy in ward three. He reminded me—"

"Of someone you know." Carmen reached beneath the sink and poured herself a drink, then placed two links into the pan. Tears welled in her eyes as she diced the onions and red and green peppers, then tossed them into the hot skillet. She washed two tomatoes and let them drain on the dish towel.

Spice opened her eyes, leaning her upper body forward and looking into Carmen's tearful eyes. "Adarius. It wasn't just the way he looked—"

"It was his voice."

"I hate to mention it, Carmen. I know it hurts. But we're friends. We're family. I want you to be able to talk to me. I couldn't call myself your friend if I didn't say out loud what you were thinking and were afraid to say. I know how much . . . it still hurts."

"Yes. But I'm fine, Spice. Really I am." Turning away from Spice, Carmen wiped her eyes. She opened the freezer door to grab some ice cubes and prayed for momentary freedom from her emotions. "What'll you have to drink, spirits or coffee?"

"Coffee will be fine."

Carmen served her friend, turned the television on to CNN, and went back into the kitchen to turn over the sausage. "Did I put too much sugar in?" she asked over her shoulder.

"It's just right," Spice said after sipping the creamy liquid. "Guess who else stopped by last week—Otis."

"And . . . ?" Carmen coated two buns with Miracle Whip before layering the bread with sizzling sausage, onions, and peppers.

"Carmen!" Spice shouted, rising and moving to the sink beside her. "Your hands are shaking."

123

"It's nothing. I'm fine." Carmen turned on the faucet and, with a dollop of liquid soap, washed her hands under the hot water until she felt herself begin to relax.

Forcing a smile, she dried her hands on the dish towel. With sturdy hands on Spice's shoulders, she steered her friend back to the sofa. "So tell me what that good-looking brother-in-law of yours is up to."

"He wants to seduce me." Spice eagerly accepted the platter of sliced tomatoes and the bulging Italian sandwich. "Thanks." She caught Carmen's eye. "I almost let him."

Both women laughed mischievously as Carmen set the tray on her lap and bit into the thick bread. "Are you surprised?"

"No. Scared."

Carmen wiped the dressing from the corners of her mouth. "Why?"

"Hell, he's still my brother-in-law. It's creepy."

"Screwing family members these days is passé. Marrying them is another matter."

"Marriage for me means love. I didn't say that I cared for the man."

"Point taken."

Spice leaned forward and asked quietly. "How's your health, Carmen? You're so skinny I can almost see your bones."

"My doctor put me on a weight-gaining program," Carmen lied. There was no doctor. Suddenly she felt nauseated and placed the sandwich on the table. "Tell me more about Otis."

Spice took a large bite out of her sandwich, chewed until the bulk was workable inside her mouth. "I feel guilty."

"About what?"

"David. He keeps creeping into my thoughts. I don't know if I ever mentioned this to you before, but the only thing that David asked of me was faithfulness. I promised him that I would always do that for him. And now, even though he's gone, when I think about another man, I feel guilty. I know it sounds crazy, but my marriage is still so real for me. But now, my dreams are always about some other man—not David. It's strange." She sipped the remainder of her coffee, then continued, "As far as my brother-in-law goes, I've imagined Otis naked and screwing me so often in my dreams that I'm ashamed."

"Why? Who could blame you? Otis is a damned good-looking man." Carmen emptied her plate down the disposal and then hugged Spice before she sat back down. "Stop chastising yourself."

"I feel like I can't get rid of my past. It keeps pouncing on my psyche."

"You need to come to peace with yourself. You and I, Spice, we're not like ordinary people," Carmen said bluntly. "If we knew when we were young what we know now, we would never have subjected ourselves to such self-degradation." She took two long gulps of Popov from her glass. Neither of the women wanted to delve any deeper into that subject.

"However, we can't change the past." Carmen turned and stared out the window. Her face was a mask. "We can only regret," she said in a hollow voice, then again, whispering, "We can only regret."

Suddenly lines of sweat broke out all over her body. She was burning up, couldn't breathe, and quickly removed the blue smock that she'd worn home. She wiped the perspiration from her forehead and sank deeper into the sofa.

The white ashes on her cigarette were ready to fall. Carmen leaned over and tapped them into a metal ashtray, watching in silence as the embers fell. She opened her mouth as if to say something, then stopped. Very softly she began again. "Do you know what I read in the paper the other day?" She didn't wait for Spice to answer. She continued, her hands shaking again. "There was a story about a father putting his two-year-old daughter in a microwave oven to punish her for wetting the bed.

The toddler was slightly bruised, but can you imagine that child's fear? Her own father. My Lord."

Carmen's voice deepened as she continued. "And then I read about this young woman whose thirteen-year-old son was shot in the back by a policeman. The young man was in the wrong. He was trying to steal a car. But in the interview, the mother felt that the officer could have shot him in the leg, in the arm, anywhere but in the back."

"I can't imagine," Spice said.

"The worst part is, she didn't even know that her only child, her thirteen-year-old son, had been shot. No one contacted her. Her son lived for four hours at Grace Hospital. And now the mother says that she'll always wonder if she could have made it to the hospital in time before he died. She wanted to know . . ." Carmen stopped and brushed back the tears. "She wanted to know . . . Did he have any last words? Was he frightened? Did he hurt? Did he wake up alone and ask for his mama? They didn't even give her a chance to say good-bye to her . . . baby."

Spice started to cry, tears falling freely from her eyes. She spread her hands across her chest, hugging herself. "Stop. Please, don't say any more."

Carmen lit a cigarette, then walked over to the baby carriage and picked up one of the dolls. She cradled the doll in the arc of her right arm and exhaled a huge gust of smoke. She paced the length of the room three times before she spoke. "When you have a child, it's deciding forever that you want to have a part of your heart walking around outside your body. You can't control it—you can only watch, and you do your best to help them avoid the pitfalls of life."

Carmen thought, Who will feel their pain? Who will forgive their mistakes? Who will have the patience? Who will kiss away their tears?

Spice got up and went to the kitchen to pour herself a drink.

"I never thought about it that way," she said, sitting back down on the sofa.

Carmen stared at her friend. Her house felt dead. "You know," she said, finishing her drink and then pouring herself another straight double shot of vodka, "there's something warm and friendly about a drink." She drained the glass and slammed it down on the table, feeling relieved, feeling empty. "By the way, have you spoken to Sterling lately?"

"No."

"Why not?"

Spice's voice was defensive. "I'm tired of hearing her sorry excuses."

"Why not try praising her, instead of downing her all the time? Sterling needs to be praised more. I've known you both— hell, all three of you—since the girls were small. Sterling has always wanted from you something no one else can supply. Don't ask me what—it's just there—how she watched you, her little arms outstretched. Even now, the way she acts so bad, she needs you."

"For what? Praise her for what? She never does anything right. You're right. You've known her all of her life. So tell me one good thing that you've seen her do?"

Carmen was silent.

"Nothing," Spice continued. "Not one mediocre thing. Oh, she's good at starting things. But she has yet to finish anything. The girl's got talent. She can draw her ass off. But will she finish school and get a degree? No, not Sterling. Even though she's already spent enough of my money for three degrees—"

"Stop talking about money, Spice. You know money isn't the issue. Besides, you can afford it. And Sterling knows that." Carmen raised an eyebrow. "Sterling needs acceptance for who she is. She needs understanding. Especially yours. She's crying out for your love, and you constantly turn her away. I don't think that you understand how much you're hurting her. Some of Sterling's problems, believe it or not, are not totally her fault. You should try listening to her instead of hollering at her all the time."

"I remember when I held her for the first time. That was nearly twenty-six years ago."

"She was a beautiful baby, wasn't she?"

"Yeah." Spice sighed.

"And she's still that baby in a lot of ways."

"No. No way. She's evil, an evil child." Spice's voice lowered to a whisper.

"Everyone's got a touch of evil in them. Even you, Spice." Carmen watched Spice roll her eyes, then look away.

"How dare—"

"I dare because I'm your friend, and I'm trying to save you the pain of grieving over a child that's alive, that's here, now. A child that needs to know that you love her."

The room filled with silent anger. In the quiet seconds that passed between Spice and Carmen, the dry sound of a branch breaking outside could be heard.

Carmen was tired now—all talked out. She felt the lull of the liquor tugging at her to seek sleep. But she knew she had to resolve this conversation while she could still focus. And Carmen knew if they didn't work it out, Spice would withdraw.

As the bitterness sat between them, Carmen felt a rush of love and respect for Spice—borne on a wave of fear. Desperate to make amends, she spoke in a passionate voice. "Reach out to her, Spice. Sterling is precious to both of us. She's special."

Spice said, "You sound like one of Golden Westbrook's tapes."

"I read my Bible," said Carmen, "I have faith. My dues aren't paid yet. But I know when they are, God will forgive me." Her voice trembled with sincerity. "I'm certain of that."

"I'm sorry, Carmen. I know I need to try more with Sterling, but she makes it so hard to love her."

128

"God knows. God knows my weaknesses, too. But I know that one day He will release me, He will heal me."

"Same here, sweetie. But I'm angry with God. Didn't He know I would need the love of my mother? How can I whole-heartedly love my daughters when I haven't been taught how?" Tears were in Spice's eyes when she finished.

Carmen's voice was solemn but full of wisdom when she spoke to Spice. "Without a mother's love, who will protect our children? How will our children heal? Who will cry for our children? Who will hear them cry? Who will love our child?" She reached for a tissue on the table and wiped away Spice's tears. "You've got to forgive your mother."

"I can't." Spice turned away, fresh tears standing in her eyes. "She gave me away."

"There had to be a reason." Carmen's words were slurred and slower now. She felt the dulling effect of the alcohol. She had to stay focused. They were both trying. There was so much past between the two women . . . and so much still yet to be spoken out loud.

"I've imagined two thousand excuses for my mother, and none of them are good enough." Spice rose and gathered her coat and purse.

In a state of bone-deep fatigue, Carmen lifted her body from the sofa and stood beside Spice in the small entryway. She embraced her friend, and they said good night. As she let go of Spice, Carmen felt her body sway.

From stints in rehabilitation clinics, she knew that alcohol, like most other depressants, created an overabundance of dopamine in the body. Right now she felt as though she were standing outside of herself, watching a movie and staring at herself. She hadn't believed this could happen, but here it was.

When Carmen caught sight of herself in the foyer mirror, she saw her face as God would see it. Gone were the dark circles under her eyes, the sallow skin, the hollow cheeks, the oatmeal-like complexion.

What she saw was the face of a woman healed—a face of glory like a Sabbath psalm. It was the face that God wanted her to see. It was a sign.

Mink

"Yes—they are good boys," said a kind father. "I talk to them much, but I do not beat my children: the world will beat them."
— Elihu Burritt

*M*ink hadn't seen her husband in over two weeks. Their schedules had never been so mismatched. She was on the final leg of a five-day trip, leaving for home tomorrow morning, and she couldn't wait to get there.

Even though it was the middle of February, the temperature in Orlando, Florida, topped eighty degrees. Most of the employees at Pyramid Airlines were out of their uniforms, and enjoying the sunny weather.

After an afternoon of sight-seeing and shopping, Mink and Julie were returning to the Marriott, exhausted. Both juggled heavy shopping bags. Once inside the hotel lobby, the flirtatious bellboy offered to help them with their packages. Mink said quickly, "No, thank you. We'll manage."

"Can you believe that little shit," Julie said, pressing the elevator button. "He can't be more than twenty."

"Hey there, sisters," a husky voice called out as they waited for their elevator.

Both women turned simultaneously toward two gentlemen stepping off an adjoining elevator.

Mink nodded hello first, and Julie followed, smiling.

Julie's warm smile turned out to be a mistake.

"Are you girls from Miami?" the taller of the two men asked, moving closer to Julie.

"No, Michigan. I'm a flight attendant at Pyramid Airlines."

"I meant to say Detroit." The taller man smiled, showing a chipped front tooth. "I can spot my beautiful black sisters from the North just like that," he said, snapping his fingers twice.

"Nice meeting you two," Mink cut in, "but we're in kind of a hurry." Impatient, she pressed the elevator button again.

The shorter man finally spoke up. "How about meeting us later for a drink in the bar?"

"Sorry. We're tied up," Mink said.

"Can't you speak for yourself?" the taller man addressed Julie. "I'm Hank, my friend here is Jeff."

"Nice meeting you, Hank, Jeff," Julie said.

Her impatience growing by the second, Mink was about to lose her cool.

"As you can see," Julie said diplomatically, "we've been shopping all day and we're pretty wiped out. Some other time?"

When Hank casually touched Julie's arm, she jumped two steps back.

"Bad move, Hank." Mink placed both hands on her hips and spoke between clenched teeth. "Don't you touch her! She said 'No, thank you.' Don't you get it?"

Hotel guests brushed past the group with an inquisitive

scowl on their faces. Laughter echoed from the bar adjacent to them.

"So, I get it now. Yeah, I thought so," Jeff said, rolling his eyes at Julie.

"You get what—" Even Mink didn't really know what was driving her to act so nastily.

"Come on, man, these bitches ain't worth it, anyway," Jeff said to Hank, nudging his shoulder. "Let's go, man."

"Naw, I remember when y'all used to be called stewardesses," Hank said, scratching his buttocks. "Now you all want to be called flight attendants. Think you too good for black men like us, huh?"

"No," said Julie. "But—"

While her friend spoke, Mink noticed the particles of lint stuck to the ends of the man's Jheri-Kurl. "We're both married," she finished, even though Julie was recently divorced.

"Oh, so y'all don't kick it with a brother every now and then—"

"Um, *brothers*, we don't want any trouble," Julie said, looking around at the passersby, who were now focusing their attention on them. "I think—"

"I don't remember asking you no questions," the little man said, moving closer to Julie.

She immediately stepped back. The raunchy scent of cheap, sweet wine on his breath polluted the air.

"Come on, Julie, let's go." Mink nodded her head toward the open elevator.

Just as they turned to leave, Julie heard the little one mumble loudly enough for them to hear, "Just what I thought, a pair of dyke-ass bitches."

Mink and Julie whipped their heads back around, saying in a soprano chorus, "Say what?"

"Y'all really need to step off us, 'cause y'all never be half the man ya mammies was," mocked Julie.

Bolder now, the little guy said, grabbing his crotch with a tight fist, "Y'all freaks done forgot what a real dick feels like." He walked back up to Mink and got in her face. She was a good two and a half inches taller than he was. "So, you da man and she the girl," he said, pointing first at Mink, then at Julie. He swayed and dipped his shoulders from left to right as he walked backward.

"No," said Mink, handing Julie her bags and walking toward him, "I'm just not interested. And neither is my friend." She was in his face now. "You got a problem with that?"

The taller man came up to stand beside his friend. "And you," he said, pointing at Julie, "don't start that shit talking 'bout my mama. Don't try and dog me, you might get hurt, girl. Believe me, honey, you ain't the shit."

"And—"

"I don't want to hurt you, girl," said the small guy, shaking himself loose from his friend. "Y'all just go on about your business and we'll go on about ours, okay? Bounce."

From the corner of her eye, Mink could see the bellboy who'd tried to help them earlier speaking with two Caucasian men at the front desk and pointing toward them. If there was one thing that would get the white establishment's attention, it was a group of black folks looking as though they were about to start trouble. That spelled riot in the minds of most whites.

Suddenly a gentle voice called, "Mink. Julie. Can I be of any assistance?"

Mink was suddenly staring into Harrison Fielding's expressive eyes. "Thanks," she said. "I've seen nearly the entire crew, except you, today."

"I do my shopping with a credit card and a telephone," Harrison said, smiling at Mink.

Mink heard the high sound of Julie giggling and turned back around. Hank and Jeff had hit the road.

"I'll take those, ladies," Harrison said, gathering up both women's packages.

"Thanks, Harrison," Mink said, suddenly nervous.

Harrison waited to speak again until they all were inside the elevator and the doors closed. "I was at the front desk complaining about the broken fax in my room and caught the end of what was happening. You girls okay?"

"We wouldn't have been. I believe that in two more seconds Mink would've slapped the tall one. Great timing, Captain Harrison," Julie said. Company policy at Pyramid dictated that the whole crew—captain, co-pilot, flight engineer, and flight attendants—always work together as a group. The strategy was they would maintain smoother relationships in the air and during the entire trip. Good communication was essential when hundreds of passengers depended on positive energy within the crew.

Before the incident with the two men, Mink had planned on going back to her room and turning in early in preparation for take-off in the morning.

"How's about the three of us meeting in my room for drinks in an hour?" Julie suggested. "I don't know about you guys, but I'm still a little hyped up."

Harrison checked his watch and said, "I've got to make a few calls."

To your wife, I'll bet, Mink thought.

"But I'll be free around eight," he said, looking directly at Mink. "Stop by my room." His voice deepened. "We can play a few hands of cards."

"Bid wisk?" Julie asked.

"No," Harrison said, smiling. "Strip poker."

Hush my mouth, Mink thought, giggling.

An hour later, Julie knocked on Mink's door. "Are you going?" she asked as soon as she entered the room.

"Where?"

"You know good and damned well what I mean."

"Oh, Harrison. I hadn't given it much thought."

Julie plopped down on the sofa. "Then why is your face painted like a china doll's?"

Mink looked away, embarrassed. "Okay, you busted me."

"Don't worry about me. Worry about Dwight."

Mink sat beside Julie, exhaling. "I don't understand the attraction myself. I've got way more than the average American dreamer. But ever since Harrison and I made that flight together last month, I haven't been able to stop thinking about him."

"Try spending more time with your family. Don't make the same mistake that I did."

"What are you saying, Julie?"

"The reason why my husband divorced me is because I was never there. I took his love for granted and put my career first. Give up the overtime—your marriage is worth it."

"Dwight—"

"Understands? Don't kid yourself. Chauncey, my ex, loved my last week's drawers. He still does. And I love him—always will." Her voice wavered. "But too much damage has been done. Making a marriage work requires more than love. I know it sounds old, but time and commitment are very important issues between a husband and wife. If you don't put that man first in your life, another woman will."

Mink gave that statement more thought than she usually allowed herself. Sure, she'd wondered if Dwight fooled around. But she'd never found anything on his clothing or in his wallet to cause her to believe that he'd been unfaithful. He was always so busy and so wrapped up with Azure. In the summer months his landscaping business took all his free time. He couldn't possibly have the time to screw around on her, could he?

"It's cold outside, honey. Even though we're sitting here in Florida in this warm weather, back home them menfolks want a warm soul lying next to them every now and then. And I ain't talking about no puppy dog, either."

ONE BETTER

Jelly Jam flashed before Mink's eyes. For some reason, she had never liked that dog.

I know my man, Mink thought. He'd never do that to me.

Like ghosts, everybody talks about true love, but few have seen it. The second night after Mink returned home and slept alone in her bed, she was haunted. She dreamed she caught Dwight in their bed with another woman. The dream seemed so real, she woke up clenching her teeth and fists. Unable to go back to sleep, she went downstairs, made a pot of coffee, and pulled out a stack of interior design magazines.

A few hours later, about eight in the morning, the doorbell rang.

"Hello, Mink." Spice kissed her cheek. "I'm bearing gifts today. Where's my grandbaby?"

"Here I am, Grandma," Azure said, running into the living room.

"I'll be back in a minute. I've something for you, too," Mink told her mother. One thing about the Witherspoons: they didn't need an occasion to buy each other gifts. Mink noticed that her mother looked a bit more fatigued than she had during their lunch date three weeks ago. Working too hard, no doubt.

When Mink returned Azure had opened her gift. "Thanks, Grandma," she said, hugging Spice.

Spice lifted Azure and her baby doll into her arms. The African American porcelain doll had black curly Persian lamb hair, pearl earrings, painted fingernails, and patent-leather shoes. Dressed in a soft white lace shift over a black velvet dress, the doll was stunning.

"Promise me that the next time you see Aunt Carmen, you will thank her and give her a big kiss. Okay? It took her months to make the baby doll."

"I promise," Azure said, slipping down from Spice's lap. Just then Erma called her for breakfast.

"Here." Mink held out two boxes, handing Spice the larger of the two. "Give this one to Carmen," she said, placing it next to her mother's box.

Spice seemed surprised by Mink's gifts. "The wrapping is so pretty, I'm afraid to spoil it by opening it."

"Go on, Spice. You're just as nosy as I am." Mink smiled, enjoying a moment of pleasure she'd given her mother.

After removing the ribbon carefully, Spice felt her eyes mist with tears as she opened the package. Inside were two bright red copper and golden yellow seventeenth-century luster pitchers. Spice gasped, turning the priceless pieces over and over. "They're beautiful. I've been looking for ages . . ."

"I know. It took some time to track down, but it's worth seeing the surprise on your face now." Mink was suddenly embarrassed. Her mother rarely showed such emotion. "C'mon. You can help me turn my house into a showplace like yours."

Dwight had promised his wife months ago that they would spend a day going through and discussing the new ideas she had for remodeling the house. That hadn't happened. Dwight had been working crazy hours at the firehouse for over a month. Soon his landscaping customers would line up like planes waiting for take-off. They couldn't coordinate their time together. Tired of waiting, Mink decided she'd make some decisions herself. Dwight would just have to live with it.

With swatches and samples spread all over the dining table, mother and daughter started hashing out a theme for the decor. The day before, Mink had scoured the Michigan Design Center in Troy, where the ideas and innovations for home decorating were sometimes five years ahead of the retail stores. She had come home with wallpaper samples, ceramic tiles, and fabric swatches.

"I've got this brass lamp in my study that would fit perfectly—"

"No, Spice," Mink said. Her mother loved that lamp.

ONE BETTER

Mink and Spice could hear Azure giggling in the kitchen. "You come on in here and help us, sweetie," Spice said while flicking through the Henredon catalog. "I never get enough time with my grandchild."

After Azure joined them, seated on Spice's lap, Mink picked up the paint samples. "We've got a lot to do. Let's dig in."

"You said French contemporary?"

"Yeah, I want something kind of funky, eye-catching, as soon as you walk in. I'm going to do the entire house, front to back, upstairs and down. This house is so cold looking, it looks like a bachelor lives here."

"Is that because Dwight did most of the decorating when you first moved in?"

"Yeah, my mistake. I didn't have the time. Then, when I saw what he'd selected, I didn't want to hurt his feelings. Now it's time that I expressed myself. As long as I keep the same bed, I don't think he'll complain too much."

A few minutes passed in silence as mother and daughter and granddaughter flipped through the samples.

"Have you heard from Sterling?" Spice asked, pretending it was a casual question.

"No." Mink added dryly, "After that little fight, I think we both need time to cool off."

"Yeah, but this long? I knew she'd stay away for a while when I cut off her credit cards, but this is too much. One of us—me, probably—should contact her." Spice picked up a magazine and started flipping the pages.

"Not so fast, Spice. You've got to accept that Sterling has to finally take responsibility for her life. You can't always be there to save her."

"Carmen believes that I'm responsible. Carmen thinks—"

"Stop right there. I already know what you're going to say." Mink shook her head and sat in the chair. "Just because Carmen and you have known each other for decades, that still doesn't give her the right to try to tell you how to parent *your* kids."

"She's my friend."

"I know. But why is it that people think they can tell you how to do something they won't do themselves? If Carmen's so knowing about motherhood, why doesn't she have kids herself?"

Spice looked away. "She's not in a position. Besides, Carmen is having a really hard time lately. I think she may crash soon. I don't want to even think a negative thought about her. She needs support."

Mink didn't want to go into Carmen and her problems. Carmen and Spice's friendship was too complicated. As close as Carmen had been to them all over the last few years, she always kept her distance. The more she drank, the more remote she became. It had been confusing to Mink in those sensitive days when she needed so much herself. It hurt her, and although Carmen had once truly felt like family, Mink didn't feel that way about her mother's friend anymore.

Noticing the sadness on her mother's face, Mink knew it was time to change the subject. "As far as Sterling goes, she's got to stop feeling sorry for herself. Just because she can't get her life together doesn't give her the right to blame you. I don't agree with Carmen. How long is a mother duty bound to her child? Is it for a lifetime? Is it until they turn eighteen? When do you stop putting your child first and start thinking about your own life? Sterling is not your responsibility anymore."

Spice shook her head. "I'm worried about her. She hasn't been the same since David died."

"You can't fix that problem. David spoiled her rotten, and now he's not here to straighten her out."

Azure exhaled loudly.

"What's wrong, sweetheart?" Spice asked.

"I'm finished. Can I go now?"

Spice kissed Azure's cheek and lifted her down from her lap. She smiled as she watched Azure exit the room.

Afterward they were quiet, reviewing paint samples. Spice pulled out a blue as crisp as winter's noon sky. Mink held it against the wall, the carpet.

Finally Spice resumed the conversation. "I can't say that Sterling's problems are not mine, but I can't intrude—could you call her?"

Mink sighed.

"Thanks, honey. Listen, speaking of David, get this—Otis comes by all the time. He's been calling a lot lately." She waited for her daughter's reaction.

Mink whistled. "That's a good-looking man. He's definitely got his shit together. So what's the problem?"

"He's David's brother."

"Spice, get real. If he was *your* brother, I'd be shocked. David's gone. No one besides Otis from the Witherspoon family lives here. There's no one to judge you but you. And if you feel right about it, it's no one else's business."

"I've always been attracted to Otis. I mean, since David died," Spice hurried to add.

"Anyone can see why," Mink said slyly.

"I'm scared."

"Of Otis?"

"No. Of me. There's something wild inside of me that I've suppressed for years. David wasn't that kind of man. Otis is like . . . he's like . . ."

"Dwight."

"Yeah. He's got that animal attraction about him that can weaken a woman."

"You have to be a weak woman to begin with. And we both know that you're not."

"You've got a point," Spice said, smiling. "You definitely have a point."

Rosalyn McMillan

*   *   *

When Dwight came home late that same night, he slipped quietly into the master suite, showered, went downstairs, and took out Kahlúa, Bailey's, Amaretto, and whipped cream. While waiting for coffee to brew, he mixed together the ingredients for a screaming orgasm, then, holding two brimming mugs, he skipped up the back stairs and turned on the music in the bedroom.

Mink grumbled as the blare of music awakened her from a sound sleep. Hooding her sleepy eyes to check the clock, she complained, "It's four A.M., Dwight."

Dwight stood six feet two. Except for the mole on his right cheek that stood out against his burnt sienna complexion, his face and head were nude of hair. Through daily weight training, his muscular body at thirty-one looked like a twenty-year-old's. Even though the guys at work kidded Dwight about his skinny bowlegs, Mink felt it only added to his sexiness.

He placed the glass mugs on the night table and, pulling back the covers, ran his warm hands over her breasts. "I miss you, sweetie," he said, kissing her from lips to belly button. "I know you're ready for some of this," he said, guiding her hand to feel his erection.

The gold cross earring he wore in his right ear tickled her skin. "Yeah, I am," she breathed.

Casually sipping the hot liqueur, both felt giddy and relaxed as they listened to Barry White blow his velvet tunes through the stereo speakers built into the room.

Before Dwight led her into the bathroom, he rubbed the bare bulbs surrounding the tub with eucalyptus oil. He enjoyed watching his wife's flattering figure as gown and underwear were removed. He was aroused and reached out for her.

Honey, jojoba, and the seductive aroma of eucalyptus filtered through the room, giving it the atmosphere of an outdoor flower garden.

ONE BETTER

While Mink sat on the edge of the tub, Dwight filled the Jacuzzi, then turned on the jets. Dwight helped her step down, then slid his long body beneath the bubbles until they covered his neck.

Mink reached out to hug him, then eased back to the other end of the tub and placed her legs outside of Dwight's. Sliding her buttocks forward until they touched his thighs, she felt the velvety tip of his penis touch her moist opening.

As he slid easily—deliciously—inside her, Barry White harmonized the music their bodies made together. Tons of bursting bubbles circled around their wet bodies and then overflowed onto the floor as they sped up the pace. It was wet, it was wild, it was *needed*, as they came together in a hurried climax. They laughed at the mess they'd made as Dwight toweled their bodies dry, then carried her back to bed.

She kissed him affectionately on the mouth, then pressed her hot body close. They lay breast against breast, hip pressed against hip, until the heat of their naked flesh demanded more.

Dwight kissed Mink tenderly as he ran his fingers through her short hair.

He entered her again, driving as far into her depths as she would allow. Mink felt him sink into her softness, not daring to breathe.

They moved as one in blissful harmony, heart to heart, mind to mind, in body and soul the way only love could bind.

He pushed steadily, steadily deeper, until he heard her gasp. Mink met his strokes with equal force, sucking in her stomach muscles to pull in more of him.

"Tell me where the fire is," Dwight said seductively, kissing her. "Tell me where it still burns."

They came together violently, each drowning in the hot desire that enslaved the raging power they felt between them.

"Are you still up for the rest?" Mink asked as she caressed the inner sides of his thigh. "I purchased a five-brush artist set while I was in Texas. Guess what I plan on stroking them on?"

"You've got so much freak in you, Mink."

Moving her fingers higher and fondling the length of his love muscle, she asked in a deep baritone, "You like that, baby?"

"I love it." He rolled over to his side and took her breast in his mouth, sucking tenderly until he heard her gasp with pleasure. "I can't wait much longer, baby."

"Me neither," Mink said, blushing. "I'll be right back." When she returned, she held a glass of ice water and a small case of fine artist brushes.

"Sweetie?"

"Lie back," she commanded. "I'm running this show tonight." She lifted a brush from the case, dipped the tip inside the glass, then stroked him gently. "This is called an angular shader." Squatting over his midsection, she angled the brush beneath his scrotum and brushed under, over, and around until she heard him gasp. "And this one," she said, reaching back inside the case," is a seven-sixteenths-inch script liner. My sensual signature says all this is mine." She brushed, then alternately licked the radius of his penis.

"Umm. Don't stop, sweetie."

"And this . . . and this one," she said, dipping, then slowly caressing his moist tip, up and around the outer rings until she felt him squirm, "is an inch-and-a-half long liner. The tip is so slender, so tender, like you, baby. Can you feel it?"

"Damn, that shit is good, sweetie."

"Wait. Wait . . . here's number four—a small fan." Mink felt Dwight tugging the sheets, knowing he was seconds away from exploding in orgasmic ecstasy.

While her right hand worked magic with the brushes, she used her left hand to explore every inch of his body, taking pleasure in the roughness of his legs, the toughness of his feet, the tender texture of chest hair, the delicacy of his eyelids, the muscles on his arms expanding and contracting, and finally the miraculously compliant feel of his penis's head.

Dwight arched his back, and his toes curled in sublime pleasure as Mink used the final wide, fanlike brush in a circular fashion over the length of his penis, pressing, releasing, up and down, fast . . . then slower, until Dwight came in spasms of erotic ecstasy.

Wanting to give as much as he received, Dwight turned his wife over onto her back and tenderly thrust the length of him deeply inside her. His orgasm so close, Mink was even more turned on. Their passion built still, and Dwight plunged deeper, thrusting lower and farther inside her as she let her love hold, envelop them, sustaining their animalistic lust until the wild pulse of savage joy could be held back no more.

There was ecstasy on Mink's face as they came together. There was peace. Their bodies had communicated in a language that surpassed words. And when they slept, her naked torso cupped in the arch of his abdomen felt intoxicating. Coupled close, they absorbed the secretions of their love. Throughout the night he uttered, "Mink, Mink . . ." and reached out to stroke her, and she fell into a deeper sleep whispering his name.

Just as the birds began to sing, Mink was awakened by a series of buzzes and loud bangs at the front door.

"Hold on," she called, letting Dwight sleep and coming down the stairs herself to answer the door.

"Who is it?" Erma asked from the top of the stairs as she put on her glasses.

"I'm not sure."

It wasn't quite eight-thirty. Standing on her tiptoes, Mink peered through the glass enclosure on the door at the stranger outside. "Who is it?" she asked.

"Is Dwight Majors at home?" the voice answered.

"Who is it?" Mink asked again.

"I'd like to speak with Dwight Majors, ma'am." The man backed up and flashed a silver badge that read "36th District Court Bailiff Common Police," so that Mink could see. "I'm a process server."

Mink was at a loss. Never faced with the law in her life, she didn't know what to do. Hesitantly she opened the door a crack. "He's asleep," she said finally.

"Could you wake him, ma'am?"

"No. You'll have to come back."

"It's important that I deliver this today. You're just making it worse."

Now Mink's hands were shaking visibly. Her voice held a nervous quaver. "What kind of trouble—"

"Mink," Dwight's voice came from the stairs. "I'll take care of this."

Without another word, Mink left Dwight alone to handle his business. She knew that he was waiting for her to get out of earshot before he spoke. So, just out of his view, on the third stair, she stopped to eavesdrop.

"Mr. Majors?" the man asked.

"I'm Dwight Majors. Is there some sort of problem, Officer?"

He handed Dwight the papers. "You've been served by the Third Circuit Court in the county of Wayne."

"Wait a minute!" Dwight shouted, opening the petition and scanning its contents. "Child support? What the fuck is this shit about?"

The man had already turned and walked away.

Mink raced up the stairs in a rage.

He'd better have a damned good explanation, she thought. Child support! That son of a bitch has been fucking around. That bastard!

She slammed the door of their bedroom, waiting for Dwight to come in and plead his case. She took a seat on the edge of the

146

bed—waiting. The face she wore wasn't pretty when Dwight finally entered their room.

Just as Mink was ready to pounce, Azure screamed. Dwight instantly made a 180-degree turn and went to check on his child. Mink followed. Azure was doubled over, heaving her guts out and wailing between heaves. A trail of vomit led from the table to the kitchen sink.

"Daddy's here, sweetheart." Dwight felt Azure heave the final load of vomit on his chest as he grabbed a napkin and wiped her mouth. Her tiny stomach was working so fast, he waited a moment for her to settle down and then wiped her mouth again with a fresh napkin. When Azure finally stopped crying, hiccups followed. "Let Daddy get his baby some water."

Stepping back from the mess, Mink left the kitchen.

Filling the tub with water, Mink poured a few drops of Chinese flower oil in the center, then turned up the jets on the Jacuzzi full blast. She shed her nightclothes, and just as she stepped in the inviting pool, she heard Dwight's voice.

"She's okay now." Dwight stripped off his pajama top.

"Take that top downstairs and put it in the washer. It stinks," she snapped. "You're dropping cornflakes and vomit all over my white carpeting."

"Sorry," he said, leaving his wife with an angry scowl on her face. "Baby-Z could use some help downstairs."

"You're doing fine," Mink answered, and eased down up to her neck into the fragrant, pulsating water.

After showering, Dwight pleaded with Mink to listen to him before judging him. "The woman has been obsessed with me for years, sweetie."

"What woman!" Mink shouted. "Who the fuck is she?"

"No one you know. I didn't want to bother you—"

"You didn't want to bother me about some woman claiming to have had your baby?" Her voice rose with every word. She knew she was on the edge of hysteria.

Dwight sat on the bed with a pained expression on his face. "She threatened—"

"So it's not yours?" Mink buttoned her blouse and watched him as she stood before the mirror. "You damned liar!" she roared. She rolled her eyes at him, then looked away, shaking her head as tears fell down her cheeks.

"Mink—"

"You scroungy bastard," Mink seethed between her teeth.

"Give me a chance to—"

She was shaking. "Get out! Leave. Get the fuck out of my house before I kill you."

"Sweetie . . ."

But Mink turned her back on him. She wouldn't let a word or a touch of his in. Instantly she imagined a granite wall around her mind and heart. "Do Not Enter, Dwight Majors" was carved in the imagined gray stone.

Dwight's shoulders slumped with defeat. His eyes pleaded for forgiveness, but Mink wouldn't even look at him. After taking a fresh shirt, slacks, and socks from his bureau drawer, he opened the bedroom door and stopped.

"Just go," Mink mumbled between sobs.

By that evening her eyes were swollen shut from crying, and she couldn't sleep. Moving through the house like an automaton, she found herself in Dwight's office. It occurred to her that she hadn't looked at the court papers—maybe they would tell her more. She lit a fire and sat at his desk, but the papers weren't there. She studied a revised blueprint for a new client's yard he was working on. The design called for an octangular pattern to be cut in the garden that mirrored the shape and theme in the dining room leading off the patio doors. Her husband's talent was awesome. Mink missed him. The wall around her heart cracked open.

"Daddy! Daddy!" Azure screamed at the top of her lungs. Before Mink could budge, the child was standing at the office door.

ONE BETTER

"It's Mommy," Mink said.

"Where's Daddy? I'm scared, Mommy." Azure hugged her mother's legs tightly and buried her head between her thighs. "And so is Jelly," she said, pointing at the puppy, who'd followed her. "I had a dream; it woke me."

Mink reached down and lifted her little daughter into her arms. She stroked her fuzzy afro puff, then smoothed her cheek against hers. "What'd you dream, honey?"

"I dreamed the devil was beating his wife, Rosemary."

With great care, Mink carried Azure back to her room and set them both down in the rocking chair beside the bed. Jelly joined them, lying down alongside the chair, listening and panting with his tiny head cocked toward Mink's voice.

"Why is the devil beating his wife?" Mink asked, intrigued by her daughter's seriousness.

"I'm not sure, but I think it's because she's pregnant."

She stifled a laugh. "Doesn't God watch—"

"The devil watches, too," Azure cut in, "since he's got to get into people. You know the devil gets into people and makes them do bad things."

Jelly turned his head inquisitively toward Azure.

Momentarily Mink thought about her argument with Dwight, and she was instantly lonely.

"You listening, Mommy?" Azure asked, turning her face with her small hand. "Lie down, Jelly," she commanded. "You're so spoiled."

Jelly whimpered and laid his head down.

"Yeah, Baby-Z. Mommy ain't missed a word. Aren't you sleepy?" she said, looking into her daughter's serious chocolate eyes.

Azure squeezed her mother's middle, putting her tiny arms around her shoulders, "No, Mommy. I can't sleep now. Can you close the door, please?" Jelly followed her to the door and back, then resumed his position beside the rocker.

"It's okay, baby." Mink felt her daughter's small body tremble. "Mommy's here." She rocked her for a few minutes.

Mink felt Azure's body relax, her breathing slow down.

Suddenly Jelly started barking. Azure looked at her closed
bedroom door. She folded into her mother. "Where's Daddy?"

I should have given him more time to explain, Mink thought.
"It's okay, baby," Mink said, rocking Azure. "Mommy won't let
anything hurt you. Daddy won't let anyone hurt us, because
Daddy loves us. He loves us so much, baby."

SPICE

We are starving our children to death at every level.

—OSSIE DAVIS

***

*E*verywhere she looked, Spice saw something green. The grass, the flowers, the trees slipping leafy bracelets out along their arms, all were bringing the pale green wonder of March to life from its winter's sleep.

Since her conversation with Mink last month, Spice began to feel more comfortable about dating. However, her thoughts weren't of Otis.

Music, starlight, the taste of vintage wine—each time her senses received the slightest nudge, Spice had felt the urge to seek out the man who had said: "Love is natural. Love is free. Love is the essence of God." It was the truth of those words that had brought her to his church today. And it was also the thought of finally seeing him again.

The sky shone a brilliant blue on this perfect Sunday morning. It seemed to her that God had bequeathed this day as her baptism into the community of Christian fellowship.

Wearing a muted gray Valentino suit trimmed with a standing mink shawl collar, chocolate Robert Clergerie pumps, and a matching clutch, Spice tucked her shoulder-length bob behind both ears, inhaled a fresh breath of courage, and climbed the steps to Divinity Baptist.

"Good morning, miss. Have a blessed day," a young man said, offering his hand to Spice as she stepped inside the church.

"Thank you," Spice said, shaking his hand nervously.

"Nice to see you today," a woman said to her, smiling.

"Thank you." Spice smiled and accepted a program from the usher. The beautiful glow reflecting through the stained-glass windows touched not only the sky, Spice thought, but the men, women, and children seated in the pews. All seemed bathed in an identical aura. Happiness and peace reigned here. Soon music started softly, and the choir stood. The church program listed the page number of every song on the morning's service, and when the congregation joined the choir in song, Spice nervously flipped through the hymnal book until she found the first selection and sang along.

As they neared the close of the last hymn, she saw Golden enter and take his place on a chair on the dais. He was clothed in a royal-blue-and-white robe with silver brocade, which Spice would come to know was Golden's trademark church attire.

She was also about to learn that Reverend Golden always put on a show. His congregation expected it, and he never let them down. He began with "Let's Just Praise the Lord" and concluded with "Walking Up the King's Highway."

"If you're not walking, start while I'm talking, walking up the King's Highway. . . . There'll be a blessing you'll be possessing, walking up the King's Highway."

Listening carefully to the words, Spice understood the message and hummed along as the choir sang softly in the background. And while the congregation was feeling the emotion and strength of the song, Golden jumped into a fiery sermon, commenting on the shortage of schoolbuses in Detroit public schools this year. "How are we going to educate our youth if we can't get them to the house of learning?" he demanded.

A few minutes later, a young member brought out a chalkboard. Golden draped a black smock over his robe, then asked the congregation to open their Bibles to the Old Testament and turn to Zechariah 8:4, then to the first chapter of Joshua.

Spice struggled to find the text. Then the man sitting next to her obligingly explained the reference and flipped the pages to Joshua 1:1–9 of the Old Testament.

"Show us!" someone shouted out. "Show us what you talking about, Pastor."

With a large piece of chalk in his hand, Golden moved to the chalkboard and began to draw a picture of children on a bus and children standing outside a high school, talking simultaneously. Using these visual and verbal cues, he began to explain the meaning of the Scripture.

"All leaders need constructive critics to keep us doing our best job. The preacher is not God." The gold cross hanging from his neck swung back and forth like a pendulum with each movement of his shoulders and stomp of his feet as he moved across the platform. "We need to be filled with Bible study, and a little bit of prayer, then most of us would realize how God has blessed us. Leaders need to wake up—do in our communities what we're supposed to do."

Spice felt the spirit of Golden's words, and she began to feel proud of him now, her chest broadening with each breath she took.

"A woman called me the other night at three o'clock in the morning. She was upset. She said, 'Pastor, do you know that they had the nerve to serve my son a chicken wing at the church picnic and give the rest of those children some spaghetti?' " Golden paused for a full fifteen seconds. "I asked her, 'Did he eat? Did he get full? Did he have a good time?' "

Everyone laughed along with Golden, including Spice.

"What nonsense she concentrated on. Leaders need to feel faith because faith cuts down on a whole lot of nonsense—bigger than the chicken wing. I'm talking about terrorism, cynicism, antagonism, and any other 'ism' that gets in the way of our faith in God."

Spice loved the rhythm, she loved the caressing sound of his voice. Without understanding exactly how, he seemed to pull her very soul to him. As she replayed the words of Golden's sermon inside her head, she felt a quiet peace, something she had never experienced before. Who was this man she wanted to wrap herself around until she found one moment of eternity?

"Amen," the congregation shouted. Spice felt euphoric as she joined those around her. The next hour went by fast, and soon the service came to an end. She left unobtrusively, wanting to think about what she'd seen here before she saw him next.

As she drove home, Spice remembered Pastor Golden's closing words: "He always says you need to take the time and listen to the quiet. Allow your mind to relax, reflect, and eventually the words of God will fill the silence, and you'll end up in prayer and left with a good feeling."

As she allowed herself to relax in silence, she felt closer to Golden—felt the silence *was Golden.*

The next day, Spice called Golden under the pretext of their developing business relationship. They decided it would be most convenient for them to meet at Spice's home.

"I've been thinking that we should form a limited liability corporation. If we can come to terms on how much we each plan on investing, I think it would be a good idea. I'm told the tax advantages make this type of corporation more desirable than a joint venture."

"True. Taxes are paid as a partnership so the individual parties can't be sued."

"I've mentioned my interests to my brother-in-law, Otis."

"Otis Witherspoon." Golden paused. "The dinner at Southern Spice; I'd completely forgotten the connection."

"Is there a problem?"

"No. But you should know going in that even though the land in Detroit is relatively cheap right now, the politics surrounding prospective projects, especially in the empowerment zones, do present drawbacks."

Did he mean Otis? She was not oblivious to the discrepancies in Otis's lifestyle, but she'd always turned a blind eye—Otis was family, and she herself was far from perfect. She put Golden's comment aside. "Thanks for the advice. But I've done my homework, and I'm ready to proceed." Spice dug into her bag and retrieved a set of plans she'd asked Morgan Bender to put together. "Here's a few ideas that I have for developing the Lafayette property."

For a moment, his liquid brown eyes rose, caught, and held hers. His soft lips formed a small smile. It was as if he intuited her reaction to him. They both blushed, then turned away, back to business.

Golden appraised the plans for a few minutes before commenting. The rough sketches were of a senior residence with graduated levels of assisted living as needed by each resident. "I'd recommend making a few changes, but I'm confident, after tracking the success of your Foxphasia complex, we won't have any problems."

"Great." Personally, the project didn't excite her—it was depressing. But it fell into the good works category for sure, and it would give them a chance to take each other's measure.

"We haven't discussed the value of the property. I'm figuring a hundred thousand."

"The land is worth more than that."

"Have you had it appraised lately?"

"Certainly. My question to you is how much do you plan on investing, given the fact that my property is half paid for?" Spice asked Golden.

"And the taxes are current?"

"Of course."

"Then I owe you fifty thousand. I can have my attorney draw up the contract and deliver it to your attorney."

"Forgive me for being so inquisitive, but how can you run a church, head a development company, and run NAABR?"

"Simple. I get three to four hours a sleep a night."

"I guess it helps to be young," she teased, wondering when it would be prudent to ask his age.

"Anyway, the NAABR is finally in the black. It's taken years, but I'm proud to say we've made it."

"Of the three, which is most important to you?" Her mind ricocheted from the pulpit to the bedroom. She prayed he didn't analyze the reason for her blush.

"That's a tough question. In one way, they're all equally important—especially in aiding the black citizens of Detroit. I wouldn't want to choose to give up on any."

"So the challenge of doing all three well is what drives you?"

He smiled and said, "You could say that. Yes, you could say that." Golden concluded their conversation by telling Spice about the current projects his company was working on and how excited he was that Detroit was finally building new homes for middle- and upper-middle-class families. "I think we've finally got the go-ahead. Needless to say, getting the inspections and paperwork together is a job for Hercules."

Spice returned his smile and then looked down at her hands,

tightly clasped in her lap. She knew she could allow some silence between them, and her mind drifted a bit.

For days she had seen his face on the ceiling when she went to bed at night. As she drank her morning cup of coffee, she saw his reflection in her cup. When she read the morning paper, the words would blur and form a surreal picture of Golden. But she couldn't talk of that. She couldn't say that she was in deeper than she'd imagined, and she didn't even know why. She could only pray that he felt the same way. Subtly, quiet as a prayer, Golden was filling all the empty spaces her lonely early life had left. Through him she was redefining love rather than hanging on to wounds from long ago.

With confidence in her unquiet heart, she took a high dive into white churning rapids. "Golden . . . I'm not sure how to say this, but I've felt that something was missing in my life. It's been a long time since I've felt this much pain and glory at the same time." Her courage building, Spice spoke to the soul in his eyes. "It's a feeling I don't even fully understand."

"I know," he said softly.

After Golden had left, Spice realized that no matter how close the situation, no matter where they'd stood, Golden had never touched her. And upon further reflection, she realized that his eyes had never lowered past her neck. Not once had she caught him admiring her breasts or buttocks.

Their relationship was beginning differently from hers with David, but her respect for each was the same. David had loved her sexually before marriage. Instinctively Spice knew that what she would share with Golden would be very different.

Time had taught her to trust those with principles. Life had taught her that to be able to trust your partner is a greater compliment than to be loved. And it was beyond question that Spice felt Golden was a man she could trust.

The next day, Spice's calendar was full. By six that evening she was back home. She'd planned on taking a shower and changing into a dressing gown, but after she kicked off her shoes and sat back on the couch in the library for a brief reprieve, she fell asleep. It was eight-thirty when she scrambled awake. By nine she had answered her phone messages and bathed.

Her thoughts were so caught up with Golden over the past week, Spice realized that she and Carmen hadn't spoken in days. Concerned, she started to dial her number when she remembered Carmen was on night duty this week, another reason she hadn't seen her. Spice decided to go down to the second floor to check on her.

Before she could follow through on her thoughts, the phone rang.

"Get down here, Spice. Now. Carmen's in trouble," Travis said quickly.

As she stepped off the elevator, Spice saw a circle of employees standing in the candy section of the second-floor kitchen.

Pushing her way through the crowd, Spice saw Carmen face-down, passed out on the floor.

"She's unconscious, but her pulse is normal. An ambulance should be here soon," Travis said to Spice. "When I couldn't revive her, I called Chamberlain Hospital, then you." He bent down with Spice as she kneeled beside her friend. "She's breathing, but it's serious this time, Spice. Real serious."

"Carmen?" Spice said, trying not to panic. "You'll be okay. Come on, kiddo," she said, lifting Carmen and struggling to cup her head in her arms. Spice yelled, "Get me a cold pack . . . somebody, please."

When her efforts to revive Carmen proved futile, she rocked her, hugging Carmen's heart to hers.

Soon the paramedics arrived. Even using all the equipment available to them, they were unsuccessful in reviving Carmen.

Although Spice tried to convince Travis that she didn't need his help, he refused to let her go to the hospital alone.

ONE BETTER

"I should have known this would happen," Spice said to Travis as she paced the waiting room floor. "I saw the signs, read the clues, and even warned her. I saw her breaking—" She stopped. Crying, she couldn't continue. She allowed Travis to comfort her and fell into his muscular arms as she let out her grief.

"Shhh," Travis said, hugging her gently. "She'll get through this."

"You warned me, too, Travis, and I didn't listen."

An ugly gray day greeted Spice the next morning. She hadn't slept a wink, tossing and turning through the night. Now, with the rain as her companion, Spice scoured the directories for a treatment center that might take Carmen.

It was Kia's day off, but she came into work and helped Spice go through the list, splitting it in half and outlining the questions they would ask each facility.

Over the years, with Spice's help, Carmen had been in numerous rehabilitation centers, including Hazelton and Smithers—the most prestigious as well as the most expensive. Carmen had hated all of them and, much worse, none of them had helped her. What she needed was a totally new approach this time around.

Temple Gardens was a facility recently built in Flint, Michigan. They worked exclusively with addicts who hadn't been successful in other substance abuse centers. The center was testing a pilot program with children of alcoholics that allowed the children to spend weekends and go through the programs along with their parents to better understand the extent and severity of their disease. Spice hoped that with children, whom she always loved to be around, and other patients with similar problems as her companions Carmen's own plight wouldn't seem so bad.

"That's it, Ms. Witherspoon," Kia said, smiling and helping Spice put on her coat. "I'll be at Crittenton Hospital by eight

A.M. to drive Ms. Enriquez to Temple Gardens. They'll be expecting her at nine tomorrow morning."

"If only I'd been able to cancel tomorrow's meeting with my new partners, I wouldn't have had to ask you to do me this favor. I can't thank you enough, Kia." Spice turned off the lights in her office. She locked the door behind them, then stretched her long arms and yawned. "It's late." Massaging the muscles at the back of her neck, she said, "Take the following day off." She lifted a single finger. "Don't argue, Kia. You've done double duty today and I'm truly grateful."

"You feeling okay, Ms. Witherspoon?"

"I'm fine." Spice walked Kia to the elevator and pressed the button.

"In case you need me, I'll be available at a moment's notice. Good night."

When Spice walked into her home, the phone was ringing. It was Otis. Listening to him talk on and on about new development projects in downtown Detroit suddenly seemed irrelevant. He was talking about the empowerment zone, a good opportunity for Spice, they could work together—she was barely listening.

Pulling back the drapes in her bedroom window and looking outside, she let her mind wander as Otis rambled on.

It was still raining. Under the cool garland woven of silver light, the silence made her think of Golden.

Three days later, Spice still had not succeeded in contacting Carmen's doctors at Temple Gardens. With shaky hands, she again dialed the facility.

"Hello, I'm Spice Witherspoon, and I'm calling concerning a patient of yours—"

"We don't give out information about our patients over the phone." The receptionist's tone was professional but sharp.

"Maybe you don't understand," Spice said, forcing a calmness in her voice. "You've got my friend—"

ONE BETTER

"Hold on, miss. Weren't you listening? There are over two hundred patients here. The doctor won't be in until Monday morning." The receptionist hung up.

Spice was stunned as she held the dead receiver in her hand.

Why were they keeping Carmen away from her? Was she okay? Did she ask for her friend?

She laid her head on her desk and cried. How she needed someone to hold her. How she needed a man to tell her that everything would be okay. How she needed . . . how she needed—oh, Lord, how she needed.

*O*TIS

*When a child can be brought to tears, not from fear of punish-
ment, but from repentance for his offence, he needs no chastise-
ment. . . . When the tears begin to flow from the grief at one's own
conduct, be sure there is an angel nestling in the bosom.*

—HORACE MANN

*S*hit!" Otis exclaimed to himself.

The belt buckle on his black leather trench coat was stuck in
the car door.

Pulling the handle, he opened his car door, releasing it. Before shutting the door, he noticed that he'd forgotten the pro-
posals beneath his gloves on the front passenger seat. He placed
the small bundle into his briefcase, then tied his coat closer, feeling a shiver creep up his pants leg. Even though he was on the
lower level of the city's downtown parking lot, he could hear the

163

March wind howling outside. So much for spring being on its way.

As he stood before the City-County Building waiting for the traffic light to change, Otis glanced upward at the vacant, eye-like windows of the building. Two more years in that brick bitch, he thought, and he could get the fuck out of there.

Against the misty background of the sky, he turned up the outer collar of his coat, then quickly crossed the two intersections and waited for the security guard to unlock the door. It was just past seven on a typical Tuesday morning. Taking the elevator to his office on the fourth floor, he reached inside his pocket for his key, only to find that the office was already lit up.

"Morning, Otis," Sandra Hunt said cheerily. Otis's boss was at the front desk, manning the telephones while going through the building inspectors' routing reports.

"I thought we were supposed to have those extra lines in this week?" Otis asked.

Sandra Hunt shrugged. Otis frowned and then continued past the main station to where the building inspectors' offices were located.

After turning on the lights in his office, he went over his schedule for the day's inspections. Today, as he did every day, he wrote the reports from yesterday's inspections. In three hours he'd go out into the field.

Smiling to himself, he added a few comments to the violations he'd discovered:

02-20-97—Out on complaint of illegal construction in progress at 11225 Charlevoix. Found: Workers on job (Renaissance Properties. 23545 Piedmont, Detroit, 48235). Footings and concrete forms are in the wrong place. Spoke to foreman, ——Cain, who could not produce a permit for work in progress, but thinks his boss forgot to post it on the job. Warned Mr. Cain I would check with our office and if permit was not issued, I would have to issue a violation notice. Recommendation: Check of tub records and cardex indicates no permits on file for work in progress. Issue office notice.

Rec. Notice: (Violation)

1—Stop all work in progress until the following items have been complied with and you are authorized to proceed with work by this department:

A—Present plans and make application to secure the required building permit. Ord. 290-H, Sec. 12-11-16.1, 12-11-27.0

B—Upon securing the required permit, contact this department and arrange for the required inspection.

Then Otis went through his in-box and found a memo indicating that Golden had made an end run around him, directly petitioning the city to yet again start up the Renaissance project—it seemed as though they went through this stop-start-petition-start-stop every week. Why couldn't he show Golden the easier way to do business? Golden was making a bad move if he planned to continue doing business in Detroit. *The bastard has nerve. Worse, he knows the process and works it to his advantage.*

This would cost him. I'll fix your ass yet, Westbrook, Otis thought, signing his name on the back of the report.

"Nice suit, Uncle O," Colby said, sticking his head into Otis's office. "Jack's Place?"

It was now ten minutes to eight, and most of the city workers had filled the offices. Colby, a twenty-five-old engineer with three years' seniority, thought of Otis as his mentor. From his first day on the job, he'd called Otis "Uncle O."

"No. L'Uomo Vogue in Southfield."

"I'll check it out," Colby said, nodding.

Otis yelled to his assistant, "Get Golden Westbrook on the phone—now!" A minute later, Golden was on the line.

"Westbrook here."

"Westbrook, it's Otis Witherspoon. I just received notice that you once again evaded the new stop work orders on your Renaissance project. I thought we could come to an understanding—"

"Of course we can. I will not play the game. I, too, have friends in high places."

"But what about our discussion at the restaurant last month?"

"You mean your contribution to my reelection campaign? I am most appreciative of your support. However, as you must know, I keep my varied interests quite separate. Since my order is now signed, I want to tell you to keep my property off your inspection list—just in case you were thinking of dropping by to inspect something else."

Golden's tone was pushing Otis over some edge. "Not just now, Westbrook, but watch your back."

"Mr. Witherspoon, as I've said to you in the past, I don't take to idle threats. Good day."

Otis slammed down the phone. Just then Sandra Hunt was in his office. "Hey, Otis, did you know that Mr. Westbrook also has plans for a senior citizens' facility? They are currently being reviewed by the planning committee." She paused and gave Otis a mischievous glance. "His partner's name sounds familiar. Spice Witherspoon."

Instant fury made the air around him spin, turn red.

"Isn't that Witherspoon related to you, Otis?" Sandra asked.

"She's my sister-in-law."

A phone rang. "Duty calls," Sandra said. "Talk to you later."

Otis's pager went off. It was a long-distance number. He dialed it.

It was Sterling.

"I can't hear you, Sterling." She was crying hysterically. "Repeat what you're saying—slower."

"Bennie isn't home. I can't call Spice or Mink."

"Hold up, now. What's wrong? What's going on? Tell me what you need."

"I fucked up. Fucked up bad. I'm in jail in Waco, Texas. Spice—"

"She doesn't have to ever find out. C'mon now, tell me how I can help."

"I've been arrested for driving under the influence. But something else seems to be wrong."

"Were drugs involved?" Otis shook his head and searched his mind for an attorney who would be available on short notice. "Never mind. I don't want to know."

"Uncle O," she said with tears in her voice, "I don't have anyone else to call. Please help me." She broke down again.

"Don't worry. I'll take care of it."

STERLING

For as children tremble and fear everything in the blind darkness, so we in the light sometimes fear what is no more to be feared than the things children in the dark hold in terror and imagine will come true.

—TITUS LUCRETIUS CARUS

What's your business in Mexico, miss?" asked the customs officer at the Texas-Mexico border.

"Shopping, sir." Sterling replaced her driver's license in her wallet.

It was late on a sunny Thursday afternoon. She'd flown into Houston that morning, rented a car, and made her way down to the border by late afternoon. She was ready for her first run—which was not to say she liked it. But it kept Bennie tied to her. Bennie had specifically stated that the best time for her to cross the border was at the end of the workday, when Mex-

169

ican nationals who worked in the States were commuting home.

The idea of crossing the border to pick up drugs made her nervous. Having been in bumper-to-bumper traffic for the past hour, she could feel her nerves becoming more frazzled. She raised her wrist and nodded meaningfully at her gold Gucci watch.

"How long do you plan on staying in Mexico?"

"Four or five hours, sir."

"Are you bringing anything into the country, miss?" His peering eyes quickly scanned the interior of her rented white Pontiac Sunbird. A small bag and change of clothes were all he saw on the backseat.

"No, sir." She felt sweat forming above her top lip and licked it off. Even as her outer body heated, inside she felt a deadly chill creeping into her heart. The thought of the customs inspector finding the money made her mind race. How would she explain half a million dollars in cash?

"Okay, go ahead."

Relieved, Sterling smiled and drove off.

Now that it was late afternoon, the bone dry Mexican heat had begun to wane. Each mile she drove, with the shadows of wildflowers along the range stretching on either side in rust to indigo, to green, and to gold, began to loosen her nerves. Sterling began to feel a ray of hope that renewed her courage to press onward.

As she drove along Highway 101 toward the city of Matamoros, she constantly checked her rearview mirror. Most cars had U.S. license plates, so she didn't stand out.

In just under twenty minutes she spotted the lighted bright green-and-white sign: Castellano's Garage.

"Hello," Sterling said to the stranger who approached her car.

Wiping his oily hands on a cloth he'd pulled from his back pocket, the man walked casually to the back of the car and checked the license plates, then retraced his steps before asking, "Need some work done today?"

Straining to see his right ear, Sterling looked for the earring. Bennie had warned her not to panic, that panic could only lead to mistakes. Being in another country all alone, she couldn't afford that luxury. With Bennie in mind, Sterling was confident that either Henriquez, Ricardo, or Gus was probably close by. This man wore oversize green coveralls with "Kiki" scripted in white, and the bulk of his muscular chest and arms strained against the tight cloth.

"Excuse me," Sterling said, sneezing. Desert dust was everywhere. "I've got a slow leak in my back tire." She exited the car and brushed invisible dust from her silver silk jogging suit. "How long would it take to fix it?"

Before he could answer, a middle-aged man also wearing coveralls, but with the jade-and-silver elephant earring in his right ear, spoke first. "Oh, probably ten minutes or so. I'll take care of it, miss."

Sterling handed him the keys and watched the handsome creature drive the small car into the open stall.

While waiting for the car, she walked a few yards away to the next building and purchased three silver rings, an ankle bracelet, and two copper mugs with "Mexico" painted lavishly at an angle in bright red.

"How far is the nearest liquor store?" Sterling asked the man when he handed her back her car keys.

The man laughed. His accent was heavy and sexy. "How did you manage to miss the liquor signs? They're all along the highway."

"I guess my mind was focused on finding this place first." She shrugged. "So I'll pass one on my way back?"

"Certainly. By the way, I'm Henriquez," he said, extending his hand. "Tell Bennie I said hello."

"Sure. Everything's all set with the tire?"

He winked. "You're good to go, miss."

"Thanks," Sterling said, trying not to stare at the jet black curls that had fallen across his beautiful bronze forehead.

Minutes later she spotted a liquor store, stopped, and purchased a half gallon of whiskey.

A few miles from the border, she checked the time. It wasn't even six P.M. She pulled off the road. She had to laugh—it had taken no time at all to transact her business. She reached in back for her toiletries bag and removed a tampon from the carrying case, then emptied a small dose of the powder she'd hidden there onto the map the car agency had provided. Lifting it to her face, she snorted the heroin.

She passed through the Mexico border back into Texas without any problems. She was heading north on Interstate 77 high as a rocket. Lighting a Salem, Sterling scanned the stations for the weather report and traffic. Glancing at her watch, she saw it was approximately six-thirty. The highway was clear. The weather report came on first.

"Okay, let's hear some music," she said, reaching over to change the station. She stopped when she heard a news report:

> Parents use their son and daughter as mules to transfer drugs in from Korea. The married couple made the children swallow the balloons filled with dope before they left Korea.
>
> Throughout the long trip, the mother kept telling the flight attendant that the child didn't want anything to eat or drink. With such a long flight, the stewardess thought it was strange and alerted the police. Unfortunately, when they arrived at Metropolitan Airport in Detroit, the boy had died from an overdose of heroin. The balloon had burst in his stomach.

Sterling turned off the radio. The part of her that wasn't totally gone on heroin felt sick to her stomach. She was sorry for the little boy and ashamed of being a part of the craven world that had caused his death. She peeled the protective plastic off the whiskey and sipped straight from the bottle.

Soon drunk as well as high, she drove through the small towns of Texas; then she stopped to purchase fish and chips at a carryout in Austin.

Back on the highway, she gobbled down her food as she drove, washing it down with straight whiskey. The odometer showed she'd driven four hundred and fifty-eight miles since leaving Matamoros and was now entering Waco, Texas.

Once again she reached for the bottle of whiskey and took a long gulp. Just as she screwed the top back on, she noticed the cop car creeping up behind her, and she slowed down—too late. The lights started flashing red and blue, and she pulled over. Pushing the bottle onto the floor, she tried to kick it under the seat.

"Can I see your license, miss?" the officer asked, shining a flashlight in her face.

While Sterling searched inside her purse for her wallet, she asked in a calm voice, "What's the problem, Officer?"

"Are you in a hurry? I clocked you at ninety."

Could he smell liquor on her breath? "I was on my way home to Michigan, Officer," she said while noticing the other officer had circled the car, checking the license plates, and was now flashing a light on the passenger side of the vehicle.

"I'll be back in a moment," the policeman said, taking her license.

She knew he was going to run a check on her license. Thank God she didn't have any speeding tickets. Sterling kept her eyes on the clock and sweated profusely through every second of every minute. He was back in four minutes.

"Mind if we check the vehicle?"

"No, sir," she said, exiting the car.

He's going to find the drugs, she thought. Please don't let him find the dope. Please, please don't let him find the dope. A part of her was scared shitless, the other part was too high to care.

He found the whiskey, three-quarters full. When he seemed to pass over the spare tire with the heroin in it, Sterling closed her eyes and offered up a silent Thank you, Lord, though the absurdity of that nearly made her burst out laughing.

After administering a Breathalyzer test, he said, "I'll have to cite you an OUIL, ma'am: operating under the influence of liquor. You'll have to come with us," he said, cuffing her.

By the time Sterling reached the police station it was one A.M. They printed and photographed her and took her to a holding cell. With the alcohol and drugs wearing off, the joy of not getting busted for possession of heroin gave way to a growing rage. The fact was, she was alone. "Can I at least have a cigarette?" she asked her guard as she stood just inside the cell door.

"Sorry, this is a nonsmoking facility."

Fuck. She took irritable steps to an empty cot and, keeping her eyes focused on her shaking hands, avoided the bold glances of four other women sharing the cell with her. Sitting down, she bit her bottom lip, trying to contain her craving. She knew that it wouldn't take long for her jones to come down, and without a cigarette, she didn't know if she could make it.

She figured it was about eight A.M. when the officer finally told her that she could make a call. She immediately dialed Bennie— there was no answer. She waited a few minutes, then dialed again. After five tries and still no answer, she had to laugh. The officer had said so nicely, "You can make all the collect calls you want to, miss." But what if no one is home? she wanted to scream.

Then she dialed Otis.

Who is not attracted by bright and pleasant children, to prattle, to creep, and to play with them?

—EPICTETUS

Our imaginary woes are conjured up by our fantasies and fostered by passionate feelings. Real hurts come of themselves and need to be opposed by a nearly superhuman exertion of mind. Mink knew well that real grievances had displaced her troubles borne of passion.

Today, as lonely as the ghost of that portentous conversation she'd had with Julie, Mink sat with her husband in the judge's chambers. Julie's statement haunted her: "If you don't put that man first in your life, another woman will."

The judge stated matter-of-factly, "Mr. Majors, the court is certain you are the boy's father."

"Hell," Dwight said, jumping up from his chair.

175

"Sir." The judge tapped her gavel, then wagged her index finger in Dwight's direction. "May I remind you that you're in a court of law?"

Turning away from Dwight, Mink lowered her head in anger and shame.

Dwight ignored the judge and stood up, shouting, "That bitch has fucked everything that could walk or crawl. And now you want to say that this child is *mine?*"

"Mr. Majors, I must warn you again—"

"Bullshit!" he hollered. "You picked the first man with a decent job—which was me—an employed black man, just to get that bitch off the welfare rolls. You will always be 99.9 percent sure an employed black man is the father!"

"Mr. Majors, are you saying you never slept with Estelle Rivers?"

Sweat streamed down Dwight's shiny head as he shifted his weight from one foot to another. As silent as fate, he turned to look into his wife's eyes, which were wet with tears.

Not waiting for him to answer, Mink got up and walked out.

After the initial hearing and the results of the blood tests, the court concluded that Dwight was the father.

That same night Mink moved into the guest room, refusing to speak to or sleep with her husband.

Like fragile ice, anger passes away with time. Not with Mink. Her heart was as frozen as the glacier that anchored her soul.

A week went by and Mink still refused to speak with her husband.

"You don't have to talk to me. Just listen to me, let me explain, okay? Look, you can be mad tomorrow!" he screamed as he stood outside the guest bedroom door.

"I'm filing for a legal separation," Mink said, finally opening the door. Her voice was hoarse from hours of crying. "Don't waste your time trying to talk me out of it." She and Dwight had been planning to celebrate their eighth wedding anniversary in a couple of months.

"But sweetie! I told you that the bitch is lying about the kid's age—if he's mine, then he's got to be older. This all happened way before you and I were married. All she wants is money."

But Mink wouldn't listen. "If you have an ounce of respect left for me and your daughter, you'll leave." She slammed the door in his face.

Dwight moved into the firehouse.

A week later, as Mink dressed for work, she flicked on the television set to the midday news. She listened with half an ear as she toweled herself dry. While spraying oil sheen on her neatly cropped 'fro, she heard a story that caught her attention.

A three-alarm fire at a two-family duplex on Linwood and Gladstone flashed across the screen. A fireman had been killed trying to save a mother and her two children.

That was Dwight's district! Her heart began thumping wildly inside her chest, and she turned up the volume and listened. Please don't let him be hurt, she prayed.

Mink sat on the edge of the bed, wrapped in a towel, waiting and dying a little inside.

In the background, the remnants of a contained fire smoldered as the reporter gave a brief summary of the tragedy that had just transpired at 28894 Gladstone. When he concluded, he moved to interview a firefighter who was sitting on the rear bumper of the fire truck.

"This is Firefighter Conyers," the reporter said, placing a microphone before the man. "Could you tell us what happened?"

Mink recognized Kim Conyers's smoke-stained face. Her body tensed, and tears fell as she prayed silently for her husband.

"I'm sorry," Kim said in tears, "I can't talk right now."

The camera panned to a fellow firefighter, this one suffering from smoke inhalation, being wheeled into an ambulance.

Mink thought her heart had stopped. Then, suddenly, there was Dwight, standing next to the reporter.

"Can you fill us in on what happened here?"

Mink's heart started beating normally again as she watched her husband speak. He looked hurt. He looked thin. He looked like the man she loved, Mink thought as she watched him speak into the microphone.

"Kim and I warned Harvey to wait for backup. This was Harvey's second week on the job and his first fire. He heard the kids screaming on the third floor and panicked. Kim and I tried to pull him from the flames. Harvey wouldn't budge. He fought us and ran farther into the depths of the fire."

The reporter's face showed genuine emotion as he hung on to every word.

"I knew that unless we left right then, we would die. We had six minutes of air left, and that wasn't going to get us up and down six flights of stairs when the fire was out of control."

Dwight stopped. He hugged Kim, who was still overcome with emotion.

Mink clutched the folds of the spread, the harsh words she'd used the night she'd kicked him out burning her ears. She hadn't seen or heard from him since. It had been seven days.

"I had no choice . . ." Dwight stopped and covered his face with his hands. His shoulders shook. Mink had never seen him cry.

Kim finished for him. "When Dwight made it outside, he fell to the ground. There wasn't an ounce of air left in his tank. I had to drag him to the truck; he needed oxygen. The bad news came minutes later . . . four lives were lost. Harvey had run out of air trying to save the kids and their mother."

Mink's fury was suddenly sidelined, but her ambivalence remained. They were miles away from each other, and she knew that she could not reach for what had been or try to control what was to be.

ONE BETTER

She picked up their wedding picture on the dresser and pressed it against her breasts. At that moment he was closer to her than her next breath. But she wondered, Am I still so close to you?

The next day, with a thirty-hour layover in Dallas, Harrison Fielding suggested they rent a small plane for an outing. Mink assumed that he was kidding and declined his offer. Three hours later he called up to her room to say that a limousine was waiting downstairs to drive them to a private airfield in Balch Springs. Forty minutes later they boarded a small rented plane.

"You were so keyed up during the flight, I thought you might like to feel like a passenger for a change."

"That's sweet of you, Harrison."

"I remember how you looked when you talked about your Cessna."

"You remember?"

Harrison's agility in the cockpit was as smooth as a mirror. They took in the sights of Dallas from the sky. Harrison pointed out each geographical landmark as accurately as a talking travelogue. Mink was used to pointing out the areas of interest in each state they flew through to the Pyramid passengers, but she did so by rote from a written instruction card. This was the first time that someone had actually pointed them out to her, and in such vivid detail. She loved it.

She thought of telling Harrison about the fire and her problems with Dwight. But as she'd learned from her mother, it was never a good idea to share secrets.

As they landed, it started to rain. The innocent time that they'd shared together had been unexpectedly exciting. Mink was struck by Harrison's wisdom and self-assurance. She admired him; she also found him incredibly sexy.

Still, in the hours they'd spent together, Harrison had spoken often and languidly of his marriage. Clearly he was a man who was totally in love with his wife.

Back at the hotel room, Mink felt wired, but instinct told her to rest. If the weather cleared, in three hours her crew would be on their way back to Michigan. She decided to take a hot bath and try to force her body to relax. As she toweled off, she received a call from Julie informing her of the severe fog and thunderstorms coming in from east. The Dallas airport was closed until tomorrow; all flights were canceled.

Mink picked up her revised flight schedule from beneath her door, read it, then called Erma and told her that she wouldn't be home until tomorrow afternoon.

She stared out the window and watched the rain come down in waves. She felt cut off from her world, disoriented. She couldn't think of home.

She called Julie. "Do you want to meet for drinks later? We both could use a distraction right about now."

"No. But thanks for offering. I'm going to call it a night."

Mink felt a bit of tension in Julie's voice. Maybe her friend was feeling disgruntled about the strike that was brewing among the flight attendants. Why else would she sound so distant?

Just then the phone rang. It was Harrison. "Mink, would you like to go out this evening?"

Suddenly Mink's whole attitude changed. She was connected once again, and she wanted to party. She took a quick shower and went downstairs. At the sight of Harrison, Mink forgot about home, husband, and child. She was enjoying the moment, even with the rain shouting like music outside. The plane ride and the rain outside only heightened the opera.

They discussed braving the rain to try the Italian restaurant two blocks away. Soon they were dashing through the pouring rain.

It was pitch black behind the hotel. Harrison held fast to

ONE BETTER

Mink's arm as they ran toward the restaurant. Even with his supporting arm, Mink tripped on a curb and fell backward, pulling Harrison to the ground with her.

In the midst of the storm, no words were necessary. The rain pressed Mink's chiffon dress against her small breasts. She could see the silky hairs on his chest through the thin fabric of his shirt. No one was around. There was not a single person to point a finger and condemn. They were less than a hundred feet from the restaurant, and the feeling hit them like a brick wall. They were helpless.

Harrison kissed Mink's shimmering lips. Overwhelmed with lust, Mink eased back on the flooded pavement and spread her legs open wide. It wasn't pretty. It wasn't softened either by the exotic atmosphere of the Italian eatery in the background or the spicy scents emanating from it. It was quick thrusts, heightened by the pounding rain. It was just what it was: sex. Hot and heavy sex that peaked at a point neither had expected.

Afterward their parting was quick and clumsy. As she hurried back to her room, Mink was torn by mixed feelings. She felt both thrilled and ashamed by how quickly she'd succumbed to her lust.

How could she face him again?

The next afternoon, as soon as Mink stepped through the doors of her home, the telephone was ringing. It was Dwight.

"How are you, Mink? How was your trip?"

"Fine. We were delayed because of the weather." Mink paused. She felt simultaneously relieved to hear his voice, angry, and suddenly awkward. Then she thought of Harrison on top of her.

"I saw you on TV the other day. That was some fire."

"The boys were pretty shaken up. But everyone is settling back down. So, Mink, don't you think it's time we saw each other and talked things over?"

"I'm sorry, Dwight, it's just too soon. I'll call you in a while."
Mink put down the phone without waiting for his reply. The
truth was she felt too guilty to face him.

The winter season had taken its toll, and several captains had
called in sick. The next day, Mink was asked, for the first time
since becoming a captain, to work overtime. With nothing better to do, she accepted.

When she returned home three days later, Kim Conyers
called. He was worried about Dwight. He'd been drinking
straight tequila for two and a half days.

Early Thursday morning, Dwight pounded on the door. This
time Mink answered.

"Hello, Dwight," she said, stepping back upon seeing the
rage in his eyes. She smelled the liquor and knew it was going
to be a scene. "Go upstairs, baby," she called to Azure, who was
playing in the hallway. Then she opened the door to let Dwight
in. Azure immediately ran to her daddy and clung to his legs.
She hadn't seen her father in three weeks.

"Daddy'll be up to see you as soon as I talk to Mommy, okay?"

Mink pulled Azure back toward her as he spoke, then sent her
little girl up the stairs. Instantly, she turned on Dwight.
"What's wrong with you? You smell terrible."

Dwight breathed deeply, trying to calm himself. He entered
his old home and kicked the door shut behind him. "I need to
talk to you."

"You're drunk, Dwight. Maybe we should wait—"

"Dammit, I said I need to *talk* to you!" he hollered.

"Okay, okay," Mink said nervously. Suddenly she was scared.
Dwight never got drunk. In fact, he hated drunks. After she
heard Azure's footsteps in the upper hallway, she led Dwight
into the library and sat on the sofa.

Dwight paced the floor in front of his wife, rubbing his forehead, sighing, and gritting his teeth. "I want to come home."

"No—"

ONE BETTER

"We can work this out. The judge says the child is mine. So I guess he's mine—on paper, that is. The point is, he happened before you and I even met—I'm sure of it."

"You think the lawyers can't determine the child's age? Is that what you really believe? Hell, you're not drunk—you're crazy!"

"Look, I'll pay the child support for the boy. You won't even know he exists."

"What!" she yelled. "You admit you've got a son, and now you want to shirk your duties as his father?"

"You've got a lot of fucking nerve. Poor Azure can't even ride in her mother's Jaguar because she might mess it up. All you care about is you, your career, your luxuries—"

"Fuck you, Dwight. I'm the kind of mother who needs to work for a living because her husband can't afford to take care of her."

"You bitch! I work two jobs. I let you have a career. I let you follow your dream!"

"After expenses, those jobs wouldn't even pay my yearly shoe bill. You spend more money every year purchasing new equipment. The fact is . . . you're losing money and you're too stubborn to admit it."

"Tell the truth, Mink. Money's never been the problem—"

"Look, maybe I'd like to be able to sit on my ass every day. Live the good life. Do volunteer work once a month, bake homemade cookies, and be at home for Azure."

"Azure couldn't stand you being here all day. You suck as a mother, and you know it. Don't try to pretend—you've never been a good mother."

"How dare you!"

Even though in her heart she knew he spoke the truth, who was he to sit in judgment of her?

"I'm sorry." His voice was suddenly tender. He reached out to touch her arm. "I didn't mean that. Forgive me."

She jerked away from him, her voice thick with tears. She was consumed with anger and guilt. "I look at you now and know myself better. Because much of what I am today is because of you."

CARMEN

No man has ever lived that had enough of children's gratitude or woman's love.

——WILLIAM BUTLER YEATS

*C*armen woke early, an iridescent sky shining through her window. From her bed she could see the roof of the greenhouse where she worked while in rehab. Under the two 1,500-square-foot glass domes, hundreds of trays of fruit and flower seedlings were growing. Carmen remembered when she had helped Spice plant the herb garden on the grounds of Southern Spice. Together they had chosen to arrange the herbs in the shape of a wheel, and the different plants grew between the spokes of old cartwheels, the outer rim edging the makeshift circle.

At Temple Gardens Carmen had planted the herbs in a traditional checkerboard design, choosing her favorites—anise, basil, tarragon, valerian, lemon balm, mint, hyssop, lovage, and rue.

185

She treated each plant with as much love as she would have her own child, and the garden reflected it. Carmen loved working with herbs and soil. She felt closer to God. One afternoon, one of the patients who'd been in and out of Temple Gardens over the past year told her that in the summertime beautiful butterflies would look for their favorite herbs—red-flowered pineapple sage and cinnamon basil. Carmen quickly ordered the seeds through a catalog.

Today was the second Saturday in April. She had an early appointment with her therapist, and then Spice would come. Carmen didn't want to move. She lay in her bed, remembering a story she had heard over a news radio station about a stepmother who allegedly terrorized and disfigured her two stepdaughters over an eight-month period. The younger child was pushed down the basement steps, and the other girl had been cut severely on the cheek and hand with a utility knife. When the stepmother confessed to the abuse, she admitted that she'd been drunk at the time.

Who will protect the children?

Now, as the dust floating on the wind swooped past her windowpane, Carmen felt the secrets hiding in the chambers of her heart. Her hands began to tremble. She rose and began to pace the room, trying to fight the craving. It had been almost six weeks since she'd tasted alcohol, since she'd had even the tiniest of sips. She began to lick her lips. She stopped, turned, and walked faster, clasping her trembling fingers behind her back.

Suddenly she fell to her knees to pray but couldn't find the relief she sought. Prayers were no substitute for her real friend. Spice would be there soon, she knew, but for how long could she lean on Spice to save her?

When Carmen first arrived at Temple Gardens, she had suffered from an acute case of the D.T.'s. To ease her withdrawal symptoms, she'd gone through first the unmedicated detoxification, then the medicated, which finally worked. But not without pain. Carmen had experienced such severe tremors that the head of the institute, Dr. Wright, had told her she'd been in danger of dying from seizures during her three-week bout in detox. The mental anguish was as severe. The hallucinations, night terrors, the whole "ball of wax," as her therapist put it, had left Carmen weak in body and devastated mentally.

During this postdetox period, Dr. Wright called Carmen into his office and revealed to her that because of an error in communication, the staff had barred Spice from visiting. He apologized profusely and promised that starting today, Spice would be given a daily update on Carmen's progress from Dr. Wright personally. Even more important, Spice would be allowed to visit.

The first visit was strained for both Carmen and Spice. Few words were spoken. The two friends merely held each other's hands.

By the third visit, Carmen had begun counting the days between visits. Spice brought along hair products, a curling iron, a blow dryer, and a makeup kit. Carmen couldn't get enough of her friend's pampering. She felt secure in Spice's love for her.

"How do I look?" Carmen once asked Spice hesitantly. She knew that Spice would ignore her lumpy complexion. Of course her hair didn't shine as much as it did when they were young. How could it, after all her years of drinking? There was no way to hide the telltale signs of alcohol. Your body told on you before you could open your mouth to argue.

"Tiny," Spice answered.

"You look good, Spice." *You always look good.*

"I didn't say you didn't look good, Carmen. I just mean you're still too thin." Spice mussed her hair and said, "You're the prettiest woman I know. If you weren't my friend, I wouldn't take time trying to make you look better than me."

Carmen chuckled a bit and relaxed some.

By the time Spice was ready to clip her fingernails, Carmen could feel herself warming up, a morning glory in the sun.

As Spice worked, she filled Carmen in on everything that was happening at the restaurant. She assured Carmen that her apartment was being cleaned weekly, and her pictures were being dusted, not to mention her beloved dolls. Carmen knew Spice was working to see a smile on her face.

And the visits were therapeutic for both of them. Spice talked about the girls.

When Spice mentioned that she hadn't heard from Sterling since their argument in January, Carmen could see the pain on her face as she spoke.

"Do you worry about her?" she asked Spice quietly.

"Of course. I don't know how she gets by day to day. Sterling is so miserable at taking care of herself. But I can't do it for her anymore. It's time she learned." Spice looked away, trying to hide her tears of anguish.

Then Spice mentioned Mink and Dwight's problems. "They just can't seem to see eye to eye," she explained.

Something told Carmen there was more to this story, but Spice wasn't sharing it. Carmen took a breath before she spoke and then said, "Spice, Mink's a lot like you. She's driven to succeed. Perhaps you can be the one to tell her that family is just as important—maybe even more. Did you ever think that maybe Mink can't handle the money and the power it gives her—mostly over Dwight?"

Spice looked at Carmen and then said, "Something's wrong there, dreadfully wrong. She doesn't seem to be thinking clearly lately. Sometimes I think she's going to crack. She's always been so strong. I don't know—"

Changing the subject, Spice talked about her building developments.

Carmen stopped listening. She saw it all too clearly: Mink was following in her ambitious mother's footsteps. She just prayed it wasn't too late for Mink's marriage. None of them could measure up to Spice.

Glancing up now toward her friend's face, Carmen didn't miss the pity in Spice's eyes as she gazed at the other patients walking around. Some talked to themselves. This was a routine sight for those who lived at Temple Gardens, but seeing them through Spice's eyes, Carmen felt pain—it hurt to watch them. As Spice packed up her things to leave that day, she said, "You need to get out of here, Carmen. I don't ever want to see you like that." Her eyes pointed to a woman who, ever since Spice arrived, had been crouched in the corner, talking to herself.

"You won't," Carmen said as she followed Spice to the door.

Carmen looked at her watch. Connie, her therapist, would be expecting her: she was due for her appointment in ten minutes. Every morning and afternoon, 12 Step meetings were conducted with groups of patients to help guide them through the process of conquering their addictions. Each resident was also assigned a therapist. It was in this more private setting that each patient tried to elude her inner demons.

Carmen felt comfortable opening up a bit of her past to Connie. For instance, she'd told her that her son had died in a fire. Of course, there was much more to the story than Carmen told her. She still couldn't utter the words aloud.

Still, there were parts she didn't need to hold anymore. This morning on her way to Connie's office, Carmen, without even knowing it, dug down deep, as deep as the herb's seeds, and made some decisions.

"I want to tell you how my son, Adarius, died," Carmen said to the therapist when she arrived. "It's been over fifteen years, but my child's charred body is imprisoned in the vault of my heart." She paused and looked fearfully at the therapist. "I want to free both of us."

Connie nodded for Carmen to continue.

"During a cold winter back in 1981, I was living in Midnight with Adarius, who was just eight at the time, and Frank Desmond. Of course, he wasn't Adarius's father, but Frank told me that it didn't matter. From the time he moved in, Adarius called Frank 'Daddy.'

"For two Christmases and two Mother's Days Frank promised me the moon and the stars and didn't produce a broom. I was brokenhearted. We'd had big plans to move away from Midnight, raise Adarius in a good home, put him in a private school, take him to church, and teach him about life.

"That didn't happen. The beatings started and I found out too late that Frank was more in love with his drug habit than me. I also finally noticed that every time we made plans, we were both high on cocaine. Sometimes I wondered if I only imagined that he'd said all those wonderful things to me. When we were sober, which was rare, Frank obviously didn't give a damn about me or my son and stayed away from home for days at a time.

"I finally got fed up, and took my son to stay with a friend for the weekend. When Adarius and I returned home on Monday Frank was gone, along with the little money I had saved. I started using drugs more often, started making excuses for failing to pursue my lofty dreams—to make the dolls to sell. To join Spice at the restaurant and continue cooking school. I got high because I didn't know what to do with myself. I had no money. No motivation.

"I was running away from my problems and running away from myself. I would look in the mirror and say, 'Carmen, you look like shit. This ain't you.' I kept the house a mess, but Adarius would clean it up. While I was high, I would lash out at Adarius, call him a bastard, a little motherfucker, whatever I could think of. By some miracle, my son never lost respect for me. Adarius would wash the clothes, fix his lunch for school, and make soup and sandwiches for dinner, or whatever he found in the cupboards to eat. I would leave for hours and Adarius would have the house cleaned when I returned.

"I would come home feeling guilty, hug and kiss him, then say, 'I'm sorry for calling you names. I'm sorry for leaving you. Please forgive me.' And he did.

"During one spell that year, I stopped drinking for two months. I was thinking better, and taking better care of my child. Then Frank showed up and the drugs started—again. He was there only a few weeks. Just long enough to disrupt two needy lives before leaving.

"Back then, I remembered my aunt telling me, 'Carmen, you need to keep your ass at home and let that boy of yours go out and play with his friends. A child is just a child for a short period of time. Let the boy have some fun for a change. He's too young to have so much responsibility.'

"Over and over again, my aunt would preach the same words. I kept silent. Who could understand how I felt? Adarius had long since outgrown his clothes, and I had no money to buy new ones or secondhand items. The bimonthly check from the government barely paid the rent and bought food—especially when I was done buying drugs and booze. I didn't know what to do.

" 'You can't expect your boy to live like this,' my mother would say over and over again. 'Aren't you ashamed of what you are? Aren't you tired of this filth? You stop this, you hear? You stop or I'm calling the social services to come and get him.'

"I told her if she called welfare, she'd lose me. She wouldn't have a daughter no more.

"My mother called the authorities anyway. I came home one morning and found my child gone. If I'd had a gun, I would have killed my mother. Luckily, I just got drunk instead. After court, I got a caseworker, who was a single mother of three herself. I regained custody of my son. While waiting for him to come from foster care, I cleaned the house from top to bottom.

There wasn't a piece of lint on the carpet when I welcomed Adarius back home.

"I remember Adarius said, 'Mama, I knew you'd come to get me.' He hugged and kissed me until I pushed him away in embarrassment. It nearly broke my heart when Adarius said, 'I'm proud of you, Mama.' "

Carmen saw that time was passing. Soon her hour would be up, and Spice would be there. She had to release Adarius's sweet memory—she had to get free of it as well. Connie's eyes led her on.

"For a few months things went well. But when Adarius went back to school, I began spending too much time home alone. I couldn't find a job, and one day, while I was downtown at the bank cashing my bimonthly check, I spotted Frank with a woman. Both were dressed in expensive clothes. He wouldn't speak to me. Dismissed me like I was a tramp.

"I got high that day, and it was the last real day of my life.

" 'You want Mama to iron your pants for you, baby?' I asked my son, reaching for the basket of clothes that he was carrying.

" 'You can't iron my pants like I can.' He sprayed starch on his wrinkled jeans. 'I'll do it, Mama.'

"I smiled. 'Mama's going out for a little while. I'll be back in a couple of hours.'

"Later, on my way home, I was higher than the price of gold, with two hundred dollars in my pocket. The taxi driver asked, 'Do you hear sirens, miss?'

"I heard a child's wail. Adrenaline shot through my veins and I was instantly sober. As I watched out the cab window, I saw flames shooting up into the sky. Smoke clouds blackened the area.

"Several fire trucks and people I didn't recognize surrounded my small house. I ran from the taxi, screaming, clutching my heart. I was in agony as I ran, storming toward my burning house.

ONE BETTER

"One of the firemen held me back. His arms felt like steel bars, locking me forever away from my child. 'My son is in there!' I shouted, trembling. 'Let me go!' I said, struggling to break free.

" 'You can't save him, ma'am. I'm sorry.'

" 'This can't be happening,' I screamed, hysterical, burying my face in my hands, then looking back at the fire. 'This can't be happening!'

"Later they told me that the iron had caused the fire. The autopsy showed that my child died from smoke inhalation. The humiliation of going to court and being charged with negligence and the tragic death of my only child was more than I could bear."

Carmen fell silent. She was beyond tears, and when she looked in Connie's eyes, she saw herself—a defeated woman.

Then Connie finally spoke. "The court records show you were deemed not guilty."

"I didn't leave the iron on—no—but I am guilty. I've replayed the fatal scene with Adarius that morning over and over again. How could I know that those would be the last words I would hear from my child? 'I'll do it, Mama.' Those simple words haunt me nightly. Why hadn't I done my job as a mother and ironed his clothes? Why?"

Carmen's voice was ablaze with passion and emotion. "I know my child is not at peace, that he's suffering. His soul is on fire."

Tears streamed down the therapist's face. Connie cried Carmen's tears.

"The pain is unbearable. Losing a child is indescribable. Tears fall without my knowing. My feelings are on automatic pilot. . . .

"Some days I can't think. I can't eat. It's a pain down in my heart that will never move. Only dope and booze can keep it quiet." Carmen's tears flowed, but she spoke as if she didn't even notice, as if she didn't expect them to ever stop. "What mother can bear to outlive her child? Who would expect that God could be so cruel? You wonder, What have I done, Lord, to deserve this? Sure, I did drugs. I acted bad. But I hurt *me. Me!* Why didn't God punish me instead of him?" Carmen paused, accepting a tissue from the therapist and blowing her nose.

"I just want some peace. Just a moment of peace when the pain will stop. When my suffering will finally be over."

Part Two

Your children are not your children. They are the sons and daughters of Life's longing for itself. They come through you but not from you. And though they are with you, yet they belong not to you. You may give them your love, but not your thoughts. For they have their own thoughts. You may house their bodies but not their souls. For their souls dwell in the house of tomorrow, which you cannot visit, not even in your dreams.

—KAHLIL GIBRAN

SPICE

Children make you want to start life over.

—MUHAMMAD ALI

━━━━━━━━━━━━

$\mathcal{D}$eceit and deception. Those were the terms she'd heard over and over again in the last few days concerning the structural engineer, Lucas Mann, whom her dear brother-in-law, Otis, had suggested Spice use on the Foxphasia project. Along with those accusations came the devastating news that not only had Mann underdesigned the buildings, but there was structural failure on sixty percent of the Foxphasia complex.

Six days ago Otis's counterpart in the town of Royal Oak told Spice the design was so deficient, it would be more cost-effective to tear down the complex and start all over again. Immediately both of her partners had backed out of the venture.

Now she sat in her company truck on the outskirts of the Foxphasia job site, numb, as the wrecking ball hit the brick wall of the half-built hotel for a second time. She didn't know what compelled her to come to the site and watch it be destroyed. At last, she turned away. Either she had to find new partners willing to invest quickly, or she needed to borrow $18 million to finish the project. Both options seemed impossible.

The double indemnity clause on David's life insurance had enabled Spice to tuck away $2 million. That was her nest egg. Southern Spice was worth between $8 million and $9 million. With her other combined assets and investments she was worth at least $15 million. But if Foxphasia failed and she used all of her own money, she faced financial ruin. Could she take the chance?

Shaking her head with disgust, she looked away from the cement devastation. And what would she have to leave her daughters? What had Carmen said? She was constantly torn between the concerns of her daughters and the catastrophes threatening her business ventures.

On top of everything else, Travis had walked out on her. What began as an extended vacation became a bold dare for Spice to call and ask him why he hadn't returned to work. They both knew why. She knew he was starting up his own restaurant. But his departure was a year earlier than she had expected it would be.

Spice dropped her head in her hand. Everyone she cared about was caught up in a web of misfortune. Her thoughts crisscrossed from Carmen to Mink to Sterling. Just that morning she'd been awakened by a call from Otis, detailing Sterling's latest incident with the law. Spice hadn't been able to reach Sterling on the phone for weeks, and the call from Otis was the realization of her worst nightmare.

"Listen to me, Spice. Sterling is okay. She needed help and was afraid to ask you."

Her voice shook with emotion. "Do you think I wouldn't help my own child?"

ONE BETTER

"It wasn't a matter of what I thought. She was arrested—"

"Arrested! My baby!" she screamed. "For what? Otis, what are you telling me?"

"DWI. It's just a year's suspended license and a two-thousand-dollar fine."

"Two thousand dollars! A year's suspension!"

"It's happened before," Otis mumbled.

"So you know about another arrest Sterling was involved in, and you didn't bother to tell me?"

"I thought it best. It was a while ago, Spice."

"How dare you," she said, and slammed down the receiver.

She opened her bedroom door and went out to the balcony. Her hands trembled. The cold April breeze calmed her, felt good against her tear-streaked face. She fixed her eyes on the willow trees bordering Paint Creek, just showing their early buds. Dewdrops still glistened on the grass, and the young foliage smelled of rain. In the distance she could hear the fresh, clean, newly thawed cold water rushing down the ravine from Clinton River and flowing into Paint Creek. Spice turned and went back inside.

I love her so. When her tiny little fists were like orchids yet to open, baby hair soft and silken, her eyes shone with such spirited gleam, I loved her so. Yet, Lord, something is missing, and I feel this terrible pain. She's still only a child, not capable of understanding the sorrow she brings. How can I make my child understand?

Now Spice, still in her truck, punched in Mink's number on her cellular phone.

"Hi. Mink?" she said, forgetting the cranes and trucks when she heard her daughter's voice. "You sound terrible." From the hoarseness still evident in Mink's voice, Spice knew that her daughter had been crying. "Are you okay?"

"Yeah, I'm fine."

"Where's Azure?"

"She's in the backyard playing with Jelly."

199

"Has Dwight been to see her lately?"

Mink's tone was sharp. "Why?"

"I just wondered."

"Look, you have no idea what I'm going through. Your marriage to David was perfect. I'm facing total ruin here. My husband has a bastard child out there." Her voice began to rise. "How am I supposed to explain to Azure she has a brother? Should I hide it? Pretend that he isn't here? Make him disappear?"

"Mink—"

"I'm sorry, Spice, I've tried to forgive Dwight, but I can't. I'm going to divorce him."

"You're moving too fast. You need more time to think."

"Fuck him," Mink said, more tears in her voice. "I've gotta go, Spice. I'll talk to you another time. Bye."

Spice turned back to the disheartening sight of the wrecking ball destroying her dreams. When she thought of Carmen, Mink, Sterling, and herself, she felt as though they were all bundled together, their lives being battered and turned to dust.

Foxphasia had also been David's dream. What would he do? Then she remembered.

Stored in the bottom drawer of David's cherrywood desk was a list of individuals and corporations he had approached when he'd first purchased the Foxphasia property in Royal Oak. Coded beside each name was the dollar amount they had committed to the project. If her memory served her right, at least three of the twenty had been willing to put up $5 million. True, the list was now five years old, and the commitment had been made to David, but she was certain she could convince enough of them to agree to raise the $18 million she needed to finish Foxphasia.

With the challenge of her future at stake, she started the engine and headed home.

Glorious nature had blessed the grounds of Southern Spice that second week in April. Spice watched as Dwight worked meticulously, making sure every blossom was at its greatest splendor for the big event, the April tea, which would take place in a few days. Seven years ago on this very day, Mink and Dwight had met. Spice had hired the young, ambitious landscaper, betting on his innovative garden design ideas.

Each year he had added to the grace and opulence of the garden setting. And since so many influential people from the city would witness his work, this event had become Dwight's best opportunity for acquiring his most affluent customers.

Spice continued to marvel at Dwight's gift for invention. One day last year, while he was working on his plans, Azure had asked why there couldn't be more water. Following his daughter's suggestion, Dwight drew the plans for two water gardens to go on the east end of Southern Spice's four-acre grounds. Both would feed from Paint Creek and be visible from three sides of the restaurant. When he presented the new idea to Spice, she'd been ecstatic.

Before long, two fifty-by-seventy-foot circles were dug on each side of the central walkway. The ponds were filled with hyacinths, water lilies, Japanese koi, and goldfish. Later, Dwight had added ducks as well.

Throughout the past week Spice had watched Dwight from the window of her apartment. Of the seven days he'd been there, Azure had accompanied him on five. Spice knew he must be distraught at the split of his family. It was so clear that he loved his daughter. And what about Mink? Their conversation the other day still rang in Spice's ears.

"Come here, baby," Dwight called after Azure, seeing that she was getting too close to the edge of the water garden.

"Wait, Daddy. Jelly wants a drink." She tried to pull the puppy back from the water by his stomach.

Dwight whistled for the dog. "Here, boy." Jelly, ears pointed, backed away from the water.

Azure followed after the puppy as Jelly Jam raced toward his master. Spice came downstairs to join them.

"Hi, Grandma!" Azure said in her sweet voice.

"Hi, Baby-Z."

"We're nearly finished for the day, Spice," Dwight told her. "Can you stop in my office a minute before you leave?"

"I've got to get Baby-Z home. It's time for her dinner."

"She can eat—" Spice stopped herself.

They both knew that Dwight would not eat the fatty entrées at the restaurant, nor had he allowed Mink to dine on Southern Spice's rich meals. He was a staunch health nut, and there wasn't anything to say about it. His daughter would not eat the restaurant's cholesterol-packed foods.

Dwight's white Blazer was a few yards away, already packed with all his equipment. "Take Jelly to the truck, Baby-Z," Dwight said, patting her head gently.

Spice knew that Dwight would be within his rights if he took Mink before the judge for contempt of court. Not once, during their month of separation, had she allowed Dwight to see his daughter. Mink had no right to keep Azure from seeing her father, so she'd arranged for Erma to leave Azure with her when Mink was flying. And she made sure Azure saw her father during those times.

"It was weeks since I'd seen Azure before you arranged these visits. I want to thank you, Spice, for letting me spend this time with my daughter. Mink won't talk with me right now."

"That's what I wanted to see you about. I'm concerned about her. She seems so different—"

He stared out into the grounds for a few moments before speaking. "She is different."

Spice could see the muscles tensing in her son-in-law's jaw. "Don't give up on her, Dwight. I don't want to pry into your personal business, but Mink is not herself. Lately she's just somewhere else. That's so unlike her."

ONE BETTER

"I know."

"And she's forgetting things. When I mention something we discussed, she doesn't remember it. Like she can't keep her mind on anything."

"I've tried talking with her. She won't listen. She keeps telling me she needs more time. But how much time am I supposed to give her?"

"I can't answer that question. Only you and Mink can."

Reuben, Dwight's assistant, who'd been working on the topiary greens on another part of the grounds, signaled to Dwight that he was finished.

"Thanks again," Dwight said to Spice before leaving.

As Spice watched Dwight walk away, she wondered if her daughter was thinking about her little baby at all. Left only with Erma, Azure seemed confused and frightened. Suddenly she thought of Carmen, wishing she were nearby to ask her friend's advice. How Spice needed Carmen now.

Spice had made dinner reservations for two at the Whitney Mansion on Woodward Avenue. Starting in March, "Hi-Falutin' Garden Parties" were held each Wednesday night, and Spice thought it would be a wonderful setting for her and Golden.

The exotic plants that covered the grounds were already in bloom, and Spice knew that the music, by David Potterman and Friends, would be engaging. Golden's timing entering her life at this point couldn't have been better. His gentleness, his patience, had given her the strength to cope when her world was falling apart. Whenever she was around him she felt more energetic, invigorated. That energy, that patience, was part of the reason for her attraction to Golden—she fed off his strength.

Spice tapped her foot to the beat. Not sure if a preacher danced, especially in public, she wondered if she and Golden would ever get to enjoy that particular ritual. As the soothing music flowed around them, Spice watched Golden's animated

203

face. When a song came to an end, Golden applauded the band and then turned back to look at her. Spice didn't miss the smile on his face.

They sat for a while, drinking coffee, not saying a word to each other, just listening to the music and nodding every now and then. Golden set down his empty cup and turned to look into Spice's eyes. He took her hands in his. "I love you, Spice."

"What?" Despite their close mood, his words truly caught her off guard.

"Yes, and it feels so right."

She felt his voice enveloping her, felt his understanding and compassion. He wasn't judging her, as David sometimes had done in silence.

"But we've spent so little time. You haven't touched me. We've never—" She blushed.

He caressed her hand and gently covered it with his. "I just know I love you."

Spice felt as if her body were made of butter, and she was melting, melting. "When did you know?" she said breathlessly, uplifted by the moment.

Golden closed his eyes. "Just now, when I felt you slip inside of me."

Her body felt as if it had taken flight, like a light, fluffy, floating cloud, and then she *felt* him. Felt the transfer of his love pouring into her.

The realization of who she was, who she had been, and what he represented awakened her like a pail of cold water thrown in her face.

Spice remembered the first time that she'd heard his voice on the tape: "God is love. God is truth. They are all connected. If you are a liar, love is not for you."

Love is not for you.

No, she thought. It had to be. She wanted love with Golden,

and that meant she had to tell him everything. "Golden, I have a past," she said flatly.

"I'm interested in what you are now, and not what you've been. We've always been something *before* in our lifetime if we've lived long enough. Everyone in the world is recovering from something."

"I wasn't in love with David when we married." She had to start somewhere; for some reason she wanted Golden to understand about David. About the way she grew to love him and why.

Golden listened with a calm, patient smile.

"Although I found love with him as our marriage grew, I didn't realize how *much* I loved him until he died. Since then, I've been afraid of another emotional commitment. I don't want to get too close. I don't want to be hurt again by a person whose love controls me." She paused and looked into his eyes. "It's scary for another person to have that kind of power over you." He touched her hand, and Spice held her breath.

She was talking not just about David, but about Sterling as well. How she hurt because of their being apart. Turning her head to the music, she listened to the band for a moment, then added in a dry tone, "I don't want to lead you on. I want you to understand. I've been betrayed by love. I'm not going to rush into it again."

"The God that is in me recognizes that in you," Golden said, kissing her powder soft hands. "And I'm ready to help you take a chance. I'm ready for you to take a chance on me." The smooth and gentle tone of his voice lapped over her like a warm tide. "I know that I've been trying to find and reembrace my other half for years. I've waited and I've found that person, and that person is you, Spice."

Later, as Golden drove her home, Spice couldn't think of what to say to him. She sat back in her seat and smiled, inhaling the love that had perfumed the night. She just wanted to enjoy the moment. But soon, thoughts from the past invaded her consciousness.

How much should she tell him? How much would he really want to know?

As if reading her thoughts, he said, "One day, I'd like to take the time to read with you Mary Magdalene's story."

She was stunned. "Mary Magdalene?"

"History says Magdalene was a prostitute. But I don't believe it. She was just a woman in pain. I think it will help you. You will gain an understanding of true love, life, and strife, and what it means to be alone and suffer. I think you'll enjoy the honesty of her life."

They pulled up outside her home, and Spice asked Golden to come upstairs. In the intimacy of her kitchen, she offered him a mug of hot chocolate.

"I wasn't always saved," he told her. "I was a troubled youth with a bad attitude from a broken home. I rebelled against my mother. In my teens, I got into trouble with the police and spent time in jail for possession. Fortunately, my mother took every dime she had and sent me away to college. I had no friends. All I cared about was survival. I learned how to push myself and, finally, excelled. I earned a scholarship, and when I received my degree in theology from Oxford, my mother was there."

"Oxford, in England?"

"The same."

"My Oxford Odd Fellow. It's so hard to believe, Golden. You seem to have yourself so together. I would never have thought . . ."

"That I was human? That I am a man? I am."

"No, I'm sorry. Most people think of pastors as—well—perfect saviors. We know they aren't, but we want to believe that they are superhuman examples for us to follow."

He pressed his warm hands against her face.

Did he feel as she felt? she wondered. She wanted him to pull her close to him, kiss her tender lips. *Is he feeling what I'm feeling now?* "Thank you, Golden Westbrook, for coming into my life. Only God knows how much I needed a man of your strength in my life right now."

For five years Spice had denied herself personal happiness. During those years her wealth had soared. Money, she knew, even before Sterling brought it to her attention, was a poor substitute for love.

"God knew, and he whispered softly in my ear, 'She's the one for you.' That's why I'm here."

"It's destiny," Spice whispered. "That it is." Suddenly she heard a noise and turned toward the door. Her tongue felt stuck to the roof of her mouth as she saw Otis standing in the doorway.

Wearing a demonic expression on his face, Otis demanded, "What the hell is he doing here?"

Spice jumped up. "How did you get in?"

"I've always had a key. David gave it to me."

"Do you want me to leave?" Golden asked Spice.

"No. Otis is leaving. And leave your keys on the table. Never mind, I'll just change the locks."

"You're making a big mistake, Spice," Otis said, staring at Golden.

Spice led Otis to the elevator in the foyer. "I'm trying to maintain my relationship with you. I know you're concerned about me, and I appreciate it, but I need my privacy."

"I was wrong. Forgive me for caring so much about you," Otis said spitefully.

Spice swallowed her tears as she watched the elevator doors close on Otis's saddened face.

When she reentered her home, Golden was making a fire. He turned and smiled at her.

Spice tossed a log onto the fire and smiled at Golden. She knew that she'd made the right decision.

Children have never been very good at listening to their elders, but they have never failed to imitate them.

—JAMES BALDWIN

"Fuck no," Otis said, hitting the cocktail table with his fist. "I'm not going to accept this bullshit." Rolling his eyes at his phone, he picked it up and pushed redial. After the third ring, the answering machine came on. Angry, he hung up.

He was stretched out on the sofa in his living room, the remote control in one hand and a tumbler of Hennessy in the other. For the next two hours he dozed, glimpsing snippets of the fights on HBO. With each punch one opponent struck, he felt his headache pounding. A part of him felt like knocking some sense into Spice.

Moving to the kitchen for a dose of two double-strength Tylenol, he thought of Spice again. He couldn't help but respect her. She'd been firm in her convictions about their relationship, even though they both knew she cared for him. She couldn't be led easily, and he'd always liked that about her—even when she was married to David. Somehow he had to make her understand what they could share together.

"I don't want to lose our friendship, Otis," Spice had said.

He wanted now to tell her, "Friends make better lovers! Some couples never reach the level of relationship that we've shared over the years."

His first wife had died in childbirth, along with his son, twenty-five years ago. Since then he hadn't found a woman strong enough, until he met Spice—who at the time was married to his brother.

Happiness is difficult to find and even harder to hold on to. After his wife died, he was nearly immobilized by depression. It was not possible for him to find even temporary pleasure in the arms of other women.

Immersing himself in his work hadn't helped. Buying cars, taking vacations, and hoarding money in the bank hadn't worked, either. What Otis realized was that up until now, he hadn't been able to express correctly to Spice how much he truly cared for her. What had begun years ago as an infatuation had blossomed into mature love.

Catching sight of his reflection in the TV screen, dressed in silver blue shadow-striped silk pajama bottoms, he flicked off the set and went into the bedroom. He reached inside his dresser drawer and removed a small box. Inside was a size seven and a half, six-carat princess-cut diamond ring. It sparkled even in the dark. He'd purchased the ring for Spice this past year while he was vacationing in Senegal. He'd planned on proposing marriage on Christmas Day.

A small card inside the box read "God was the first that marriage did ordain, by making one, two and two, one again." Otis felt even though he and Spice had begun their relationship singularly, through marriage, a union of love, of intimacy, they would become as one.

I shouldn't call her when I'm drunk. But what difference did it make? He held the same conviction sober or drunk. One day soon she would be his wife. He was tired of waiting. And if it went on too much longer, Golden would persuade Spice that he was the man for her. No, he had to find a way to remove Golden from Spice's life.

Easing back on his king-size bed, he turned on the television—the main event was on. He knew he needed something to take his mind off Spice. The alcohol definitely wasn't working.

"Oh, yeah," he said to himself, propping several pillows behind his back. Julio César Chávez, one of Otis's favorite boxers, was just entering the ring. His opponent, Dustin Melford, was two years younger and had a three-inch height-and-reach advantage. Melford had taken the title away from Julio eight months earlier. Scheduled for twelve rounds, the fight promised to be a great show. Otis sat back, urging Julio on to regain his crown as junior welterweight boxing champion for the WBC.

As he watched the action begin, Otis thought about Spice and Golden. At first he was angry, then he knew in order to win her back, he had to have patience.

But he needed more than patience with Golden. He needed a plan. And suddenly he had one.

On the southwest side of Detroit, all new construction plans were reviewed by the Departments of Planning, Engineering, Building, Fire, and Traffic Safety. This combined committee made recommendations to the planning commission about any proposed site. Once a site plan had been approved by the planning commission, the plan was sent to the building department.

Golden had submitted the site plans for his low-income housing development on February 9. They'd been approved by the planning commission and sent to the building department—

Otis's department—on March 28. And that was where they would remain.

Over the next few days, Otis put his plan into action. With a smile on his face and $1,000 bribes to the heads of the plumbing, electrical, mechanical, and structural departments, he doomed Golden's plan. Otis saw to it that each of the various departments would go over Golden's documents with a fine-tooth comb. Even if Golden could have the problems they cited corrected, each inspector would present yet another list of mandatory corrections. Otis figured it would take at least six months before Golden's plans would be approved.

Six months. It was all the time he needed. Otis would be able to bleed Golden dry and pull him off his holier-than-thou throne. NAABR would want nothing to do with Golden if he couldn't deliver on his promises, and Spice would certainly be showing Golden the door.

Otis's next plan of attack was to help Sterling. He knew that was one way he'd win favor with Spice. Not that he didn't have genuine concern for his troubled niece. But this way he'd get two birds with one stone.

His last visit to Sterling had been upsetting. She obviously hadn't taken in a word he'd said about looking for a job or made one step toward enrolling in architecture school.

Instead Sterling had been high. It had taken a while for her to even open the door to let Otis in. Sitting once again in his bedroom with a tumbler of Hennessy, he looked back on that visit.

"Can I fix you a drink, Uncle O?" The lids of Sterling's eyes were not fully open. Her bottom lip drooped, looking as though gravity were tugging at it.

"No thanks." He handed Sterling an envelope, then his coat, and took a seat in one of the leather side chairs. "Happy belated birthday."

"What's this?"

"Pamphlets and literature on drug abuse." His niece, he remembered, had thrown aside the envelope. "I don't know why I love you so much, Sterling. You're spoiled, you're lazy, and you're strung out on drugs. But for some reason I feel I need to help you."

"What are you talking about, Uncle O?"

"First of all, you need to get off that shit." He gave her two business cards. "Here. Call them."

Sterling read over both cards and sneered. "Why?"

"For God's sake, look at you." Otis half carried, half dragged her tiny body to the mirror and said, "Look. I remember when you were pretty. Now you're nothing but skin and bones. Your face is all puffy and splotchy, and your hair isn't even combed." He turned up his nose, sniffing. "And you haven't bathed, either."

Pulling away, she caught his wrist and glanced at the time. "Oh." She shook her head. "It's seven already." Otis was positive she didn't know if it was seven in the morning or at night.

"You're strung out. Don't try to deny it. But I've seen addicts worse off than you make a complete recovery."

Sterling struggled to make it back to the chair.

"Look, Bennie's days as a hustler are coming to an end."

Sterling looked up. "How would you—"

"I know what you're doing, Sterling. You're lucky I got you out of that situation in Texas unscathed. Haven't you learned anything?" Otis sighed, shaking his head, thinking of how he could make her understand the seriousness of this. "Running drugs is not a game, Sterling. Stay away from Bennie, and get off the heroin." He bent down beside her and placed a gentle arm on her shoulder. "If you respect yourself, if you care about . . ." Otis stopped, seeing the tense expression on her face. "Look, we both know you love your mother. Who do you think you're kidding?

"You know you can trust me. I never told your mother about what happened in Texas," Otis lied. "But your mother loves you, Sterling. She worries about you. Think about Spice, think about yourself, goddammit. We care about you. Bennie Locke doesn't care about anything but money."

Sterling, high as a kite, was still sensitized—on red alert. Otis watched her eyes blaze the moment his conversation veered toward Spice.

"I hope you find out before it's too late. You mean less to Locke than his beloved money does." Otis wanted to deliver Sterling to her mother clean. As he was leaving, he turned back and looked at her. "I'll be back, Sterling."

Otis stepped out of the city car that was part of his pay package and moved toward the Chesapeake Park building site, a new subdivision of roughly sixty manufactured homes erected on eight acres of land on the southeast side of Detroit. Dozens of backhoes were digging foundations. Several cranes were lifting mobile homes and placing them on the foundation-ready concrete slabs.

Moving toward Jonas, one of the park's supervisors, Otis raised his voice over the sound of trucks hauling away dirt and rubble. "We've discussed this before, Jonas. I can't authorize your company to cut the metal frames."

"Listen," Jonas pleaded as he watched Otis jot down notes on his inspection sheet, "can't we work something out? I've got families waiting to move in."

"That's not my problem." Otis walked over to one of the homes that had recently been completed and opened the door to look inside. He pointed to the ceiling. "See that? Some of the support beams are starting to show. The two halves of this mobile home don't seem to be married to one another."

Jonas was silent. He followed him through a few more structures, with Otis making more and more "Stop" notations on his pad. "Chesapeake Park is going to have to do better than this. No way can I let families move into this kind of situation. It's not safe," he said, pointing to the floor. There was a one-inch gap running along much of the floor in the kitchen area.

ONE BETTER

Otis heard Jonas's heavy footsteps following him as he made it back to his car.

"If we hire on another crew, it might take us maybe . . . another three weeks to fix the problems you've ticketed."

From the corner of his eye, Otis glanced at Jonas. "I can't let the violations linger that long, Jonas. We have codes to follow. I've got developers lined up for inspection. I don't have the time to reinspect properties three and four times. If these violations aren't complied with by next week, I'll have to recommend closing the park down. Meanwhile . . ." He handed the man a copy of the report.

Jonas accepted the paper from Otis. He was clearly too mad to speak.

"Aren't there going to be families with young children living in these quarters? I won't have someone's life on my conscience. No, sir," Otis insisted.

Jonas mumbled under his breath.

They both knew the deal. They'd been through this before.

"However"—Otis rubbed his fingers together—"if you can hire, say, two crews, I could be persuaded . . ."

Jonas reluctantly pulled a packet from his inside pocket and handed Otis an envelope filled with cash.

"Thanks." Otis scribbled a few notes on his inspection sheet and said, "Even though you've got an early okay, I still want these violations fixed."

Jonas rolled his eyes at Otis as he drove away.

Once inside his car, Otis checked his route sheet for his next inspection. By bypassing the next stop, which he didn't need to inspect, he could save two hours. Chuckling to himself, he signed his name on the back of the next inspection sheet, then drove in the opposite direction toward Southern Spice. He wanted to give Spice an update on his "progress" with Sterling.

STERLING

God sends children for another purpose than merely to keep up the race—to enlarge our hearts; and to make us unselfish and full of kindly sympathies and affections; to give our souls higher aims; to call out all our faculties to extended enterprise and exertion; and to bring round our firesides bright faces, happy smiles, and loving, tender hearts. . . . My soul blesses the great Father, every day, that he has gladdened the earth with little children.
                                                                    —MARY HOWITT

If anyone asked, Sterling would say that she was better at describing unhappiness than happiness. She searched for the sublime in sorrow. Sometimes she found it. But one thing was sure, everything that she'd learned in life, and learned well, she had learned from pain.

Sterling was giving some serious thought to what Otis had said. She even called the rehab facility listed on one of the cards.

Refusing to admit where she'd gotten the name of the clinic, and not agreeing to come in, she hung up after the woman kept insisting that Sterling give her name and number.

With the blinds closed morning and night, Sterling hadn't left her home since returning from Texas. Had it been a month? Now it was April, and she was ready for a fresh start. Since the Texas run, she'd hoarded her money. Fuck Spice, fuck her money. Sterling would take care of herself.

Her basic needs were met with weekly groceries, highlighted by weekly sex and heroin delivered by Bennie. Until now, there had been no need to go out.

But over the past four days, Sterling had been unable to keep anything in her stomach. She felt as if dozens of acidic bubbles were surfacing and busting inside her belly, relentlessly and slowly, one by one. Bennie wanted her to do a run to Arizona, but there was no way. She had to start taking care of herself. She knew she had no choice: it was give up drugs or be sick, then die. She worked up her nerve to tell Bennie.

"Okay, babe. I'll get Jamie to make the run to Phoenix."

"Are you coming by tonight?" she asked.

"I'm leaving right now. I got some good shit, too."

"I'll pass," Sterling said, suddenly feeling stronger than she had in months. It had been almost a week since she'd touched heroin or alcohol.

But no one knew Sterling's addiction better than Bennie. She was his hostage; he was her addiction. In lucid moments, like now, Sterling could see clearly that each time she'd try to get clear of Bennie, he'd propose. She'd feel blindsided, unable to say anything but yes.

That's the way it happened before Christmas, Sterling remembered. Sterling had told him she was through. Then Bennie had arrived, his arms filled with flowers, champagne, and, of course drugs. They'd made mad love for a solid week, and on the final day, Bennie had proposed. He'd suggested they get the marriage license by Friday. And with barely six full days to prepare, Sterling had made arrangements for a small ceremony at the Little Wedding Chapel in Taylor, Michigan.

All that Friday, Sterling had sat without watching television or radio, waiting for a phone call, the doorbell, any sound saying that Bennie had come for her. Sterling hadn't realized how compliant she had become. She hadn't realized how much she depended on Bennie.

She'd rechecked the contents of her suitcase and taken one more look at the wedding dress that it had taken her eighty hours of shopping to finally settle on. At eleven P.M. Sterling had turned out the lights and, without shedding a tear, unpacked her suitcase and gone to bed.

True to form, Bennie had stood her up again.

But now she lay in bed, queasy.

There, she felt it again. The stale bile percolated in her stomach and rose, rose and rose still, until she was forced to run to the bathroom.

Her hair stuck to her face as she vomited again and again into the toilet. She lifted a weak hand to flush, then tried to lift herself. In a half stance, she felt her body convulse and she heaved in the porcelain basin once again. After wiping her face and mouth with a cold towel, she forced herself to shower and change into clean pajamas. She brushed her damp hair, twisted it, then pinned it on top of her head.

Feeling a little better, she knew she had to eat. When she opened the refrigerator door, the strong aroma of garlic from yesterday's half-eaten spaghetti made her stomach lurch. She slammed the door and held her breath for a moment before barely making it to the bathroom.

As she staggered out after vomiting again, the phone startled her. "Hello?" she asked.

"Hi, Sterling."

"Spice?" Her heart fluttered like a fan. Spice had left many messages on her machine, which Sterling had ignored, but they hadn't spoken since their fight all those weeks ago.

"I miss you, baby. Can we meet and talk?"

Sterling was overwhelmed with emotion. Having been psychologically dependent on heroin for so long, she hadn't realized the pain of being estranged from her mother. It seemed to overpower even the pain of withdrawal from the drug. "Name a place and time. I'd love to see you, too."

Mother and daughter scheduled their momentous reunion for four P.M. the next day at the Golden Mushroom restaurant.

Sterling arrived a few minutes late. She saw Spice getting out of her seat, coming toward her, an eager look on her face.

"Hi." Spice greeted her daughter with a quick hug.

Sterling felt herself stiffen.

"Hello." She followed Spice to the booth and sat across from her. "It's nice to see you, Spice. You look . . . good." Sterling was shocked by how youthful her mother's complexion looked. Her soft brown eyes, lined with a navy kohl pencil, positively sparkled. Most little girls thought their mothers were pretty. Sterling could honestly say that about her mother today. She was beautiful.

"Let me buy you lunch?" Spice offered.

"It's nearly dinnertime."

"Dinner, then."

Sterling smiled nervously.

Both chose to ignore their last meeting, which had ended in screams and accusations. Instead they asked each other safe questions until they placed their orders. After ignoring several pages from her beeper, Spice finally excused herself for a moment to make a phone call.

When she returned, Sterling was sipping on a diet Coke and flicking the leaves of a chicken salad.

Spice sat down to her tuna salad and said, "You're not eating, Sterling."

Sterling shook her head and turned away from the food.

"I haven't seen you in a while, but you look like you've lost some weight," Spice continued.

"No," Sterling lied. "I'm still a perfect size four."

Sterling hadn't touched a forkfull of her food, and when she looked at the beautifully served entrée, she felt repulsed.

Spice looked worried. Finally breaking the silence, she asked, "Sterling, are you sick?"

"Of course not."

"Are you pregnant?"

Sterling took longer than she should have to answer. "No."

"Are you sure?"

Sterling fought back tears and fixed a steel gaze out the window. Was that why she was sick? How fitting that Spice would know even before Sterling knew herself.

There was a long period of silence between them.

"Is it Bennie's?" Spice asked.

"Why would you care?"

"I've always cared. And I hate to see a man like Bennie taking advantage of you."

"I love him. Can't you understand that?"

"Does he love you? Does he know about the baby?"

"There is no baby, Spice." Sterling pressed her fist to her mouth, suppressing a cry. She felt hot. And she was positive that her face revealed what a mess things were. She hated to hear Spice bad-mouth Bennie. He was like black charcoal, burning deeper and deeper into her heart—and even though she tried to extinguish the flame, it still burned, smoldering the embers of her soul.

"I don't want to argue, Sterling. We've been through too much already. Listen, if Bennie is the man for you . . ."

"We're going to be fine. I know it."

Spice reached out and took Sterling's hand. "I'm dating someone now, too. His name is Golden Westbrook. I've grown to care about him. Deeply."

"Isn't he a preacher?" Secretly she hoped that the preacher would break it off just as Bennie had with her over and over again. She knew she should be ashamed for thinking this way, but she wasn't.

"Yes. How did you know?"

Sterling laughed. It was a nasty laugh. "Travis told me. I heard he left Southern Spice to open his own business. Is that why? Jealousy?"

"How would Travis know? Anyway, I can get along fine without him."

"Even without fucking him?" Sterling didn't know where that had come from. Certainly Travis was ancient history to both of them.

"I shouldn't have mentioned men. I asked you to meet me so that I could say I'm sorry. I miss you. I want to be your mother again. I'm sorry about cutting off the money, Sterling, and the credit cards."

"I don't need your money."

"We both know you need the help. And now with a baby . . ."

"Stop talking about this phantom baby! All you can think about is money! The day is long gone when I would kiss your ass for some money."

Spice looked shocked.

But Sterling continued, "All that money has made you cold. Money doesn't give you pleasure, it doesn't comfort you at night." She turned away from Spice. "Neither does a scripture. A man does. I'm sure you get my meaning. Let's face it, Spice, you've never been a mother to me." Her steel gray eyes challenged Spice's.

"You should take a good look at yourself. All you've ever given me is money." Tears filled Sterling's eyes, and she felt the heat rising between her breasts. "I'd rather be broke but be able to feel something for another human being every now and then. Maybe Golden needs to work a little harder to make you more human like the rest of us. Even if I have to suffer pain from Bennie, at least he makes me feel something." She stood up to leave. "You don't know what love means."

"Sterling, you're my baby. I love you."

"No, you don't." She picked up her purse to leave. "You love success."

"These ill feelings have gone on too long between us."

"You're right. Keep your money, Spice. I wouldn't take another dime from you if you begged me to." Sterling pressed her purse securely beneath her bosom, then walked away.

Wiping the tears from her face, Sterling unlocked her car door and slid inside.

Spice still didn't understand how simple it was to offer love. Love was free, it wasn't bought. She tried so many times to define it, evaluate her and Spice's ongoing problems. She knew without anyone telling her that she was at a disadvantage trying to cope with the pain alone. Pain and pleasure, like light and darkness, succeeded each other. She needed someone to take her out of the darkness and into the light, where nothing shone but love.

She let the tears fall.

The next day she went to the doctor. She was pregnant all right. Noticing the needle marks on her arms and her ill health, the doctor talked to her about an abortion. Then he asked if she was married. Sterling resented his intrusion into her privacy and stormed off in a fury.

Did the doctor think she was heartless? This child was her miracle, her one chance at making something good come from her life. She would make certain her child would be safe. That meant more to her than her own safety. No way would she use drugs again.

What she hadn't told Spice, and what she did not want to admit to herself, was that Bennie had promised to move in with her last week, in preparation for their getting married. It was a trial run, Sterling had insisted to him. And he'd agreed. But she hadn't heard from him since that conversation. She knew that her trump card was the baby.

She wasn't ready to tell Bennie. She wanted him to love her for herself, not for carrying his child. But how else would she get him to commit to her?

CARMEN

If you don't have children the longing for them will kill you, and if you do, the worrying over them will kill you.

—BUCHI EMECHETA

_____

*C*armen had now been at Temple Gardens for almost ten weeks. And as much as she attended the daily AA meetings and talked to Connie, her craving for alcohol never vanished. Some days, like today, the craving was so keen that she thought she would die unless she had a sip, just one sweet sip.

Carmen could get no peace. She couldn't quell the need filling her, coursing through her veins. Her arms itched so badly, they burned. She quaked inside while her outer shell remained still. With each breath, she felt as though her chest were being squeezed tighter and tighter and she was suffocating little by little. Her body was crying out for alcohol.

Today Spice was scheduled for one of her visits, but as Carmen looked down at the fresh scratches on her arms, she knew she couldn't face her friend. She was afraid that Spice would know what was really happening—that yet again Carmen would fail. Or was it something more? After her session, when she broke down and told Connie more about the fire that killed Adarius, Carmen had a dream. She was a little girl, tiny for her age, malnourished. She was standing at the edge of a stream. Her dress was in tatters. She was watching her doll float down the stream, and not knowing how to swim, she couldn't jump into the water to save it. She stood there on the muddy bank, crying out, and then the dream shifted and it was she who was floating down the stream. And on the banks she saw Spice, who was reaching out to her, yelling, "Carmen, Carmen, let me save you, please let me save you!"

Even to this day, the fearful dread of the dream stayed with Carmen. Finally, unable to bear the pain, Carmen casually dropped a hundred-dollar bill on the floor as she walked past one of the male nurses. She continued to walk ahead, stopping only when she heard him say, "Carmen, you dropped something."

"No, it's for you."

"I can't accept this."

"Please, I need a drink. Anything. Just bring a bottle to my room."

The guard looked at her and shook his head.

Her therapist brought it up in their next session. Carmen couldn't speak, she was so humiliated.

Now, from the solarium, where visitors came, Carmen saw Spice park her company truck in the visitors' section. Then Azure jumped down from the cab. Carmen felt a moment of elation as she rose to greet them at the solarium door.

"Hi, Azure. I'm so glad your grandmother brought you." Carmen hugged Spice, then took each by the hand and led them to one of the sofas near the coffeemaker. "Let me fix you a cup of coffee."

ONE BETTER

"Can I look at the magazines, Aunt Carmen?"

"Sure, baby."

As soon as the girl walked away, Spice took Carmen's hand. Carmen knew she hadn't been successful in hiding her tension from her friend.

"You look so afraid, Carmen. What is it, what's happened?" Spice asked, her voice gentle.

"I don't know. Just people, I guess."

"You were doing so well. But you don't look well now. Tell me what's wrong."

Turning her head to the side, Carmen looked directly into her friend's soulful eyes.

"Can't you talk to me about it?"

"I'm sorry. I'm sorry," Carmen said.

"I hadn't realized that you were in this much pain."

Suddenly Azure appeared. "Can you read this book to me, Aunt Carmen?"

Carmen took a deep breath and began to read. Azure stopped her by the third paragraph. "Stop. I don't like this story."

Thinking for a moment, Carmen said, "Wait, I know a story that you might like to hear." She walked to the shelf and picked up a worn copy of the children's Bible. She flipped the pages to the story of Solomon and the Queen of Sheba.

"The Queen of Sheba was a beautiful black woman like your mother and your grandmother."

"For real?" Azure asked.

"Um-hm. When the Queen of Sheba heard of the fame of Solomon, she came to see him—"

Before she read much further, Azure had fallen asleep. Visiting time was over. Carmen handed the sweet bundle to her grandmother. All the while she tried to think of a way to explain to her friend that she really suffered from two diseases—alcoholism and depression. The two diseases fed off each other, in a downward spiral. The depression caused her to drink. The drinking depressed her.

Carmen blinked away tears, turned to Spice, and said morosely, "I've been studying butterflies. Did you know butterflies have no ears?"

"No. But I do, and I think you're trying to tell me something. I don't know what to say to you anymore, Carmen," Spice said. "I don't have the words. I don't have the power. I don't know *how* to help you."

"You can't. And you can't understand how I feel because in order for you to understand, you would have to experience the pain of causing your child's death." Even though Carmen loved her friend, there were lines between them.

"I want to help you. Tell me what I can do."

"I'm hoping that as my best friend, you'll honor my request."

"Anything. Just ask."

"I think it would be best if we didn't see each other for a while."

"Carmen?" Spice asked, shocked. "I'm not hearing you correctly." She pressed her fingers to her forehead. "Are you saying you don't want me to visit you here again?"

"I'm getting better. The doctor said that detoxification is not a cure. I need to do more work, Spice, and I need to do it on my own. Dr. Wright has told me that I'd be out soon." Refusing to give in to defeat, Carmen knew she was out of options. She was facing an ultimatum: Stay sober or die. If her son's life meant anything to her, sobriety was her only choice.

Spice breathed, speaking fast. "Of course you need a few days to sort out—"

"No. I need more."

Spice didn't speak.

"I hurt. You hurt. Who's to say which of us hurts more—does it really matter? I love you, Spice, but I can't survive with your love. It's smothering me. If I don't make it, I'll die of guilt, not alcohol. I wish I didn't love you, so that I could say 'Kiss my ass, Spice.' But no matter how much I love you, I have to get sober for me. I have to shed the tight strings holding us together. That's what friendship is about, Spice. It's about loving someone without thinking, without questioning. You give it freely without a second thought, like your next breath. It's that easy. To give this to you, Spice, I feel I have to ask you to let me find my strength without borrowing it from you. You've been my rock for so long, I feel I have to break free."

Lifting Azure, Spice transferred her dozing granddaughter from Carmen's lap to her shoulder. She collected her purse and moved to the door. Cupping Carmen's arm, she gave her friend one last sorrowful look before turning away. "I love you, Carmen," she said over her shoulder.

The echo of Spice's words reached Carmen's heart, and then the glass doors closed between them.

When Carmen was released from Temple Gardens, she asked her new AA sponsor not to call Ms. Witherspoon. Then she took a taxi to her bank and withdrew $10,000 from her savings account, money that she'd saved all the years she'd worked for Spice.

She walked to a nearby diner and purchased a newspaper and, after ordering a cup of coffee and a slice of pie, checked the Want Ads for a job. Her hopes fizzled when she saw that there were no listings for a chef—not even a cook. Before she tossed the paper in the trash, she noticed the real estate section. A full-page ad of new homes and businesses in the town of Novi piqued her interest. It was just far enough away, and close enough to come back home if she chose to.

She got another taxi. "How much to drive me to Novi?" she asked the driver.

"That's quite a ways, miss."

"I know. How much?"

"Probably forty to fifty bucks."

"Let's go."

As soon as they left I-96 on the Novi exit, Carmen was overwhelmed by signs and shops on both sides of the highway. Twelve Oaks Mall was surrounded by several places to dine. Furniture stores, linen shops, bookstores, and craft stores were just a few blocks away from a Red Roof Inn. Carmen asked the driver to stop there. She had found her home.

During the next week, she temporarily put aside her search for a job and shopped for clothes and crafts. She felt lighter, free, and was enjoying the hell out of her freedom.

The small town of Novi was booming. Newly constructed shopping centers and businesses were being developed all over the affluent community. Carmen placed fifteen applications at different establishments. Within three days she had secured a decent job working the late shift at Cicero's Truck Stop Restaurant, which was open twenty-four hours a day.

At Cicero's there was room for three hundred trucks at night. Sometimes they had to turn some away. There was a twenty-room motel adjoining the stop that was usually full. Inside Cicero's there was a minitheater that could seat sixty truckers and showed the current video releases. The truck stop also contained an ATM machine, Laundromat, party store, and drivers' lounge. Lot lizards, prostitutes by trade, bargained their bodies outside while truckers conducted their business in an eighteen-unit phone room. In the rear of the building was a bank of twenty-five showers; it cost five dollars to use them, although they were free with a fill-up. On the second floor was a ladies' lounge and shower room, barbershop, a certified psychotherapist—and even a masseuse by appointment.

Throughout the evening, truckers of all shapes and sizes came in to eat. Carmen watched the flow of men and women dressed in plaid flannel shirts and jeans stream in and out. They looked as though they'd come off the *Roseanne* show. When Carmen's shift was over, she scouted out the apartments in the area. Already she knew she was going to like her job. It was the middle of May, and the apartment complex that she'd decided upon wouldn't have another two-bedroom apartment available until the first of June. Carmen was disappointed that she would have to stay in a motel for two more weeks, but she wasn't willing to settle for a one-bedroom apartment. As soon as she got her new place, she planned on packing up her things at her old apartment and resuming making the porcelain dolls that were part of her plan for her future.

After a week of working, she scouted the area for a cheap car and settled on a Honda Civic hatchback. Now she could get away during the day, and soon she'd be able to see Spice; she would be living on her own, alcohol free. She had been sober for almost three months, and her life was falling into place. Could it be?

Right off, she contacted the welcoming committee in the small town and received all kinds of information about the area. She checked for information on local AA meetings close to her home. But Carmen felt uncomfortable when she attended the small meeting. She was the only Hispanic female in the group. Actually she was the only minority, period. She felt alienated, with no commonality with the other members.

The day she finally moved into her two-bedroom apartment, she overslept after the exhausting work of getting settled. Late for work. It was 1:15 A.M. when she punched in. Cicero's was nearly packed.

Carmen worked nonstop until her break at four. The weather was warm. She sat outside, watching the large rigs going in and out while she ate a bagel and drank orange juice. It amazed her how the truckers maneuvered the large rigs so effortlessly. She thought the trucks looked like pretty, dressed-up women with all their red glittering lights. Some of the trucks were painted with naked women on the side, their chrome wheels shining like new money even in the darkness of the night.

Carmen noticed a shiny, purplish opal truck filling up at the truck station. She was fascinated as she watched the huge machine with its silver pinstripes, four antennas, and blinding chrome wheels. It was beautiful.

Then she saw him.

He parked the truck and headed toward the restaurant. Carmen felt the goose bumps start to rise on her arms. But she had to stop herself dead in her tracks. AA members were encouraged to wait at least a year before dating or getting involved in anything romantic. Getting sober and staying sober were supposed to be your priority.

The tall man with muscular biceps and soft brown eyes was walking toward her. He looked up at Carmen, and their eyes met. A flood of feeling washed through her body. He said, "Hi," and, trying to sound casual, Carmen responded in kind. He took a seat inside at a counter as Carmen sat still, finishing her cigarette before resuming her shift. This feeling reminded her of what she had imagined David and Spice had shared at the beginning.

Suddenly she missed Spice terribly. She'd picked up the telephone several times to call her, but she was determined to contact Spice only when she felt really secure in her newly won sobriety. Somehow Carmen knew that she couldn't rush seeing Spice. But that realization didn't stop her from fearing that she'd lose the friend she loved so much, lose Spice as she had lost so much else in her life.

Later that morning, as she lay in bed waiting for sleep to come, Carmen couldn't erase the calm face of the man at the truck stop. She knew she wasn't ready for a romance yet. But just the fact that she'd felt an attraction for a man, that she'd been sober long enough to allow an emotion like that to come through, reassured her that she was on her way to getting better.

Mink

Be ever gentle with the children God has given you. . . . Watch over them constantly; reprove them earnestly, but not in anger. . . . In the forcible language of Scripture, "Be not bitter against them."

—ELIHU BURRITT

*M*ay is for remembering. The month in which we remember our heroic men who died for their convictions. It is a time for the recalling of suffering and defeat as well as victory. Some say we should forget our personal errors, erase our mistakes, expunge the past, and go forward. But Mink did not feel that all errors, sins, or the wrong turn in your path should be entirely erased. She felt that all these troubles and griefs should be remembered.

What had she done about it? How deeply had she repented? How much had she learned from her mistakes? Her sorrows?

The reality of what might have happened six, seven, or eight years earlier with Dwight stung deep in her heart. No matter how hard she tried, she couldn't stop remembering.

Like tiny triumphs of spring, wildflowers had sprung up along the freeway and in vacant fields near her home. But what she really loved, what made her feel especially lonely for love, were the wild lilac bushes that grew near her home. As she drove by, she inhaled their sweet perfume.

She had four days until she had to return to work. She was never good with idle time, but she tried to focus on being with Azure and redecorating her house. She was trying her best to keep her thoughts away from Dwight.

To her surprise, Harrison called. He was free, he said; his wife was visiting her mother for the weekend. And when Mink suggested they take a ride in her plane the following morning, he agreed.

Made of luscious peach tones, the sweatsuit she wore fit snugly around her sultry hips. Harrison wore navy twill Dockers, a white cotton pullover, and blindingly white K-Swiss gym shoes. Mink had to tear her eyes away from him. She loved the way his white pullover highlighted his immaculate gray sideburns and his smooth, golden brown skin.

She pulled her Cessna out of the private hangar at Metro Airport at two o'clock in the afternoon. As they taxied onto the runway, both knew where the excursion was headed.

Their seat belts secured, Mink waited for the clearance from the small airport tower before taking off.

"I've got to be back before nightfall, Mink." They had an unspoken agreement never to discuss their families.

"You seemed a little tense earlier. Is something wrong?"

"Nothing that you should concern yourself with."

"I've got a bottle of Harvey's Bristol Cream in the back." Her take-off into the broad blue sky was smooth as a lake.

"Thanks, I'd forgotten to bring anything." Harrison criss-

234

crossed his arms behind his neck and closed his eyes. She could tell that, like her, he loved to feel the plane rising and rising until they reached thirteen thousand feet. They both seemed to love the solitude of being beyond the reach of others.

"I thought we could find a nice open field to land and sit and talk awhile."

"Sure."

They fell into a companionable silence.

"Harrison! Harrison!" Mink called as she shook his sleeping form. "We're almost there."

Harrison shook the sleep from his eyes and focused. "We're landing?"

"Just a few miles up ahead in Lexington, Kentucky. There's a private airstrip."

"Kentucky?"

"The bluish green hills and open meadows in Lexington are breathtaking this time of year. I rarely get to see this when I'm not working."

"Have I been asleep long?" He reached inside his pockets and popped a mint in his mouth.

Mink didn't bother to answer. They had left Detroit at nine-thirty A.M. and headed southwest, flying over Ohio and Indiana and then into Kentucky.

Bathed in the pale afternoon light, they landed in Kentucky around one P.M., had lunch at the city airport, and purchased snacks, drinks, and sandwiches for a picnic later.

"Have you spoken to Julie lately?" Harrison asked.

"For some reason, she seems to be avoiding me. I've suggested that we meet and talk, but she doesn't appear to be interested in my company." Mink knew that Julie was uncomfortable with her affair with Harrison, that she didn't want to be privy to Mink's dubious choices.

Back in the plane, Mink showed Harrison the spot on the

map where one of the pilots she'd talked to had suggested they land. The secluded area was just ten minutes away by air.

Mink found the spot more by instinct than by navigation. Spring was forcing tender green shoots to perk their heads up, and the meadow was plush with Kentucky's famous bluegrass. It was in just this color that Mink planned to make love with Harrison.

Mink taxied the airplane to the end of the landing strip and stopped. She slipped her lips over Harrison's mouth to remind him of the pleasures to come. They had just a few hours, and she wanted to savor every moment.

They deplaned and set up their picnic. In an instant, they were naked and in each other's arms. Butterflies floated above, moving with the wind as puffy cloud shadows raced up and down the hill, enveloping the two naked forms pressed against the tall grass bed.

They sipped Harveys out of paper cups and listened to crickets singing a melody. Talking wasn't necessary. Right now both wanted only to imprint their sexual signature on the other.

Mink lay on her back, with her arms spread wide, her lips moist, eagerly awaiting a kiss. With a smile on her lips, she drew his head against her breasts and felt his cool maroon lips encircle her nipple. Pushing her deeper into the grass, he kissed her stomach, sliding his tongue in and out of her navel. A low moan emanated from the back of her throat, and she arched her body beneath him. Harrison ran his tongue over his lips, then her small breasts, enveloping himself in the softness of her young flesh, kneading and sucking each one. A pleased sigh escaped her lips. Then, cupping her head with one hand and kissing the soft flesh beneath her chin, he teased the tight curls of her womanhood, still not giving her what she wanted. Something didn't feel quite right.

Dwight knew when to stroke her, when to tease her, when to enter her. When they made love it was charged with the urgency of animalistic lust. What she shared with Harrison was more earthly, like an expedition of unadulterated vanity.

Finally Harrison touched her—there. She trembled as he slipped his fingers inside. He manipulated the inner and outer layers of her vulva.

Mink felt her clitoris swelling, expanding as his fingers moved quicker, in and out, out and in, until she felt her muscles grabbing, tugging him back inside. She gasped when he suddenly withdrew.

"Mmm. I love it when it's wet like this," Harrison said, looking into her eyes. He coated her breasts with her wetness, then took his time licking it all off while his hands returned to her vagina. She was close to an orgasm.

Harrison lifted one of her long, lovely limbs over his shoulder, then the other. Sliding both hands beneath the sides of her hips, he pulled her closer to his head resting on the grass. His tongue outlined the fluffy triangle, making lazy circles, tickling the tiny gem; then, upon hearing her breathing quicken, he plunged his tongue inside the moist center.

Mink licked her tongue over the top of her lips as she reached out to clutch the back of his head and felt the tingling warmth travel from her abdomen to her inner thighs. Moaning with pleasure, she rolled her hips rhythmically toward the sweet satisfaction of his probing tongue. Hot as hellfire, she felt the flames of passion shoot through her body. Her small jewel began to tingle, tighten, and then she felt a deliciousness take her over. She shivered, felt her body levitate and ride the carnal waves of passion, then floated downward, slowly, and slower still. Her body felt weightless.

As she guided his head back to her breasts, like hot, buttered love, she slipped into his arms and pressed her dampened hand against his hardness. Her legs flung open. On his knees, he entered her slowly. Mink uttered a sigh and, lifting slightly, reached out her arms for him.

He cupped, then stroked her breasts, all the while pushing her back against the soft bed beneath them and moving deeper and deeper inside of her. Mink stroked her heel against the back of his thigh, biting her lower lip with each stroke of his calculated, accelerated thrusts. And a voice inside her cried: *He hasn't kissed me.*

His balls slapped sporadically against the roundness of her buttocks as he moved in and out, in and out. It was a long and delicious plunge, as she gripped him, pulling him deeper toward her womb, until both succumbed to their sexual gratification.

For a long time afterward, they were speechless. Exhausted, Harrison fell forward and placed his head between her breasts, panting.

"Oh, my God, Harrison," said Mink, stroking the back of his head. "That was intense."

"Yeah." He could manage only to grunt that single word.

Was he thinking of his wife? All that he had back home? Could he make love to her like this and still prefer his wife?

They dressed as they'd begun, in silence.

She held him.

And still he hadn't kissed her.

Their bodies swayed with the grass. The sea of green waved good-bye to the parting lovers.

Mink felt disquieted. Their lovemaking seemed pale. She knew well that beauty inspired love, because it was nature's gift and had God's handwriting all over it. But there was no beauty here.

The following weekend, Mink was on tour again. But instead of mingling with the others, she kept to herself. She ignored everyone, and when they checked into the hotel, she went straight to her room. Once inside she double locked the door and closed the curtains. Turning away, she glanced at the telephone.

Maybe I should call Dwight? No. It's better if I speak with him in person.

Mink worked on her flight manual, something required by Pyramid Airlines and the FAA, neglected lately because of Harrison. Periodically, the routing from different airports changed, and the pilots and flight attendants were required to change it in their manuals and update them constantly. If the FAA asked to see the manual and it wasn't in order, a pilot could be fined up to ten thousand dollars. Pilots and co-pilots were required to keep the manuals on them at all times.

Usually there were about thirty to forty pages in the manual to change every month. Employees had to document in the front of the manual what changes they'd made and highlight the changes. Some captains paid a service to update their manuals, but the dedicated pilots made the corrections themselves.

Mink had considered using the service but in the end had decided she shouldn't take such an important part of her job for granted. Midway through her manual, she couldn't concentrate and put it down.

Once in a while Mink came down to earth and stopped lying to herself about Harrison. He never called her at home just to talk, even though he knew that she was separated. He avoided her when they flew together, which was just about always. It dawned on her slowly that she was being used.

She decided to go down to the hotel bar and have a drink. Harrison had left a message that he might drop by the lounge. Now it was ten o'clock and she was on her fourth Manhattan. Most of the crowd were middle-class and upper-middle-class businessmen and -women who spoke softly and directly into the eyes of their companions. A mixture of black and white clientele, the quaint establishment was three-quarters full and there were no loud noises, no arguing, no raps whining on the radio.

Mink felt alienated from the crowd and ached inside. She'd waited three hours for Harrison to show up. She checked the desk for messages, but he hadn't even had the decency to call and cancel.

"Bartender. Bartender," a man called out, then slid next to Mink on a barstool. "Can I get you another one of those, young lady?" he asked Mink.

"No, thank you," she said, trying to stand up. "I've had enough." Her words were slurred, and her body swayed into his a little.

The bartender's eyes told her he knew that she had been waiting on someone for hours. "Good night, ma'am," he said as he polished the already sparkling countertop.

Ignoring the gentleman who still tried to engage her, she smiled at the bartender and left. The faces turning this way and that seemed to float before her as she walked toward the door. Her body felt detached from her head as she tried desperately to balance the two.

Amid stares, she persevered and was thankful when she spotted Julie walking in her direction.

"Girl, I've been calling your room—" her friend began.

"Help me, Julie," Mink said, grabbing hold of her arm. "I think I'm going to be sick."

"Hold on." Julie put her arm over Mink's shoulder and placed Mink's arm around her waist, holding it in place with her own.

Mink held out until they reached her room on the forty-eighth floor. Once inside, Julie lifted the toilet seat. Mink fell to her knees and released an explosion of vomit. Julie bent to her knees and patted Mink's back until the attack subsided.

Julie rinsed out a cold towel and handed it to Mink. "You okay now?"

"Sure, I'll be fine." Mink flushed the commode, pulled herself up, and plopped down on the hard plastic. She placed the cold towel over her forehead, cupped her hands over her eyes, and shook her head. "I'm sorry, Julie. Thanks for helping me."

"Girl," said Julie, sitting on the side of the bathtub, "you're gonna have a humongous headache in the morning."

Then Mink was crying.

"You want to talk about it?"

Julie immediately called room service and ordered a tray of cheese and crackers for herself, a cup of vegetable soup for Mink, and a couple of ginger ales for each of them. By the time their late night snack arrived, Mink was well into her story.

"It was so exciting. I thought I was living out a fantasy."

"There's a reason why they call it fantasy," said Julie, easing back in the armchair. "Now it's time to wake up."

"But Harrison is—"

"Married. And anyway, so are you! Face it, Mink, he isn't going to divorce his wife anytime soon."

"But I thought—"

"You thought the same as all the women he had before you. Don't kid yourself. Harrison knows what he's doing. He's been doing it for years. I've got to admit something to you, Mink. Something that I'm ashamed of. I knew that you'd fall for him. And at first I hoped that he'd break your heart, just as he does to everyone."

"What? Why?"

"I thought you deserved it. At first I didn't like you. I was jealous of your being a captain and all, but I've gotten over it. Hell, you know that most of the flight attendants can't stand the pilots. But I've grown to respect you. I can honestly say I like you."

"Why are you telling me this now?"

"Because I see you destroying your marriage over a man who isn't worth it. Harrison, like a lot of the male pilots, is a whore."

"But Harrison cares for me, Julie. He really does."

"Listen to me, Mink. When it comes to women, men like

Harrison are like customers in a Baskin-Robbins shop, trying out each selection, black cherry tonight, tutti-frutti tomorrow night. You got married young, so maybe you don't know—men get bored."

Men get bored. Mink remembered hearing Spice telling her those same words before she married Dwight.

"They don't know and they really don't care. The woman is *supposed* to understand that it's time for him to change flavors, without questions, without interference. Not necessarily their wives—probably not their wives—just the women who dress up good enough, put enough cherries, whipped cream, and toppings on. So they're just enjoying the flow for however long the dessert lasts."

"Me," Mink stated.

"Exactly. Harrison hasn't done anything new to you that my man hasn't done to me. Love is constant, passion is up and down."

Julie piled cheese on top of a cracker and said, "You should be making a lifelong commitment with the man you're married to, honey. Not a dog like Harrison."

"You don't know the entire story about my faithful husband." Mink turned away, embarrassed. "Anyway, I did try."

"Yeah?"

She would miss Dwight, then catch herself, remembering. "As you said, I married too young, Julie."

"You never marry too young if you've got the right man. Anyway, I can't help you in the marriage department. I've married and divorced twice; made two wrong choices, but I knew that going in. What's meant to be will be. If you and Dwight are meant to be together, no matter what happens between you two now, you'll work it out."

Julie paused, then continued, "Seems like young women use their bodies to get a man; older women use their heads to keep him." She swallowed the last of her ginger ale and placed the empty bottle on the table. "I don't believe you really want to leave Dwight. I think you know he'll always be there. Love, family, and friends are healing to people. Divorce is lethal, and I don't believe you've considered the domino effect it'll have on your daughter. There are prices to pay when you play."

Mink sat still, stunned by the truth of her friend's words.

Infidelity cures nothing that is bad. It only ridicules and denounces all that is good. It tears down but never builds up; destroys but never imparts life; attacks religion but offers no adequate substitute. Mink knew her affair with Harrison was wrong. But as of yet, she'd found no substitute for the thrill.

After Julie left her room, Mink fought the urge to call Dwight. She knew she had to completely give up Harrison. Her next step was to beg Dwight's forgiveness, because Julie had spoken what Mink knew all along. She was wrong, and she was going to ruin her life if she didn't straighten it out now. But how was she going to do it all? It seemed so clear in her head, but she felt anxiety creep up her neck as the image of herself alone reared its ugly head. She was scared. She couldn't imagine being alone.

When she got home, May blossoms filled the air with their sweetness and covered the ground with pastel petals. Love was in bloom. Mink called upon all her courage and picked up the phone and called Dwight. Under the guise of celebrating Memorial Day together for Azure, Mink invited Dwight and his parents for a barbecue at the house. She'd finished all of the last touches of the redecorating and was eager to show her in-laws and Dwight.

Even though they were still separated and close to a divorce, neither had spoken again about his son or the paternity suit. Mink had no idea how he settled it, if he saw the child—nothing. She couldn't face it. Sometimes she wondered why, if she had feelings for Harrison, Dwight's other life mattered so much.

Now, with the holiday upon them, they pretended to be a family—sort of. Dwight volunteered to help Mink cook the ribs and shish kebabs, while his mother and father sat and enjoyed the blessings of their only grandchild.

The few hours the husband and wife spent together through revolving doors from the patio to the kitchen passed with minimal dissension. It was almost like old times in the Majors household. Dwight apprised Mink of the latest problems at the fire station, and Mink filled him in on Pyramid business.

Since the temperature hadn't reached sixty degrees, cool for May, they elected to have dinner inside. At dinner Slim Majors complimented Mink on how well the house looked since it had been remodeled, and everyone raved about the exquisite dinner. Mink was delighted.

Dwight's mother, Justine, was not so kind. She complained that she had not found a single item that she'd picked out for her granddaughter in Azure's room. In truth, Mink had donated all the furnishings and bedding Justine had given them to the Salvation Army. But she kept silent. Justine had never liked Mink.

While the in-laws enjoyed drinks in the library, Mink put Azure to bed, then joined Dwight, who was busy cleaning the kitchen. The tension had started to build over dinner, and Mink knew that Dwight was waiting for the right moment to drop a bomb.

"I heard about your friend," he finally said.

"Who?"

"You know, the other man."

"I don't know what you're talking about, Dwight."

"No?"

"No. And I don't think my friendships are any of your business."

"We are still married."

"We're legally separated."

"And that gives you the right to fuck around?"

"Okay. If this is how you want it. You had an affair; now I am. And I'm woman enough to tell you face-to-face who I'm fucking. His name is Harrison Fielding. We take the Cessna out and get some foreplay in while we fly. Remember, whatever you can do, I can do better."

"How dare—"

"I've got more balls than you've got. 'Cause if you think you're going to fuck around and I can't, you're wrong. I like a little strange, too. That first time, it's thrilling."

"You bitch."

"Glory hallelujah, I think you've got it, buddy. But when *I* go out fucking, I bring a pack of rubbers with me so I don't have any bastard babies. I'm just like a man. I want my pleasures just like you do. I can come home and take a bath and come out 'Ivory Snow' clean, *just like you*!"

Even as she spat out the words, even though they were true, Mink immediately regretted saying them, and she ran out of the kitchen and up to her room. She decided she'd just stay there until all her guests were gone—she wasn't going to wait politely downstairs. She felt completely frazzled. She couldn't take another thing. As she was closing her eyes, she heard the sounds of Azure playing.

Mink opened Azure's bedroom door and found her daughter in the middle of the floor, surrounded by all her toys.

"Time for bed, young lady," she said a little harshly. She was tired and didn't want Azure to give her a hard time.

"Please, Mommy, let me stay up a little longer," Azure whined.

Mink looked at her watch. It was almost ten o'clock. "Absolutely not. Now get undressed and get into bed this instant." She grabbed her daughter's thin wrist, and without realizing her strength, she pulled Azure into a standing position. Then she noticed the water seeping out of the bathroom. She opened the bathroom door and found the tub overflowing and Jelly Jam soaking wet. "That's enough! I just can't take another thing tonight!"

Azure started to cry.

"I'm going to whip your little spoiled ass!" Mink screamed at Azure.

"Please don't hit me, Mommy," Azure cried.

Suddenly Dwight rushed into his daughter's room. "Don't," he yelled, stopping Mink in midstride. "If you touch that child, I'll kill you."

Shocked, Mink lowered her hand to her side. She looked over at Azure, who was huddled in the corner with a wet Jelly Jam shivering against her small chest.

Mink was stunned. She felt his hot words creeping upon her and the breeze of Dwight's body running past her toward the small child. She fell to her knees, crying. "I'm sorry, Azure. I didn't mean it, really I didn't." Dwight held Azure in his right arm and the soap-soaked Jelly in the other, rocking them gently. He kissed his baby, not looking at his wife as he spoke.

"I'm taking Azure to my parents' home. She'll be safe there. I'm letting you know straight out, I'm going to sue for custody."

Mink held on to his arm. "Don't, Dwight. I'm sorry. I didn't mean it." Looking around, she realized now how obvious it was, with the floor flooded with water, what Azure had done. Obviously the child tried to give Jelly a bath.

Dwight ignored Mink's cries as he prepared to take daughter and puppy away. Pushing aside his wife, he threw a few of Azure's things into her little knapsack. "I'll see you in court, Mink."

Mink sank onto the bedroom floor, listening to the door slam behind them.

With Dwight taking her child away, she had no choice. She had to believe in Dwight's love; she had to believe in him.

SPICE

I love these little people; and it is not a slight thing, when they, who are so fresh from God, love us.

—CHARLES DICKENS

$\mathcal{E}$ven if it was a dream, let it stay, this wonderful dream about Golden, Spice thought as she opened her eyes. She felt the warmth from the smooth satin sheets touching every inch of her naked body. It was early, and the birds had not yet begun to sing. She felt ready for anything. Today was the special day that she looked forward to all year long—the annual May tea dance, held the last Saturday of the month. Unfortunately Golden was away on church business and would not be there. Missing him already, she hummed a spiritual melody as she showered and dressed.

Holding a cup of hot coffee and wearing nothing but a breath of fresh air, Spice pushed back the curtains and studied the threatening gray clouds. Every day for the past week, she had checked the weather forecast. Rain hadn't been predicted until the following week. It couldn't rain, though honestly she believed more in the power of prayer than the forecast.

Today would mark Southern Spice's eighth annual tea party. So far, rain had never intruded upon the big event. Now, with the windows open, Spice felt a moist breeze from the willows caress her face, and she inhaled the sharp scent of new grass growing, covering the grounds and mingling with the sweet blossoms.

There were just two days throughout the year that the restaurant was officially closed: the annual tea party and Christmas Day. The theme of this year's tea party was "Back to Romance— the 1920s." It had taken months of planning. The invitations had announced that attire was formal and should be 1920s style. Out of the three hundred and fifty invited guests, only nine had replied that they would be unable to attend.

Spice dressed, then went downstairs to check on the work in progress. Usually her employees were as excited as she was about the party, knowing they would receive a special bonus in their check the following week because of their efforts.

It was seven in the morning, and the kitchen was filled with hustle and bustle. Most of the food preparations were close to completion. Spice looked over the shoulder of one of her most valued employees, the pastry chef, Verna Eagle. She'd worked for Spice for twelve years. The only employee Spice valued more was Carmen. And with Carmen away, Spice had to rely more heavily on Verna.

"How's everything going, Verna?"

"Mighty fine. Mighty fine," Verna said as she moved to place a tray of patterned pastry crusts into the commercial oven.

The flaky pastries were cut into shapes of flowers, leaves, and shells. Later that morning they would be covered with shrimp spread that had been prepared the day before, garnished with dill and fresh greenery, then rerefrigerated.

"Try the strawberry sorbet," said Alice, another employee, offering a tablespoon.

Smiling, Spice thanked the small woman. "Excellent," she said, cupping her hand beneath her chin. "I'm sure the guests will be begging for the recipe."

"That's our secret," said Alice, wagging a finger in the air before she turned and headed back to her station.

Hearing her name called at the other end of the kitchen, Spice said her good-mornings to the rest of the small staff and moved on toward Laura, who worked in the fresh fruit section.

"I put a little more white wine in the peach soup than the recipe called for." Laura was a bit more nervous than usual this morning. She glanced at the hazy weather outside the window, then looked back at Spice. "Do you think it's okay?"

Spice sampled the cold peach soup. "As a matter of fact, it tastes better," she said, winking at Laura.

"It does, doesn't it?" Laura smiled mischievously at Spice. Chocolate fluted party cups with berry filling, cucumber sandwiches, madeleines, asparagus-and-cream sandwich petit fours, and lemon tarts filled several rows in the spacious commercial refrigerator. Spice peeked inside for a quick check, then appraised her findings silently.

Even though Verna was doing an exemplary job, Spice still missed Carmen. It had been two weeks since they'd last spoken to each other. As much as it grieved her, she had to respect Carmen's wishes and wait until her friend contacted her.

"It looks like rain, Ms. Spice," Verna called to her.

Spice shivered, hugging herself, then moved toward the window. "It wouldn't dare rain, and spoil our party."

But it did, just five minutes later.

Six young men were assigned to decorate the tables and garnish the walkways and porch railings with garlands of ivy and ivory ribbons entwined with gossamer white and yellow lotus flowers. Now they rushed inside, escaping the rain.

"Develle," Spice called out as she left the kitchen, "make sure that everyone inside continues on schedule. The rain *will* stop."

After Travis had quit, Spice had promoted Develle to the job of head chef. Truth was, Develle had a better rapport with the workers than Travis had and was doing an exceptional job.

Back upstairs, she dialed Sterling's number for the third time that day. A few weeks ago, when Spice had last spoken to Sterling, her daughter had barely mumbled a hello. Spice had apologized for the nastiness at their last lunch together. She yearned to question her baby about the pregnancy but bit her tongue. Now was not the time in their tattered relationship to play the role of smothering mother. She'd simply asked Sterling if she would attend the spring tea. Sterling assured Spice that she'd be there. Spice had left several messages since then, but Sterling hadn't returned the calls.

Now the machine came on again and Spice left yet another message: "Did you get your dress? I assume you'll be here. Mink will be here around noon. Let's start being a family again, sweetheart. You know I love you." And she added a profound "Please" to the end of the message.

At nine-thirty, just as Spice predicted, the rain had played its soft, pleasant tune and the umbrella of fast-flying colorful clouds passed like a whiff of smoke. Spice closed her eyes and gave a prayer of thanks.

Then, suddenly, like the smiling daughter of the storm, the sun broke through. The party would start in three and a half hours. Spice picked up the phone and called downstairs.

"Do you see it, Ms. Spice!" Develle asked excitedly.

"Yes, the rainbow is lovely, Develle. Now hurry. Write this down, we've barely got three hours, and there's so much to do."

Against the light, the colors of the rainbow shone like the

hues of the soul against the darkness of the world. It arched above Southern Spice like a promising beam of hope.

Mink arrived early and helped Spice finish dressing.

"I thought you were bringing Azure," Spice said to her daughter.

"She's got a cold. Erma's nursing her at home."

"You shouldn't have left her, Mink." Spice was genuinely worried. Azure was never sick. "I wouldn't have minded if you'd called and said you couldn't make it. The baby should be your first priority, not some stupid tea."

"You worry too much." Mink clasped Spice's pearl necklace, then placed her hands on her mother's shoulders. "Azure has a slight temperature, but otherwise she's fine. Erma knows how to reach me. Now stop worrying."

"I know. I know I need to relax."

"You might not realize it, Spice, but these teas mean a lot to me."

Spice knew Mink was thinking of Dwight. It was clear that her daughter was hurting.

Mink took Spice's hands in hers, looking into her mother's eyes. "You told me years ago how special these teas were to you. You said it wasn't about putting on a grand show. It was more about the intimacy of friends, the quiet comfort of all types of people talking and sharing an afternoon together. That made it special."

Though Spice hadn't voiced her concerns to Mink, she felt that this tea would bring their family back together again. Spice smiled. "And each year I'm struck by how many leave here so happy and relaxed."

"The same will happen this year."

"Without Sterling?"

Mink patted her mother's warm hands and helped her to her feet. "There's still time for her to show up. You know how much she loves attention."

251

Spice finished applying her makeup, then slipped into her dress. "I left her three messages just today, begging her to come. I haven't seen her since we had lunch weeks ago."

"I saw Sterling last week." Mink helped Spice into her silk chiffon floor-length costume and began buttoning the forty satin buttons that ran down the back. "Azure and I were shopping. Sterling sneaked up behind me at Lord and Taylor's and scared the shit out of me."

"Was she alone? How did she look?"

"She looked the same. Although her roots had grown out, which was unusual for Sterling. Otherwise she looked like Sterling, color coordinated and conceited. And yes, she was alone. In fact, what really gave me a chill is how alone Sterling seemed. She acted as though she'd just seen Azure the day before, as if she hadn't missed a beat in her short life. She talked about taking her to the Detroit Zoo, the new African museum, the Science Center downtown, and even designated a time that she'd pick her up. Before leaving, she kissed Azure on the cheek and said 'I've missed you, baby. Your auntie Sterling will be by tomorrow.' High as a kite"—Mink sniffed—"as usual."

"Don't talk about it, Mink." Spice's eyes drifted to the window. "I hate thinking about it." And what about her baby? Spice worried to herself—but she kept this news from Mink. There was no telling what the future held for that poor little baby. And for her poor little baby as well.

Spice placed the final touches on the three-foot-wide straw extravaganza that she was wearing on her head, sticking a hat pin in the front and the back. The hat was definitely a conversation piece, ten yards of tulle along with seven yards of multicolored flowers. "Your dress looks lovely on you," Spice said, eyeing Mink's gown.

Mink's silver blue chiffon dress, cut in a 1920s chemise style with a floor-length matching silk chiffon scarf of iridescent bugle beads, mirrored her mother's.

ONE BETTER

Spice took one last look out her window at the garden. And though the scenery below was a beautiful sight, all she saw was Sterling's absence.

Mother and daughter entered the party looking like exquisite sisters. Since each year it proved difficult to find just the right dress for the tea party, Spice had had three similar dresses made this year by a designer in Chicago, one for herself and one each for the girls.

For the next hour Spice welcomed her guests and thanked them for coming. Governor Michael Mitchell, Congresswoman Donna Bradley, Mayor Quincy Cole, accompanied by his wife, Judge Judy Cole, and several local recording artists strolled into the restaurant with a casualness of coming home for the holidays. With her oldest friends, she discussed the teas from the previous years.

From one P.M. until five P.M. the tea party unfolded with the charm and elegance that were the fruits of Spice's unique savoir faire.

May was Spice's favorite month for the garden. Throughout the month, peach, purple, and yellow three-foot daylilies embraced the four-foot white picket fence running the entire circumference of the three-and-a-half-acre grounds of the restaurant. Along the outer edge was a deep and lofty enclosure of conical and pyramidal evergreens in contrasting textures and shades of green. The brick-laden walkways crisscrossing the two pools were lined with low hedges and mirrored on both sides with Stella d'oro miniature daylilies, peonies, black-eyed Susans, three-foot dwarf cosmos, Siberian irises, and rosy pink coreopsis. Four rows of mounded crimson pygmy Japanese bayberry bushes provided a scarlet-toned color foil for shades of green. The effect was a kaleidoscope of color.

Each spring Spice was surprised by the fresh radiance of the flowers and the sweetness of their fragrance. The ground was swollen with moisture and the temperature was just right so that the plants could rapidly transform light energy into grow-ing tissue.

It had taken years for Spice and Dwight to create the archi-tectural landscape of Southern Spice. Spice again remembered when her beloved daughter, now so distraught, had first met Dwight. Spice had hoped to have a garden wedding for them, but it wasn't to be. They'd jumped the gun on her. Now Spice could only hope that one day Sterling would walk down the gar-den path and unite with a man whose first name wasn't Bennie.

By one-twenty most of the guests had arrived, elegantly clad in stunning clothes from the twenties era. The people looked like a page ripped out of a storybook. Couples walked together, arms linked, chatting or laughing like children and enjoying the pleasant atmosphere as waiters passed through the crowd, offer-ing silver trays of hors d'oeuvres. More than a hundred exotic teas, available to the guests, were served in steaming pots of bone china.

On the opposite end of the grounds a grand topiary cre-ation—Sleeping Beauty made of yews on a bed of corkscrew wil-lows—created an equally impressive view. Together, Spice and Mink made their rounds and introduced themselves to the guests. Politicians were paired with businessmen. Artists were tabled with entrepreneurs. It was an interesting mix of old and new money. Most knew Spice from years of patronizing her restaurant; others were pleased to meet the famous restaurateur and her widely publicized daughter.

Spice didn't miss the admiration in Mink's eyes as she re-sponded with pride to a female radio personality who asked about the landscaping that her husband had designed all of Southern Spice's grounds.

A warm breeze blew the ribbons of the elaborately designed straw hats tacked around the dessert tables. The ribbons of the hats fluttered over the tops of the tables. The centerpiece, a spec-tacular hat design for Marlene Dietrich, sat atop the table in its original box from Saks Fifth Avenue from the 1930s. A half hour before the tea ended, each hat would be raffled off to forty lucky ticket holders.

Antique billowing lace tablecloths kissed the immaculate lawns. Iridescent silver china and delicately shell-shaped sterling silver stemware graced each table.

When the cold peach soup was served, with fresh blueberries and sprinkles of cinnamon garnish, the guests raved. She'd have to thank Laura; the additional wine had gone over well. Even the chilled berry soup with orange juice, yogurt, lemon juice, honey, and fresh blueberries, raspberries, and strawberries with no alcohol received rave reviews.

Just as a reporter had finally gotten Spice's attention for a quick interview, she noticed Travis speaking to one of the guests. He held a stack of papers—fliers of some kind. Their eyes met, and he moved toward her.

Spice quickly read the flier he handed her.

Foxx's Fancy Foodplace at 33178 Grand Circus Park, opening June 1.
Spicy Louisiana Cuisine.
Use this flier for 15% off your meal.

He was using her tea to promote his own restaurant! "What's this, Travis?"

I just thought I'd drop in for a friendly visit."

She kept her face indifferent. She'd be damned if she'd stoop so low as to mention his inappropriate behavior.

"When you own your own place you can afford to give yourself a raise anytime you deem necessary."

"Is that what this is all about? The raise that I failed to give you?"

"Certainly not."

Spice spoke in an unconcerned manner. "At the time, you

didn't deserve one. I thought I made that clear," she said, handing him the cream-colored flier.

Travis smiled. "I thought you'd be happy for me. It's what I've always wanted. You knew that when you hired me."

"You still owe me fifty thousand dollars. Where'd you get financing?" Spice asked, knowing that his credit wasn't good and that he'd had a cash flow problem for the past two years.

"I've got a private partner."

"A partner willing to pay off your fifty-thousand-dollar debt?"

"Possibly," Travis said, smiling and walking away.

Spice shrugged off the unpleasant exchange—good riddance to bad news. The tea had been a grand success, and Spice smiled, waving to the guests as they left. She knew though her personal life was in turmoil, she still could pull off a grand occasion with style.

Later that evening, Spice slipped into comfortable clothes, poured a cold glass of milk to wash down some Mrs. Fields oatmeal-and-raisin cookies, and, sitting on the recliner, gathered up a pile of *Archie's Pals 'n' Gals* comic books.

Archie and Reggie's dialogue was written on puffs of white clouds with sharp hooks pointing to each. The words began to blur and run together into one jumbled text. She dozed.

Spice imagined she was a teenager once again. She found herself swooped into a world where Golden was Archie, she was Veronica, and Carmen was Betty. It was fun times at Riverdale High. They were all telling jokes and pulling pranks on each other with no worries whatsoever.

The phone startled her awake.

"Archie?"

"Who the hell is Archie?"

"Otis?" Spice asked, rubbing the sleep from her eyes. Collecting herself, she pushed the recliner to the forward position.

"Now you got it."

"Oh." She was silent for a moment, trying to shake off the sweet fantasy. Damn! she didn't feel like talking to Otis tonight. Spice glanced at her watch and jumped up. "It's twelve-thirty, Otis. Why are you calling me so late?"

They hadn't spoken since Otis had boldly entered her home without an invitation. The following day, she'd had the locks changed. Clearly Otis was doing as Spice had asked, allowing her space and respecting her privacy. She knew how much he loved mingling with the crowds during the annual tea.

"I didn't want to disturb your day with the preacher, but I felt I had to talk to you." He stuttered, "I—I wanted to come, I wanted to come over. Too late, though. So I decided to give you a call."

No matter what, Spice knew that she and Otis would always remain friends. There was something special about a disavowed relationship that made you give respect to what might have been. Nothing could break the bond they'd formed over twenty-five years. For others it might seem inappropriate; for Otis and Spice, it was just how it was—a fact.

By the pronounced slur in his voice, Spice knew that Otis was drunk. "Thanks for your concern. But I think we need to put this conversation off until tomorrow." She yawned. "I'm real tired, Otis."

"I've just got two questions."

Spice let out an exasperated sigh. "Okay. What is it?"

"What does Golden Westbrook mean to you? And what direction is our relationship heading?"

"First off, I don't feel like defending my feelings about Golden to you. And second, you're too intoxicated to remember anything I'd say to you tonight."

"Was he better than you and I could have been together?"

By his lowered tone, she knew he was referring to sex. Why did men feel that in order to win a woman, they had to compete with each other sexually? "Is that the first thing that comes to your mind? My God, he's a preacher, Otis."

His voice was slow. "How does he treat you?"

"What a stupid question."

"I don't know what you've heard, Spice—"

"I've heard enough to know that I can't trust you, Otis. The sad part is, you nearly convinced me that dating my brother-in-law wasn't such a crime. I was starting to have feelings for you."

Spice had read the rumors, headlined in the local newspapers, about city officials taking kickbacks. She was certain that Otis was involved, even though specific names weren't mentioned. His lifestyle and income had never matched in Spice's mind. How could she trust Otis, build a life with him, if his ethics were questionable? But she didn't want to get into all that now.

"Spice, I—"

"No, now that you've brought it up I need to let you know that what there could have been between us can never be. I'm sorry, Otis." She placed the phone down before he could respond, feeling somewhat guilty but glad to get it over with. Otis would have to understand sooner or later that Golden was her first and only choice for a future husband.

The irony that Otis hadn't come that day to the tea because he'd wanted to avoid Golden didn't escape her. And although she understood that Golden's obligations kept him even busier than she, she was disappointed that he hadn't been there to share in the beautiful day. The day he returned, in apology, Golden took Spice to a dinner at the exclusive Rattlesnake Club. With a view of the Detroit River, Canada, and the Renaissance Center, the Rattlesnake Club boasted a chef who had studied in France and made his own sauces from scratch. Among other divinely inspired dishes, rack of lamb was the chef's specialty. But more to the point, the Rattlesnake was Southern Spice's only real rival.

Under the watchful gazes of three fawning waiters, Golden

and Spice discussed upcoming events at Golden's church, then went on to their business concerns.

"How's the refinancing going on the Foxphasia complex?" Golden asked.

"Better than I expected. I am fortunate. Lucky, actually. Four corporations with whom my husband had business dealings years ago were willing to invest in Foxphasia."

"You should have contacted me."

"Truthfully, Golden, I wasn't sure if you wanted to take on a project outside the city, knowing that most of your development projects are in the empowerment zone, including the retirement center."

"You've got a point, but under the circumstances, I would have been willing to make an exception." Golden smiled and took Spice's hand.

Spice watched the lights suddenly go on across the Detroit River and felt there was nothing more breathtaking than Detroit's riverfront or Canada at nightfall.

"But there is something we've got to talk about, Spice."

"What's that?"

"I got violation notices from every department on our project."

"Our project?" Spice was surprised. Otis, she thought immediately. "Is there anything we can do?"

"I'm not sure. Working with these people is a bureaucratic nightmare." Golden paused.

Spice knew that Golden was also thinking about Otis, and she respected him more for not voicing her brother-in-law's name.

"What can we do?" she asked quietly.

"If worse comes to worse, we can sue the council."

"This is so unbelievable." Her voice reflected a tinge of anger.

"Try not to worry. I'm in for the long haul. I don't care how many postponements we get, I'm determined to build this retirement facility."

Spice smiled. "That's the kind of partner I like." She held up her hand for a high five with Golden. He tapped her hand and held it.

"Don't look so serious, Golden. It's just business."

"No. It's more. It's us. You've made me see that no matter how much success you have in life, it's empty unless you share it with someone. That's what a marriage means. It isn't about just sex, it's about making you my center."

"Golden, I don't know what to say—"

"The Lord says, 'Lean not in thine understanding, but in all thy ways acknowledge me.' I knew that when the time was right for me to choose a wife, I wasn't just going to go out and pick one. I knew the Spirit would guide me. And I've been led to you, Spice Witherspoon."

"I love you, Golden. God knows that I do. But I'm confused by so many things. I've prayed over this. I've prayed for this, for our love to blossom into something deeper, into something permanent. But as much as I've prayed, I'm scared now that it's actually happening."

"In the natural world we expect prayers to happen overnight. But in the real world that instant may take tens of years or a century. Sometimes prayers are not answered because it's not the will of God. The Lord's Prayer says: 'Thy will be done.' Everything we do is a part of God."

"So you're telling me that you believe it's destined for us to be together?"

"Yes. I'm telling you, my love, that my dream is over. No longer shall I long for the ethereal; I've no share in paradise. I want on this earth to live plainly and honestly. I will never again ask the Lord what exactly is this thing called love because until it came I had not yet been born, and now I know." He stopped and turned to face her, and placed her hands in his. "Spice Witherspoon, I love you very much, and I'd be honored if you would consent to be my wife."

"But there's something I have to tell you."

"It's not necessary, Spice."

"Oh, yes, it is. Please. Hear me out." Ashamed to look into his eyes, she turned away before she began to tell her story.

"I don't remember my mother after the age of four. I've told you this before, but what I haven't told you is after being shuffled from one foster home to another and being sexually abused by two of my foster fathers before I turned twelve, I lost all respect for men. One of the men I was intimate with was a preacher."

Spice stopped, trying to judge Golden's reactions. When he said nothing, she continued. "By age fourteen I was pregnant. After Mink was born, my foster parents kicked me out. I had nowhere to go. I met a girl in Midnight, Mississippi, who was living in a home with three other unwed mothers. That woman was my friend Carmen. Even though she didn't say so, I knew how they were making a living.

"I moved in, lived with them, hustling, until I became pregnant again. Soon after, I met David, and my life started to look up. I was working at a diner, then Carmen and I set up a catering business. Life seemed possible for me, and it was David's belief in me that pushed me to believe in myself.

"I never lied to David. He knew where I was from, what I'd been doing. And he loved me anyway. But I have never gotten rid of the shame of giving myself to strangers for money." Spice stopped, shoulders hunched, the pain pounding over her left eye, throbbing to the words "Will he still want me?" "I don't know if I deserve you, Golden."

With an aura of peace in his voice, Golden finally spoke. "There are many places in the Good Book that teach us to forgive, to not judge. I know how pure your soul is, Spice Witherspoon. And I know too that God has forgiven you, and that you now must forgive yourself. In other words, I can't judge you without first judging myself. We all have crosses to bear. In forgiving your sins, I ask forgiveness for mine. The reason why your past prostitution doesn't matter to me is simple. Some men say that they'd rather marry a whore than a virgin because she's already been out there—she's already experienced. Most women who have only slept with one man dream about other men. She daydreams about the thrills and frills of multiple sex partners."

Spice sat back in her seat, the tension easing from her shoulders.

"What happened to you over twenty-five years ago merely made you a better woman today than you ever might have been. You're wiser because of it, smarter. You are a complete woman, the kind of woman that any man would be proud to call his wife."

Spice was in tears. Her body shook as she released the shame that she'd clung to for years. Golden reached out and placed his hands in the center of the table. She looked into his face and saw hope and life in his eyes. She placed her hands in his and smiled.

"Again, I ask you, knowing all that you know about yourself: Spice Witherspoon, will you marry me?"

Overcome with love, her hands trembling in his, she whispered, "Yes. Yes, I will marry you."

_O_TIS

_Before you beat a child, be sure that you yourself are not the cause
of the offense._

—AUSTIN O'MALLEY

_T_he bartender set a fresh drink in front of Otis.

"I didn't order this, Chappy."

"The lady paid for it." The bartender pointed to a well-
dressed woman near the center of the bar, her face angled rather
arrogantly toward Otis.

Otis smiled at the woman, and she was instantly off her seat
and heading toward him. "I'm Shaylynn," she said, extending
her hand. "Are you with anybody?"

Otis hesitantly shook his head no.

Taking the empty seat to his left, the woman said, "I'll have
another Alizé, please."

It was late. One-fifteen A.M. But he wasn't ready to go home yet.

The Soul Twist Bar, a favorite night spot for businessmen and -women, was situated on the corner of Livernois and Tuxedo. Ordinarily the place was packed. Tonight, the door to the street was open and Otis could smell the early summer night wafting in—a small comfort.

Sipping his drink, he appraised the woman, who looked to be about forty. She said she owned a travel agency located in the Renaissance building downtown. Apparently she'd been there for ten years and was pissed that General Motors had bought the building.

"So where are you considering moving your business?" Otis asked flatly.

"Someone told me about a development in the inner city—I thought I'd look into that."

Otis nodded, knowing that she was talking about Golden's Renaissance project. "Oh yeah, what's its name?"

"The Renaissance project."

Otis laughed resignedly.

Shaylynn began to babble on for a few minutes about her job, and Otis listened placidly—or, rather, heard her from a distance.

Suddenly she stopped, and was looking at him, her right shoulder dipped and her neck cocked back. Otis recognized this posture; many black women he knew responded this way when they felt defensive.

"Listen, I don't know if I'm the best company tonight." Otis was trying to be polite. Usually he could summon some interest in a good-looking woman.

He spotted her wedding ring. *Thank God.* "You're married?" he asked, smiling.

"No. Recently divorced." He could feel the woman's hot breath on his cheek as she scooted a little closer to him. Otis stiffened.

He hoped he'd masked his displeasure.

"What about you?" she asked.

"Sad to say, I'm a widower and still single." His every thought was of Spice as he spoke the words.

"I live just a couple miles away. You could follow me. I always keep my bar well stocked."

Otis signaled for Chappy to refill his drink. *How in the hell am I going to get out of this?*

To his shock, Shaylynn pressed her breasts against his shoulder. What was he going to do? Suddenly he heard a familiar voice call out his name.

"Hey, Uncle O."

Otis looked up and there was Sterling. He grabbed his niece and kissed her on both cheeks. "Sterling," he said, "this is Shaylynn."

"Hi," Sterling said, removing her coat, all the while checking out Shaylynn.

"Hello."

"This is my niece." Otis asked the man next to them if he would move down one seat so Sterling could sit beside him. One look at Sterling's blond hair and blossoming bosom and the gentleman obliged.

"Thank you," Sterling said to the man in a sultry voice.

"Chappy!" Otis called out a tad too loudly. "Bring my niece a double shot of Courvoisier."

"Thanks, Uncle O, but I'll have a Shirley Temple."

Otis beamed. As Sterling arranged herself at the bar, he noticed how clean her hair looked, how her skin seemed taut, her eyes rested. He smiled and got up. "Excuse me for a moment, ladies," he said, and headed for the bathroom.

Otis felt temporary release from his despair about Spice. He'd looked after her daughter. That mattered. It had to matter to Spice. Maybe if he showed Spice, brought Sterling back to her, she would understand how deeply he loved her.

As he was returning to the bar, he saw Shaylynn handing something to Sterling. He quickly drew closer and realized it was money. The woman was obviously offering Sterling money to leave—the old "get lost, little sister" trick.

"What's going on here?"

"Uncle Otis, get this bitch out of here."

"Sterling," Otis said admonishingly. "Excuse me, Shaylynn, I think we need to say good night."

Both Sterling and Otis watched the angry woman's face as she picked up her purse. Shaylynn rolled her eyes hard at Otis as she twisted off the seat and left. When she was gone he turned to Sterling. "Whew, that was close. What brings you out tonight?"

"I went to see the play *Your Arms Too Short to Box with God*, at the Fisher Theatre. I had a hunch I'd find you here—"

Otis fingered his drink. He knew that she was lying about where she'd been—Bennie's apartment was only five minutes away. But he couldn't deny how good she looked.

"So, Sterling, you look like you've cleaned up."

"Yeah, Uncle O—thanks in large part to you. I couldn't have done it without you."

"Sterling, you know I'd do anything for you. You're like a daughter to me." Otis's heart tweaked as he said the words—he knew the depth of their truth. "You really do look wonderful. I am so proud of you."

"Thanks, Uncle O. Actually, I have some good news. Besides the getting clean part." She paused. "I'm pregnant." She was smiling.

"Well, I guess that's good news, Sterling."

"Oh, it is! I think I'm finally going to be happy."

"Does your mother know about this?"

"Yeah—not that I told her. You know how she has a sixth sense about things."

"What did she say?"

"She didn't have to say anything. You know and I know how

266

she feels. She doesn't trust me, believe in me, so why would she believe I can take care of a child?"

"Sterling, you need to trust her. Give her a chance."

"Why should I?"

"Because she loves you."

"You mean because you love her?"

Sterling's words were angry but true, and they cut through Otis's heart like a scythe. He downed his drink and ordered another.

"Your mother had a hard life, Sterling."

"Oh, I'm sick of that shit—just because she didn't have a mother! Well, neither did I. Why do you stick up for her? She treats you like dog shit. She doesn't give you any respect—you should hear what she says behind your back."

Otis felt something boiling deep within his stomach. Was it true? All these years caring for Spice, and what does she do?

Sterling was still ranting. "She's nothing but a whore. Why bother?"

Otis was very still as his rage surfaced. "You're right, Sterling. Your mother is nothing but a whore. Once a whore always a whore."

Sterling looked at Otis as if he were possessed. Maybe he was. Something was triggered, and he couldn't help himself any longer. He gulped down his drink and ordered another.

"She made a better whore than she ever could a mother."

"What did you say?" Sterling's eyes narrowed.

"She's gone back to her roots, cavorting all over the city with a man at all times of the day or night, a man almost ten years her junior. No class, acting just like a whore."

Sterling shrugged, assessing the strained expression Otis was wearing. Spice and Golden's engagement was in all the papers. The story had even managed to make *People* magazine's hot singles list of 1997.

"I don't get it, Uncle O. You weren't calling Spice a whore before she decided to marry that preacher."

"You don't know the half of what I know about your mother."

"Maybe we should stop, before this conversation gets ugly."

But Otis couldn't contain himself. "There's lots you don't know—like Mink's daddy was her pimp."

"What?"

"She's just a low-down whore."

"You're drunk, Uncle Otis."

Otis gulped down his drink. "David knew what Spice was before he married her—a common whore. He told me all about it. Hell, the whole town of Midnight knew. Why do you think she and Carmen are such good friends? They've got a lot in common."

Otis's mind was flailing, the alcohol making his thoughts incoherent.

"Why should I believe you?"

"You'll have to. Her past has a lot to do with you, and Carmen."

"Are you trying to tell me something, Uncle O?"

Otis looked at Sterling. What had he just said to her? Had he really betrayed Spice? Suddenly he felt nauseated. He removed a fifty from his pocket and threw it on the bar.

"If all this is true, Uncle O, then how come you want Spice so bad?"

Otis again looked at his niece and said without any emotion, "I love her."

STERLING

The plays of natural lively children are the infancy of art. . . .
Children live in a world of imagination and feeling. . . . They
invest the most insignificant object with any form they please, and
see in it whatever they wish to see.

—ADAM GOTTLOB OEHLENSCHLÄGER

The next morning, Sterling woke up early. Her head was clear, but her heart was heavy. Had Otis spoken the truth? What did he mean about Spice having been a whore? Could it really be true? She rubbed her hands over her stomach and imagined it swelling, growing as her baby grew within her.

Who was her father? Sterling picked up the phone and called her sister.

"Mink, it's Sterling."

"Well, well."

"How are you?"

"How am I? Since when did you think to ask?"

"I think about you, Mink."

"And what about that promise you made to Azure? Sterling, children have very good memories."

"Mink, there's something I've got to tell you. It's important. It's about Spice."

"I don't want to hear about your problems with Spice, Sterling. You need to grow up. I'm not getting in the middle of this shit. I've got enough problems of my own. I can't—"

"No, it's not about me. Well, not directly." Sterling paused. How was she going to say this? "I saw Uncle Otis last night and he was drinking—I guess upset about Spice and Golden getting married. Anyway, he said something about Spice, about when she was younger."

"What, Sterling? Just spit it out," Mink said.

"He said that Spice used to be a prostitute."

"Sterling, you're on drugs—why don't you get a real life!"

"No, it's true. I think it's true. She and Carmen—when they were young and living in Mississippi."

"That's bullshit. I don't believe a word of it!"

"Uncle Otis said that David told him."

"I don't believe a damn word. How dare you! How dare Otis talk about Spice behind her back?"

"Think about it. Neither one of us knows who our real father is."

"You know what, Sterling? I'll soon be thirty years old. And if a son of a bitch came up to me now saying he was my father, I'd just as soon spit in that bastard's face as call him Daddy." Her voice was shaking now. "I don't care what Spice has been or was. I don't give a fuck about some man who shot his seed into my mother's womb. The only thing . . . the only thing I care about is the people I've known and loved all these years. Anybody else can kiss my ass."

Sterling held the humming sound of a dead receiver in her

hand. Her sister's rage seemed big enough for both of them. Mink was right, she thought. Otis was probably lying about Spice. Then again, what did it matter? She had more important things to think about. She had the father of her own baby to deal with. Pushing the button to clear the line, she dialed Bennie's number. She had to tell him about the baby.

Bennie picked up on the second ring.

"Bennie, I've got something to tell you. It's important."

"What's up, Sterling? You sound so serious. Are you sick?"

"No. Can you come over?"

"Give me an hour."

That was too easy, Sterling thought to herself. Why? She pushed her doubts aside as she started building a fresh fire in the living room grate. She covered the lamps with wispy red, black, and silver silk-printed scarves. From the back corner in her bedroom closet, she removed a huge white sheepskin rug and centered it before the burning fire. Next she doused a drop of Chinese silk oil on the rug, the light bulbs, and into the burning embers. She put on a jazz CD and turned the lights low. The effect spelled sex, which was exactly her intention.

She was nervous. *Maybe just one hit and I'll be okay. Just one won't hurt the baby.*

It had been five weeks since she used any drugs. She'd kept a half ounce of heroin wrapped inside a sock in a shoe in her closet, just in case. Now with shaky fingers she inhaled the heroin and sat back on the bed, reveling in the sublime feeling flowing through her body.

Afterward she took a shower, then checked her watch. Bennie was due to arrive in ten minutes. Sterling prepared two drinks and set them on the ceramic mantel.

When Bennie arrived, Sterling was floating. She greeted him with a warm kiss on the mouth. "What's the big secret?" he asked, handing her a small bag.

"I'll tell you later." Sterling led him by the hand to the rug on the floor before the fireplace.

The music in the background covered all the communicating they needed to express at the moment. Cupping her hands around his chin, she slowly brought her hands to either side of his face, then higher to his forehead. Without applying any pressure, she used the tips of her fingers, followed by her palms, to caress his face. Then she kissed him.

Sterling felt his hand roving, probing her back and buttocks, as she slowly inserted her middle finger inside the fullness of his mouth. Moving her body to the rhythm of the music, she touched the inside of his lips, his gums, the inside of his cheeks, luxuriating in the wetness she found there. Each beat of the music heightened their growing excitement as she removed his clothes and he removed her robe.

In the throbbing firelit darkness, the air was suffused with the erotic scent of Chinese silk. Sterling felt as if she were floating on a sacred river. The tenderness she felt for Bennie could only be expressed by how they loved each other's bodies.

"I'm going to make love to you all night, baby," Bennie said, reaching over to retrieve the brown bag. "Tonight, like no other night."

Again Sterling felt a twinge of doubt. Why was he so enthusiastic tonight? What was going on? He seemed genuinely happy to be with her.

Inside the bag were black figs that could have come only from the South. He laid her back on the furry rug. With his teeth, he peeled back the skin of a ripe fig. After opening it, he split it into four sections, revealing the glittering, rosy, wet, honey-petaled fruit. He took the wonderfully moist fruit and inserted it inside her hairy veil. Moving the fruit back and forth inside her, he teased her warm pink slit with its coolness, while licking her lips and tongue into a mad fury.

One by one he fed her, then himself, the sweet fruit, now

scented with her. When he finished, she felt his eyes feasting on her body, moving from her heaving breasts to the juncture of her thighs.

Pressing his mouth against her lower lip, he touched her with his tongue, pressing hard until he heard her scream.

While placing his head above hers, he made a necklace with their arms, inhaling her sweat-soaked silken hair. "Your sweat is the odor of sweet musk," he said.

She exhaled and closed her eyes. She wondered if he noticed her swelling abdomen.

With the burning flames of Bennie's fingers and the throb of the fruit, which pulsated in and through her, she came with a thrilling tremor, shaking from head to foot. Before she could re-cover, Bennie buried his face between her legs, kissing the length of them, sinking his nose in the tender curls of her vagina, until she fell back, her ivory thighs opening and her hands clutching the hairs on his head as she sank deep into the fur rug's deep pile.

Seconds later, she came again. Leaning back on her elbows, she admired the gleaming energy of his erection, throbbing proudly at her. At that singular moment her body as well as her mind was weak with the desire to give more, more—so weak now that she confused her body with her soul.

Then she felt him. Thick fingers slid inside her vagina, smoothly, fully, and began to move up and down. Though her head shook backward and forward, she could have sworn she was frozen with pleasure.

Reaching down, she pressed her long nails against her outer lips, feeling his fingers touching hers, felt the pressure of his fin-gers about a third of the way inside her vagina, stroking her inner muscle. She began to fondle herself to the same rhythm.

As Bennie speeded up his thrusts, her excitement grew with each motion. Knowing she was about to come, she stopped. In-serting one knee between his thigh, she urged him to turn over onto his back. Straddling him, Sterling eased her buttocks closer to his face, then lowered her head toward his feet to feel the tip of his member with her tongue. She felt him, at the same time, stimulate her clitoris with his teeth, mouth, and tongue.

Kissing each side up and down and around, she made her way to the silky tip and felt its heat on her tongue. Taking his organ halfway inside her mouth, she sucked hard. Then, feeling him enjoy the sensation, she shook his entire organ into her mouth, feeling him pushing, pushing it farther and farther back, as far as it would go, as if he wanted her to swallow it. With his pulsating organ, warm and wet inside her mouth, her lips engorged, she lavished the tightness of his mushroom tip, dragging her lips slightly over the smooth surface to create friction.

He shuddered.

Tasting the sweetness of his first orgasm, she shuddered as well. Her vagina throbbed as she felt a waterfall of orgasms spill over her.

Bennie lifted her naked body to the leather chair and sat her down. After placing a pillow beneath each knee, he pulled her hips forward until she felt the full extent of him enter her. With his stomach rotating in and out he stroked Sterling until she cried out for release.

"It's not over yet, baby," he said hoarsely.

Crossing both her legs, he raised her feet over his shoulders and quickly eased back into her wet triangle.

His powerful thrusts left her weak. She felt as if a part of her had separated, then dissolved, her own molecules like motes of dust, every atom of her being completely blown apart and then recombined. With less than a second to recover, she felt another spasm of pleasure, a final surrealistic shudder pass through her body—lasting seconds—lasting forever—the sound that came from her like a death knell.

Knowing Bennie was prime for his final climax, Sterling, thoroughly exhausted, held him inside her, drawing him in tighter, like a repeated suction, squeezing and again holding him within her for a long time until she felt him stiffen, then felt him coming inside her in hot spurts: one, two, three times it came out. With her hands on his buttocks, she felt him quiver, then stiffen again. Bennie fell forward on the chair beside her, his breath coming in short pants. After a minute he looked over at her. They both smiled and fell into a deep sleep.

When Sterling woke up the next morning, Bennie had already showered and dressed.

"I've got to make a run," he said to her as she sat up in bed.

"How long will you be?" She still hadn't told him about the baby.

"A few hours. Then I'll be back."

Sterling left the bed and wrapped her arms around his neck. "Don't you love me, Bennie? Don't you want to marry me?"

He slapped her naked buttocks softly. "I know what I promised, Sterling. We'll get married soon."

"Then I can count on you to keep your word this time?"

"Absolutely, babe," he said, kissing her on the forehead. "Gotta go."

This time would be different, she thought, because soon she would tell him about the baby.

When Bennie finally turned up a few days later, Sterling pretended as if nothing had happened.

"Are you coming in or what?" She forced a smile on her face.

Wearing his impeccable manners on his sleeves, he looked cool in his lemon polo shirt and matching cotton twill slacks. The smooth copper-toned skin of his face was covered with a six o'clock shadow. His perfectly symmetrical dimples were balanced by the cleft in his chin. He looked good enough to eat, Sterling thought. He stepped inside, both hands in his pockets, sunglasses pushed down on his nose, totally nonchalant.

"What's up, Sterling," Bennie said as he automatically went

to the refrigerator for a soda. He had a way of walking around the place as if he owned it. He never asked for anything. Whatever Bennie wanted, he could have. He seemed to have known that from the start.

"Why are you playing games with me, Bennie?" She sat on the leather chair, opposite the sofa where he was now seated.

"If you want to know why I haven't returned your calls, say so, Sterling. Don't try to get coy with me. It's not you." He sipped the soda.

It was ten o'clock at night. Her skin and hair were glowing: inside, she felt like shit. "Are you still planning on moving in or not? It's been almost two weeks since you promised."

"I'm here, aren't I?" He pulled her toward him.

"When?" she asked, relaxing into his embrace.

"I'm already packed." Bennie was smiling.

"Really?"

"All my things will be here tomorrow. I've already made arrangements to put my furniture in my buddy's basement. Just make sure you've got enough room for my clothes."

"Bennie," she said, kissing him on his eyelids, his lips, his neck. Then he pushed her back.

"Let's save all that till tomorrow night, okay? I'm tired."

He'd taken the next day off from work, and he was there, just as he'd said, with an army of garment bags and bulging suitcases. They listened to music, made love, hung up the clothes, ate lunch, made love again, and then called Domino's Pizza for dinner. Sterling couldn't remember Bennie being so attentive toward her. Maybe, she thought, seeing the fullness in her breasts and her normally flat buttocks filling out, he'd guessed about her condition.

They set up housekeeping arrangements immediately. They split the housework in half. Sterling agreed to cook during the week; on the weekends they would eat out.

It was her dream come true. Finally, Sterling felt secure

enough in Bennie's love to tell him about the baby. Sunday she prepared a special dinner, lit candles, and chilled expensive champagne.

"Bennie, remember I had something to tell you?"

"Yeah, what's up?"

"I'm pregnant." Sterling tried to smile, but she felt tears welling in her eyes. What if he wouldn't be there for her? Suddenly, one of the vague doubts she'd been pushing away came into full view: If Bennie was being so nice, it only meant he wanted something from her.

Bennie sat across from her, his head leaning into his hands. He didn't move. "You're what?"

"Pregnant."

Bennie gulped down the last remnants of his champagne and not too gently placed the glass on the table. "Shit, Sterling, why did you do that?"

"I didn't do it on purpose. Bennie, I thought you'd be happy."

"It's not even mine."

"How can you say that?"

"Listen, Sterling, I can't really deal with this information right now. I gotta go." And he walked out the door.

Bennie didn't come home that night. Or the next night. Monday she was in a daze. Tuesday came and went without a word.

Wednesday morning, she called Bennie's job and found out that he'd taken a week's vacation time.

Sterling panicked. Each time the two of them made up, she convinced herself that this time would be better. She called his friend Jamie.

"I think he's down at the hospital," Jamie said.

"Is something wrong?" Sterling's heart began to thump inside her chest.

"Nothing's wrong—just Sandy havin' her kid."

Sterling felt her heart drop into her stomach. "Which hospital?"

"I think William Beaumont in Royal Oak."

She got into her car and drove to the hospital.

When she walked into the lobby, her hands were shaking. She wasn't sure what she planned on doing. She only knew she had to see for herself. Sandy's surname was Greene. She remembered seeing it on Bennie's health insurance. When she asked the receptionist for Sandra Greene's room, the young woman promptly gave her the number and floor.

As soon as she stepped off the elevator into the maternity ward, her heart sank to the pit of her stomach. Her legs felt like rubber. She lost her courage. She broke out in a cool sweat as she trudged down the hall. No matter how much she tried to accept it, she knew she couldn't embrace Bennie's children the way she would hers. Holding her head erect, and bracing her heart for the hurt that she was certain would come, she took deep breaths the closer she came to the room of doom.

Sterling stopped just outside 571. She could hear Bennie's voice and that of at least two women, one sounding elderly.

Taking three deep breaths, Sterling walked casually into the room. "Hello."

The new mother, sitting among dozens of fresh flowers, turned to Bennie. He looked at her and said, "This is Sterling, Sandy. She's a friend of mine."

"Hello." Sandy smiled at Sterling, as did the older woman. Sterling was appalled at the huge woman holding the newborn baby girl. Sterling took in the color of the woman's skin and hair, the shape of her lips, the color of her eyes, the raise of her brow, the shape of her fingers, and the length of her weaved hair. She was unattractive and obese. Sterling was embarrassed that Bennie was even able to make love to such a slob.

In a state of shock, she stood there mute, until she felt Bennie's arm under her elbow, escorting her to the door. Bennie had spoken so sweetly to her that Sterling hadn't realized she was outside the room.

"Let's go," Bennie said, steering Sterling from the room.

He didn't say another word until they reached the elevator.

"What are you doing here?"

"Why haven't you been home? I've been worried sick."

"Go home, Sterling. You don't understand."

"Tell me why I'm not enough for you, Bennie."

"Sterling, go *home!* I'll call you later."

"Bennie—"

"Please, just do as I say," he said in a low voice laced with venom.

At first, she was in shock. When that wore off, she knew despair. The hurt was too deep now to repair. Her baby would be hers alone. And maybe she'd have a reason to be better. One better, Spice had always told them, my daughters are one better. Well, now she'd see if she could fulfill that promise.

In the stark days that followed Bennie's exit from her life, Sterling was barely able to function. Over and over again, she replayed the years that she and Bennie had shared together.

In the beginning she had believed it was the children that made Bennie leave. His son needed him, he'd said to her over and over again. And now there was the daughter. He wouldn't allow another man to raise his children.

How could Bennie leave her for a fat, unattractive woman probably on welfare? Did he love her?

Sterling tried to fight off depression as she asked herself continuously, Why want *her?*

When you gaze at something, but see nothing; when you listen for a sound but hear nothing; when you try to grasp it and find it has no substance—was God telling her to leave it alone?

Sterling waited until he finally called.

"Look, you and I have had problems from the start."

"None that we can't solve together."

"I'm not coming back, Sterling. Not right now. I've already left one son; my place is here with my daughter. It's time I became a real father."

"You're planning on marrying that bitch?"

"No. But I've decided to move in with her."

"What about my baby—our baby?" she screamed.

"It's not mine." And Bennie hung up.

Part Three

Nobody who has not been in the interior of a family can say what the difficulties of any individual of that family may be.

—JANE AUSTEN

 M<small>INK</small>

Your child does not belong to you, and you must prepare your child to pick up the burden of his life long before the moment when you must lay your burden down.

—J<small>AMES</small> B<small>ALDWIN</small>

---

*L*ying awake in a sterile hotel room in Houston, Mink realized her life meant close to nothing. All she had to hold on to was her job. She'd lost Dwight, and now she might even lose custody of her daughter. Suddenly Harrison seemed a distant memory, an afterthought, a total and complete mistake.

How could she have been so stupid? With dread working its serpentine way up her body, Mink felt shock pervade her soul: she loved Dwight.

It had been a few weeks since Dwight had decided to sue for custody, and though Azure was safely at Spice's house, Mink still could not sleep from worry about her daughter. Had she really almost struck her?

How could she make Dwight understand if she didn't?

Erma agreed to move into Spice's duplex with Azure until Mink and Dwight's divorce was settled. Dwight had moved into a house with his co-worker, Reuben. The night before, Mink had finally read through the legal papers concerning the custody suit against Dwight. She realized that the child was eight years old—born six months before she'd met Dwight. Why hadn't Dwight told her? That made a huge difference! Did he try and had she just not listened? Did she just not take the time to read the papers? Mink shook her head in frustration. Before she'd left for Houston, she had gone to see Dwight at the firehouse.

An emptiness had ached at the bottom of her stomach. "I've made a lot of mistakes, Dwight. I was wrong." She had tried to reach out to him.

Dwight had pulled away, his eyes cutting deep into her. "I love you, Mink. That's a fact. But I love my daughter just as much, and she deserves to live in a home where her parents don't argue and fight all the time. We can't change what's happened between us."

"But we can try," she had offered weakly.

"I can't help but wonder if you want your family back because the man you've chosen over me has kicked you to the curb." Coldness had filled Dwight's eyes.

Mink cast her eyes down before she spoke. "The truth is," she had begun, "the truth is, I never appreciated what I had until I lost it. I always took for granted that you and Azure would be there."

"You've never loved her like I've loved her."

"I do. I do, Dwight. I just didn't know how to show it. My career came first. That was wrong, I know. I know I've been selfish. I thought you understood that about me when we married."

ONE BETTER

"And now, just like that, you're trying to tell me that you've changed." He had snapped his fingers and turned away from her.

She had explained that she had read the papers. "But I never realized the kid was so old. I've had a chance to think things over."

Dwight had then explained that he'd found out from a friend that the woman's husband, who had the boy, read about Mink's recent promotion and suggested that she take Dwight to court for back support. Michigan law states that after a child reaches the age of six, the mother could file a claim for child support, but she could not receive retroactive pay from the date of the child's birth—her claim was two years old. Expecting close to $60,000, the woman was pissed when the settlement totaled only $7,000. The court ordered Dwight to pay $600 in monthly child support.

"If it mattered enough for you to leave me, then I have to question whether you've ever really loved us at all," Dwight had said.

As he walked away, Mink had to face the facts: it was she who was unfaithful. Her position as captain of an airline, that which had always been the driving force of her life, the source of so much pleasure, suddenly meant nothing at all.

She'd had it all: a beautiful, healthy daughter, a nice home, financial security, and not just the love of her husband, but complete erotic fusion with him in the framework of their marriage. She'd had it all and lost it all. And Dwight was very clear—he wasn't ready to take her back.

She cried all the time now. And as she hauled herself out of bed and began to pack her clothes, she started to cry again. She washed her face and cried again. Even after putting on a fresh coat of makeup, she cried.

Realizing she was out of tampons, she went downstairs to the hotel's drugstore. In the lobby she looked around at the couples

285

smiling and talking to one another. How can these people look so content, Mink thought, when I'm so miserable?

Not waiting to pay, she got out of the short line. Not even going to her room, she telephoned Dwight at Reuben's house from the hotel lobby.

As soon as she heard the first ring, her heart leapt. The second ring seemed to take a lifetime. By the third, she was losing hope. When the answering machine came on and she heard Reuben's voice, she was too overwrought to leave a message.

A woman in the hotel lobby laughed, and Mink turned away from the phone and the last memories she had with her husband.

Memories are like books that remain a long time shut and need to be opened from time to time to exhume the dust that's collected. It is necessary, so to speak, to open the leaves, so they may be ready in time of need.

Waiting for the elevator to go back upstairs, she inhaled the citruslike scent from the sweet white Daphnes planted in huge pots in the skylit atrium. The pink-flowered Daphnes, which had grown into three-foot-tall globes, were not yet in bloom. Their pointed clusters looked positively tantalizing against the leathery green foliage.

Stepping inside the elevator, she took a last glance at the beautiful blossoms and thought of Southern Spice, Azure, Spice, and Dwight. Mink missed home. She missed Dwight. The Fourth of July was just eight days away.

I love you, Mink. I love you, Dwight. I love you, Mink. I love you, Dwight. Where did it go?

Should she have believed him when he'd said she was the only woman he ever loved? Could she ask him to come home now? Would he want to be there?

She looked out the window. It was raining again. She sat still, waiting for a call that the Pyramid van was ready to take them to the airport. Mink tried to shake off her dream, but its eeriness haunted her. In her dream the dead body of a trodden-on crab lay on the side of the road. A papier-mâché cat was being scrutinized by the early sun, revealing scratches and worn edges.

Windblown raindrops splattered against the wall of windows, merged, then flowed downward. Mink, cradling the telephone between cheek and shoulder, stood looking out her hotel window into the darkness. This was the third time she'd tried phoning Dwight, and as of yet she hadn't been able to reach him. She'd also tried reaching Spice to check in on Azure. But no luck there, either. Mink had pushed aside her thoughts concerning Sterling's information about Spice. How could it be true? But somewhere, deep inside of her, she shuddered.

The dreary weather mirrored the eerie coldness deep down in her bones, a melancholy chilling her spirit. She felt the weirdness continue as she boarded Pyramid Flight 2408. With two previous marks on her record for missing flights—days she'd just been too depressed to report to work—Mink had already been warned by her superiors that absenteeism without a doctor's explanation would not be tolerated by the airlines. Eyes always scrutinized her performance. Whom could she tell that she felt something foreboding? Who would believe that she was anything but a tormented, teary-eyed woman, with no husband and no prospects, who seemed to be losing her mind?

"This is Rescue One. We're on our way." The fire chief spoke into the two-way radio.

"We're in standby position on runway two-two."

"Copy that."

Pyramid Flight 2408 was on a collision course, about to land at Detroit's Metropolitan Airport in roughly eight minutes. Mink called ahead when the problems first began to surface in the aircraft, and ground control was alerted to take all precautions for a probable crash.

After leaving Houston, the plane began having problems with the hydraulic system at thirty thousand feet. By the time

Flight 2408 reached Ohio, the fuselage had caught on fire. When Mink attempted to land in Ohio, the landing gear malfunctioned. Their only option was to try to repair the problem or manually fix the gear in the fifteen minutes it would take to make it to Detroit-Metro Airport.

Captain Mink Majors and co-pilot Chester McQuilla worked with the equipment to extinguish the fire, but their efforts proved futile. Gloomy thoughts pervaded her mind as Mink tried to calm herself before calling tower control in Ohio to inform them of their urgent situation. They were low on fuel, and the rain and thunder made landing with only one brake operational even more dangerous, but it was necessary.

"There's a small airport at ten o'clock approximately fourteen miles away," the tower responded.

"Negative. Our landing gear still isn't functioning properly," Mink said into the microphone. "We'll head for Metro Airport in Detroit."

Instructions were given from tower control to all outlying areas to be on alert for a possible crash.

"Okay, listen, everyone. This is Captain Majors. I'd like you to listen very carefully to everything the flight attendant tells you to do. As I stated earlier, we're experiencing difficulty with the hydraulics system." She paused to clear her throat. "Some of you may see the fire from the left wing . . . don't be alarmed. We're going to land safely at Metro Airport. When I give the signal, I'd like everyone to crouch down low, and place the pillow that the flight attendant gave you over your head. The signal will be 'Brake, brake, brake.' "

Julie entered the captain's quarters a few minutes later and relayed to Mink that everything was secured and ready.

"Don't worry, girl. We're going to make it."

Julie smiled and tried not to look frightened as she closed the door behind her with a cheery "Good luck."

ONE BETTER

Chester was able to get the landing gear down, but he couldn't be certain the wheels were locked in place.

Mink said to her co-pilot, "With no hydraulics, and the landing gear malfunctioning, we're really going to have a problem landing." She looked at McQuilla. "Let's pray for a miracle." She wiped the sweat from her forehead. "You okay? Ready?"

"Yeah. Let's do it."

After relaying the headings and the approximate miles the plane was now from the airport, Mink heard from the tower, "Approach is looking good." McQuilla looked quickly at the brilliant lights lit up all over Metro Airport, then sighed.

Mink and Chester simultaneously stared at each other a second after they heard an explosion down below. The control panel lit up and started blinking like a Christmas tree.

"You are clear to land on any runway, Pyramid 2408."

"I can't make the turn on three-one!" Mink screamed into the microphone.

"Can you make three-two?" the tower asked.

"Negative! The landing gear is on fire."

"Clear runway two-two," Mink heard the tower say. "Go! Go!"

They felt the landing gear clicking, clicking, clicking, unable to engage, and for the first time in her career, Mink was frightened.

Pyramid 2408 was barely 1,200 feet from the ground. She was going to try to land. She didn't have a choice. She turned on the speaker. "Okay, brake, brake, brake."

"Ease the power back now!" Mink screamed at McQuilla. "Easy! Easy!. . . . Left . . . left . . . easy."

Then she heard the second explosion.

Thousands of feet in the air dark purple clouds billowed. The crew in the tower stared in horror at the wreckage in the making. Every service vehicle on the scene moved toward the carnage.

The police department arrived on the scene first. With all available trucks and equipment, Captain Mosely of the Detroit Fire Department had called in all firefighters in the Wayne County area. Dwight Majors was one of them.

With over three hundred passengers on board, and the possibility of the landing gear not working properly, the airport had prepared for a major disaster. Three hundred and seventy-five national guardsmen and one hundred soldiers were poised to assist the firefighters and rescue units at Metro. One hundred backboards were set up in area four by the airport's rescue team. Dozens of red-and-white rescue vehicles were on the scene and waiting to plunge into action.

Members of the ground crew began shouting orders as flames shot into the air. It took only seconds to come to an agreement and coordinate everyone into a single effort. Everyone was talking at once. Captain Mosely issued the command: "On the double. Move! Move!"

Choppers circled overhead, talking to the tower as they heard from the radio, "Move in!"

Dwight fixated on the shouts of the survivors. He ran toward the crash. Men and women running away from the plane screamed. But when he heard the helpless screams from the children, he plowed into action.

Blood coated the survivors' faces. Panicked passengers fled for their lives. Some were able to jump down the airplane's inflated ramp, until suddenly there was a third explosion . . . then an eerie, odd silence.

Fellow firefighters worked fearlessly to pull the passengers away from the plane. Dwight ran toward a small body he saw trapped amid the flames. He stumbled, fell, and injured himself on a piece of metal from the plane's wing flaps. Blood squirted from his leg, but he plowed ahead to save the small child. The little boy's legs were stuck under a heavy piece of metal. Dwight managed to pull the child out and carried him to one of the ambulances. The smoke was blurring his vision. All of a sudden he heard a woman scream. On his hands and knees he crawled toward the woman, whose face was so blackened it was unrecognizable. When he reached her, he wrapped his protective arms around her, hugging her, until the screaming stopped. Only then did he realize he held his wife in his arms. In the distance someone was hollering "Medic! Medic!" Dwight's energy was depleted. He pressed his wife's head against his chest and said, "Hold on, sweetie. We're going to make it."

CARMEN

In praising or loving a child, we love and praise not that which is, but that which we hope for.
—JOHANN WOLFGANG VON GOETHE

*C*armen had things under control. She had a decent apartment and an okay job. But doubt kept creeping in. She'd gone back several times to her AA meetings, but she still felt like an outsider. Maybe she just couldn't make it, maybe she was fooling herself. She missed talking to Spice.

Two days before, when her sponsor called, Carmen lied about going to meetings regularly and quickly hung up the phone. Today her mind began to glorify the high she'd felt while drinking, how good it was, how good it could be again.

Being cooped up in the apartment was wearing on her nerves. Her hands shook so badly when she tried to work with the dolls, she'd gotten frustrated and stopped. There had to be something else that she could do. Work another job? No. The added stress would probably make her want a drink more.

Deciding that it was time to get some exercise, she went out for an early summer walk. There was a small park two blocks away from her apartment complex, and listening to the laughter and gaiety of children of playing and couples chatting relaxed her.

She sat in a swing, pushed off, and swung her feet up and back until she soared higher and higher into the air. From across the street, she could see in the window of a quaint café a woman and a man smiling at each other as they sipped glasses of wine. Carmen felt an immediate resentment. Why could they drink like "normal" people and she couldn't?

She watched the waiter refill their glasses and saw the pleasure sweep across their faces. Carmen's tongue began to feel thick inside her mouth. She bit the side of her bottom lip and held it. She felt a twinge of anger as she continued to watch them. Feeling dizzy, she stopped and got off the swing.

Turning away, Carmen reminded herself that she had to take it one day at a time. But right now she didn't feel that she could make it through *this* day. Her hands began to shake, and her mouth felt bone dry. Her heart pumped up, faster and faster, as the craving she tried to suppress gained strength. *Damn! Damn! Damn!* She was growing breathless.

Who was she kidding? She couldn't make it. Somehow she'd always known that she couldn't. Carmen pulled herself up from the bench and walked six blocks to the liquor store that she had passed every day on her way to work. Just touching the bottle inside the brown bag gave her comfort. And as she walked home, she felt uplifted by a sense of impending elation. She walked faster. Her entire body was coated with sweat when she shut the door of her apartment behind her.

She set the bottle on the coffee table, went into the kitchen to retrieve a glass, then sat down. When she reached over to grab the bottle, something stopped her. Placing a clump of fingers inside her mouth, she bit down hard, stifling a scream.

Don't do this. You can make it.

Slowly she eased her arm back, clenching both fists on her thighs. Carmen told herself that she'd been sober longer than this before. Four months was nothing.

She willed herself to think, to tell herself that she was stronger than the bottle, that she wouldn't be defeated again by alcohol.

The clock over the sofa ticked and ticked. Carmen felt the sounds reverberating inside her heart. She felt as though she were a time bomb ready to explode. She looked at the bottle and the glass again, then back at the clock. In nine hours she would leave for work. Telling herself she could make it, she went into the spare bedroom and covered the bed with newspapers.

For two hours she tried to paint. During that time, her hands shook more and more, and her head throbbed. But she completed six faces. None of them were any good.

In the kitchen, she tried to prepare a small meal and popped open a soda. She sat at the table, nibbling at a pastrami sandwich and pickle. An ice cold Vernor's soda burned her throat and eased some of the rumblings in her stomach.

It wasn't working. She needed a drink.

Pounding her fist in her palm angrily, she watched the vodka bottle watching her.

Back in the bedroom, she again tried to paint. She had to make it until midnight. If she concentrated a little harder, she could do it.

Carmen thought about Spice and how much she missed her friend. Even though a part of her still resented her success, the sane part remembered that Spice would begrudge her nothing and that always when it came to Carmen, she acted out of love.

Three and a half hours to go. She was beginning to feel stronger. She selected three faces from her unfinished porcelain dolls and took them into the kitchen. The painting was getting a little easier, and she had actually made one look almost real, the way she used to.

By eleven-thirty she knew she'd made it. Walking by the lonely bottle, she smiled. She showered and dressed and felt relieved for having conquered the evil that threatened her sanity.

When she picked up her purse and car keys, she stood at the door for a moment and stared at the bottle of vodka. She told herself when she returned home that morning, she would keep the bottle in that exact same spot to remind herself of her weakness and her strength.

"You are not my friend," Carmen said to the bottle, and walked out.

The very next afternoon, Carmen returned to AA. This time she no longer felt alienated from the others; she finally understood their common cause. With victory as her source of inspiration, she spoke with other members after the session was over. Each night thereafter, she found friendship. She found understanding. And she finally found salvation.

After a full week of going to regular meetings, Carmen got up her courage to call Spice. Specifically, she wanted Spice to attend an AA meeting with her.

As she dialed Spice's familiar phone number, Carmen prayed that her friend had not deserted her. Did Spice understand her need for silence? Carmen knew she had to make the call regardless of her fears.

"Spice?"

"Carmen? Is that you?"

Carmen could hear the relief in Spice's voice. "Yeah, it's me. I'm alive!"

"Oh, thank God. Not that I ever doubted you. I knew you had to go away in order to come back."

"Oh, Spice, it's so wonderful to hear your voice."

ONE BETTER

"Oh, Carmen, I've missed you—we've all missed you. When are you coming home?"

Carmen thought of her little apartment. She had paid a mover to go there and pack up so she would not risk seeing Spice before she was able to.

"Well, I'm not sure. I kind of like my life here—not that it's nearly as entertaining as Southern Spice—" The women laughed together. "But I am calling for a specific reason. I was wondering if you'd attend an AA meeting with me."

"Of course, I'd be honored."

"It's what they call a qualification meeting. After someone has been sober for a certain number of months, when they feel ready, they stand up and begin to make amends with the world."

"I would be so happy to be there for you, Carmen. Just tell me when and where."

When Carmen hung up, she couldn't believe the inner light she felt coursing through her. She felt strong, as though her life were finally taking a positive direction.

Moments before she was to meet Spice, Carmen stood just inside the vestibule of St. Peter's Church—jittery and biting the last fragments of her nails. Then she saw her friend approach.

As always, Spice looked magnificent, walking into the church like a princess.

"Carmen, talk to me. Are you okay?" Slipping off her lace gloves and stuffing them in her purse, Spice continued, "I know you're ready for this. Otherwise you wouldn't have called me, right?" She pulled Carmen closer, and Carmen once again felt her friend's strong grasp.

"I'm just a little nervous. I'll be fine. Come on, let's find a seat."

One hour and six testimonials later, it was Carmen's turn.

"And now, I'm sure most of you know our newest member." The speaker turned to Carmen. "She hasn't been with us long, but today she's ready to share her story with us. She's a little ner-

297

vous. This is her first time speaking, so ladies and gentlemen, please welcome her with a hearty round of applause."

Carmen glanced quickly at Spice before heading up to the lectern. She took a deep breath, exhaled. "Hi," she said bravely, "I'm Carmen, and I'm an alcoholic."

The audience applauded in their usual manner, and it gave Carmen the courage to continue. As the group members continued to applaud, Carmen forced herself to look at the white wall ahead of her and not the onlooking faces. She couldn't bear that . . . not yet.

Her sponsor had told her that she should talk for at least thirty minutes. "I can't talk for that long," Carmen had whispered to herself. Now she stepped back, lowered her head, then stepped forward again.

She was about to begin when a gentleman brought her a cool glass of water with a twist of lime, placing it on the lectern. Carmen took a long sip, relishing the fresh taste.

She met Spice's smile, recognizing it as a bit of encouragement. Carmen was scared. She was ready to run right off the stage, but somehow she gathered the strength to go on. She thought of Spice's old refrain: *Promise me that you'll take better care of yourself.* With that loving thought in mind, she began.

"Just three days ago, I was here at a meeting. A young woman, a fellow member, got up and spoke. She talked about her mother, how much she hated her. When she mentioned why, I felt sick to my stomach. She'd been an incest victim, her father had abused her for years, and her mother knew about it, and didn't stop him. That night I couldn't sleep. I dreamed the next night and then the next about my mother. This went on for days before the truth hit me. The therapist had told me that I was suppressing something that I couldn't deal with. I hadn't believed her. Wouldn't listen to her constant proddings to dig deeper."

Carmen took another gulp of water. "Many of those who care

about me think my drinking problems stem from the death of my beloved child in a fire." She stopped. "That's partially true." She stopped once again and took another drink of water. "But what I've really been hiding, even from myself, is the fact that I was abused also, like the young woman I mentioned a moment ago."

Carmen saw the shock in Spice's eyes, and she looked away. If she looked at her for another second, she wouldn't be able to continue. "I did some soul-searching in those days in the clinic, getting in touch with the pain and shame of how my child died in a fire and how I could have prevented his death if it weren't for my drinking.

"Through suffering we learn wisdom. It opens our minds to all that is hidden inside us. Lord knows, God knows, that I'm no better than any of you."

By now she was crying, but not bothering to wipe away the tears. Carmen felt strong, euphoric. "What I've hidden . . . what I didn't want to face . . ." She stopped, caught her breath. "After the birth of my son, when I was all grown up and living on my own with some other single mothers . . . it was then that my father raped me. I was just visiting, had just come over to my parents' house, and my mother wasn't there. I had been drinking, but my father, he was drunk. And he raped me. I became pregnant. The shame, the humiliation of bringing this child into the world, this innocent child I didn't want, didn't ask for, was more than I could bear. I tried talking to my mother, but she spurned me, slapped me, telling me that I was no better than she was. What I wouldn't know for a while was that she, too, was a victim, like all the women in my family, moving from generation to generation like a virus, spawning babies out of unnatural acts. The hatred I felt toward her began to build. I started drinking, and the alcohol took the place of my parents' love."

Carmen paused and then continued, "They say I experienced alcohol-induced amnesia. But I know it was my soul unable to reconcile itself with its pain. You expect your parents to take care of you, to protect you. You trust them because you love them."

I trusted them.

"It's difficult when you learn that you can no longer trust your parents. It's hard. It hurts. It hurt me. But I was lucky, because at the time this happened, I was living with . . . my friend."

Tears streamed down her face. Because her story was so real, so true, many of the listeners were in tears, too. "If my friend . . . my friend . . ." She stopped.

"And I say once again if *my friend* hadn't loved me so much, I might not have survived."

Carmen broke down crying. It took a few minutes for her to regroup. "When I bore that second child, my daughter, I gave her away. I couldn't bear to look on this child of incest. People say that children born from incest are retarded, look funny, or something is wrong with them. Don't believe it. My child was beautiful. But I couldn't take the humiliation."

Carmen paused again to gather herself. "Even though I knew the person who became my daughter's mother saved my daughter's life, and saved my own, I have never been able to forgive myself. Never. Until now."

Carmen looked up and found Spice's eyes. "I want to let you know," she said, extending her outstretched hand to Spice's aisle, "that you saved me. I thank you, my friend, for saving my life."

Spice was crying as everyone around her began to applaud.

"After my parents died, I went home to Midnight and did some digging into my family history. That's when I discovered that the woman I thought was my mother was really my grandmother. And that my mother was really my older sister, who was so fractured by the rape by my father, she killed herself.

"I'd like to conclude by saying that any of you men out there who are abusing your children, stop. Please stop. A child shouldn't have to suffer such a shameful sin, such an invasion of their privacy, and carry this burden and shame for the rest of their lives. Some never get over it, like my mother." She paused. "Some die."

A man in the audience broke down crying.

"Please, know that your children are worth loving, worth saving, and worth treasuring for just what they are—children seeking the love and respect of their parents. Help them, love them, save them."

When Carmen stepped down from the stage, Spice met her in the aisle with a handful of tissues in her hand. Together, the two women walked shoulder to shoulder out the door. There were no words necessary between the two friends. Understanding and love was what they shared, and it was all that mattered.

SPICE

*She was nurturing within her what had gone before and would
come after. This child would tie her to that past and future as in-
extricably as it was now tied to her every heartbeat.*

—GLORIA NAYLOR

---

*W*hen Pastor Taylor said, "I now pronounce you man and
wife," Spice felt as though her feet were not attached to the
ground. It was as if in this one instant, all the tendrils of her
life—both light and dark—had come together. And when
Golden took her in his arms and kissed her, she felt as if she were
floating up to heaven.

Could she know such happiness? Was this moment real?

At first, Spice had wanted to invite Sterling, Mink, Dwight,
Carmen, and Otis to their private ceremony. But with so much
going on in everyone's lives, she decided to invite only Carmen.
She looked over at her best friend and smiled. Dressed in a

turquoise blue silk shirtwaist with violet piping and violet shoes, with her face and figure filling out, Carmen looked terrific. She looked as radiant as the bride, Spice thought. And Carmen's expression told Spice how she shared her happiness. It was true: only Carmen could fully appreciate Spice's road to this place.

Ever since attending the AA meeting with Carmen, Spice had felt a new source of strength in their friendship, as if Carmen, too, were a vehicle to release her own pain. Their shared history strung them together—only Carmen knew Spice then, and only Spice knew Carmen. And to see the misery gone from Carmen's face made Spice rejoice.

For almost two months, since the crash landing of Flight 2408, Mink had been kept in the hospital. Physically she was recovered, but she struggled with a deep depression. Her doctors felt that, given her fragile state, she might be a danger to herself. The psychiatrist had no idea when Mink would come out of it—every case was different. Spice had consulted with him about her upcoming marriage. The doctor had suggested that she go on with her life. Mink was in good hands.

As for Sterling, all Spice knew was that she was pregnant. Sterling still wouldn't return her calls. Spice had to assume and believe that maybe this—the coming birth of her own child— would finally bring Sterling some peace so that she could have a fuller, more directed life.

Otis was different. Spice knew he would be too angry or embarrassed to attend her wedding.

Now Spice and Golden were on their way to Mackinac island. There was a thirty-minute layover in Chicago before their flight continued on to the small town of Pellston on the island. While the newlyweds waited, Golden went over their travel plans. But it was clear that the main item on both their minds now was their private time together tonight.

September was coming, and the unfolding of autumn's living

sculpture of vibrant greens, reds, golds, browns, and purples as the temperature dropped was fast approaching. This was why Spice had wanted a fall wedding. Fall was her favorite season.

She read the paper while Golden left to call his office. An eerie feeling clouded over her heart when she read about a young woman's death. The headline read "Ex-Boyfriend Charged with Slaying His Girlfriend." The young woman, thirty, was stabbed and shot after the killer removed a live, full-term fetus from her womb. The newborn was in the hospital and in good condition. Relatives were caring for the baby, whom they had named Noah.

Spice thought of Sterling and Bennie. Even though this was an unrelated incident, it made her worry about her daughter, and she went to the phone to try calling her again.

The telephone rang, but no one answered. Carmen's voice rang in her ears: *Without a mother's love, who will protect our children? How will our children heal? Who will cry for the children? Who will hear them cry? Who will love the child?*

Tears fell from Spice's eyes as she hung up the telephone.

Spice had assumed that Sterling's silence was a way of holding out for the ultimate drama that she loved to create. But what if she were wrong? With another grandchild due soon, Spice decided that when she returned from her honeymoon, she would make amends with her baby daughter and get the family functioning as the strong force she knew it could be.

For now, though, she tried to let go of her worries about her family. She supposed that part of being a mother was learning to allow her children to tend to their own troubles. Spice drew in an enormous breath and imagined her wedding night with Golden. Life was going to be good to her after all.

The Westbrooks had reservations at the Grand Hotel on Mackinac but declined the honeymoon celebration package. They'd made plans to charter a fishing boat, go horseback riding, attend some of the nightly hayrides, and check out the historical sight-seeing, and Golden had brought plenty of videocassettes to film their entire honeymoon on the historical island.

But as soon as Golden and Spice arrived, thunderclouds circled the sky above the small island. Trickles of light rain touched them as they hurried inside the hotel. It was just after twelve in the afternoon, and already the sky was beginning to turn a soft gray, the color of infinity and eternity.

After their luggage was set inside the door and Golden gave the young man his tip, Golden dutifully carried Spice across the threshold of their suite, kicking the door shut behind them.

Spice felt a little scared. She wasn't sure if Golden expected to make love now or later. She felt awkward for a moment, wondering about the correct thing to do, but Golden quickly took control of the situation.

"Spice, I'd love to take you in my arms, and love you for a while."

Thank God! Spice thought, and she answered him with a kiss.

Golden closed the drapes, and when he did Spice turned on the lamps on the nightstand, rolled back the covering, and sat on the bed, waiting for her husband.

He removed his suit jacket and draped it over the sofa, then unbuttoned his shirt. Sitting beside her, Golden cradled her in his arms and hugged her tenderly. He sensed that Spice was nervous. "Relax." He tipped her chin up and pulled her toward him. "You don't have to be afraid of me. I told you, I'm just a man. And now you're my wife, and I want to show you how much I can love you."

Spice took a deep breath. "Golden, I love you, too. I want to make sure that I—"

"Please me."

Spice blushed.

"We talked about this before, remember?"

"Yeah."

ONE BETTER

He gathered her in his arms again. "Do you know how long I've fought these feelings?" He kissed her deeply on the mouth. "I've wanted you so badly, I ached all over. But I'm honor bound by my religion. From the moment we first met, my desire for you was so strong, my soul was tormented nightly. The love I felt for you deepened along with my desires. Marriage—which made the inevitable inevitable—was the only answer."

Spice smiled now as she listened to him tell her how beautiful she was, how just being near her made his skin tingle. He told her how he remembered the first time they met; what the weather was like, how the light shone on her lovely face, the dress she wore, the scent of her perfume, and the smile on her face that was meant just for him.

No other words were needed when he touched her face and kissed her full on the mouth. His hands outlined the swell of her breasts, and Spice was shocked and aroused by the new sensation.

Spice kissed him now, freely, without holding back. "Wait," she said, and stood before her lover. She undressed slowly down to her garter and nylons and watched his eyes taking in the voluptuous curves of her body. The smile she felt inside was nothing short of rapture. She hadn't felt this much like a woman in years. She felt sexy, desired, and the lust she saw in Golden's eyes fueled her into showing him so.

As Golden undressed, Spice helped him, telling him how she loved the scent of his skin. In turn, he told her how beautiful her body was, and he touched her here, and kissed her there, and they fell into bed.

Spice lay on her back and reached for the man she loved. The ecstatic joy expressed on his face when he sank deeply within her was well worth the wait. Their bodies locked in blissful harmony, blending, adjusting, and blending once again. They were synchronized and moved as one, riding the crest of ultimate passion until they were spent.

When he entered her again, her body was languid, floating, like the rippling sound of the lake outside. The sweat on their bodies fell like dewdrops upon their skin, which quivered gently and tingled until the beads of water rolled down, down, stopping at the tips of their toes. They moved, rotated, and pushed, sending the beads of sweat back upward on another journey, making love until both were exhausted.

While Golden caught his breath, Spice reached into her suitcase and brought a small bag to the bed. It was full of fresh mint from her garden. The sweet perfume was overpowering. She broke off a piece, crushed the leaves in her hand, and rubbed it over her cheek and mouth, relishing the cool taste of mint on her lips; then she pressed the crushed leaves on her bare breasts.

When they came together again, colors, sounds, and the moment opened up as if they were Adam and Eve in a rain forest. There was nothing to prove, no one to be better than the two of them.

They slept, locked in bliss.

The next morning, a storm was brewing outside. The terrifying beauty of cerulean blue and iridescent silver phantom bursts of waves slashed and crashed with a fortissimo of percussion that awakened the honeymoon couple.

Spice looked out at the storm and felt a bad vibe deep inside. Something was wrong. She got out of bed while Golden was still dozing. She tried to shake the bad feelings by taking a shower. The rush of water on her body felt invigorating, causing her to think back on the last conversation she'd had with Carmen before leaving for her honeymoon. Spice smiled to herself as she dried off, remembering.

"I remember when I was a petite size seven. I'm not small anymore," Spice had said, turning away from the mirror.

"Last time I checked, men weren't concerned about how small their women were, because they all knew one size fits all."

"You devil, you," Spice had teased, looping an arm through

Carmen's as they'd left the bedroom and walked down the hallway to the living room.

"Got any gray hairs down there yet?" Carmen had queried.

"A few. How about you?"

"Loaded with them. But I think it's cute."

"I can't seem to picture me and Golden together yet—I mean sexually, that is."

Carmen had been silent for a moment. "Why can't you see Golden as a man? As your lover?"

"Golden taught me about my salvation, my redemption. Even though I know he's a man first, my mind won't give up the glorified vision I have of him as a preacher. Yet there is also the special bond that we've shared, a chemistry that was instantaneous."

"You're telling me that it was love at first sight?"

"Yeah."

"I don't believe in that bullshit."

"And I never believed in it, either, until it happened to me." Spice had sucked in her stomach and held it. "Do you think Golden will think I'm too old?" she had added nervously.

"Do you?"

"I'm still not comfortable with him yet. How will he feel when I'm fifty and he's forty-two?"

"You ain't got nothing to worry about. One thing about a woman's vagina is that it don't wrinkle."

"They don't?"

"I ain't seen a wrinkled one yet."

Spice hoped that Carmen would move home soon and take her old job back. But she would be patient—as long as it took for her friend to feel and be independent. Her job and apartment would be waiting.

Smiling now as she slipped on her dress, she heard Golden shifting, awakening in their bed. It was a new experience between them, something that she'd have to get used to. A sound she knew she would always want to hear.

Spice lifted her eyes, feeling Golden once again watching her. She rose and felt the silky silver ribbons from her whisper-thin garter caress her naked thighs under her long black dress. With every step she felt her power building. Their eyes met. She captivated him—they both knew it.

And Spice remembered the conversation they'd had eight days earlier. They had been discussing trust. He was overwhelmed when she told him that it was difficult for her to trust anybody. With all that was happening now, Spice wanted to confide in her husband the last secret. She wanted to trust him, but still she held back.

Golden had told her, "I trust those who trust me. More important, I trust those who have no faith in me because what I give, I receive twofold."

"I don't have any idea how I can learn to trust again," Spice had said.

His answer was simple. "Like a child."

Imagine a young woman afraid of love for most of her life. Imagine a woman who never knew where she came from—who had just now, for the first time, discovered faith, learned its strength, and experienced for a second time what it felt like to be in love—yet still needing to hold back. Restraints created in the past tainted her present. She had to break out of them; perhaps Golden's love would free her.

Later, after the newlyweds had dressed and gone downstairs to the dining room, Spice told Golden of her feelings about something being wrong at home. He volunteered to call for her. He assured her that her hysteria wasn't warranted, even though the storm had revved up since the early morning.

So she sat now alone at the table in the near vacant dining room of the Grand Hotel and witnessed the storm in two dimensions: surrounded by mirrored columns in a room whose walls were windows, she looked out on destruction.

While she waited for Golden, Spice could hear electric wires whipping against the hotel's exterior and witnessed high-voltage wires spewing from downed power lines. Winds had forced the wires to become dangerous dangling strings at the mercy of the elements. A generator temporarily provided power. Couples had dispersed themselves throughout the airy hall, seated at candlelit tables, watching in awe the spectacular show outside. As the couples chatted, beads of molten wax trickled down the sides of their candles like slowly rolling tears. The great hall was filled with the candles' wild-cherry scent.

Turning up the volume on the radio public address speakers, the hotel manager said, "Excuse me, ladies and gentlemen. Your attention, please . . ."

The voice reported, "Just one hour ago, a young girl, between the ages of fifteen and eighteen, went unnoticed by the police and was killed by the sheer power of the winds while attempting to cross the Mackinac Bridge. With wind gusts producing ten-foot waves along the coast, the Coast Guard has issued a warning to remain inside until the storm passes."

Spice turned to find a bellman handing her a fax. She read it just as Golden returned:

"Mink relapsing in hospital. Asking for you. Come home as soon as you can. Dwight."

In temporary shock, Spice was unable to speak. Then she said anxiously, "Mink was okay when I left. The doctor told me not to worry. I have to get home."

Golden went directly to the phone and started making calls.

Twenty minutes later, her nerves on edge, Spice slipped an arm around her husband's shoulder and felt the warmth of his cheek touching her. Then she asked hesitantly, "Still no luck?"

"Not yet," he whispered, covering the mouthpiece. "Trust

me. I'll get us off this island. Don't worry, I'm praying that Mink is okay." He went on calling.

From across the room, Spice watched Golden at the bank of telephones. Sensing her, he looked up, and for a split second their eyes met. They smiled in unison, but just as he turned away, she saw the defeat in his eyes. There was no way they could leave the island—they were trapped.

After several hours on the phone, Golden finally reached someone back in Detroit who would risk the flight to come get them. Spice was relieved but frightened. "Is it too dangerous, Golden?"

"I'm not going to mislead you, Spice, but as I see it, we need to go. This storm could last several days. I know this man—he's an excellent pilot. We'll be in good hands."

Spice thought back to the joy of the night before the puzzling intuition had come. She knew she could trust those vibes in the pit of her stomach. She half smiled. She could just imagine her daughters teasing her about being psychic.

Two hours later, as they flew over the depths of Lake Michigan, Spice felt as if someone were speaking to her, warning her of her imminent suffering, one heartbeat at a time. So she tried to focus on the memory of last night, when she'd heard the thunder the first time and seen Golden's body loving hers, that felt like, that began like, that sounded like . . . music.

When Spice and Golden arrived in Detroit, they went directly to Chamberlain Hospital to see her daughter. Mink was so doped up with medication, she couldn't speak. Her psychopharmacologist told Spice that they'd begun reducing Mink's dosages, but that had caused her to relapse. Mink's psychiatrist was also present. He said little. Spice could tell the doctors were holding back on her.

"What happened?" she asked.

"Well, she tried to hurt herself."

312

ONE BETTER

Spice felt her heart sink. Her daughter's pain was unimaginable. How could she be so helpless?

"She stopped swallowing medication, which of course is why she relapsed. An orderly luckily found the stash of pills when he was cleaning up."

"Oh, my God," Spice cried.

She tried to be patient as the doctor assured her that the trauma of the plane crash, coupled with her upcoming divorce from her husband, was more devastating to Mink's mind than anyone had expected.

Spice left an hour later, moving numbly to her car. How could a woman as strong as Mink suddenly break? The doctors were wrong. Mink's problems went deeper.

The doctors told Spice that Mink was experiencing a sense of personal inadequacy, disillusionment, and depression. Spice knew her daughter's pain about the divorce must be ripping her apart. If Mink only knew that Dwight had never really left her. What was it Carmen had said in that long-ago meeting? *Through suffering we learn wisdom. . . .* If only that were true for Mink.

Dwight was there from day one after the crash. He'd taken a leave of absence from work and moved back home. The custody issue was a moot point at the moment. He brought Azure home and got his house in order. Erma was back. Without saying so, Dwight showed that he had no intention of complying with Mink's suit for divorce.

Spice had always thought of Dwight as the son she'd never had, and he proved it now. Without his dedication to their marriage, his love for Mink, Spice wouldn't have been able to rest, knowing that her child was experiencing so much pain. So, having felt that she'd done all she could for Mink, she left her daughter in Dwight's capable hands.

But she had another daughter to deal with.

The following day, she called Sterling.

313

"Hi," she said as if nothing were wrong between them. "I was wondering if you needed anything. Maybe I should come over."

"I'm fine, Spice, really."

Spice guessed that Sterling was roughly thirty weeks along in her pregnancy. "How are you feeling? Keeping healthy?"

"Don't start in, Spice."

Spice decided to take another tack. "I've spoken to your aunt Carmen. I thought maybe if it was okay with you, Carmen could come and check on you sometime?"

"What's the matter, you too busy?" There was a pause in the conversation. "I'm sorry, Mother, I'm cranky."

She called me Mother! Spice's eyes filled. "Hey, baby, I've been pregnant. It's those catty hormones. So, it's okay?"

"Carmen?" Sterling paused. "Yeah, that'll be fine. So how come you're home early? How was the wedding and the honeymoon?"

Spice was careful not to make too much of her happiness with Golden. "Everything went well until Mink relapsed. We came home immediately."

"Mink relapsed? What happened? Is she going to be okay?"

Spice was surprised by the real emotion in her daughter's voice. "Would it be too much to ask you to go and see her?" she asked.

"I have. She doesn't want to see me. I don't want to lose this baby, Spice. I feel if I take on Mink's problems, I won't be able to cope with my own. After all, Mink has Dwight. Bennie, as you had warned me, doesn't give a damn about this baby."

"I understand."

"I've sent cards to Mink. To Dwight and Azure. It's a little late in the season for forgiveness, but I'm hoping they'll understand. This baby means everything to me, Spice. No way I want to lose it."

So Spice went back to work. She began concentrating her energy on the grand opening of the Foxphasia project. Months before, she had planned the gala black tie affair set for a week from today. She knew that her reliable staff had followed through on every last detail of the celebration.

After the two investors signed on, Spice changed the name from Royal Oak Southern Spice to the Southern Spice Royale because one of the new partners had requested it. The grand opening was planned for two thousand guests. Although the doors of the hotel and restaurant didn't officially open until Friday, the $100-a-ticket, black tie affair was sold out in early September.

The decor of the sister Southern Spice was a mix of French and African styles. With the help of a renowned interior designer in West Bloomfield, Spice had chosen only top-grade fabrics, carpets, and furnishings in chocolate browns, copper, rich golds, and iridescent white. Now she watched as the guests, wandering about munching on salmon Wellington and sipping miniature bottles of Chandon champagne through curly colored straws, commented on the elaborately detailed Goli dance masks, the just discovered reproduction pieces of African art by Picasso and Matisse, and the Kongo and Chowke figures that were carefully arranged on walls and pedestals throughout the three-hundred-seat facility.

The guests were all her regulars—the wealthy, the politicos, the entertainers. It was obvious, by their intense interest, that some would leave under the spell of African art.

Wearing a Chinese white silk shantung evening gown by Bill Blass that clung to her every curve, she, not her restaurant, was the topic of conversation. Spice seemed out of step, not her usual gracious and graceful self. It wasn't like her to let her nerves show in this way, but she was married, and unescorted. Everyone knew the unasked question: Where was her new husband?

And it was a good question. Without either her daughters or her husband by her side, Spice felt vacant. The occasion on its own didn't mean as much as it would have in the past. Nowa-days her priorities seemed to be shifting.

Ever since she and Golden had returned from their honey-moon, the only time they'd spent together was at night. Golden for the most part had been unavailable. His numerous develop-ment projects were taking precedence above anything else. In order to fulfill his duties as a pastor and balance his personal proj-ects, he had to work sixteen-hour days. She shouldn't have been surprised. Golden had told her before they married how much his businesses meant to him. But with Mink ill and the stress of her own projects, she was needy. She found herself grasping for his attention, and frequently he wasn't there.

Spice had moved temporarily into Golden's house. She'd agreed to do it so he could be closer to his first love—Divinity Baptist. Golden owned five acres of prime riverfront property, surrounded on three sides by the Detroit River. In eleven months, their new home would be built there, although Spice always planned to keep her apartment above the restaurant.

Sex was great, but that wasn't enough. She wanted Golden by her side tonight, and he wasn't there. She poured herself another glass of champagne. How many did that make? She'd lost count.

After making a wonderful speech and complimenting both her partners and other members of the project on a job well done, she headed once again for the champagne. She felt herself weaving as she mingled with her guests.

"Let's go, Spice." Suddenly Otis was by her side, taking her by the arm and leading her away from the couple she was talk-ing to. "You've had too much to drink. I'll take you home."

Spice snatched her arm away. "No," she said, stomping her foot like a child. As she turned around, she found herself sud-denly facing Golden. Her immediate thought was, Well, it's too damned late.

"It's a lovely party, Spice. I'm sorry I'm late."

ONE BETTER

"You should have been here earlier, Golden. The best part is over."

"You knew I had church business to attend to. It couldn't be helped," Golden said, ignoring Otis.

Spice was hurt. "I'm the guest speaker at another party in Birmingham." She tapped a finger on his chest. "I thought you weren't going to make it. I've asked Otis to escort me."

"I'll take her," Golden said to Otis, fuming.

After Spice made excuses to both men to get her fur coat, Otis spoke up. "Don't fuck with my family, Golden. You'll find you'll lose every time." And when Spice moved toward them, he grabbed her arm and pulled her with him to the door.

Once in the limousine, Spice began to sob into her hands. Otis rubbed her back as she said, "I just can't take it. Everything is falling apart. I just don't know what it all means anymore."

"Let me take care of you, Spice. You know I love you."

Spice pushed open the door. She had to find Golden. Just then she saw him pull away in his car.

Momentarily defeated, Spice climbed into the car and rested her head against the backseat in exhaustion. Then she looked at Otis and said, "Otis, I love Golden. I wouldn't have married him if I didn't. I've just had a few really difficult weeks."

"I'll back off then. Truly, Spice, I'm trying real hard to understand why."

They sat next to one another in silence, Otis respecting Spice's pain.

OTIS

*The smallest children are nearest to God, as the smallest planets
are nearest the sun.*

—JEAN PAUL RICHTER

_I_t burned to the ground last night."

"What!"

Otis's boss, Sandra Hunt, rose and sat at the edge of her desk.
"Two lives were lost—a twenty-one-year-old student painter,
who was putting in extra hours for the finishing touches on the
interior—and Travis Foxx. They both died from smoke inhalation."

"Foxx?" Otis began to sweat. He shifted in his seat, knowing
somehow that this was the third sign of his condemnation. He
kept silent, waiting.

"Weren't you supposed to inspect the electrical specs on that
property?"

"Um-hm. I did. Everything was up to code."

Sandra slid off the desk and moved around behind Otis. "Not exactly. We're told that department officials suspect that it was an electrical fire, and substandard components were used."

"That's bullshit, Sandra! You know—"

"Look, you're a good employee, Otis. I'm behind you in this. But I want to prepare you for the inevitable. When a life is lost, there's always an investigation. Our department has never gone through one. I hope, for your sake, that this one will prove unwarranted."

"I don't understand how this could have happened."

"I'm sure you noticed the activity in the office this morning. They're pulling the plans for the Foxx building and checking what happened between the time the building permit was issued and our department's numerous inspections on the site. Also—"

"They will want to speak with the person who made the final electrical inspection."

Fuck! Fuck! Fuck! Otis wanted to scream out loud.

"If anything is found to be questionable about a city employee's performance, criminal charges can be brought against him or her and the department. As you know, wrongful conduct by a public official is punishable by prosecution and termination of employment."

As soon as Otis had walked into his office earlier that morning, he had sensed something was wrong. At just past seven on Monday morning, the office was unusually full of employees hard at work, talking animatedly to one another. Their averted eyes had given them away. That had been the first sign.

With a scalding hot cup of coffee in his hand, he'd ignored the whispers behind his back and gone into his office. Before he could hang up his coat, the telephone had begun to ring. The second sign.

"Hello," Otis had said hesitantly.

ONE BETTER

"Otis, I need to see you in my office as soon as possible," Sandra had said, hanging up before waiting for a reply.

Calmly removing the previous day's reports from his briefcase, he'd canvased his mind about the probable cause for a meeting with his boss this early in the day. No way, he'd thought, could she know about the kickbacks. Moving through the maze of hallways that led to Sandra's office, Otis had flexed back his shoulders before knocking on her door.

"Come in, Otis."

"Morning, Sandra," he'd said, taking a seat.

"Otis." She'd looked up from her desk, pushing her glasses down to the tip of her nose. "I don't know if you've heard, but the office is under investigation."

"What for?" Otis had eased back in the chair, uncomfortable but not showing it.

"Are you familiar with the establishment on Grand Circus Park, known as Foxx's Fancy Foodplace?"

And then she had told him the bad news.

It couldn't be. Termination of employment. Prosecution! He had less than two years before retirement. How could he cover his tracks? Everyone would rat him out. Why hadn't he seen this coming? Could he be responsible for the deaths of two people?

He thought about the night before, sitting next to Spice in the limousine. How could he face her? His life seemed over.

Otis left the office in a hurry, sprinted to the underground parking lot, and steered his Cadillac toward I-75. Before he knew it, he was sitting outside Spice's restaurant. He'd never been in this position before, never had to ask for help.

Spice wasn't in her office. It was still early. Was she home or at Golden's? He'd completely forgotten she'd said that she was moving to Golden's place once they were married.

Moving like an automaton, Otis got behind the wheel of his car and drove out to Golden's house. He noticed that Golden's car was gone, but that Spice's was still in the circular driveway.

321

He rang the doorbell, and then there was Spice, standing in front of him.

"Otis, last night was a mistake. I told you—"

"No, Spice, it's not about last night. It's, it's . . ."

"What, Otis? What's happened? Is it Sterling?"

"No. It's me. Travis's restaurant burned to the ground."

"Oh, my God."

"That's not the worst of it." Otis paused. "It burned to the ground because I let him get away without proper safety precautions."

"Did anyone get hurt?"

"Yes. A young painter, and . . ." He hesitated. "Travis Foxx."

"Oh, my God," Spice said, covering her mouth with her hand.

"There's going to be a major investigation. And, well, I don't know if you're aware of this, but I have a few enemies. Some people might hold me responsible."

"Otis, why don't you come in. Let's talk about this inside." Spice led him into the kitchen, which was bright and sunny, the autumn colors glowing in the plush brown woods of the kitchen.

"Start from the beginning, Otis."

He told Spice everything—about the kickbacks, the inspections, the contrived stop work orders. He even told her how he had tried to sabotage Golden's Renaissance project.

"You will hate me when I tell you this—"

"What? That you were Travis's silent partner?"

"You knew?"

"I guessed." Spice was silent for a moment. "But wasn't Travis aware that you were skimping on the inspections?"

"Sure, that was the whole point."

"Well, then you can't take on the entire blame for the fire. Travis was also responsible. It was his restaurant."

ONE BETTER

"I guess." Otis let his head fall into the palm of his large hand.

"Otis, but how did all this get so out of control? Why did you do it?"

"I'm not sure anymore. It was the money at first; then the power. But when it comes to Golden . . ." Otis paused and looked at Spice. "Well, that was about you. You can guess the rest."

"Do you have enough money for a good lawyer?"

"Some. But I've wasted so much money. Spice, I don't want to do jail time."

Otis turned away from Spice. He was ashamed to look her in the eye.

Spice patted her brother-in-law on the shoulder. "If Golden and I can do anything to help, please let us know."

"Why would you help me after all I've done?"

"You're family, Otis. You'll always be family."

STERLING

You cannot teach a child to take care of himself unless you will let him try to take care of himself. He will make mistakes; and out of these mistakes will come his wisdom.
—HENRY WARD BEECHER

———————

Sterling hadn't heard from Bennie for almost three months, ever since the day in the hospital. Sterling understood that it wasn't just the sex that she loved and missed about Bennie. She knew that even when the physical allure was gone, she would still be fascinated by him. She was sure that her lover wasn't even aware of his own mystique, his expressions, his intelligence. There was a fire, a yearning, that was constantly burning in his eyes. She wanted those eyes to look upon her now. She wanted to feel his arms caressing her now.

Sterling massaged her stomach. Her body was like a piano, as happiness was to music—she needed to have the instrument in

good working order. Her miracle of life was becoming more evident. Soon she'd have a child in her arms. Nothing on this
earth, she thought, could be better.

Part of her couldn't really believe that he'd forsaken her; part
of her believed it. She thought of all the warnings she'd had
about Bennie, then her mind went to Spice.

Some of her anger at her mother was waning, but Sterling
wanted to prove to Spice that she really could be independent,
that she could and would care for her child without her mother's
help.

But Sterling's checkbook revealed she was down to her last
$200—$220, to be exact. What was she going to do? She was
almost seven months pregnant and she had no cash. No one
would hire her like this. What was she to do?

As the thought entered her mind, she tried to brush it aside.
Could she do just one more drug run? Fast, easy cash? Enough
to get her through for a while?

But she didn't want to call Bennie. She decided to call Horacio, her backup supplier.

"Hey, Horacio, it's Sterling."

"Hey, Sterling, how's it going?"

"Okay, I guess. Listen, I need some work, if you know what I
mean."

"I thought you quit."

"I quit doing the stuff, but frankly, I need the money."

"Does Bennie know?"

"What does this have to do with Bennie?"

"Everyone knows about you and Bennie, Sterling, it's no secret."

"Bennie and I are history. Now, are you going to help me out
or not? You've got to get your dope from somewhere, Horacio."

"Watch what you say, where you say it, girl." He paused.
"Now let me think. I may be able to put something together for
you. But you've got to be willing to travel."

ONE BETTER

"I like to travel."

"I'll call you tomorrow. Be available."

When they hung up, Sterling experienced the first heroin craving she'd had in a while. She knew it was because she was scared.

By the next afternoon, Sterling was on her way to Texas and then Mexico. On this trip she'd be hauling a half million in cash. The exchange was almost identical to the one Bennie had had her do the last time. This would be easy. She was barely nervous. Her take, when the deal was over, would be ten thousand—better than she'd thought.

It was hot, scorching hot. The temperature had topped a hundred for the fifth day in a row, unusual for late September in Michigan.

In a strange way, Sterling felt relieved to be putting things together on her own—even the run. This child was her motivation in life. No way could Bennie love this child the way she could—too much had happened. And how could she ever trust him? Rely on him? It was better this way.

After Sterling landed at the Houston airport and took the shuttle to the rental car agency, she retrieved the keys and paperwork, put the duffel bag with a half million dollars in cash in the trunk, and steered her car through Texas.

She drove to a house twenty miles over the Mexican border and waited in the designated parking lot. Minutes later she was shocked to find that the red rental car, scheduled to meet her, was empty.

As she approached the car, the smell of gasoline was strong. She looked in the open trunk and found nothing. There were no drugs. She searched under every piece of carpeting in the trunk—still nothing. Snapping the trunk shut, she saw the shadow of something inside the car.

Very slowly she approached the driver's side. The door was shut, but the window was down. Then she saw it.

In the backseat a body was covered with a heavy, old blanket. One perfect hand was dangling out of the blanket—a hand she recognized immediately.

Sterling turned and ran blindly, driving her car through Mexico, back into Texas, and then north toward Michigan. She could smell the repulsive scent of burning flesh miles away from the victim—Bennie.

She stopped for gas and snack food. She used the rest rooms and kept driving.

She kept pushing Bennie's burned body out of her mind.

Having nowhere else to turn, she drove straight to Horacio's house.

"What the fuck are you doing here, Sterling?"

"Bennie's dead."

"You don't think I know that? Get the hell out of here. The cops are going to be all over me."

"How did you know that Bennie was dead?" Sterling was shocked.

"It's a small world, girl." Then Horacio laughed. "I used to work for Bennie, don't you get it?"

Sterling got it. She was looking at Bennie's murderer. She remembered Bennie telling her that he didn't trust anyone. Now she knew why. "Did . . . did Bennie know I was going to Mexico?"

"Yeah. He found out—that's why he went down there."

"What do you mean?"

"He must have got the word that something bad was gonna happen." Horacio laughed again, and Sterling realized Bennie had tried to stop her from getting mixed up with Horacio, who was clearly crazy. And he'd died for his efforts.

Horacio began looking outside, to the left and right of his

door. "Now, you gotta go, Sterling. But where's the money I gave you? I need the fucking money."

The money? Sterling had forgotten about the five hundred thousand buried in her trunk. *Think fast, Sterling, think fast.* "It's . . . it's in the car." Sterling was terrified.

"Get me the fuckin' money now! I've got to get out of here."

Sterling was frozen with fear, talking to the madman who had killed her lover. All she could think of to say was, "Can't I get a hit? Just one? Please?"

Horacio gave her a hard look and then laughed. "You're pathetic," he said, and retreated into the apartment. Sterling followed him. He handed her a bag of heroin.

Drugs brought her life back into focus. Soon she was as high as heaven itself.

Horacio looked at her. "Now go get me the money from the car and stay clear of here."

Sterling nodded in reply and walked out to her car. Dust covered the rental car, and she imagined she looked just as bad. She held on to her little white bag and kept walking. When she reached the car, she fumbled in her bag for her keys. Her hands were shaking badly. She was feeling faint. She wanted another hit, but she couldn't do it in broad daylight. She sat on the edge of the curb and tried to pull her keys out of her bag.

Just then she heard a car pull up. She looked across the street as two men walked quickly toward Horacio's door. They didn't knock. They just barged through. She heard two shots.

She was already behind the wheel of her car and driving away.

Sterling stayed in her condo for a solid week. She didn't answer her phone. She didn't make any calls. She finished the last of the heroin and fell into a living coma.

Any and every child born into the world deserves all the dignity and respect there is—in short, love, which is not a privilege, but a natural right.

—KEORAPETSE KGOSITSILE

ou're lying!" Mink screamed at Dwight. "You're trying to confuse me again. They're all dead, I know they're all dead—I killed them!"

"Sweetie," Dwight said, sitting beside her on the bed. "No, they're not all dead. You did a wonderful job—you saved lives. If it weren't for you, no one would have survived." He cradled Mink's head in his arms and stroked her forehead.

There was a tap at the door, and Spice came in. Dwight met her at the door.

"How's she doing?" Spice whispered.

Dwight shook his head. "No better." Then he left mother and daughter alone.

Spice looked at her daughter, her afro grown out to a full three inches now. She didn't look like herself. Though Spice and Dwight had tried to get Mink to agree to let the nurses cut it, she wouldn't let them touch it.

Usually, when Spice came in, Mink would turn away from her, sitting on the opposite side of the bed for most of the visit.

"I told you not to come back in here," Mink hissed.

"Baby . . ."

Mink lifted her long legs from the bed and circled Spice's stiff form, then stood in front of her. "Why you looking at me sideways like that?" Mink eased up closer to Spice now, with her head turned to the side. "Why do you flinch when I get next to you?" She was inches away. Her close breath warmed Spice's face. "You think I'm gonna hurt you or something?"

Spice looked uncomfortable. "No," she said steadily. "You don't scare me. It's you who's afraid. If you—"

"Go slow," Mink said, glaring at her, "I can't understand what you're saying." She clamped her hands over her ears. "You're trying to drive me crazy. All of you!" she screamed. Her eyes widened as she spoke in high whispers. "I won't listen to you. I won't listen to any of you."

Spice sat at the edge of the bed, weeping. Then Golden was in the doorway. He looked at Spice and said, "Can I come in?"

"Who's that?" Mink asked angrily. "A john? Like my father?"

Spice gasped.

"Your mother loves you, Mink, no matter what. No matter what she's done, who she's been." Golden approached Spice and put his large hand on her back.

"Mink? Baby?" Spice tried again, reaching out for her daughter's hand.

Mink looked into her mother's eyes. She felt afraid.

"I'm here, sweetheart. You're going to be fine, baby. Just fine."

Suddenly, at the top of her lungs, Mink screamed and lunged at Spice, pounding her in the chest with both fists.

"Sterling told me that about you! Who's my father, Spice?" Mink stared at Spice, her brown eyes bold in confrontation. "Tell me the truth," she yelled.

Unable to speak, Spice reached for Golden in tears.

Then Golden said quietly, "Mink, your mother truly loves you. Forgive her trespasses, forgive yours. My prayers are with you both, Mink."

Mink watched her mother and Golden leave her room. The cruelty of what she'd done to her mother made her cry.

Eventually her doctor found the right combination of anti-depressants, which seemed to lift the veil of depression that cloaked Mink. She returned to the world around her, confused but not as damaged.

She and Dwight began to talk about her affair. Mink got in touch with her intense guilt over having slept with Harrison.

"But Dwight, if I hadn't had an affair, I would never have crashed the plane."

"Sweetie, the two are unrelated. You couldn't help the mechanical failure of the plane."

"But it feels that way, that it's all my fault."

"No, it's not. Not even your affair is all your fault. Remember, it always takes two."

"You mean me and Harrison?"

"No, I mean you and me. I am just as much responsible for the disconnection in our marriage as you are." Dwight paused. "Can I tell you something that Golden said to me?"

Mink nodded in reply.

"He said, 'All marriages are imperfect, and probably a disappointment in one way or another. That's reality. Being in love doesn't protect people from lust.' I think he's very wise."

Mink smiled. "Yes, he's very wise." She had thought that because her affair was secretive, it was about dishonesty. It enhanced the thrill of the relationship. The secret sealed the conspiratorial alliance of the affair, making her relationship with Harrison intense, dangerous, and therefore exciting. Dwight had a secret. Why not she?

But Mink saw now that there was no safety in denial, but there was hope in admission. Perhaps now their marriage could be saved and might even be stronger than before the crisis.

"Dwight . . ."

"Don't talk. We've both made mistakes. We love each other. That's all that matters."

"I'm sorry—"

"It doesn't matter. Nothing matters. We've got a child. We've got a future. We can make it work."

"More than my job, more than my life, I love you, Dwight."

"And I love you, sweetie."

"Can you forgive me?" Mink asked.

"Yes. Can you forgive me?" Dwight asked.

"Yes," Mink said, crying. "So much has happened. Will we ever get back to the way we were?"

"Absolutely." Dwight embraced Mink.

Soon Mink was released from the hospital. Her heart was hungry with need. Armed with medication, Mink felt strong enough to return to the tender love of her family. And after all that had transpired, coming home turned out to be wild, wonderful.

Earlier, Mink had tendered her resignation with Pyramid Airlines in writing. Although he hadn't said so, she knew that Dwight wanted her to reconsider leaving the airline. Her decision had been impulsive. She'd known it at the time but couldn't retract her decision—or so she thought.

When she arrived home, there was a registered letter from Pyramid, letting her know they all wished her well and hoped she'd consider coming back to work.

The Jaguar was parked next to the Blazer. Dwight carried Mink's suitcase inside.

"You sure you can handle some rhythm today, baby?" Mink asked her husband.

"Sweetie, we're past rhythm. I'm talking about percussion. It's time I showed you that there's a symphony going on in the Majors' house—and we don't need an audience, or any applause."

Dwight put down her suitcase and carried his wife into the living room.

They were completely alone. Erma was shopping, and Azure was still at school.

He kissed her.

It had been so long. Dwight's lips felt like toasted marshmallows, first soft and hot, then creamy, warmer and sweeter, the longer you kissed them.

Mink rested her head back against the cool marble. "Oh yeah," she said, pulling him toward her.

They made love on the piano. Mink enjoyed the feel of the ivory keys against her buttocks. It was spontaneous on Dwight's part. He undressed her while he played, then lifted her naked body up onto the piano. At first he played a short tune, then subtly he entered her, and they moved in harmony along the surface. The sound, the feel of the cold keys on her bare skin—it was wild, it was fun. They laughed together as Dwight balanced his body and worked the keyboard.

Later, Mink led him upstairs to their bedroom. They undressed in silence and went into the bathroom. Mink and Dwight sat opposite each other in the double Jacuzzi. The gentle rumbling from the jets pulsated around and over their nude bodies. Their eyes met over the rim of the fluted champagne glasses.

"Dwight," Mink said, tracing her toe along the length of his leg, then blushed.

"What is it? Tell me."

"Nothing, really," she said in a half laugh. "I was just thinking about this morning."

"It was good, wasn't it." He paused, then said, "Tell me about flying the plane, Mink. Tell me how you feel when you're up there."

"You've never asked me that before."

"It's time I did."

Mink sipped the champagne and smiled. "The best part is the take-off. When I feel those wheels lifting off the ground, it's a rush." She felt herself getting aroused. "And then when I'm up there and the clouds are just below, it's like visiting heaven. And I think, This is me flying this plane. I'm in control. I can feel the power of the engines starting, and hear the loud purring sound in my ear. My adrenaline is rising, and rising, and I feel so light, so free, so—"

"Sexual."

"Yeah," Mink said softly. She reached out and smoothed her hand over his smooth, wet calves. She could hear her breathing accelerating, and his eyes bored into hers. "Tell me about fighting the fire, Dwight. I want to know how you feel."

"It's a rush, similar to what you feel. The roar of the fire is seductive. You want to tame it, control it, calm it, until it's quenched beneath your feet."

Mink placed her hands between her legs as he spoke, as he described the feelings, and she closed her eyes, and she began to see, to understand the energy that transformed into power, the power that was sexual. She heard him speaking, almost whispering, about the rush of the water, the flames licking him, and the heat between them as he talked was building, building.

She felt him on top of her, sliding, gliding his body into hers. She opened her eyes and felt the taste of his mouth on hers. They moved fluidly, slowly at first, then faster, until Mink felt her body exploding. His body shuddered as he exploded inside of her, and she could feel the contractions of his penis, and the relaxation of his entire body as he surrendered himself to ecstasy. Feeling that singular sensation, Mink knew that Dwight would never belong to her more than he did at that moment.

The short adjustment period they went through before they resumed their lovemaking was eased by their intimate conversations about what they'd missed about each other.

It was so ironic; they talked a lot more now than they ever had before, even while they made love. Usually Dwight would find something funny to laugh about, and make her laugh, as they made love. And this would help to relax them and break some of the tension between them. Their love was growing and building; it was better and stronger than before.

Maybe Dwight was right. Maybe she'd think about going back to work. She'd give the idea some thought in the coming weeks.

Carmen

Save the children! Save the children from dope, miseducation, and
poverty. Save the children from gang warfare and adult abuse.
Save the children from the apathy and indifference and timidity
of their elders.

—JOHN H. JOHNSON

*L*ike the joy of a leaf that unfolds in the sun, Carmen felt a
new warmth in her heart. Ever since she had learned about Sterling's pregnancy, it was as if her life had come together. Each
child born into the world was a new thought of God, Carmen
believed, an ever fresh and radiant possibility.

She'd given notice to the truck stop that she'd be resigning.
She'd taken Spice up on her offer to return to the restaurant as
second chef under Develle. She still felt a bit dizzy at the challenge that lay before her.

Many a night when Carmen wasn't at work at the restaurant,

she'd drive to Sterling's condo. A few times she even went as far as the doorstep. Through the blinds she could see Sterling pacing back and forth. Carmen knew that scene—the baby was kicking. She wanted to knock, to go in, but she had so little to offer. She was afraid to be with Sterling—what would happen if she did the wrong thing? She would reach out her hand again to knock, but she wasn't ready. So she'd leave, defeated.

Until the day came when she was suddenly ready. Eight months sober and more like herself than she had ever been. She tried calling Sterling, but the line was busy for over an hour. When the operator checked there was no one on the line. Without wasting a moment, she sped out to Sterling's apartment. Something was wrong.

On the way, she turned on the radio. There was an update of a story about an infant who had lost her foot to a Rottweiler puppy. When the incident occurred, the court had taken the child away from her parents. During the time that the little girl had been in foster care, she was learning to walk with a prosthesis. Now, four months later, the parents were petitioning the court for custody.

Hasn't the child suffered enough? Carmen thought. The parents don't deserve—Damn! Her thoughts strayed briefly to her own sad childhood.

Soon she arrived at Sterling's condo. Out of breath, she rang the doorbell. No answer. Furiously she pounded on the solid wooden doors. Still no response.

Carmen checked her Timex. It was 11:55 A.M.

With her heart pounding at the pit of her bowels, she walked around the condo to peek inside the bedroom window. She didn't care what the neighbors thought and hoped that they'd call the police. Just then she heard a weakened voice calling out for help.

Peering inside through the opened white miniblinds, Carmen wiped a clear circle with her hand and pressed her face against the window. From the angle of the bed inside, she could vaguely make out a small patch of Sterling's blond hair.

"Sterling!" she shouted, banging on the window. "Sterling, baby!" she said again, pounding on the glass.

Carmen went back around to the front door and spotted a neighbor who was motioning to her.

Thank God.

Suddenly the rain poured down as she made her way to the neighboring condo. The downpour nearly drowned out her words. "The young woman next door has passed out. She's pregnant. Please, can you please call an ambulance and the police?"

Holding back tears, Carmen ran back to Sterling's condo. Her mind and heart racing, she knew that she wouldn't be able to face Spice if something happened to Sterling.

Straining, and with rain running into the stream of her tears, she lifted one of the vases on the front doorstep. Her small body ignored the pain she felt as she heaved the vase and ran forward, plunging it against the glass into the bedroom window. Immediately the alarm system went off.

She kicked a hole large enough to get through and entered the apartment. The foul scent of urine caused her nostrils to flare open. Racing to the bed, she found Sterling, an eerie shade of blue, semiconscious, inches away from the telephone, which was off the hook, lying next to the bed.

Shocked when she saw Sterling's neck and limbs jerking wildly and the opaque white bubbles foaming around her mouth, Carmen dropped to the floor. "Sterling, baby!" she shouted. "What's wrong?"

She cradled Sterling's head in her arms and watched in horror as her eyes rolled up in her head and her tiny body continued to jerk and shake violently in spasmodic convulsions.

Less than five minutes later, the paramedics transferred Sterling into the ambulance and whisked her off to nearby Chamberlain Hospital.

Tears raining inside her soul, Carmen punched in Spice's page number. No response. Where the hell was she? Carmen left message at Spice's home and her apartment, then rushed after the ambulance.

Driving ninety miles an hour, Carmen thought of Sterling when she was first born. Should she die, Sterling would never know the truth—that she was Carmen's baby. The baby born of rape, the baby she hadn't been able to keep.

It was now 12:35 P.M.

Carmen caught up with the ambulance just as they wheeled Sterling into the emergency room. Sterling's eyes opened. Even though she seemed barely conscious, she managed a small smile at Carmen.

"Get the mag!" the emergency room doctor shouted as he quickly assessed Sterling's condition. "Push the mag!" he shouted louder.

Carmen was told by the doctor that he was giving Sterling a dose of magnesium sulfate that would stabilize her seizures without harming the fetus. He explained that Sterling was suffering from pre-eclampsia, or toxemia, which meant that if she did fine, they would give the baby three to four hours to calm down and then proceed with inducing labor or delivering the child by C-section.

While the doctors scheduled a series of tests to determine Sterling's condition and the extent of the injury to the fetus, Carmen kept calling Spice. No answer. She paged her again. Several minutes passed—still no answer. Carmen dialed Mink's home. The machine came on, and she left a message. Carmen was beside herself with worry.

Who else should she call?

Without the doctor having to tell her anything, Carmen knew that Sterling's blatant drug use, coupled with ten years of chain smoking, had compromised her system. The stress she lived under, Carmen surmised, was the icing on this bitter cake.

ONE BETTER

After Sterling's initial examination, the team of doctors informed Carmen that in the past twenty-four hours Sterling had experienced perhaps as many as two hundred seizures. Until the patient was breathing on her own and could confirm their assumption, they couldn't know for sure.

"How long has she had this pre-eclampsia condition?" Carmen asked.

"It's hard to tell. Ms. Witherspoon might not have known. Unless her obstetrician ordered a dip-stick protein check during her checkup, this problem could virtually go undetected."

"So you're saying that Ms. Witherspoon—"

"My assumption is that Ms. Witherspoon experienced periods of high blood pressure, severe headaches, and possibly swelling of the hands and feet lately. It's possible with her continued use of heroin that she failed to factor in the danger of these symptoms to her person and her fetus."

Drugs. Would this be the only commonality that mother and daughter shared? Carmen thought.

Silence.

As they stood just outside Sterling's room, the strident steps of a nurse broke into Carmen's thoughts.

"Doctor, we've intubated the patient, but she isn't responding well to the medication." She handed him Sterling's chart.

Dr. Katbi turned to Carmen after the nurse left. "Ms. Witherspoon's heart rate is at one fifty, which is extremely high. I'm concerned that if we wait too much longer, the fetus won't make it."

Please stop talking. Please stop talking, I can't think. I can't lose my child. Oh, Lord, what am I going to do? I don't understand a word he's saying.

"I don't have any jurisdiction over Ms. Witherspoon. I'm just a family friend," Carmen said. *You're her mother, tell them you're her mother.* Her voice broke as she added, "I don't know how you should proceed—" Her chin touched her chest, with tears closely following. What would Spice do?

"We cannot predict the possibility of another seizure." The grave look on Dr. Katbi's face said that Sterling's chances for recovery were tenuous.

Carmen dialed Spice's home and beeper over and over until her fingers were numb. Then she had another thought. What if Spice called the restaurant? Carmen smacked herself in the forehead with her palm. *Damn!*

The familiar sound of Develle's voice offered a polite "Hello."

"Could you punch me in to Kia's office, please?" Carmen asked, keeping her voice as steady as she could.

"Certainly, I'll connect you now."

"Kia, listen carefully. Sterling is in the hospital—it's serious. Spice isn't at home, and I can't reach her anywhere." Carmen's heart and body ached with an indescribable emptiness. "I've been dialing her pager for the past twenty minutes. She hasn't called back yet."

"Today's Sunday—her day off. Usually she doesn't turn her pager on. Wait. Are you dialing her new number?" Kia rattled it off.

Minutes after Carmen coded in the new pager number, there was a call at the desk for Carmen.

"Carmen," Golden said, "you sound terrible. What's wrong?"

"It's Sterling."

"What's happened?"

"I found her at home, unconscious. She'd had a series of seizures—the doctor—Golden, she's very ill. Where's Spice?"

"At church. She's conducting her first new membership meeting. Don't worry, I'll get word to her."

Five minutes later Spice was on the line. Her voice was shaking as she spoke. "Carmen, if she doesn't make it before I get there, tell her everything."

"Spice—"

"No. Hear me out. Tell her our story. And tell her I love her."

"Spice, she won't die." With tears falling down Carmen's face, her heart tearing in two, she hung up the phone.

Five miles from town, living in an old dilapidated house, Carmen and Spice couldn't afford a phone. The nearest house was a mile and a half away. Both Carmen and Spice were pregnant. The night Spice was ready to deliver, Carmen was drunk and couldn't take Spice to the hospital.

"Ms. Enriquez," the doctor said, walking toward her briskly, "Ms. Witherspoon's had another seizure. We've got to take the baby, now. If there's a choice over the mother or the child's life, we need a decision now from her mother."

"Her mother. Her mother"—Carmen choked back the words—"would want you to save her daughter. Save Sterling, Dr. Katbi. I'll be responsible."

Spice tried to walk the distance to the neighbor's house, and halfway there she passed out on the side of the road. Waking up from a drunken stupor, Carmen spotted the blood and went looking for Spice. When she reached Spice in the cold darkness of February, the baby, between her bloodied legs, was stillborn. Days later, with Carmen's guilt overwhelming her, Carmen and Spice had a conversation.

"I don't want my baby," Carmen said, crying. "When it's born, you can have it."

"No, that's wrong. I can't take your baby."

"It's my father's child. I can't love it. I know you can."

Carmen sat there holding her daughter's hand, waiting for the doctors to take her into the OR.

By the time Carmen's baby was born at home, she'd finally persuaded Spice to care for her daughter. "No one else can love her as much as you can, Spice. I wouldn't trust my baby with anyone but you."

The surgery didn't take long. The doctors delivered the little baby boy by cesarean section. It was two o'clock when they wheeled Sterling into the recovery room, and Carmen went to her side. Sterling was groggy, but her eyes were open.

Carmen gripped her child's hand. "It's a boy, Sterling."

"A boy. That's nice." Her voice was hoarse and her eyes a sunken gray, like the reflections from the visage of an angel.

"The doctor said that you could see him when you woke up. He's beautiful, Sterling."

"Carmen. Where's my mother? Why isn't she here?" Sterling's voice bordered on panic.

"Don't worry, baby. Spice is on her way."

Together, Carmen and Spice went down to Tupelo General Hospital, so the doctors could examine the baby and send off to Jackson, Mississippi, for a copy of the baby's birth certificate. "I'm the mother," Spice said.

"I'm a witness," Carmen added.

Nothing more, in twenty-seven years, was ever said.

A telemetry monitor, tracking Sterling's heart rate, was at the head of the bed. At present, the monitor showed the patient's heart was stable.

Sterling glanced at the numerous plastic tubes taped at her wrist and winced. Carmen could only imagine the pain that Sterling felt. Even though painkillers were being administered through an IV into Sterling's arm, her intense discomfort was still evident. "The doctors say you're going to be fine, Sterling. You and the baby are going to be okay." Carmen wiped the moisture from Sterling's forehead.

The afternoon sunlight streamed in through the windows. From where she stood she could see the red, gold, and green treetops that typified the tints of autumn. How beautiful, she thought. How melancholy.

Outside, the flowers were falling like her hopes, the leaves falling like her years, the clouds fleeting like her illusions, the rivers becoming frozen like her life—all bore secret relations to her destiny.

Carmen turned when she heard fast footsteps coming through the door.

ONE BETTER

"Hey, sis," Mink said as she entered the room with Dwight, trying to appear cheery. Mink hugged Sterling, then kissed her forehead. "How you feeling?"

Overwhelmed with tears, Sterling couldn't answer.

"Spice is going to be here soon. Don't you worry." Mink looked up at Carmen with desperation in her eyes. Carmen looked away.

Sterling's voice was weak. "She's not going to make it in time."

"In time for what, Sterling?"

Sterling looked away, and lopsided tears slid down the corners of her eyes.

"Ms. Enriquez," the nurse said, "there's a telephone call for you."

"Thank you."

Carmen followed the woman to the desk.

It was Golden again. "Is Spice there yet?"

"No—Golden, not yet." She wept silently for a moment and felt Golden's pacific presence. "I forgot to tell you earlier that Sterling is in the intensive care unit at Chamberlain Hospital," she said. "She's just delivered a baby boy. She's in a lot of pain."

"I'll be right there."

"Where's Spice?"

"She left a half hour ago. I'm on my way."

"Please pray for Sterling, Golden. Please. Pray."

When Carmen returned to Sterling's room, the young woman said, "Please don't leave me." Sinking deeper against the pillows, breathless, she scrambled to reach and touch Carmen's hand. "I don't want to be alone. I don't like the darkness . . . the quiet." Her eyes widened with fear.

"I'm right here, baby." Carmen closed her small hand over her child's, fighting back the tears as she watched Sterling struggling for air.

"My head hurts, Aunt Carmen. Oh, my God, my head is killing me." Sterling started to cry.

"I'll get the doctor," Mink said, running from the room.

Dwight turned to look through the glass walls of the intensive care unit at the duty nurse, who was already leaving the desk.

"Nurse," Mink said once they were back in the room, "my sister is in pain."

"That's subjective," she said briskly, leaning over and listening to Sterling's chest with the stethoscope.

Sterling was fighting for air. Fresh beads of perspiration covered her forehead.

Carmen noticed the stale scent of urine again, as it had been in Sterling's apartment. Neither Mink nor Dwight seemed to notice the smell, but Carmen could inhale the sour scent from Sterling's perspiration as well. And she knew then that Sterling might not make it.

The fear on Sterling's face was greater now.

Everyone stepped aside when the doctor entered the room.

Carmen watched Sterling struggling to keep her wits. So like Spice, she thought, putting up a brave front. How funny that she should turn out so like Spice and nothing like me.

"Ladies, sir, can you step outside for a moment?" Dr. Katbi said. He joined them in the hall. "Ms. Witherspoon isn't responding to the medication as we would have liked. I'm sorry. We're doing the best we can. Under the circumstances, with the patient's substance abuse and current condition . . . She's too unstable now to get a CAT scan. I sure hope it's pre-eclampsia, because the mag will eventually fix it. If she's had an aneurysm, the mag sulfate isn't going to help her at all; she could have another seizure." Dr. Katbi glanced at his watch. "I've scheduled a CAT scan at three. If necessary, we'll have her ready for neurosurgery should the test confirm that theory."

Dwight sniffed, then wiped his nose with a handkerchief

from his back pocket. "The baby, I keep forgetting about him. Somehow he doesn't seem real, you know."

Mink shook her head. "I know."

"What's taking Spice so long?" Carmen checked her silver Timex.

Mink looked up at Dwight. "I'm ashamed to say, I don't know how to pray. Anyway, maybe God's not even listening."

Dwight wrapped his arms around both his wife's and Carmen's shoulders.

"If I didn't know better, I'd say that this is payback for all our sins," Carmen said. "But you know what, the Bible says that we 'all have sinned and fall short of the glory of God.' That means that no matter how well we try to disguise our sins, God knows our thoughts, even those we've tried so hard to hide. And even though he hates sin, he loves us."

Neither Dwight nor Mink understood that Carmen was speaking of herself and the ultimate sin of lying to her child.

The three of them returned to Sterling's bedside.

"I didn't believe at first that this was happening to me," Sterling said softly. The curtains were drawn, and even though it was daylight outside, the room was lamplit, and their shadows appeared as ghosts along the wall.

"You should rest, Sterling. Don't talk now." Mink took her hand, rubbing it slowly. "Shhhh."

Though Carmen was closer to Mink and Sterling when they were younger, she couldn't feel more love for either of them than she did at this moment.

Carmen sat on the end of the bed, leaning in toward Sterling. "Take it easy, baby. The doctors are taking good care of you. You're going to be fine."

Sterling flinched. "No, I won't." She blinked several times, trying to control the breathlessness she felt before speaking again. "I've got to face this."

"Sterling," Carmen said. "Don't. I can't—"

349

Carmen, feeling the shivering of Sterling's small body, and knowing that she was suffering a great deal of pain, turned away from her, letting the silent tears fall.

"Listen to me," Sterling pleaded, gasping. She was obviously fighting the pain that made her body convulse in rhythmic waves. "I was jealous of you and Spice, Mink." She grimaced, and her body stiffened, then relaxed. Beads of sweat were more prevalent now, outlining her lips.

Carmen imagined her Timex was ticking loudly. It was 2:45.

Moving forward, Dwight mopped the sweat on Sterling's face with a tissue. "Shhh now." He forced a brave smile.

"Carmen, Carmen," Sterling called out. It was increasingly difficult to hear her.

"I'm right here, baby." Carmen wiped her eyes, then turned to look at her.

"I want you to know that I've never forgotten all the wonderful moments you spent with me and Mink. You taught me how to color when I was six years old. Remember? You always listened when I played a new tune on the piano. And even . . ." She stopped, smiling. "And even when Mink and I were little you used to break up our fights. You even tried to break up the fight we had when we were big girls. Remember?"

"Don't," Carmen whispered through tears.

There was no self-pity in her voice when Sterling asked, "I'm going to heaven, ain't I?"

"Yes," Dwight stated.

Mink wiped away her tears, unable to speak.

"Of course you will," Carmen added. "But not now, honey. You're going to get better. You're coming—"

Sterling stretched out her arm to touch Carmen's arm.

Should I tell her? God knows I want to tell her. Right now! Help me, Lord. It's not fair! Help me help my child.

"I've made a lot of mistakes, but if people really, really knew me, they might not judge me so harshly."

ONE BETTER

Both Mink and Carmen were crying openly now. The look on Sterling's face showed relief. Obviously she needed to bare her soul.

It was then that Carmen knew for sure that Sterling wasn't going to make it. She was struggling to gain understanding and respect on her way out. Carmen could read Sterling's thoughts. "Please listen to me. Please. I've got to let you know." Sterling tugged her bottom lip in with her teeth. She clamped the sides of her head with both hands. The monitor beeped, informing them she had just gotten another severe pain, but Carmen knew with certainty that Sterling felt something else, too. She felt peaceful even through the pain.

Carmen watched the wavy lines on the monitor moving more rapidly now, erratically. She looked up through the windows, pleading with the nurse who was monitoring Sterling from the circular station.

Mink cried soundlessly, turning into Dwight's chest, whispering, "I can't take this."

Dwight signaled Carmen with his eyes. He had to remove his wife from the scene. It was too soon after her own illness. "I love you, sweetie." He kissed Sterling's clenched fist over and over, then, hugging his wife's shivering form, left the room.

"Carmen? I should tell the doctors about my drug use." She strained to speak. "I'm worried about my son. I used so much dope."

"They know, Sterling. Your baby is okay. He came into this world weighing almost five pounds. That's a miracle in itself. Don't worry, he's a fighter just like you. Hush now."

"Carmen? Listen to me. I'm begging you. Adopt my son. We both know Spice can't handle a heroin-addicted baby. It's beyond her. Let me know you'll be his mother."

I should tell her the truth, Carmen thought again.

"Oh, my God. Carmen, where's Spice? Where's my mother? Doesn't she care about me anymore?"

That was the sign that Carmen needed. Sterling wouldn't have to know the story. No matter what Spice said, there could be no words, no amount of tears, to undo years of love from a woman who'd substituted as her mother. It would be wrong to try to correct that now.

"Sterling?"

"It's okay." Sterling pressed the button for the nurse to come in. "Can you help us, please?" With Carmen's help Sterling sat up in bed. When the nurse came in, Sterling asked for a paper and pen.

"What are you doing?" Carmen asked her.

Sterling spoke out loud as she struggled to write: "I, Sterling G. Witherspoon, hereby request that my aunt, Carmen Enriquez, adopt my son, 'Gray Sterling Witherspoon,' previously known as 'Baby Witherspoon.' " Sterling signed her name.

"Spice would want—"

"No. If my son turns out to be addicted to heroin, Spice won't want him. I want you to care for him, Carmen. I know you'll love him like he was your own."

Carmen couldn't have felt more proud. They signed their names, then the nurse brought Mink and Dwight back into the room to witness the paper.

Death is the foreshadowing of life, the life of a newborn child. Carmen knew that, if it weren't for the child, her soul would fall down, right at this tender moment. Without any forewarning, Carmen found herself in the arena where she had to play out the struggle of life versus death.

She was overwhelmed with emotion as Sterling handed her this declaration of love.

"I've got a half million dollars in a safety deposit box. Use it to care for my son," Sterling told her.

"You don't—" Carmen stopped. She didn't care where it came from.

"Stop," Sterling said, smiling. "I want something good to

come from my life. The key is taped under the crystal panther figurine at my house. Take care of him, Carmen. Tell him how much I loved him—how much I wanted him. Tell him he was a miracle. My miracle."

Sterling looked into Carmen's loving brown eyes. "Before, while I was sleeping, I dreamed of peace. It was a beautiful dream of understanding, and I was loved just for me." She paused to catch her breath. "Look, Carmen. Do you see?"

"What, honey? What is it?" Carmen's voice broke. Tears closed her throat and she was unable to speak again.

"On the blinds, through the windows, there's a pattern. A picture."

Carmen looked at the windows, then back to Sterling, questioning. Then she remembered: when she was high, she always used to ask Spice if she could see the pictures, the patterns, that were there. No one could ever see them but Carmen. And now Sterling was seeing patterns of her own.

"I see it, baby." Beyond pain, beyond emotion, Carmen couldn't move; something was coming, and there was nothing she could do to stop it.

As she slipped into unconsciousness, Sterling asked, "Carmen, do you believe in angels?"

Closing her eyes, Carmen felt Dwight's arms around her shoulders. Her eyes fought the tears as she, Mink, and Dwight stared down into Sterling's angelic face. Yes. Carmen certainly believed in angels now.

At 3:00 P.M. Sterling experienced a grand mal seizure and lapsed into a coma. At approximately 3:10 P.M. Sterling Gaye Witherspoon was gone.

SPICE

It always grieves me to contemplate the initiation of children into the ways of life when they are scarcely more than infants. . . . It checks their confidence and simplicity, two of the best qualities that heaven gives them, and demands that they share our sorrows before they are capable of entering into our enjoyments.

—CHARLES DICKENS

---

*G*olden caught up with Spice on the way to the hospital. She had run her car off the road in her fear and hysteria. She wasn't hurt, but it was an isolated section of highway and no one had stopped to help her. Later, she couldn't help but wonder if the hand of God hadn't been involved in her delay in reaching the hospital.

As soon as Golden pulled into the hospital parking lot, Spice jumped out of the car and raced inside. Golden caught up with her and led her to the elevator. When they stepped off on the fifth floor, Spice felt her heart was frozen.

355

Turning, she heard Carmen scream, "Spice!" Right then, at that precise moment, she knew for sure that her baby was gone.

"Where is she!" Spice screamed. "Where is *my* baby?"

Golden was beside her then, covering her crumpling body with his.

"Spice, baby. Hold on, baby." Spice looked at Carmen, and all their secrets, all the pain, all their good intentions, went floating by in an instant. Carmen reached for Spice's hand without saying a word.

"Is she really gone?" Spice asked Dwight. "What about the baby? Is it alive?"

"I'm sorry, Spice. Yes, she's gone. The baby is in intensive care."

With Golden's arms around her, her shoulders shook violently. There was no gauge to measure her pain. Slipping through his arms, her body as light as the whispers of a dream, she had no feeling when her legs suddenly gave out, and she accordioned onto the cold tile floor, screaming Sterling's name.

Her head flopped between the tops of her knees, and her boneless arms dangled on each side of her body.

Golden, off balance, was unable to hold her, and he slipped down with her. They sat there on the floor, and Golden pulled Spice close to his chest and comforted her with his lips and hands. Finally she whispered in his ear, "I need to see her." She looked up into Golden's loving eyes and implored him, "Please let me see her."

Golden lifted his wife up and nodded to the nurse.

The nurse led Spice and Golden into Sterling's room. The young woman pulled back the sheet from Sterling's face. Spice swallowed a sob. There was a small smile still on Sterling's face. Her soft gray eyes were half-open. Spice moved closer, and as she did so, she could hear Golden praying over her child's soul—praying for the family, for their strength and hope.

Without taking her eyes from Sterling, Spice addressed

Golden. "I am sorry I doubted you that night, Golden. I will never doubt you again. Please forgive me."

"All is forgiven."

Spice thought of Golden's words, his prayers, that no one should leave this world without accepting Jesus Christ as their personal savior—Spice prayed that Sterling had.

When Sterling was born, Spice had tried to envision her as a precious, tiny angel but found it impossible. She'd been given to her secondhand. But now in death, she could.

By the grace of God, Spice felt peace when she stared down at her baby. Spice rubbed her hand lovingly over every surface of Sterling's body. She rubbed her feet, then looked into her eyes. She smoothed both legs, touched her swollen stomach, where she could feel, through the gown, the prickly stitches from the cesarean surgery. She let her hand rest there for a while.

Smiling now, Spice moved her hand over her arms, her shoulders, the slope of her neck, then she stopped again. She outlined Sterling's face with her thumb. With Sterling's eyelids half-closed, Spice wasn't frightened, but grateful to stare into her daughter's beautiful sterling gray eyes.

Tears touched her smile when she bent and kissed her daughter. "I love you, baby. Mother's going to miss you so."

"See the smile on her face. She's with God now, baby," Golden said to his wife.

Stepping back, Spice felt Golden's arms encircling her shoulders, and she fell back deeper inside of them, breathing softly. She turned around, sinking her face into his chest, pulling the lapels of his jacket over her face. Unable to stop the sobs, she cried, "Hold me, Golden. I don't know if I can make it."

"I'm here." He rocked her body back and forth, feeling her pain sinking deeper into his chest and into his heart. He waited until she had exhausted her tears and her body stopped trembling.

Finally she said, "I'm okay." She turned to look back at Sterling and, brushing back her tears, smiled.

"C'mon, let's go see the baby."

"Wait." Spice turned to the nurse. "Is there a chapel in this hospital?"

"Of course. Follow me."

Spice couldn't hold back the tears as she and Golden walked into the small room. She felt Golden's strength building from within as he prayed. Kneeling on the altar, she closed her eyes and steepled her hands in prayer.

Golden prayed aloud. He said another prayer for Sterling. Afterward he prayed for his wife: "God, I know you have the power to heal, the power to save. Have mercy, dear Lord, on my wife. Heal our souls, dear God. Forgive our sins and stitch us more closely together, Lord."

Spice let the tears fall.

"I kneel before your throne of God and your throne of mercy. I ask you to touch me, touch her. Because you, Lord, only you, are the author and finisher of our faith."

If Golden can love me this much, Spice thought, knowing all the terrible things about my past, I have to trust him. Maybe there is something inside of me that will teach me more about how to love.

As Golden knelt beside Spice, she felt something stronger, lighter, like the brushing of an angel's wing, against her shoulder as she knelt beside him. Then, as she opened her eyes, a split second of evanescent brilliance flashed before her, and she thought, Who will save the children? Who will love the children? Who will help them? Whom can they trust?

Ironically, in this instant, when Spice knew the strength of her married love, she also knew that there was something stronger, something better, than her love for Golden—and that was her love for her children, herself, and God. Reaching out, she touched his hand. When she felt his hand cover hers, she lifted her tear-streaked face to his and asked, "Can we see the baby now?"

With his arms around her shoulder, Golden guided Spice to the neonatal intensive care unit.

Death is the foreshadowing of life; we die that we may die no more. The pain Spice felt losing her child, her daughter, was unbelievable, indescribable. Carmen was right—Carmen had wished to spare Spice the pain of a child's death. Truly, now, Spice understood what her friend had meant.

When they entered the neonatal ICU, Carmen was standing, outside the clear pane, looking inside at Baby Witherspoon. He was no longer on the respirator and weighed just under five pounds. The nurse boasted to Spice and Golden that the feisty newborn had just consumed two ounces of milk.

Spice smiled. The smile went all the way down inside her, and she could feel Sterling's strength stirring there as well.

Carmen and Spice looked at each other, without a word between them.

Golden started to ask something when he felt Spice's arm holding him back.

"Who's that man?" Spice questioned, pointing with her eyes.

An elderly gentleman in a rocking chair sat holding a small infant in the half-darkened room. He appeared to be speaking to the child or singing, she couldn't be sure.

"That's Mr. Jamison. He's our guardian angel."

Mr. Jamison held a tiny infant in the palm of his hand.

"The child's name is Joy Lee." The nurse eased in between them, saying, "At birth she weighed just eleven and a half ounces and was just ten inches long. Joy was born more than three months early. She is the smallest premature infant to survive at Chamberlain Hospital. And now, after three months of being on a respirator, Joy is breathing on her own."

The nurse went on to explain, as Spice, Carmen, and Golden watched the blind movements of their baby, Gray Witherspoon, who seemed to be reaching out for something, moving his hands and feet wildly into the air, but quietly, grabbing at nothing. Spice watched Carmen volleying her gaze back and forth from the angel to *her* baby.

They all turned at the sound of Gray's soft cry.

"Can I touch him?" Carmen asked the nurse.

"Which of you are the grandparents?"

"I—" Spice started.

"We are," Carmen said, her gaze boring into her friend's eyes.

"Carmen," Spice hugged her. Tears hot on her cheeks, she was unable to speak. "I want you to raise him. It's what Sterling would have wanted."

"I'll love him, Spice. Because he's a part of my own blood."

"He's yours," Spice whispered to her.

Spice watched as Carmen placed her carefully scrubbed hands inside the incubator and touched *her* tiny grandbaby. She could feel his power being transferred to Carmen, and she felt Sterling coming alive inside of the newborn. When they heard him cry again, low at first and then louder, Carmen looked up, and they both realized they could hear Sterling in the newborn baby's tears.

The baby cried louder. Cries, Spice thought, each one better than the last.